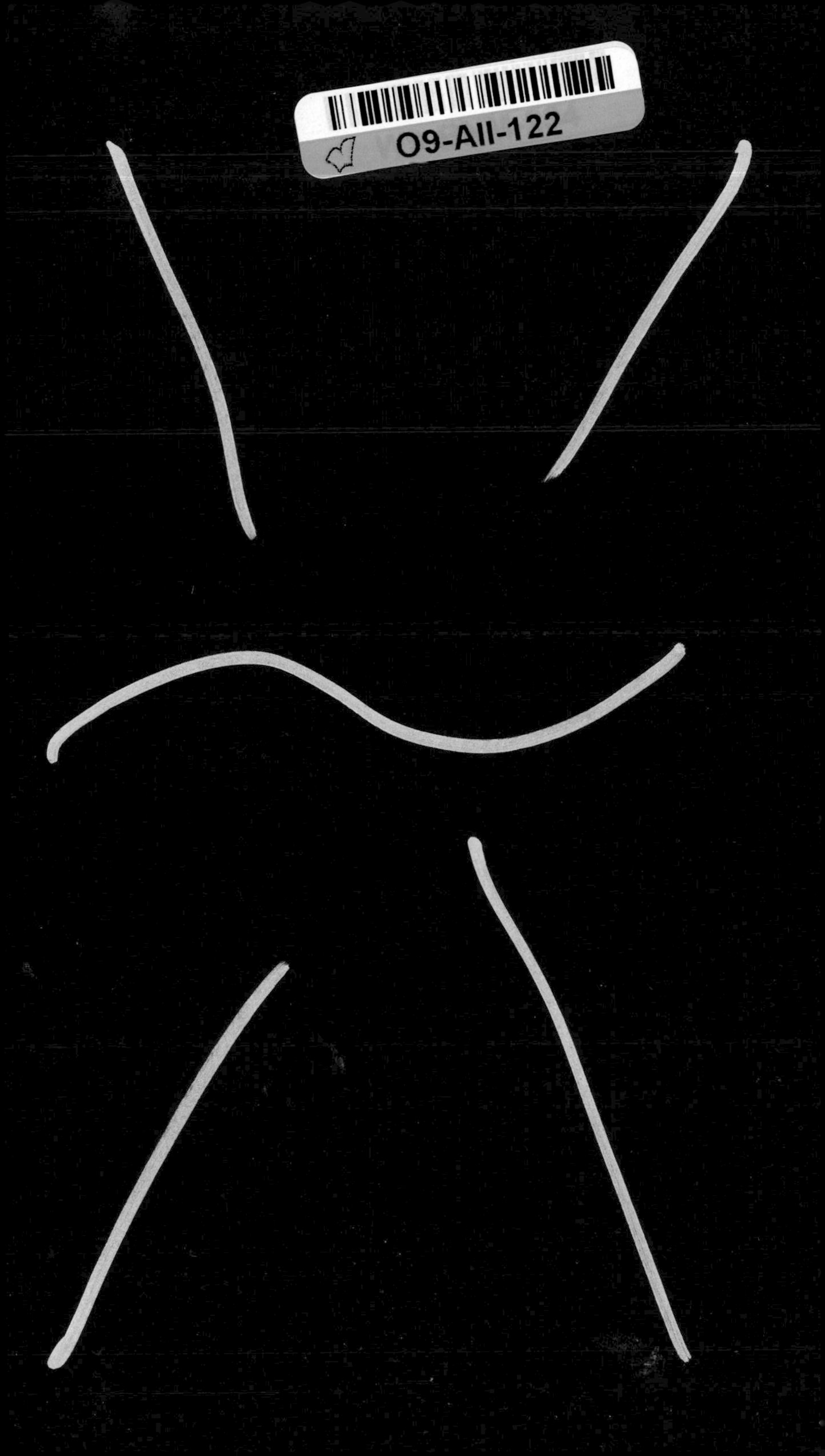
O9-AII-122

FATAL SUNSET

BY THE SAME AUTHOR

NON-FICTION

Duende: A Journey in Search of Flamenco

Andalus: Unlocking the Secrets of Moorish Spain

Guerra: Living in the Shadows of the Spanish Civil War

Sacred Sierra: A Year on a Spanish Mountain

The Spy with 29 Names: the Story of the Second World War's Most Audacious Double Agent

THE MAX CÁMARA NOVELS

Or the Bull Kills You

A Death in Valencia

The Anarchist Detective

Blood Med

A Body in Barcelona

FATAL SUNSET

Jason Webster

Chatto & Windus
LONDON

1 3 5 7 9 10 8 6 4 2

Chatto & Windus, an imprint of Vintage,
20 Vauxhall Bridge Road,
London SW1V 2SA

Chatto & Windus is part of the Penguin Random House group of companies
whose addresses can be found at global.penguinrandomhouse.com.

First published by Chatto & Windus in 2017

penguin.co.uk/vintage

A CIP catalogue record for this book is available from the British Library

ISBN 9780701189389

Typset in 12.5/15.5 pt Adobe Garamond by Jouve (UK), Milton Keynes
Printed and bound in Great Britain by Clays Ltd, St Ives Plc

Penguin Random House is committed to a sustainable future for our business,
our readers and our planet. This book is made from Forest Stewardship
Council® certified paper.

For Mary Chamberlain

‘He knew the detective’s world is not the sunlit world of the eighteenth-century philosophers, but a nighttime world where hunch and chance are more important than ratiocinative acuity.’

Josiah Thompson, *Gumshoe*

Hardly a sea of presents; only five. Left, as usual, outside his door. No cards: the game was to guess whom each was from.

He picked them up and walked back to his bed, throwing them down in a pile. He stared, then reached for the nearest one: a golden box wrapped in a turquoise ribbon tied with a bow. José Luis tugged at it. Would it be something specially chosen – crafted even – for his sixtieth birthday? It did not have to be big, of course; he was no child. Besides, the box was no larger than a cocktail shaker. But just then he required something of quality, and consideration.

The bow came undone and he slipped a finger under the lid to prise it open. He lifted out purple tissue paper that spewed from the top, tossing it on to the floor. Inside was a bottle of some kind, with a black plastic lid. Not so promising. His lips pursed: he felt certain he knew who this was from. Still, there was hope. Perhaps he was more of a child than he admitted to himself.

For the briefest moment he was with Mamá again, clutching her single parcel with nervous anticipation, her eyes expressing so much tenderness, so much anxiety, so much desire that it would please him. He had learned quickly to shower her with kisses, no matter what the wrapping contained. It was never – could never be – just what he wanted: even supplemented by her night work, the pension of an airman's widow only just kept them alive. Lying alone in their bed, staring at the shadows moving across the ceiling with each passing car in the street – and shooting them down through imaginary sights – he had tried, on occasion, to remember his father, but his uniformed image only grew dimmer, outshone by the glow radiated by his mother. He would pretend to be asleep when she returned, analysing the smell she carried with her of alcohol, tobacco, and sharp, urgent sweat. She would wash herself at the sink in the corner of the room, splashing cold water over her face, neck, chest, and finally – quickly – underneath. Droplets of water would cascade down her thighs, catching the faintest reflection from the street lamps, and he would watch furtively as they hurried down her skin, racing towards the floor, before a towel extinguished them. Dry and freshened, she would plant a kiss on his restless forehead, slide under the sheets beside him and quickly fall into exhausted sleep. She worked hard, Mamá. Harder than anyone knew. Except him.

He paused as he fingered the present sitting impatiently in the golden box. Nothing had compared since. The pretence to his mother had only been partial, and with the years became no pretence at all, for despite the disappointments he had treasured every gift she had given him – every tin car, every wind-up train, every wooden whistle – because he understood the sacrifices that she made to afford it. And he had never let them go, not even when he left for training college and she threatened to clear them out, make some space in their little apartment. Now they were his mascots, staring down every day from the mirror-backed glass cabinet made specially for his rooms. Mamá had left him long before, but what she gave him, what she taught him, would stay for ever.

Sixty years old; he would have given anything to be with her today. Perhaps later, if there were time, he might visit the cemetery, put some flowers on her grave. It had been a while.

He closed his eyes, gripped the object inside the golden box, and extracted it. It was metallic, some kind of tin, with a liquid inside. Gritting his teeth, he peeped through one eye to see what it was.

A spray-on cologne. One of those advertised on the television, with a young man wearing a bright, white, too-tight shirt grinning knowingly at the camera while girls clung to his arm, trotting down a street on their way to a club. Or home from one. It wasn't always clear. What was clear was the message: one spray of this stuff and you were guaranteed a fuck. Simple, primitive and – presumably, because he was being given it now – effective. He was only glad no one was there to see his face: no need for pretence. There was something shocking, colossal even, about its inappropriateness.

He gave the thing a shake and pulled off the lid. What did this stuff smell like, anyway? He pushed the nozzle and particles shot out into the air near his face, lingering in the streaks of sunlight piercing the shutters. He sniffed, and coughed: it was sweet and earthy, like fresh tar sizzling on an empty road. Did people really wear this stuff? He laughed to himself. Perhaps he should give it a try. Perhaps, on his birthday, he might get lucky. The first clients would be arriving shortly after dark – one of them, at least, could be tempted; he still had it in him.

With a silent prayer, he held his breath, closed his eyes and sprayed the cologne over himself, giggling. It was the last thing he would dream of wearing.

He coughed again and walked to the bathroom, placing the can on the shelf with the rest of his collection. The other presents could wait. Sweat was beginning to form around his neck as the sun rose and the heat became more intense. The air conditioning hadn't been working for a couple of weeks: he would have to get it fixed. June was just the beginning, a foretaste of the inferno that July and August brought. At least here in the mountains the nights were still cool. Down in the city the hours of darkness were already as sticky as the day. It was one thing that his nightclub had over the others: clearer, lighter air, and a sense of being elsewhere, away from the city and the usual faces: a place to lose yourself, become someone – or something – different.

He stared at the mirror, pulling with affectionate despair at the jowls sagging beneath his chin. They only ever got bigger, no matter which diet he was on. '*Mos refem*,' Mamá used to say: we remake ourselves with age. 'There's more of you to love,' others would – pathetically – insist, trying to cheer him up. But he had given up worrying about his looks years before. The threat of illness – diabetes, God knew what else – concerned him most about his increasing size. He might at least, if he managed to shift some of the fat, have more energy. Simply getting out of bed was becoming a challenge.

The phone rang as he cleaned his teeth. He gargled and spat, wondered about picking up, then wiped his mouth dry as he crossed back into the bedroom, trying not to notice the overhang of his gut in the mirror on the far wall. He pulled the phone to his ear and listened wordlessly, then he grunted an acknowledgement and hung up. More problems to sort.

He sighed and stepped over to the wardrobe, swinging the door open with intent. He needed something bright and cheerful, something that would announce to the world that today was his birthday: as loud a statement as possible. Birthdays – his birthdays – were about flamboyance and gaiety. He had sworn, when money had finally started to come, that there would be no more need for pretence: he owed it to the memory of Mamá. She would not approve of how he lived, had never, in fact, learned the truth – although at times he had suspected that she knew – but she would admire what he had built up, the creation of his own kingdom in the sierra, where nothing was wanting and no one told him what to do.

He picked out a white trouser suit with multicoloured sequins embroidered on the chest and arms. The fabric was stretchy: it would still fit – just, if he breathed in. And it was figure-hugging: perfect for making clear that even at his age – and size – he was as sexy as any of them, could do and take anything that the kids were into. He'd been there long before many of them were born: there was nothing he didn't know.

The suit slid on; it felt like a second skin, silky to the

touch, sequins glimmering. From a side table he picked up his favourite sunglasses: bright pink and oval with fake diamonds studded in the frames. His Dolly Glasses, he called them, as in Dolly Parton; at once both scandalous and ridiculous, which is why he loved them. Finally, he picked up a large straw hat with a dark red silk scarf wrapped around the head, placing it firmly over his bald scalp and tilting it to the side with a coquettish glance at himself in the mirror. That would do it. That would scandalise the bastard, teach him to call him out on *this* day. Urgent meeting? What could be so urgent about it?

His little dog, Blanquita, barked softly as she saw him leave, anxious to come.

'Later, sweetheart. Daddy's got work to do.'

Despite the hat and glasses, he squinted in the harsh flat sunlight outside. Evenings could be beautiful here, when the light softened to reveal hidden crags and undulations in the limestone mountains. And mornings too, if he was still up to see them. But the early afternoon was a time to stay indoors, a blanched, shadowless world where the sun ruled without mercy. A grey-skinned lizard sped away under a rock at the beat of his footsteps. He looked around: there was no one in sight; they would all be working. Or sleeping.

He took the path through the undergrowth towards the pine trees, breathing in their sharp, calming scent. The Chain was just a few metres further on. With luck he could get this over with quickly and then return.

A breeze, light and threatening, blew through the tops of the trees. When it dropped he heard something new, something he had not noticed before. There, in front of him, was the Chain, yet he was alone. Had the old man given up and gone already? But the sound came back to him: a buzz, circling, darting, changing course around him. Angry, and growing louder.

Confused, he felt an unexpected piercing stab in the side of his neck. The suddenness and intensity of it caused his knees to buckle, and he fell with a heavy thud to the ground in shock, clutching at the pain. But within an instant the skin on the back of his hand was punctured as well, as though by a hot needle, agony shooting like molten lead up his arm. More pricks and jabs came in quick succession: on his chest, his knee, his back. Harsher, quicker, striking again and again. Like fighter pilots swooping in for the kill.

His glasses fell from his face and his eyes became agonised orbs of glistening, bloodshot jelly. He opened his mouth to scream out against the unexpected violence. But the air caught in his throat, slamming against his tongue as it bloated and blistered at the back of his mouth like fungus on a dying tree.

He collapsed, shuddering, fighting. His face like a mirror, as blue as the sky.

Mamá!

Where was she? Hot, shamed tears streamed across his cheeks. He needed her now. Urgently.

Mamá!

But Mamá wouldn't come.

Only the sun, patrician and unforgiving, staring down with a single, all-seeing eye at its child convulsing on the ground. Far, far below.

ONE

Her first act as commissioner had been to do away with the late starts. The idea that ten o'clock was a reasonable hour to begin the policing day was criminal itself. No more slinking in when it suited them, no matter what: all officers were obliged to report for duty by eight a.m. Non-compliers were punished by having their pay cut in incremental amounts for every five minutes late. Crime did not rest and neither should they. It was what the new masters insisted on: value for money. God knew most of her staff were already overpaid.

It had worked, and after only a few days the Jefatura had started to run – with only a handful of exceptions – according to the stricter regime that Rita Hernández insisted on. This was her ship now. Lower-ranking officers might carry out actual policing tasks, but everything was done under her supervision, her very watchful eye. Without her – paying their salaries and giving them their respective tasks – there would be no crime-fighting to start with. And she didn't care what those ungrateful bastards thought.

Punctuality, however, was only the beginning. There was much clearing-up to do. Commissioner Pardo had received his distinguished-service medals and very generous pay-off, but in her eyes he should have been crucified for the mess he had bequeathed. Figuratively, of course, although if she were honest about her feelings – which was rare – she did sometimes fantasise about hammering the nails into his hands and feet herself. Blasphemy, perhaps, but he certainly deserved it.

Where to begin? Every morning Hernández's thoughts followed the same routine as she drove her Range Rover down Fernándo el Católico, turned right by the main entrance to the Jefatura, down the back alleyway and past the policeman – never forgetting to smile and wave – who stood guard by the barrier to the central courtyard, where the highest-ranking staff were allocated parking spaces. She would begin by considering the aching perplexity of the finances – Pardo had frittered away thousands of euros in a complex web of accounts with names like 'special measures', or 'emergency funding', none of it ever explained.

This was the least of her worries. There had been attempts in the past to force officers to wear uniform at all times when on duty, yet the measures had never stuck. Pardo hadn't seemed to care very much one way or another. In fact, it appeared that in his last months he had barely made an appearance at the Jefatura at all. Now, thankfully, uniforms were being worn as a matter of course by practically every member of staff under her watch. The only refuseniks being the same small group of individuals who were failing to adhere to her time directive and generally placing the greatest obstacles in her way as she turned the Jefatura into the police force that a major city like Valencia deserved.

Madrid was backing her all the way. It was why they had appointed her in the first place. She wasn't Valencian and neither had she ever served in the city. Born in León to a churchgoing family, she was Castilian – patriotic, hard-working, and, most of all, endowed with a seriousness that was clearly lacking here on the east coast. Valencia had become synonymous in recent years with malpractice, the most rotten apple in a basket of admittedly poor-quality fruit. She would do what was needed to cut out the infection within the *Policía Nacional*. It was a difficult and necessary path, her own cross to bear. And she was damned if she was going to fail.

By this point of the morning she would be passing through the door of the Jefatura building and pressing the button for the lift to take her to the third floor. And it was here, at this point, that the darkest thoughts would come. For despite her growing successes with the finances, the discipline, and eradicating the whiff of corruption about the place, there was one issue that never ceased to furrow her brow as the lift doors closed behind her. And that was the issue of personnel.

She had, it must be said, some very good officers on her team, men and women who justified the expense of their salaries by working hard and bringing in the kinds of results that made her, the accountants and even Madrid happy. Results that could be fed back into the statistical machines which provided the kinds of news stories every high-ranking officer dreamt of: lower crime figures, higher rates of citizen security, lower operational costs: the Holy Trinity of policing.

And, she told herself, as her blood pressure rose with the

lift, she had achieved much in the two months that she had been in the job. Every uniform, every skipping pair of feet rushing to get into work on time, was a victory. Yet when it came to personnel matters, her hands were tied in ways that caused her to lose sleep. Contracts, labour laws, workers' rights! God in heaven! How she dreamt of being able to point her finger and eliminate the worst offenders. But no, sacking a police officer was near to impossible. She had looked for every loophole, had even paid a lawyer to see if she could rid herself of the worst of them. Even if only one. For there was one man on her staff that she must, at all costs, free herself of.

The doors of the lift would open at this point, and Rita would sigh as she made her way to her office. Usually she would determine to focus on other matters by now. Yet this morning there was a change. This morning, as she walked out into the corridor, there was something resembling a skip in her step, even, to a closely observing eye, something of a smile on her thin, lightly painted lips. A plan had formed in her mind. Not particularly sophisticated – in fact it was so simple she wondered why she had not thought of it before. If, in the end, she wanted someone to leave, she could simply make life so unpleasant for them that they would remove themselves of their own will.

She turned the handle and walked into her office. Her secretary, Mari-Carmen, was at her desk. Rita looked up at the standard-issue clock on the wall: it was three minutes to eight. Good. Mari-Carmen stood up and saluted.

'*Buenos días, Señora.*'

'Good morning, Mari-Carmen. You may sit down.'

'Thank you.'

Mari-Carmen returned sharply to her chair, her eyes fixed on her computer screen.

'We have much to do today,' said Rita.

'Yes, Señora,' Mari-Carmen answered.

'Is everything prepared?'

'Yes, Señora.'

'Good.'

Commissioner Rita Hernández of the *Policía Nacional* walked over to her desk, placed her bag on the floor and hung up her coat on the stand near the window. She pulled the lace curtains to one side and looked at the traffic below, the buses taking people to work, the pedestrians hurrying to and fro, living their lives in quiet, industrious safety. As the world should be. With her, high above, making sure that nothing should harm them or get in their way. It made her feel maternal – a duty, given to her by God, to serve His creation and curtail the attempts of those inspired by evil to bring destruction on their heads.

And there was no greater sinner than a bad policeman.

A policeman whom she was now, finally, about to have done with.

She let the curtain fall and turned back towards her secretary. The clock on the wall showed a few seconds to eight o'clock.

'Mari-Carmen,' she said. 'Tell Chief Inspector Max Cámara I want to see him here . . .'

She paused, watching for the second hand to sweep past the 12. Then she glanced back.

'Now.'

TWO

'Max?'

The sound of Alicia's voice was drowned by the noise from the toilet bowl, where the efforts of a satisfying bowel movement were being flushed away into the labyrinthine and only partially effective hellhole of the Valencian city sewerage system.

'Max!'

He pulled up his trousers, buckled his belt and went to wash his hands.

'Is that you?'

He could hear a bleeping coming from the other side of the door.

'Is that . . . ?'

'It's your mobile,' called Alicia.

Cámara finished washing his hands, dried them on the towel, made sure the window was fully open, then emerged from the bathroom. Alicia was standing with her dressing gown half-open, holding the bleating, vibrating thing in his direction.

'What time is it?' he said.

She shrugged, trying to relieve herself of the offending object.

'Late enough, obviously,' she said. 'Here, take the damn thing, would you?'

'Who is it?'

'Who else is it going to be?'

He took the phone, wondering why it was still ringing and hadn't gone to voicemail by now. Could a caller override something like that? Holding the screen at arm's length, he recognised the number, closed his eyes, took a deep breath and pressed the answer button.

'*¿Sí?*'

He listened patiently to the order barked at him efficiently from the other end.

'Of course, I understand,' he answered.

He was already showered and dressed, but hadn't had any breakfast. Then it would take him five minutes at least to get to the Jefatura on his motorbike. Ten minutes if the traffic was bad.

'Tell Commissioner Hernández I'm on my way,' he said. 'I'm downstairs in my office right now. I'll be with her in two minutes.'

More barked comments from the secretary at the other end of the line.

'Immediately, I understand. Yes. I'm leaving my office right now.'

The phone buzzed back in his ear.

'Yes, and goodbye to you.'

He switched the thing off and threw it on to a side table.

'You in trouble again?'

Alicia was in the kitchen, from where the smell of a toasted croissant was drifting down the corridor towards him.

'Is there any coffee made?' he said.

'No, but I can put some on.'

He walked into the kitchen, planted a tender kiss on her neck and slid a hand over the curve of her hips.

'Are you in a hurry?' she asked.

He shrugged and sat down at the table, admiring her semi-naked figure.

'No. Not really.'

Commissioner Rita Hernández's face was a picture of rage when Cámara finally entered her office.

'Something urgent came up . . .' said Cámara.

'It's past nine o'clock,' replied Hernández.

Cámara looked at the clock on her wall.

'So it is. Doesn't time fly when you're—'

'And I've been down to your office,' she interrupted. 'Twice. You weren't there. Nor was there any sign of you having been there at all this morning.'

Rita Hernández was the kind of officer who made Cámara despair, someone for whom police work was nothing more than a path towards power. She might believe that she was working for the greater good, but deep down, as his friend Inspector Torres had accurately perceived, she was an apparatchik, a political animal who would be better placed in some corporation selling life insurance or engine parts or artificial fertiliser – anywhere but the *Policía Nacional.* Cámara glanced around the room. Filing cabinets lined two of the walls, a third was taken up by Mari-Carmen's little desk, and the fourth was filled by aluminium-framed windows. There were no plants or decorations, the only break in the monotony being a crucifix, and a dozen plaques and awards for distinguished service that the commissioner had received over several decades. Most of them were the kind that no one else bothered to display, being handed out simply for turning up.

'As I said, something urgent came up.'

One of the most curious things he had noticed about this office was that there was nowhere for visitors to sit. Hernández had her own chair, and then there was Mari-Carmen's, but nowhere else. Cámara walked round the side of the main desk and, in the absence of an alternative, eased his behind on to the edge.

Hernández shot to her feet.

'Get off my desk this instant!' she barked. Cámara made to look for somewhere else, then turned back to her with an innocent shrug, as if to say, 'Where else am I to go?'

The commissioner paused, realised that Cámara wasn't going to back down, then smiled. It was unimportant: soon she would be rid of this insolent buffoon and life would be so much easier.

She positioned herself at the other side of the desk, opposite Cámara, forcing him to twist in order to look at her.

'I want a progress report on your investigations in the Special Crimes Unit,' she said.

'Now?' Cámara asked.

'Yes.'

'Verbally?'

'Yes.'

'You received the written report I sent two days ago.'

'I want to hear it from you,' she said. 'What you've been . . . what you think you've been doing down there.'

Cámara got off the desk and stood squarely opposite her, hands on hips.

'As you already know,' he said, 'Inspector Torres and I are investigating radicalisation programmes by Islamic terror groups inside the country.'

Hernández raised an eyebrow.

'Go on,' she said.

'They're targeting ordinary Spanish kids,' Cámara continued. 'That is, ones with no Arab or North African background – to convert them. The danger is that such people will be harder for us to identify and pick up later on.'

'And how far have you got with this investigation?' said the commissioner.

'How far?'

'Yes, Chief Inspector, how far? I mean, how many arrests have you made? How many of these people have you managed to put behind bars? How many ordinary Spanish youths have you saved from this threat you describe?'

Cámara screwed his eyes.

'You already know the answer,' he said.

'I want you to tell me,' said Hernández. 'I want to hear it from you.'

'Memory playing up?'

'Damn you!' shouted the commissioner, beating her fist into the desk. 'You will obey an order from your commanding officer, so help me God!'

Cámara sighed, picked up a pen and a sheet of paper from the desk and deliberately drew a large circle on it.

'There,' he said.

'No arrests,' said Hernández. 'Not one.'

'As you already know.'

'That's right, Chief Inspector. I do know. And for how long have I known? Hmm?'

Cámara gave a hollow laugh.

'Is this necessary?'

'Only two days,' said the commissioner. 'Only two days because it was only two days ago that you deigned to tell me what you were up to. And then only after I'd given a direct order in writing for you to issue a report on your activities. Which you then took a month to write.'

'We were busy.'

'Oh, I'm sorry. Were you too busy rounding up suspects and making arrests during that time?'

Hernández paused. Cámara glanced up at the ceiling, pressing his tongue into the side of his mouth.

'You and Inspector Torres have been wasting everyone's time for the past six months on this nonsense,' she said. 'And have nothing to show for it. I wouldn't have minded you starting your own lines of inquiry if at least it had led somewhere. But you have nothing – just months of police time clocked up, thousands spent and resources wasted in what has turned into a farce.'

'We were making progress,' said Cámara. He knew it was hopeless: everything about her – her body language, her tone of voice, the manner of this summary meeting – told him that there was little left to fight for, but he persisted nonetheless.

'These kinds of investigations take time – they don't bring in immediate results. But what we're doing is useful. The potential for pulling off something big, something spectacular, is there. We just need to be left alone.'

Hernández wrinkled her nose.

'You see, this is exactly your problem, Chief Inspector. Some of us get on with ordinary police work. But you? In your eyes, you're special. No boring investigations for you. There always has to be an element of performance, doesn't there? That business at the Sagrada Familia in Barcelona – I believe the Catalan government gave you a medal.'

'I didn't join the police force for medals.'

'Oh, but I think you did, Chief Inspector. Deep down you long for the limelight. They say your earlier investigations helped bring down the previous government here in Valencia. Then there was that councillor in the Cabanyal, and the bullfighter case. All good headline material. You're almost a household name these days.'

'Not my intention, nothing to do with me.'

'Good, good,' said Hernández. 'I'm so glad to hear it. You won't mind, then, what I'm about to do.'

She called to Mari-Carmen, who had been listening throughout.

'Mari-Carmen, would you please tell Chief Inspector Laura Martín to join us. It's time we talked about Chief Inspector Max Cámara's future.'

THREE

Less than a minute had passed before a knock came at the door. Mari-Carmen went to open. Chief Inspector Laura Martín walked in holding a file, looking almost like a schoolgirl sheepishly entering the headmaster's office.

'*Buenos días, Señora,*' she said as she closed the door behind her and approached Commissioner Hernández. Cámara noted the formal means of address, and from somewhere in his memory he recalled some directive on the matter issued within the past months. Laura was clearly in uniform. Cámara was dressed in his usual shirt and jacket – no tie – but with nothing on him except the police ID in his pocket to say that he was a law-enforcement officer. He didn't even have his pistol: a new consignment of Glocks was due, and rather than waiting for them to arrive first, many officers had had their old ones already taken away for 'reassignment'. He was unarmed as well as inappropriately robed.

'Chief Inspector,' the commissioner beckoned Laura over. 'Join us.'

Cámara turned to his old colleague, trying to catch her eye. They had worked together in the past, never quite as friends, more as friendly rivals. Laura liked rules. She was neat and ordered and instinctively reeled from Cámara's haphazard and intuitive methods. If indeed they could be called methods. In fact, there were strong similarities between Laura and Rita Hernández – both high-ranking women in a traditionally male environment, both driven to succeed through hard work and a rejection of anything approaching flair or 'luck'. Yet a key difference separated them, and that was the fact that inside Laura's breast there beat a human heart, one of blood and flesh, which responded to suffering and which could be reached – for Cámara had done so – when necessary. Despite all her neatness, Cámara knew that inside, Laura and he were the same: moved, essentially, to do their jobs by something that could only be described as love – love for their fellow human beings.

Cámara kept his eye steadily on Laura as she crossed the room, willing her to turn his way, but she refused. And yet, he felt certain, there was a silent communication that spoke of understanding, pity even. He braced himself.

'Thank you,' said Hernández as Laura drew closer. 'Now, Chief Inspector,' she said, turning to Cámara. 'As of this moment the Special Crimes Unit is dissolved.'

She held up a hand.

'Don't argue. That's an order.'

Cámara hadn't said a word.

'Your written report and our earlier conversation make it clear enough to me, at least, that it is a waste of resources.

I've been clearing up my predecessor's mess from the day I arrived. It was his decision to set you up in that unit, and it's mine to bring it to a close. I hope that's clear.'

Cámara was silent.

'I said I hope that's clear.'

He looked confused.

'What am I supposed to do?'

'A simple acknowledgement that you've understood will suffice.'

'Oh, I see.'

The commissioner waited a moment, realised that she wasn't getting anywhere, then continued.

'I'm assigning you back to *Homicidios*, where you'll be working under the command of Chief Inspector Martín here.'

Laura nodded in his direction, still refusing to meet his eye.

'You are, of course, both of the same rank, which is unusual, but I'm sure that won't be a problem, will it?'

'No, Señora,' said Laura.

'As I say –' she addressed her words to Cámara – 'you will be under Chief Inspector Martín's direct command. No more ad-hoc investigations, no more taking off and following your own whims. You will do exactly what she says and you will report directly to her. I hope that's clear.'

After a pause, Cámara nodded, remembering what was expected of him.

Working for Laura was the least of his concerns at that moment: he was thinking of the months of work with the Islamic groups, the long hours of research, the tentative steps towards making contacts. He had felt certain that Torres and he were on the brink of establishing a mole, a disaffected young Spanish kid passed over for promotion within the group hierarchy and bent on revenge, with tales of something big, a link with the drug trade. Could Cámara still work it, pretend to be in the homicide team while actually continuing to develop his contact? It would be difficult, but not impossible. He and Torres had formed a semi-official unit-within-a-unit inside *Homicidios* before. They could do it again.

'Your partnership with Inspector Torres has come to an end as well,' Hernández continued. 'I'm passing him to Narcotics. You won't be seeing much of each other any more.'

Cámara gave a silent, stifled groan. His partnership with Torres was almost an institution within the Jefatura, the two mavericks joined at the hip. Other officers used to joke about their 'marriage' while secretly admiring the work they did, if despising their politics. Years of association had created a kind of telepathic connection between them that others were sometimes aware of. Splitting them up felt like an abomination of a natural order. Even Laura seemed to wince.

'And there's no need to go back to your office,' the commissioner went on. 'There's a team inside clearing up as we speak. Your new desk in *Homicidios* is waiting for you. Although . . .' She paused and looked at Laura with faux concern. 'I understand you may have to share with someone? Is that right?'

Laura nodded.

'Not much space at the moment. But I'm sure you'll cope.'

From the side, Laura raised an apologetic eyebrow in Cámara's direction.

'Right.' Rita slapped her hands together, smiling. 'Now

that's done, Laura can give you your new case. Something came in late last night and you're the perfect man for the job.'

She indicated to Laura.

'Chief Inspector Martín, please do the honours.'

'Yes, Señora.'

Laura opened the file in her hands and began to speak in a monotone.

'José Luis Mendoza Uribe. Died yesterday, his sixtieth birthday. Was the owner of the Sunset nightclub in the Sierra Calderona just north of the city. Body found on the premises by one Abdelatif Cortbi. Cause of death still to be determined. Body currently being held at the Centre for Forensic Medicine. Autopsy is scheduled for tomorrow.'

'Why is this our case?' asked Cámara.

'Is there a problem, Chief Inspector?' said the commissioner. 'Is this case not high profile enough for you, perhaps?'

'You said the body was found at the club,' he said to Laura, ignoring Hernández. 'That's *Guardia Civil* territory. Why's it with us?'

'He was found at the club, that's right,' said Laura. 'But he was brought to La Fé hospital in an ambulance. It was only here in the city that he was declared dead. Which means that he's on our patch.'

'He was still alive when they found him?'

'Possibly. It's still not clear. Hopefully the autopsy will provide more details.'

'OK,' said Cámara.

'Satisfied?' asked the commissioner.

'The *Guardia Civil* aren't going to be happy about it.'

'They'll just have to accept it,' said Laura. For a moment the two of them were speaking like colleagues, as though their commanding officer were not present. Cámara caught the connection between them and silently thanked her.

'The *Guardia Civil* will cooperate in every way,' Hernández butted in, sensing what was going on. 'I think that is the last thing you need to be worrying about, Chief Inspector.'

'What do we know about this man?' asked Cámara.

'At the moment, very little,' answered Laura. 'Apart from the gossip, of course. We've all heard of Sunset. And of the kinds of things that go on up there.'

'I'll look into it,' he said. 'What about this other guy you mentioned? Abdel-something.'

'Says he was José Luis's partner.'

'Business partner? Or partner partner?'

'Partner partner.'

'*Cherchez la femme*,' said Cámara with a grin. Neither woman laughed.

'Is that a homophobic comment, Chief Inspector?'

Cámara shrugged.

'No one's taken a statement from him yet,' said Laura.

'What about the científicos?'

'One thing at a time, please, Chief Inspector,' said Hernández. 'I know you're used to charging off, spending police resources with little or no justification, but things have changed. We're not getting the crime-scene investigators involved until we know that this is an actual murder.'

'I'm sorry?' said Cámara.

'I said we don't know if this is a murder yet.' The commissioner smiled. 'My apologies, we should have made it clearer at the beginning.'

'It's just a routine case?' asked Cámara.

'That's right. A routine check.'

The commissioner placed her hands on her hips.

'You may find you have to get used to this kind of police work from now on. A bit of a step down.'

Cámara sniffed. It was clear enough what was going on. Laura handed him the file.

'OK,' he said. 'Leave it with me.'

He paused.

'Just one thing,' he said. 'Why even pass it to *Homicidios* at all? I mean, if there's no suspicion of foul play?'

The commissioner was silent. Laura spoke.

'A call came in last night,' she said. 'Anonymous, relating to the death. Certainly a hoax, but suggesting that it wasn't an accident, that José Luis was killed.'

'I see,' said Cámara. 'Who took the call?'

'The details are all in the file, Chief Inspector,' said the commissioner. 'Now if you'll excuse us, I have some matters to discuss with the head of *Homicidios*.'

Cámara looked at Laura, but she stared at the ground. Clinging to the file, he walked out of the office, closing the door as gently as he could behind him.

FOUR

His old office was out of bounds, and the thought of walking into the dark, cramped, ground-floor offices of *Homicidios* where a cool reception and a shared desk awaited somehow failed to appeal. Instead, he took the lift to the basement, where a small room with a cement floor, strip lighting, two bare tables and a couple of vending machines pushed against a wall had been designated a 'canteen'. No one used it, preferring to frequent the several bars in the local neighbourhood. But the room allowed some pen pusher in the system to tick a box on a form with a list of 'employee facilities' on it.

Cámara stepped in, switched on the lights, and breathed in the hard, metallic, musty smell that he recognised from the previous time – the only time – he had been here. One of the machines was supposed to produce something resembling coffee, but it was never used and he doubted it could make anything now. The one next to it had cans of soft drinks, brightly coloured packets of nuts and crisps – almost certainly well past their sell-by date – and bottles of water. He placed a couple of coins into the slot, heard the machine swallow them, and pressed a button. With a clunk a plastic bottle fell out at the bottom. He picked it up: it was dusty and warm.

He placed the water on one of the tables and sat down to glance through the file. It stared back at him, unopened. He already knew, simply by holding it in his hands, that it was thin and held very little information. Almost certainly nothing more than what had been mentioned in the commissioner's office. The question was whether he should bother reading it at all. What had happened earlier, what was going on in the Jefatura, felt like a palace coup: bright new faces with a bright new mandate busy sweeping away the old guard, introducing their bright new world. The plan was transparent enough. He thought for a moment about giving Torres a ring, but checked himself: his colleague would doubtless be in Rita's office receiving his own dressing-down.

Instead, the question for Cámara now was how to respond: accept what had happened and carry on, or do what Rita really wanted and hand in his resignation.

The fact was, leaving the police force was always a possibility somewhere at the back of his mind. He had no problem with putting criminals away. The problem came when it was no longer – and when was it ever? – a simple matter of catching 'bad guys'. Cámara came from a long line of anarchists – his grandfather and his great-grandfather before him – active members of libertarian groups who had suffered and even, in his great-grandfather's case, been shot for their beliefs during a more authoritarian past. Deep down, Cámara knew that he shared their views, if in a less militant form. Years before he had managed to come to terms with being both a State employee and not believing in the State to begin with: in the absence of an anarchist revolution, working for the common good was good enough. And it did well to have the odd anti-authoritarian within an organisation that tended to attract his polar opposites: something about trying to balance things out, or so he told himself.

Only Torres, a lone Socialist – although he hinted at the presence of others – was on any similar kind of wavelength. It was why they worked so well together. But now even that relationship was being taken away from him.

Daydreams of a life outside the police had come and gone, getting him excited for a few days or even weeks before fading. And he would share them with Alicia. Things were good with them again, the sparkle returning to their relationship after the difficulties and scars of the past. Now both in their late forties, they had enough life behind them to know what they liked, enough life ahead of them to build something new if they wanted.

And now this. The door out of the police had been opened and he had been given a sudden push in its direction.

He nibbled the side of his mouth, eyes unfocused as he let his mind wander. Reaching for the water, he unscrewed the lid, tossed it on to the tabletop and lifted the bottle to drink. It tasted old and stale: how many years had it been sitting in the vending machine? He coughed as the liquid hit the back of his mouth, lurching forwards to clear his throat.

He stood up, coughed again, and shook himself out of

his dream state. The bottle of offending water seemed to laugh at him from the table.

'Only one place for you,' Cámara mumbled, snatching it up. He rescrewed the top and took a step towards the vending machines, sending the bottle flying towards a small, empty dustbin sandwiched between them. The bottle ricocheted off their side walls and clattered with a heavy thud into the metal container below.

'Fucking poison,' said Cámara.

He turned back to the table: the file was still there, undisturbed by his little drama.

'And what am I going to do about you?' he said to it.

No answer, and as if expecting it to tell him what to do, he flicked it open, casting an eye over the scanty contents. He had been right: everything had been mentioned already back in Rita's office.

Everything except one name that seemed to wink up at him from the page, someone involved in the case who had definitely not been mentioned earlier. Someone Cámara wouldn't mind having a chat with just now.

He grinned, picked up the file, and headed towards the door.

FIVE

Carlos watched the ambulance carrying his agent's dead body drive up the street and disappear around a corner. He checked his hands and clothes for any blood, nodded at the policeman charged with securing the crime scene, then climbed into his Audi, fired the engine, and put it into gear. It would take almost an hour to cross Madrid and reach the HQ of the *Centro Nacional de Inteligencia*.

After he had sped up side streets, zigzagging partway, the traffic began to slow: roadworks on the A6 were causing tailbacks as far as the Plaza Moncloa. In the hard morning light the city felt stiff and wheezy like an old man trying to cough his dying lungs into life. Across the pavement, the doors of the metro station opened and belched out another huddle of commuters: men with ill-fitting suits, elderly women laden with bags, students making their way with grim purpose to classes in the nearby university complex. All was movement and noise: the crashing hammer of a pneumatic drill tearing into the tarmac, the crackling buzz of a swarm of mopeds filtering past to reach the front of the traffic lights, the tearing roar of a thousand combustion engines. Carlos watched the bustling hordes: they knew nothing, saw nothing, understood nothing. Which was how it should be.

He turned his attention away as the traffic moved in a short burst along the clogged-up avenue. His schedule would suffer, and his right hamstring was beginning to tire from shifting his foot from accelerator to brake and back. And yet, he told himself, he was calm. Carlos was always calm. It was who he was, who he needed to be. Uncontrolled passion – rage, lust, greed – were a source of weakness in a man. And Carlos had no time for weakness. Which was why he had got where he had, been given the responsibilities that only he could take on.

Nonetheless, he had to admit that despite his usual sense of control, a sensation of annoyance, even mild frustration, was stirring somewhere within him. He put it down to a lack of coffee: it was fast approaching ten o'clock and the two cups he had drunk with his breakfast at six – washing down the bread, olives and fried eggs with cumin that had been his staple since living years before in Morocco – now faded into memory. Yet somewhere he knew that insufficient caffeine was not the sole cause of his discomfort. Despite being only four hours old, this morning had already brought its fair share of problems, of which the traffic jam was merely the latest.

Carlos had a rigid system of categorising people. There were three basic groups: idiots; useful idiots; and the enemy. The majority fell into the first – the crowding thousands now surrounding his car; the commuters and office workers;

the students, housewives and unemployed; the bus drivers and shopkeepers; the tourists and street cleaners – these were all, unless demonstrated as otherwise, idiots, the dumb, the stupid, the uncomprehending. The very people whose lives it was his job to keep safe. And the less they knew, the safer they were. And the easier his task became.

But the work of a security-service officer could not be performed in a vacuum – that would be absurd, if, admittedly, an attractive proposition at times. No, people – the idiots – could not be held at a complete remove, hence his second category: useful idiots, easily the most complicated of the three. A useful idiot could take several forms: almost anyone who worked for him, for example, was viewed as a member of this category. A useful idiot was, naturally, of use to him, but lacking knowledge he or she was still, technically, an idiot. Others who entered his world in a less hierarchical manner, like a colleague working in a different government department with information or leverage that could be helpful, were also part of the second group. Then there were those whom Fate occasionally sent his way: a one-time informant passing on a tip, or a person who could be turned into an operative of sorts. The great advantage of these informal contacts was the ease with which any association with his organisation could be erased: no paperwork to destroy, all connections denied. And the assistance of the mainstream, which tended to regard with suspicion claims about government 'dirty tricks' or conspiracies. No one of consequence took them seriously. Besides, endemic corruption had so muddied the waters of public life that few people believed very much at all these days.

The problem with useful idiots, however, was an inherent instability within the category itself. Ordinary greed meant that few could remain in the group for sustained periods of time; one small, very partial taste of Carlos's world led almost inevitably to them wanting more, as though intelligence were some kind of secret pantomime, a hidden theatre offering forbidden fruits of excitement and limitless entertainment. Such people had to be dealt with in a variety of ways. Some could be given a drip-feed of attention and low-level information to keep them ticking along. Others had to be pushed in one way or another back into the category of mere idiot, all usefulness removed. For a handful this could be done through fear. Others were simply starved out – cut off and left to wither. Yet this strategy could bring danger, for instead of decaying back into the status of idiot, such people could sometimes shift into Carlos's third category: the enemy.

Defining the enemy was simple enough: anyone not in the first two groups was automatically in the third. Ideology, race, religion or any other categorisation was superfluous. The only question was how to deal with them, how they could be managed, controlled or crushed. And the most difficult to deal with were former useful idiots.

Dealing with such a situation had taken up the earlier part of Carlos's morning. A week before, a member of the group known as the *Guardia Suiza* – not their real denomination, yet the name had stuck nonetheless – had gone absent without leave after completing an operation. It was normal in his line of work to be given a short term of leave after debriefing, a time to decompress, come to terms with any moral issues – although mental and physical fatigue tended to far outweigh any internal doubts among such people. Yet this man – Sergeant Mimon, a former soldier from the Ceuta-based *Regulares* unit – had vanished. An investigation revealed a complication in the man's emotional life – human passion once again causing difficulties: his girlfriend had formed an attachment to another man. Mimon had found out and, as soon as his mission was complete, immediately went home to sort things. Carlos had admired the fact that Mimon's discipline had held sufficiently not to have broken before his target was dispatched, yet once the trigger was pulled his training had snapped. After which things became ugly: his girlfriend ended up in hospital with a broken jaw and fractured skull and remained, as far as Carlos knew, in a coma. Not that he was overly concerned for her welfare – she was a member of the idiot class, and while he cared for them as a collective, he could not dwell on their individual sufferings. The problem was with Mimon, who had demonstrated a lack of self-control that could not be tolerated. From being a useful idiot, Mimon had moved into the camp of the enemy – a problem.

In the end it had been relatively simple to persuade the girlfriend's new lover to perform the task, and for a brief time this man too had become a useful idiot: supplied with a firearm and the necessary information. His rage and desire for revenge took care of the rest. Mimon was now dealt with, his body taken away by the ambulance, and his killer in police custody for murder, facing a lengthy prison term.

It had been successful, that much was true. But it had been a distraction. And what was worse, the *Guardia Suiza* – an already depleted body – had one fewer to its number. Finding someone to replace Mimon would be difficult. And this was the main concern on Carlos's mind as he edged his way along. Not just that he had lost an operative, but that he had done so at a critical time, when the services of the *Suiza* might be called upon at any moment. Things were moving into a critical phase and security for the entire operation was of paramount importance. What was more, just as he was mopping up after Mimon's disposal, a report had reached him of a possible security breach, one which, as soon as he reached his desk, he would take a closer look at. No sooner was one problem dealt with than another cropped up. Hence the need for steel-like calm, even here in the clogged-up artery of a decaying city.

Despite the gloom, however, there was one thing to be more cheerful about that morning, and he reflected on it as, for the first time in what felt like an age, he was able to move up into second and even third gear. An email had come through just as he was cleaning up Mimon's liquidation that *Operación Covadonga* was now complete. Valencia and Seville stations had both reported that the necessary measures had been taken and that National Police and *Guardia Civil* investigations into Islamic extremist groups had been successfully shut down in their respective areas. As of now, no unmonitored or uncontrolled agents of the State would be sniffing around anything that they shouldn't. It was a key element in the overall security operation, a necessary, centralising move that would make the rest flow that much more easily. Knowing that there was one less thing to concern him caused Carlos's jaw to relax. For a moment, with annoyance at his lack of self-control, he realised that he had been biting the inside of his cheek so hard that he had drawn blood.

He turned off the A6, heading along the slip road leading to the three-pointed-star office block at the side of the motorway which was home to his country's intelligence and security service – the *Centro Nacional de Inteligencia* – the

CNI. By the time he found a place to park, the bleeding in his mouth had stopped. Coffee would soon remove any aftertaste. The relief at having finally arrived came with a sigh and a stifled yawn as he picked up his shiny black leather briefcase from the passenger seat and uncurled himself out of the car.

Yes, he thought, there were things to be grateful for that morning, and he should do his best to concentrate on them. One particular detail about the completion of *Covadonga* had caught his eye – a new member of the useful-idiot category within the Valencia Jefatura: a commissioner by the name of Rita Hernández. Patriotic, religious and obedient, and seemingly delighted to follow this particular request. And an offer to do more if ever her services were required in the future. Yes, Hernández could prove useful at some point. Carlos had had dealings in Valencia in the past. It could be a tricky place at times.

SIX

Félix Azcárraga didn't like the new set-up in the operations room. The rotas had changed, meaning officers could be called in at any time for duty over an eight-day period, even if that meant – as had happened on more than one occasion – doing an impromptu double shift through the night and into the next morning. It was meant to make the police a more flexible organisation, part of the drive to create a 'modern' law-enforcement agency that could operate in a 'changing world'. Whatever that meant. What it actually meant, for people like Azcárraga, was that life had effectively been reduced to these four walls, with the giant, multicoloured screen at one end, showing a map of Valencia with moving dots representing the various squad cars – the *zetas* – on duty, with further, colour-schemed lights flashing at various points indicating incidents. Thankfully, this morning had been relatively quiet so far, but the incessant sound of the police radios – several at once – crackling away from across the city, and the hawk-like eye of the duty officer staring down at them from his glass-walled office meant that there was never any rest. Pretending he was busy took up far more energy than actually being so.

He was keeping an eye on his surroundings, trying to gauge whether there might be a chance to take a quick look at the reports on the weekend's matches – Athletic Bilbao, his team, had destroyed Seville at home 5–0 only the day before – when he caught sight of someone walking in from the side door. Someone he hadn't seen for some time, who didn't often make it into the ops room.

'Morning, Chief Inspector,' he beamed. 'To what do we owe the pleasure?'

Cámara shook Azcárraga's hand, grabbed a spare seat from the adjacent desk and sat down next to him.

'Good to see you,' he said.

'You come all this way just to see me?' Azcárraga said, surprised. 'I'm flattered.'

They had barely worked together before, in fact they had merely been in the building together briefly, late one night when the place was virtually closed down, in the days before moves towards 'twenty-four-hour policing' had been introduced. But it had been enough for the two of them to create a bond – two naughty boys playing pranks while the teachers weren't looking. A few shared cigarettes outside and an understanding that the system was there to be dodged, not obeyed, had been enough to make them recognise each other as kindred spirits.

'How're things going?' asked Cámara.

Azcárraga shrugged and pulled a face, and was about to say something when he glanced behind Cámara's shoulder and flicked his chin up. Cámara turned to see.

'Morning. It's Chief Inspector Cámara, isn't it?'

Cámara saw the figure of a portly, red-faced inspector in his late fifties grinning anxiously down at him. Peralta's drink problem was well known throughout the Jefatura – it had cost him two marriages. As was his temper.

'Can we be of assistance?'

Peralta's smile broadened, eyes narrowing into folds of fatty skin. The message was clear: the operations room was his kingdom – if anyone from outside came in, they had to go through him first.

Cámara tried to think. So far that morning, the only police work he could see in action was policemen trying to police their own colleagues. The Jefatura was beginning to feel more like a prison camp than an operations centre.

He stood up and reached for Peralta's hand.

'Forgive me,' he said, giving it as warm a shake as he could. 'I got carried away. You know how it is when you're on the chase.'

'On a case, are you?' Peralta said, baring his teeth as the grin began to morph into a grimace. 'I heard there were changes afoot. Something about you being reassigned.'

Cámara let go of his hand.

'I would expect you, of all people, to be well informed,' he said.

'Oh, not just me,' Peralta said breezily. 'Pretty much everyone's heard about Special Crimes being closed down. Must be quite a blow. Don't know what I'd do in your shoes. Probably think about quitting. After all that work you'd put into it. What's the name of the inspector who was with you?'

'Torres.'

'Must be tough for him as well. But even more so for you. I mean, he's just a lowly inspector, like myself. But you're a chief inspector. *A gran subida, gran caída*.' The bigger they are, the harder they fall.

Cámara grinned. Was this man really trying to use a proverb? No one in the entire *Policía Nacional* had as many refrains at his fingertips as Cámara: they had been drilled into him by his grandfather since childhood and formed a kind of parallel bloodstream within his body, a life force that he could draw on at any moment, like a subtle, invisible web of knowledge stretching back through time.

'But as *you* also know, Peralta,' he said, '*mala hierba nunca muere*.' A bad plant never dies.

Peralta sniffed, failing to find a riposte.

'I suspect I'll be around for some time yet,' Cámara continued, and as he did so, a way out became clear to him.

'Commissioner Hernández herself sent me,' he said. 'The matter's urgent and Azcárraga here can help us on a small detail. As to my position, let's just say things aren't always what they seem. You get my meaning? I'm not at liberty to say any more at present.'

Peralta stiffened. He was trapped: he doubted very much that Cámara was involved in any undercover work, yet the doubt was enough for him to pull back.

'One minute,' he sneered. 'Not a second more.'

Cámara sank back into his chair; Azcárraga watched until he had gone, then nodded to Cámara.

'Let's make this quick,' he said. 'Bastard's making my life hell enough as it is.'

'OK.' Cámara rubbed his face, as though trying to clean himself.

'Yesterday,' he said. 'You took a call.'

Azcárraga tilted his head to the side and gave him an exasperated look.

'Can you be more specific?'

'José Luis Mendoza,' said Cámara. 'Owner of the Sunset. A call came in.'

Azcárraga nodded. He understood: Peralta was right. Cámara had very clearly been kicked in the pants if he was being given stuff like this to deal with.

'Just some crazy guy,' he said. 'Nothing to—'

'What did he say?' interrupted Cámara.

'Not very much.' Azcárraga shrugged. 'It was over almost as soon as it started. Call came in, guy on the phone, wouldn't give his name, squeaked something about the death not being accidental, being deliberate.'

He threw up his hands.

'But you know the kind of thing. We get this stuff all the time. Especially when it's a famous person, or someone people have heard of, like José Luis. I mean, he's no celebrity or anything, but most people in Valencia have probably heard his name mentioned. Or at least enough people have. So it's just another one of those types who have to make everything more sinister, like a conspiracy. That's all. Really, Chief Inspector.' His voice changed: less informing, more consoling. 'There's nothing in it. Some bored idiot trying to make his day more exciting, that's all.'

Cámara nodded.

'Did he say anything else?'

'No, that was it.'

'You said he squeaked. What do you mean?'

Azcárraga frowned.

'Well, I don't know. He had one of those squeaky kinds of voices.'

'Squeaky?'

'High-pitched, a bit nasal.'

Cámara squinted at him.

'You know what I mean,' Azcárraga said, lowering his voice; Cámara leaned in. 'Typical *maricón*. A poof.'

Azcárraga glanced around, making sure no one could hear.

'Got to be careful what you say these days. Never know who's listening.'

'So you're saying he was gay?'

'Well, I don't know. He wasn't trying to chat me up or anything. But, well, he certainly sounded like one, or a bit like one.'

Cámara sat back in his seat. From the side office, Peralta glanced in his direction, tapping at his wrist with his forefinger.

'All right,' said Cámara, 'I'd better go before I get you into more trouble.'

He made to get up.

'Listen,' he said. 'We need to trace that number, find out who made the call.'

Azcárraga blew out his cheeks.

'I can't do that,' he said. 'Not without going through the proper channels. And besides, we need a permit, get a judge involved.'

'It's got to be done,' Cámara whispered. 'I'm serious.'

'You sure you're not—?'

'Get in touch with Judge Jurado,' said Cámara. 'He's one of the old school, total trust of the police, doesn't give a shit about citizens' rights. Get him to give you the necessary go-ahead.'

Azcárraga stared at him, eyes bulging.

'I'll get the sack.'

'Any trouble,' Cámara went on, 'get in touch with Inspector Torres. Tell him it's through me. He'll understand.'

Azcárraga shook his head in disbelief.

'Not get me into any more trouble, you said. This'll land me deep in the shit if it goes wrong. And for what? For some case that's just a simple accidental death? You can't expect me—'

'Listen,' Cámara said, leaning forwards and gripping him tightly by the upper arm. 'I've never been more serious. The fucking inmates are taking over the asylum. There aren't many sane ones left. We're a shrinking minority and we have to stick together. Do this for me. Do whatever it takes. Afterwards you can ask for whatever you want.'

'I want to get out of here,' said Azcárraga. 'I want a real job. A job in *Homicidios*.'

'Do this,' said Cámara, 'and I'll get you in. You have my promise.'

He stood up to leave.

'I don't get it,' said Azcárraga. 'What's so important to you about this?'

'We have to make a difference,' said Cámara. 'While we still can.'

Azcárraga watched him walk out and down along the corridor until he disappeared. Then he turned back to his desk.

Sane ones? What the hell was he talking about? There wasn't a crazier person in the entire building.

SEVEN

Cámara parked his motorbike on the pavement outside the glass-fronted courtroom buildings alongside half a dozen other machines in the shade of a jacaranda tree. He took off his helmet, locked it inside the top box behind the pillion seat and prepared himself. He'd been to the courtrooms before, many dozens of times, yet it was his knowledge of what lay inside the smaller structure that abutted it – where he was headed now – that always caused a swirling tightness to form in his stomach. The Centre for Forensic Science had a relatively innocuous name, but it was where autopsies were carried out, and having witnessed more than a few over the years, Cámara could almost smell the dead bodies lying within its walls before he even opened the door: the acrid, tinny stench of coagulated blood; the metallic lemon of the disinfectants; the animal pungency of faeces scooped out for analysis from sliced-up intestines. He would do anything not to have to be there right now – ever, even – yet it was a necessary first stopping-off point before he could proceed.

Nervously, he stuck his hands in his jacket pockets, where he felt the smooth casing of his phone against his fingertips. Yes, he thought instinctively, this would be a most opportune moment to make the call.

He found a wall to lean against. After a few seconds, the line at the other end was ringing.

There was a pause before it was answered.

'Hello, chief.'

Cámara's shoulders dropped. Just two words from his colleague and he knew that everything was going to be all right.

'I was wondering when you were going to call,' said Torres. 'Bit miffed you took so long about it, to be honest. I've got feelings too, you know.'

'How's life treating you?' asked Cámara.

'What? Since I saw you last night in the office? Well, I've had better mornings, tell the truth.'

'People in Narcotics treating you well?'

'Almost too nicely.'

Cámara registered the sarcastic tone.

'Enjoy it while it lasts. Got your own desk?'

'Well, I've got to work somewhere.'

'Lucky bastard.'

'What?' said Torres. 'No room for you in *Homicidios*?'

'Haven't been in yet.'

'Where are you now?'

'Outside the Forensic Science Centre.'

'Oh,' said Torres. There was no need to explain: he knew how much Cámara hated the place. If he was there it must be for a reason.

'Got a case already? That's quick. It's only half-past ten. You were sacked – sorry, transferred – just over an hour ago.'

'It's almost certainly nothing,' said Cámara. 'Routine check.'

'What are you going to do?' Torres asked.

'Well, eventually, perhaps after a cigarette or two, I'm going to steel myself and go inside, I suppose.'

'No, I mean about this. About Rita.'

'You OK to talk?'

'I'm not in the middle of the Narcotics office, if that's what you mean,' said Torres. 'When I saw your call I stepped out. So, you sticking around or what? I was half-expecting you to tell me you were quitting.'

Cámara paused.

'I'm tempted, course I am.'

'Can't live without me, that's the problem. Life in the police without me at your side is no life at all.'

Cámara chuckled.

'Something like that.'

'But?'

'But I need something to leave for,' said Cámara. 'Some other project first. Once I find that, I'll jump.'

'Sounds a bit sensible for you. You feeling all right?'

'I'll be fine. What about you?'

'I'm not going anywhere,' said Torres. 'My son's still at school, I've got maintenance to pay and rent to keep up with. They've got me by the balls, and they know it.'

'So have Narcotics put you on to anything yet?'

'Letting me find my feet, is what I was told. They'll be checking me out, see if they can trust me. You know how this unit is.'

Torres was right. Barely a year went by without some Narcotics officer being sent down for dodgy dealings of some sort: the huge amounts of cash that moved within the drug world were too powerful a temptation for many policemen, particularly when compared with their own modest salaries. Cámara knew himself: years before he had been a member of the unit and witnessed colleagues stuffing the occasional – or not-so-occasional – note or two of drug money into their back pockets. There were others, however, who were actually in the pay of the drug barons. The air of suspicion and lack of trust between fellow officers had driven him out in the end.

'OK,' said Cámara. 'If you've got some spare time, and you're comfortable with this . . .'

'Hah!' laughed Torres. 'You kidding?'

'Great,' said Cámara with a smile. 'Can you do some background checks for me?'

'That never was your forte.'

'José Luis Mendoza,' said Cámara.

'The Sunset guy? What's happened to him?'

'Well, I'm sure he's felt better.'

'Is that why you're . . . ?'

Cámara glanced towards the entrance of the Forensic Science Centre.

'Yes,' he said.

'Murdered?'

'Dunno.'

'All right. What do you want?'

'Anything. His past, background. Anything that stands out. Anything that doesn't stand out.'

'All right,' laughed Torres. 'The usual, then. Any time pressure here?'

Cámara clicked his tongue.

'No worries, chief,' said Torres. 'I'm on it.'

'Thanks,' said Cámara. They were back, a duo again, almost as if nothing had changed. As though Rita didn't even exist.

'Oh, and listen,' he added. 'Someone in the ops room might be in touch. Guy called Azcárraga.'

'No problem. What do you want me to do?'

'Help him in any way you can,' said Cámara. 'He's one of the good guys.'

'Got it.'

'OK, I'd better go.'

'I'll give you a call.'

The line went dead. Cámara put the phone back in his pocket and felt his packet of cigarettes nestling at the bottom. It was time for a smoke.

The taste of tobacco on his breath only served as a partial barrier, however. His head swirled for a moment as the usual cocktail of scents greeted him in reception. The woman behind the desk recognised him.

'*Hola*.'

'Is Dr Quintero around?' asked Cámara. 'I'd like to have a word.'

A couple of minutes later, sitting in a visitor's chair, Cámara heard his name being called.

'Max!'

Cámara stood up, watching as an erect, slim, grey-haired man approached, a beaming smile on his face. Cámara could never quite understand how someone who spent his day cutting up bodies could be so unfailingly cheerful. His white coat alone – as bright as the ones those fake doctors wore in TV adverts – seemed to reek of death.

'Darío,' he said, shaking the man's hand warmly. 'Thanks for seeing me like this.'

'Not at all,' said Quintero. 'I've got a few minutes. Come with me.'

They passed through swing doors into a corridor. Double metal doors at the far end marked the entrance to where the dead were kept.

'I heard something about changes at the Jefatura,' said Quintero in a lower voice. 'Not affecting you, I sincerely hope.'

'I've been reassigned,' said Cámara. 'Back in *Homicidios*.'

'They've put you in charge?'

The look in Cámara's eye said everything.

'Oh, I see,' said Quintero. 'I . . . well. *No hay mal que por bien no venga*.' Every cloud has its silver lining.

Cámara smiled.

'Yes, you're right,' he said. 'It's what I've been telling myself all morning.'

'So,' said Quintero, 'if you're back in *Homicidios*, I assume you're here to see one of our guests.'

'José Luis Mendoza,' said Cámara. 'Should have checked in yesterday.'

'Ah, yes. Owned one of those nightclubs, didn't he? Somewhere up in the mountains?'

'Never been myself.'

'No, of course not. Well, I haven't had a look at him yet. I think he's scheduled for tomorrow. We've got a bit of a glut at the moment. Bad case of food poisoning at an old people's home.'

Quintero checked his watch.

'But we could take a very quick look at him now if that would help.'

Cámara nodded, more out of duty than actual desire.

Quintero headed towards the double metal doors. After a pause, Cámara followed.

An assistant was inside, writing name labels to put on the drawers. Quintero asked her about José Luis and she pointed to his slot.

'That's right,' said Quintero to himself. 'We tend to put the heavier ones in the middle,' he explained to Cámara. 'Gives us more room to manoeuvre them about. Problem is, everyone's getting heavier these days.'

He pulled open the drawer. Cámara swallowed. The sheet was removed, revealing the cold, naked body of a fat, middle-aged man. The assistant handed over a file before heading out the door.

'Thanks, Luisa,' said Quintero.

'Those are the ones I need more of,' he said to Cámara once she had gone. 'Proactive, doesn't need asking first.'

Cámara was staring down at José Luis. There was a resemblance there to the photos he must have seen on occasion, perhaps in newspapers or on TV. It was difficult trying to get a reading from a corpse: death changed and disfigured people, took them worlds away from who they had been while still alive. Yet despite the ghostly grey of his complexion, the sinking of his chin, yellow front teeth sticking out from his mouth, Cámara thought he could detect a kindness there, perhaps a generosity and sensuality in what had once been full lips. Lines around his eyes seemed to speak more of laughter than concern or anger. Even stiff and emptied of life, an echo of the jollity of the man was almost perceptible.

Quintero scanned the file.

'Not much here,' he said. 'He was found up near the nightclub. Declared dead once he got to La Fé.'

Cámara glanced over the body, alert for clues. Several blue marks – small, slightly raised circles on the neck and hands – caught his attention. He pointed them out. Quintero leaned across, putting on his glasses to get a better view.

'Look like some kind of insect bite or sting, at first glance,' he said with a frown.

He knelt down, peering closer.

'I'll check properly tomorrow, but that might be a sting still inside.'

He pointed, but Cámara couldn't make anything out.

Something on the dead man's arm caught Quintero's eye. He prodded at a couple of tiny dots in the inside elbow.

'Looks like our friend injected himself from time to time. An occasional drug user, perhaps?'

Cámara frowned.

'It would fit, I suppose. That kind of lifestyle.'

'Or maybe he had a medical condition that required using a syringe sometimes. There's nothing more I can say right now. We'll take a closer look tomorrow.'

He closed the drawer and they stepped back out into the corridor.

Quintero put a hand on Cámara's shoulder.

'You want this to be a murder, don't you,' he said. 'Need it to be a murder.'

Cámara sniffed.

'You know if I could I would make it one,' continued

Quintero. 'But only the results speak the truth. I'm afraid you may be disappointed.'

'Don't worry,' said Cámara, shaking his hand. 'I appreciate you taking the time.'

'I'll be in touch,' said Quintero. 'As soon as I know.'

EIGHT

Her mobile started to ring as she finished dressing, flattening out the wrinkles in her jeans around her thighs and bending at the knees to make the cloth stretch into shape. She had a feeling it would be Max with some nonsensical romantic words to complete and sustain the liquescent joy of their earlier lovemaking. She brushed her hair off her face and went to pick up: the number on the screen looked unfamiliar.

'*¿Hola?*'

'Alicia?'

'Yes.'

'It's Nacho.'

She paused, dimmed lights from the past beginning to glimmer inside her.

'Nacho? My God! What . . . ? How . . . ?'

'Are you doing anything this morning?'

She was trying to work out how long it had been. Six,

seven years – perhaps more – since their last get-together, when half a dozen from the old university crowd had managed to be in the same place long enough for a dinner and a chance to rediscover one another. She had spent most of the evening talking to Marta, she recalled, and Pablo. But Nacho had been there, tall and angular, with that sparkle in his eyes that spoke of both fear and excitement, as though he had something extraordinary and terrifying to tell. Nacho had always been different, present yet at one slightly darkened remove from the others. It gave him a sense of mystery, although not necessarily of the attractive kind.

And now, true to form in some strange way, he was on the other end of the line, forgoing the usual rituals of friends from the past reconnecting. What did he want?

'Are . . . are you in Valencia?' she asked.

'Yes.' He sounded tired, his throat constricted. 'But only for a few hours. I just thought, perhaps, seeing as I'm here, and if you weren't too busy with things. But really, I understand. You're tied up. Should have rung before. It's just that . . .'

'It's fine,' she said. 'It'll be great to see you. Why don't we . . .' She tried to think about where they could meet.

'San Vicente,' he said. 'By the old convent.'

'OK.' It wasn't the most obvious place, and it was a little out of the centre, but she could still walk there from the flat. 'What time?'

'Twelve o'clock good?'

'That's fine.'

'See you then.'

'Great,' she said. 'Looking forward to it.'

There was silence from the other end: Nacho had already hung up.

She spent the rest of the morning checking emails and reading the news. The apartment was in a mess and needed a tidy – actually more than that, a damn good clean – but she put her domestic self in its place and concentrated on more important matters: the papers were filled with stories of the recession and its growing repercussions. The government in Madrid looked more unstable than ever; a new civil-disobedience movement was gaining strength, feeding off a growing sense that voting never brought any actual change. Then there was the persistent, nagging threat of more Islamic terror attacks, creating a collective anxiety that became deeper rooted every day. Plenty of news was there to be reported, but the economic outlook meant that her chances of getting full-time work again as a journalist were worse than before. Yes, people wanted to know what was going on, but they weren't prepared to pay for it. And part of her didn't blame them – many had more important things like paying the rent or feeding their children to worry over. But it did mean that she had to think in different ways about how to relaunch her career.

The past few years had been difficult – first losing her job at the paper in Madrid, then scratching around as a freelance. It had worked for a time. Until the medical-funding case and the episode in the underground. She still found it hard entering enclosed spaces, a kind of claustrophobia that was, a doctor had told her, a normal reaction to what happened. Others might have suffered greater psychological damage, she was informed. They admired her ability to cope. Yet scars did remain, she knew. Not just on her skin where the thugs had put out their cigarettes, but deeper inside. Scars like that could not be erased. But that did not mean they had to take control, either. She saw them, she recognised them, and she did her best to keep them at bay. Life threw stuff at you and how you dealt with it was the important thing. Becoming a victim, wallowing in what had happened, was not the kind of person she was.

Not that recovering had been easy. Max had helped – as he always did. And she knew she had made him suffer as a result, had even blamed him for a time. But it was, she had told herself – had told him when she was able – never her punishing him: it was the scars. And now the scars were dormant. No need to inflame them any further by dwelling or remembering. It was not and had never been his fault: she had leapt at the chance to help him with the case, and what they had exposed together – the rotting corruption scandal at the heart of Valencian politics – had brought some degree of change, had opened eyes to what was going on. Which meant that her pain had not been without cause. She could reason it into stillness this way, give it shape and meaning. And finally place it out of her way.

And now, yes, she felt ready – ready to embrace her own world once more. Nothing like that could ever happen to her again, she reasoned: lightning didn't strike in the same place twice. There was no need for fear. And she felt a longing for a proper story to follow, like a dog lusting for a bone. Some, she knew – editors, potential employers – saw her as being too old: she was in her late forties and had been out of the game for some time. But she had beaten off bigger problems before. And she knew exactly where they could stick their prejudice.

She jotted down a few notes – questions arising from the news stories she was reading, possible articles or lines of investigation that she could follow on her own – and checked the time: it was past half-eleven. She would have to go.

The crumbling Gothic stone doorway to the convent had no shade, and she stood in the blistering late-spring sunshine, shading her eyes with her hand and searching for Nacho. He was normally easy to spot, towering over most people and with his pronounced, mule-like features. Yet it was already five past twelve and she could see no sign of him. She pulled her phone out of her bag, thinking that she would wait another five minutes before calling. Cars roared into motion as the lights changed, and the wide avenue was filled with bellowing noise. At first the hissing sound appeared to be coming from the traffic – perhaps some wheezing old engine or the brakes on a bus. But it was insistent and after a while she realised it was coming from another direction. She turned her head to the right and caught sight of a figure in the shade of a tree, beckoning her with a low, suspicious movement of the hand.

Nacho?

She hitched her bag up on her shoulder and went to see.

'Alicia,' said the figure as she stepped closer. 'It's me.'

He was standing behind the tree, beckoning her closer. Alicia slowed down. Had it finally happened, what they had always feared for him?

'Nacho,' she said with a nervous laugh. 'What's going on?'

'Follow me,' he said. 'Not too close. Just follow. We can't be seen here. I'll explain in a minute.'

He took a step away and walked in the opposite direction, quickly and with a light, uncertain stiffness. Alicia found herself glancing around the street to see if anyone was watching – genuinely or simply to play along, she couldn't say – then started following, careful not to get too close. At the first opportunity he turned right up a side street. When she came round the same corner, he had vanished – presumably into the small neighbourhood bar, whose grimy red-and-white canopy was the only decoration in an otherwise drab prospect.

She resisted the temptation to check behind her as she stepped inside. The place was half full; Nacho was sitting at a table at the far end, his back against the wall and with a full view of people coming and going.

He pulled out a chair for her, its aluminium legs scraping on the tiled floor. A cup with the remains of a *café con leche* sat in the middle of the table. Had he been here some time already?

'Thanks for coming. So great to see you.'

She tried to look into his eyes as they kissed each other on the cheeks, searching for signs of . . . what? Would she even recognise it if it were there?

'I have to give it to you, Nacho,' she said. 'First the surprise call, now this.' She kept her expression light, playful, intrigued.

'Listen,' he said as they both sat down. 'You're still a journalist, right?'

A couple of minutes later, two fresh cups of coffee were on the table before them, Alicia having got them herself after sensing Nacho's reluctance to leave his chair, his eyes flickering every couple of seconds or so towards the door.

'Do you want something to eat?' she asked. The bar had some tortilla that looked edible, and some ham-and-tomato sandwiches recently made by the bar owner's wife. She had ordered one for herself. But Nacho shook his head.

'Sure?'

He stared out over the bar, watching the door, no reply.

The drugs, they had all blamed the drugs. Nacho had taken them along with the rest – it was what you did at university back then. But the impact had always seemed greater in Nacho, some inner balance disturbed, perhaps irrevocably. For the others it had been about having fun, breaking rules, even a degree of some psychological exploration – although never in any self-conscious kind of way. There had been one or two freak-outs, moments when the fun had given way to darker experiences. And as a group they had more or less given them up. But Nacho had continued – or so they suspected. The damage became more visible in him, if not in a clearly definable way. Yet now, as they sat in this little bar, Alicia had the feeling of being with a wreck of a man, a paranoid, shaking husk of a person who had once had so much promise, a token scientist among their humanities-dominated group and easily the brightest and most academically promising of them all.

Almost automatically she clicked into listening, sympathetic mode, like some sort of therapist. She was already thinking of people she knew, health workers, experts in this kind of thing who might be able to help.

'What's happened, Nacho? What's going on?'

NINE

Back at his motorbike, Cámara pulled his helmet out, and paused. Should he give Alicia a quick call? Their lovemaking that morning felt like a distant memory, yet he smiled at the thought of her, wondered what she would be doing right now. She had been speaking recently about trying to get back into journalism, perhaps find a job at one of the local papers. It was still a bad time, yet there were people out there trying new things, not giving up on quality news reporting. They might, she reasoned, appreciate her experience.

Cámara had encouraged her. The good thing was that they could get by on his salary alone. But now, after what had happened, her finding paid work would be an even better idea: he had no idea how things might develop in the coming days or weeks.

He wanted to ring her, wanted to tell her about the morning's events, Rita, his effective demotion. But he didn't want to worry her. She might blame herself, say that she had made him late that morning. And it would only put more pressure on her to get a job, perhaps push her down a wrong path, make the wrong choice.

He slipped his helmet over his head and climbed on to the bike. It could wait. She would hear everything when he got back home later that night.

The bike fired into life and he wheeled it off the pavement on to the road before feeding into the traffic, crossing the old river bed and heading north through the city. A wide, tree-lined avenue took him past modern, square buildings, with shiny square windows looking into box-shaped apartments. The most expensive homes in the city were in this area, with views over the new but already crumbling complex of museums and theatres that had become the symbol of Valencia. The City of Arts and Sciences had cost hundreds of millions, with large amounts of the cash being siphoned off to line the pockets of politicians and officials. Some of these were now in jail or facing charges, but not enough to remove the stench of decay about the city, its reputation as Spain's capital of corruption. It would take generations, and many more successful prosecutions, to change that.

He spurred the bike on, twisting the accelerator to push past the cars, finding gaps down the middle, speeding through traffic lights just as they turned red. Once he got past the old fishermen's quarter – the Cabanyal – he turned and rode up through the university campus before connecting with the motorway and pushing out of the city.

The sea to his left was a gently ruffled carpet of deep indigo, with barely a wave breaking its surface. A row of elderly men lined the sea wall, sitting shirtless in fold-up chairs and sipping cans of beer pulled from iceboxes as the floats on their fishing lines bobbed up and down in the quietly rolling surf.

He peered up at an almost cloudless sky. The heat was rising and the wind pulsing through his clothes brought welcome relief to his skin, yet the air was still relatively clear: the humid haze of high summer had yet to come and the mountains ahead in the distance were clearly visible, green and lush after the late-spring rains. He looked forward to breathing the lighter, drier air up there. He could be up at Sunset in less than half an hour.

He turned off at El Puig and entered the sea of orange groves to the north of the city. Their blooms had all but gone by now, replaced by small shiny green balls of fruit. He caught sight of a lone farmer tending to some of his trees, a straw hat on his head and espadrilles on his feet - attire that hadn't changed for centuries.

Cámara sped on, working his way along winding country roads, a slope rising as he began to reach the foothills of the sierra. The orange groves gave way to fields of carob and olive trees. After passing the town of Náquera, with its fin-de-siècle summer villas and neatly tended gardens, he broke out into the mountains, greeted by pockets of tight cold air sitting in shaded folds of the rocks, and the prickly, embracing scent of pine as the trees around him warmed and glowed light green in the late-morning sun.

The nightclub was close, a few kilometres further on and up a turning to the right. Most people knew how to find Sunset, even if they'd never actually been. You could see the building from afar, some claimed, from the city itself on the clearest days. It was one of those swaggering country estates that some newly enriched Valencian grandee had built for himself in the early 1900s. Cámara suspected that the man would be turning in his grave if he knew what went on today at his former home.

Cámara had been to other nightclubs often enough. For years, in the eighties and nineties, Valencia had been famous for its Ruta de Bakalao, the string of discos around the city where gut-thumping electronic music played through the night and well into the morning. It had been rivalled only by the Ibiza scene, a badge of pride among the city's youth, who decorated their Seats and Vespas with brightly coloured stickers from their favourite venues. Now the Ruta itself was no longer what it had been, and many had declared it dead. Yet a handful of the old places were still going, names like Barraca and Bananas that were legendary among a certain generation. Cámara himself had taken mescaline for the first time inside the Barraca toilets, as had almost half the city in the eighties. The drugs had been cheap and of good quality back then; people were experimenting and having fun. The ugliness came later.

A culture of some kind had attached itself to most of the venues. The Face was the trendiest and most expensive, with a snob value that cut against the grain of what having a night out was all about, as far as Cámara was concerned. Barraca had its top-class DJs; Bananas its strip acts and live sex shows. Yet Sunset had always been different. Set apart from the others, high in the sierra and looking down on the fertile city plain, it had an otherness about it. Some said that it had become a favourite among the gay community. Certainly everyone knew – or at least assumed – that its owner, José Luis, was gay. Yet Cámara knew of women going there – he had overheard a group of Alicia's friends saying they had been at least once, perhaps several times. Others who mentioned the place would also contradict the rumour that it was strictly a gay disco. Anyone went there, and people of all ages – a greater range than at many of the other haunts. Yet what went on at Sunset was the subject of dark rumour.

Cámara remembered a case from perhaps a year before. A young man in his early twenties had been found dead there. The autopsy revealed a powerful cocktail of drugs in his system, some combination of cocaïne, methamphetamine and GHB injected into his bloodstream. Sunset was the kind of place where the latest hedonistic trends tended to be tried out first, almost a testing ground for what became the fashion down on the coast months later.

Needless to say, there were many voices clamouring for it to be closed, condemning it as a den of vice, a centre even – in the eyes of some – of Satanic ritual. No priest or bishop was worth his salt, it seemed, unless he made a public denunciation of Sunset at some point in his career. In fact it was a wonder, given the enigmatic, suspicious air about the place, that someone hadn't found an excuse to shut its doors.

Yet here it still was, a crowning presence among the pine forests. Cámara wondered what would happen to it now that José Luis was no longer around.

He found the turning, with a sign showing a red setting sun, and steered the bike up the last kilometre or so. The road narrowed dramatically, twisting sharply as it climbed. In patches the tarmac had ruptured where tree roots had crept underneath and burst through to the surface. Cámara gripped the handlebars tightly, dodging them as best he could. A long drop to a dark gulley fell to his right, with no crash barrier to stop him should he make a mistake.

Through a gap in the forest he thought he could make out the main nightclub building, flashing white and yellow in the sunlight. He heard the low rumbling of an engine on the road not far away, although with the tight corners it was impossible to tell whether it was behind or in front.

Around a bend, the tarmac came to a sudden halt, rocky dirt track continuing beyond. Cámara resisted the temptation to slam on the brakes: he could easily lose control of the bike on a surface like that. He felt the bump of the suspension as he rode over a large stone in his way, his backside momentarily losing contact with the seat.

He dropped the revs and cruised for a second, trying to spot other obstacles in his path.

The sound of the engine suddenly burnt in his ears. He looked up and saw a black BMW with tinted-glass windows come hurtling round a corner, heading straight at him. Instinctively, Cámara hurled the bike to the side, trying to dodge it. But the car swerved in the dirt, pointing its nose again towards him and accelerating. Breathless, Cámara pulled on the handlebars, angling the bike away from the approaching car, yet his path was blocked by a rockfall on to the track. Spotting his only escape – a tight gap between two boulders on the other side – Cámara sped across and delved into the forest undergrowth just as the car whizzed past, inches away from his back wheel.

As it did so, Cámara turned to see: the driver's window was down. A swarthy face, unshaven and puffy, stared back at him through mirror-lens sunglasses. Behind him, in the passenger seat, was another man, shaded from view.

The car slowed for a moment, as though the driver was thinking about reversing, trying once more to run over the motorcyclist he had found in his way. Yet the second man gestured that they should drive on. The engine screamed and the wheels spun in the dirt, kicking up stones and dust, before speeding away.

Cámara tried to get back on to the road, take down the licence number, but before he could catch a glimpse, it had disappeared.

TEN

The station for the fast train to Madrid was back across the avenue and a few blocks further up. She accompanied him partway, then watched as he broke into a run and dashed across the plaza towards the entrance. The AVE was leaving in five minutes. He would just make it before they closed the platform. It took about an hour and a half to reach the capital these days, down from the three- or four-hour journey of the past.

As she turned to head back the other way, Alicia realised that they hadn't really said goodbye. But then there was so much now on her mind after what he had told her that it was perhaps not surprising. There was a pregnant, buzzing feeling in her, a need to get it down on paper. She went straight back to the bar, hoping to sit at the same table and recreate the conversation as clearly as possible, but it had already been taken. Another table was free, but the place was busier and noisier now with the first workers – dusty builders from nearby roadworks – appearing for an early lunch; instead she walked up the street and found a bench near a small children's playground, empty but for a battered pigeon pecking for invisible crumbs among the cracks in the rubber-matted ground.

She pulled out a notebook and pen, sat down and started writing as quickly as she could, trying to recapture every word of Nacho's story while it was still fresh. His train would have pulled out by now.

'Don't call me,' he had said as he broke off into a run. 'Whatever you do, don't call my mobile.'

She started by writing down what she knew about him, his position and his work.

Ignacio (Nacho) Alberola, 49 (?), Valencian. Graduate from Valencia Politécnica University. Current residence: Madrid? Employer: Complutense University, Madrid. Occupation: marine biologist.

Story:

Carrying out research into colonies of bryozoa in the waters around the island of Cabrera – small, uninhabited rock just off south coast of Mallorca. [Q: How far? Check.] Over 100 different species there – very rich and diverse – excellent venue for studying their behaviour. Clear, largely unpolluted water due to lack of human habitation of the island. This summer was his third season there, working as part of a Complutense team that included two others (didn't give names).

Cabrera is a National Park and has been since the 1990s (?). Formerly a military base. Scientific research there has been ongoing for many years. At the end of this season, however, Nacho and the others were informed by the authorities that permission to continue would not be forthcoming. No reasons were given, any inquiries had to be directed to the Captaincy General in Palma. The announcement was sudden and unexpected.

Nacho's two colleagues were already en route to the mainland when the news came through. Nacho, however, still had to complete some final analyses and had left a piece of equipment back on the island. Not thinking he was doing anything particularly offensive, he borrowed a friend's motorboat and set off to Cabrera at first light, hoping to sneak in, collect his materials and leave without disturbing anyone. Almost as soon as he came in sight of Cabrera, however, he was intercepted by a naval vessel; officials hauled him out of the boat, handcuffed him and told him he was under military arrest.

According to his account, he was blindfolded and taken to the island. There, he was led off the naval vessel and walked up a slope to an old castle (all this became clear to him later), where he was placed in a cell – some kind of dungeon, perhaps. The blindfold was removed and he was informed that he had violated military law by trespassing on Ministry of Defence property. He tried to tell them who he was, that he was a scientist who had been working on the island only the day before, but no one appeared to listen. The door was locked and he was left on his own – for how long he's not certain, but several hours at least.

Then, some time in the early afternoon, the door

opened again and a man in civilian clothes appeared – until then Nacho had only seen men in uniform. The man, who was dressed in a grey suit and tie but gave no name, spoke to Nacho in softer tones, appeared more conciliatory. He apologised for what had happened, explained that Nacho had been foolish not to have taken the order to leave the island seriously, that he quite easily could have been killed. Military manoeuvres of some kind were taking place – war games of some description – hence his rather harsh treatment. However, he – the civilian – had managed to sort things out and Nacho would now be escorted back to Mallorca. He would even be allowed to collect his materials and equipment before leaving. The only condition was that he would have to sign a non-disclosure agreement promising not to tell anyone about what had happened or what he had seen.

Nacho tried to argue that he had been blindfolded and hadn't seen anything, but the man insisted. Nacho asked him who he was, who he worked for. The man refused to give a name, said something about working for the government and stressed that Nacho's signature had to go on the papers before he would be released.

Nacho finally agreed and signed, using his own pen to do so. The man then took the papers along with the pen. A guard was summoned and told to escort Nacho back down to the bay, where the borrowed motorboat had been tied up and his materials and equipment placed inside. As he left the castle, Nacho looked around, but the island looked as it always had. The naval vessel had gone and everything appeared more or less as usual. The only visible change was in the castle itself, which seemed to have been turned into a makeshift military command centre of some kind, with antennae and even a couple of satellite dishes installed on the battlements. These had not been there before.

It was at this moment that Nacho realised he had left his pen behind. He dashed back – the guard must have had no time to react – and re-entered the castle, looking for the man in the grey suit. He found him talking on the phone with his back turned. He appeared to be giving reassurances to the person on the other end that everything was fine, no damage had been done. Then he mentioned a word: 'Clavijo'. It meant nothing to Nacho, but seemed to be of some importance.

When the man in the suit realised Nacho had returned, he rang off and admonished him, using much harsher language than before. Nacho explained that he only wanted his pen back. The guard appeared and tried to explain that Nacho had slipped away. He too received harsh words, was reminded that allowing prisoners to escape was a court-martial offence. Nacho insisted that he wanted his pen back, but the guard simply hauled him away, gripping his arm tightly and marching him back outside and down to his boat. There, an officer of some description read Nacho the riot act yet again and ordered him at gunpoint to get into his boat and sail away. A second vessel escorted him out of the bay and some distance off the coast back towards

Mallorca before turning round and leaving him on his own. He was told that should he try to return he would face a lengthy prison term.

This happened two days ago. Nacho spent that night in Mallorca before flying yesterday into Valencia. Today he has travelled on to Madrid by train.

He is clearly shaken by what happened. Nacho is not the most robust of people – there is a history of mental instability, even illness perhaps, probably brought on – or at least not helped – by drugs taken in his youth. He is frightened. Or paranoid? It's not easy to tell. And he insists there's a story here, that something big is happening on Cabrera and that the authorities are trying to hush it up.

But what, exactly? Admittedly there are reasons to be suspicious, but the explanation that the island is being used for military manoeuvres sounds reasonable and would explain what happened; civilians wandering into a firing range might be expected to be treated harshly, if only for their own safety and to prevent any repeat appearances. Nacho insists there is more to it, however, stressing this word 'Clavijo' that he overheard, as though it were of some significance.

The blindfold, imprisonment, being escorted away at gunpoint . . . Yes, it does seem heavy-handed, but is there a story here? On the face of it, no. And although I believe him, and although he is an old friend, it has to be said that he is not the most reliable of witnesses. Did the officer really draw a gun on him? How much of the story has been embellished by Nacho's delicately balanced imagination? He claims that he has been followed since leaving Mallorca – he saw the same car three times in the street where his parents live, made comments about seeing faces in crowds, men in sunglasses who studiously failed to look straight at him . . .

It's all a bit flaky, not unlike Nacho himself.

She finished writing and glanced up at the swing in front of her: a small girl was being hoisted on to the seat by her grandfather, giggling as her legs got caught in the chains. A moment later, she was being pushed gently back and forth.

'Higher! Higher!' she called. 'Make it go higher.'

Her grandfather smiled.

'Not too much,' he said. 'You don't want to get hurt.'

'Higher!' called the girl.

Alicia put her notebook and pen in her bag and got up from the bench. She could get back to the apartment in twenty minutes or so. Then, perhaps, she would make a couple of calls.

ELEVEN

The track curled around three more corners before widening out for the final approach to the club. Cámara kept the revs down, riding slowly, taking the place in: there was no sign of people, yet a Mercedes was parked at the far side of the building in the shade of a broad-leafed mulberry tree. The land in front of the building was a gently sloping open space of rocky earth, presumably used as a car park judging by the criss-crossed lines of tyre tracks. Cámara pulled in at the edge, flicked out the side stand with his foot and slipped off his helmet, hooking the chin strap on the handlebars.

He was shaken by the incident with the BMW, but reluctant to place any importance on it. Who were they? Joyriders heading home? Drugged-out youths, perhaps, too pumped with chemicals to know what they were really doing? Right now his concentration was focused on the disco, this curious oasis of vice and hedonism in the verdant heart of the mountains.

The main structure was a large, two-storey building painted mostly white with dark yellow detailing on the mouldings around the doors and windows. It was a style more common to Seville and western Andalusia than Valencia. Above the main entrance was a small balcony jutting out from a first-floor window with a flagpole attached. No flag was flying this morning. Most of the windows were closed, with iron bars and wooden shutters bolted on the inside. Cámara approached and looked closer: the hinges on the walls were rusted solid: these windows hadn't been opened for many years: inside, darkness clearly reigned.

He wondered how long José Luis had owned the place, how long it had been a nightclub. He dug into his pocket for his phone and dialled Torres's number again: he might have something already on the dead man. But after a few seconds' silence and several more staring in puzzlement at the screen, Cámara realised that there was no mobile coverage. He pursed his lips: Sunset really did occupy some different, separate space.

No matter: he could find a way of getting in touch with Torres later. For now he would continue sniffing around.

Across the car park, through a gap in the pine trees, he could just make out the shimmer of the sea. The sun had climbed high now, nearing its zenith. Heat burst out of the surrounding stones like popcorn in a pan. He imagined that from the upper storey Valencia itself would be visible down below, with the curl of the coast stretching towards the Montgó mountain at Dénia. Quite a view, if it interested you. He imagined that the many people who frequented this place felt little call to stare out at the horizon, yet something about the positioning of the main house, and what looked like tree stumps in the distance – perhaps of pines that had previously stood in the way of the vistas – suggested that he might be wrong. The grounds, at first glance, were better kept than he might have expected for such a place, with only a slight scattering of rubbish and nightlife detritus on the ground, not the piles of it he remembered from other venues.

He stepped away from the main house, getting a feel for the place. It was ornate and solid – whoever had built it had spent money and energy on creating something special, if rather grand for Cámara's tastes. Still, as a country retreat for the summer months it must have been magnificent. The paving outside the front door was made of cobblestones, with swirling, spiral patterns like snails or seashells. There wasn't a weed growing among them, and each stone shone in the high sunlight, a sheen forged by frequent brushing and mopping. Cámara imagined a small army of assistants and helpers here: gardeners, cleaners, managers, barmen, delivery-men, bouncers. Dozens would be required to keep a place like this going. Yet there was no sign of any of them. It felt very deserted.

He continued strolling around the grounds: clipped box hedges lined the far side of the car park and formed a path-way leading to the side of the house. He could see that at the back were some outbuildings: more modern constructions perhaps, and smaller, but painted in the same Andalusian colours. It was shaded down there, trees at the side of the house forming a kind of tunnel. He turned his feet towards it, all senses open for signs of life.

Something near the ground caught his eye, wedged near the bottom of the box hedges. He knelt down to see: half-shredded toilet paper had embedded itself in the tiny branches and sat listlessly in the motionless air. Cámara tugged at it hesitantly:

it was white, but stained dark, rusty red. He pulled again and more revealed itself, appearing from under the soil where someone had hurriedly tried to bury it. He lifted it to his nose and sniffed: the stains were clearly blood. Whoever it had once belonged to had lost large quantities of it. He pressed it between his fingers: there was still a stickiness to it.

'What the fuck are you doing!'

A voice bellowed from the side. Cámara turned and saw a narrow-shouldered man with a loose belly and shaved head pounding the earth as he stormed towards him.

'We're closed. Go on, get off with you!' said the man.

Cámara stood up.

'Didn't I make myself clear?' The man came closer. Cámara watched his right hand dart behind his back, as though about to draw a weapon.

'Police,' Cámara said.

The man stopped. His hand fell back to his side.

'ID?' he demanded.

Cámara pulled out his wallet, with his police identity card inside. The man took it. Cámara noticed his hands: they were pale and weak, unused to any physical labour. Whoever looked after the grounds, it clearly wasn't him.

'You're the manager, I take it,' he said. The man was still looking at the ID.

'You're a bit far from home, aren't you, Chief Inspector,' he said, handing it back. The emphasis placed on Cámara's rank was deliberate. 'The *Policía Nacional* keeps itself busy down in the city. This is *Guardia Civil* country. You sure you haven't got lost?'

'It's to do with José Luis,' said Cámara.

'That's right,' said the man. 'He died. Yesterday. What the fuck's it got to do with you?'

Cámara nodded. This kind of open hostility towards policemen had become more common in recent years. No one had dared speak to an officer like this in the past, but that had been when memories of having to fear the police were still fresh. This was an ordinary citizen exercising his right to be suspicious of a law-enforcement officer, Cámara told himself. He was no reactionary and held no rose-tinted views about the good old days, but he had to admit that general respect for the law had made life simpler back then.

'Let's start with the formalities, shall we?' he said. 'First of all, what's your name?'

'Paco. And yes,' he added before Cámara could continue, 'I am the manager. And I'm asking you for a second time what you're doing up here.'

'What's your full name?'

Paco left an indignant pause before answering.

'Francisco Jaén Díaz.'

'José Luis died at La Fé hospital,' said Cámara, 'which is why it's a police matter, not *Guardia Civil*. And I'm here making routine checks.'

Paco snorted.

'Must be overstaffed if they can send a chief inspector round for this kind of work. Come on, don't treat me like an idiot – what's the real reason you're here?'

'I came on a motorbike,' said Cámara. 'On my way, two men tried to run me off the road. Just here on the track leading up to the club.'

Paco shrugged.

'Two men driving a black BMW with tinted-glass windows,' continued Cámara. 'Know them?'

'No idea what you're talking about,' said Paco.

'Had any other visitors here before me this morning?'

'No one.'

'Car sound familiar?'

'There are loads like that. Besides, I didn't see it, so how would I know?'

He grinned through small yellowing teeth, dark gaps between all of them.

'Are we done? I've got—?'

'Hold it,' said Cámara. 'A few more questions first. Is Abdelatif around?'

'Never heard of him.'

'Abdelatif Cortbi. José Luis's partner.'

Paco looked confused.

'You mean Abi,' he said at length.

Cámara nodded.

'Never knew his full name,' Paco said. 'Sounds Moroccan or something.'

'Is he around?' asked Cámara.

'He rang earlier. Said he'd be coming back later today.'

'Anyone else here?'

Paco looked to the side, as though trying to decide whether to answer.

'The *Abuelos* will be somewhere, I suppose,' he said.

'*Abuelos*?'

'Vicente and Vicenta. Elderly couple. Which is why we call them the "grandparents". He gardens, she cleans. And cooks sometimes. Don't know where they'll be.'

'I'll find them,' said Cámara.

Paco looked uncomfortable.

'Yeah. Suit yourself. It was an accident, and we're all cut up about it, to be frank. It was his birthday, meant to be a happy occasion, presents and a party and everything.

Instead . . . Not the best time to have police wandering around.'

'Where did it happen?'

Paco waved a hand behind the house.

'Up at the top. Few minutes' walk.'

'Did José Luis often go up there?'

Paco shook his head.

'Do you know why he went up there yesterday?'

Paco shrugged.

'There was a call from Enrique, the guy who owns the land beyond. Said he wanted to meet José Luis, said it was urgent. I passed on the call. Next thing I know . . .' He stopped.

'You took the call from Enrique?'

'Yeah, then I passed the message on.'

'Anything else you remember from yesterday?'

'Isn't this all a bit unnecessary?'

'Routine, as I say,' said Cámara.

'Right, I've got stuff to do.'

Paco turned to leave.

'Have many enemies?' said Cámara. 'José Luis?'

Paco gave a hollow laugh.

'Not many people round here love this place, I can tell you,' he said. 'I imagine there'll be a few bottles of cava opened tonight.'

TWELVE

'Yeah, I'm pretty sure I saw something about it from the news agencies. But, you know, it's just not the right time for something like this. There are bigger stories around at the moment. As you know.'

'I'm aware of them, Sergi. I read the papers from time to time. It's just—'

'I really don't think there's a story there.'

'I just wanted to do some background checking, see what people were saying.'

'Well, as I said, the agencies picked it up, but even they were playing it down and as far as I know no one's running with it. I mean, I can check if you like.'

'That's fine. Don't worry.'

Alicia could see where the conversation was going. Sergi was a former colleague at the Valencian newspaper *Llevant* and nominally in charge of environmental stories – although he could be asked to write on anything from local politics to the sport these days after all the cuts, a generic staff writer, a mere word machine, like everyone was becoming. He was busy and overworked and had a finely attuned nose for what was or was not news. And the Cabrera story was not engaging him.

'Just remind me quickly, will you?' Alicia could sense him itching to hang up. 'What's the actual status of Cabrera?'

'It's a nature reserve. Has been since 1992.'

'But the military . . . ?'

'The military still own it. Some arrangement was reached to allow it to become a nature reserve, but at the same time the military retain control. And can use it how they like. I admit it's a bit strange. But to be honest, with the way things stand, everyone's more concerned about whether they'll still have a job in the morning than the plight of some jellyfish or a handful of birds on a rocky island. At any other time it might be a story – but even then only a small one. I'm sure some of the ecology magazines might be interested. But, you know, they don't pay well. Perhaps not anything at all these days.'

'OK.' Alicia smiled. 'Thanks, Sergi.'

'Look, Alicia,' he said. 'I don't want to be rude or anything, but shouldn't you be looking for bigger stuff than this? I don't know, it's just . . .'

'I'm sure you're right, Sergi. It was a tip-off from a friend. I was simply following it through. But you're surely right.'

'Try the press office for the Captaincy General.'

'I doubt it's worth it.'

'No. But at least get the official word on what's going on, from the source itself. Just saying.'

'Thanks. I'll see.'

'You should come round some time, drop in, say hello.'

'OK. I'll make sure to do that.'

She rang off and tossed her notebook on to the desk by the phone. The apartment felt silent and hollow.

The press officer took her call on the third attempt.

'Yes, this is Lieutenant Espinosa, chief joint military press officer at the Palma de Mallorca Captaincy General.'

Quite a mouthful, but he had perfected the delivery so that it tripped off his tongue with unhesitant fluency. She wondered if being able to do so were a prerequisite for getting the job.

'And you are . . . ?'

The tone was friendly but insistent. She gave her details and named a national newspaper in Madrid. The one she used to work for, but no longer did. But Lieutenant Espinosa didn't need to know that.

'How can I help you?'

'I'm interested in what's going on at the island of Cabrera,' she said.

'The military manoeuvres. Yes, I'm assuming you saw the official statement we sent out about that. Didn't it reach you?'

'Yes . . .'

'I can send you another copy if you like.'

'That's fine. I've seen it.'

'Good,' said the officer. 'So how can I assist you?'

'I was wondering if you might fill in some of the details. Cabrera hasn't been used by the military for anything like this for over twenty years. I'd like to know what prompted the sudden change.'

'Oh, I can assure you there's nothing sudden about it at

all,' said the soldier. 'It's been planned for some time and everyone concerned given ample notification.'

'Really?'

'Yes, yes. I have records of all our communiqués about the matter going back several months. I can send you copies if you like.'

She wondered for a moment – her old email address from the newspaper no longer worked. If she gave him her private address he might suspect something.

'Perhaps I can get back to you on that. But could you clarify what's behind the change? Why now? Why is the military carrying out these exercises now?'

'You will of course understand, Señora Beneyto, that I am not at liberty to discuss everything with you – these are military matters after all. But we are carrying out exercises in preparation for much larger manoeuvres in conjunction with NATO which will be taking place at a future date. That's all I can say. But it was deemed necessary to use Cabrera for this purpose. The island remains a military property and all non-military personnel have – regrettably – had to be evacuated. For their own safety, you'll understand.'

'So you've imposed an exclusion zone around the island?'

'That is correct. We are obliged to exclude all non-military traffic from approaching the island.'

'Is this temporary or permanent?'

'Have you visited Cabrera yourself?'

'No,' said Alicia. 'I haven't.'

'Well, rest assured that you will get the opportunity at some point in the future – it is a beautiful place. But I'm afraid I'm not at liberty to say now when that will be.'

'Thank you,' she said.

'You're very welcome,' said the lieutenant. 'And please do

not hesitate to get back in touch if you want copies of any of those papers and files I mentioned.'

'Thanks.'

'It's been a pleasure.'

'Oh, wait,' said Alicia before he rang off. 'Sorry, just one last quick question. Is the term "Clavijo" linked to any of this at all? *Operación Clavijo*, perhaps? Is that the name given to the exercises?'

There was silence from the other end.

'Lieutenant?' Alicia said.

'Urgent call,' said the soldier. 'I have to go. Goodbye.'

THIRTEEN

Paco slumped off, heading for the main door of the house, and disappeared into the dark interior. After a pause, Cámara turned and walked the other way, continuing down the side of the building and round the back, where a paved patio area opened up. What looked like former stables lined the far side, converted perhaps into offices or apartments: as with the main house, their windows were firmly barricaded with shutters and metal bars. To the side stood a wooden post with an ornate iron handle sticking out on one side and a spout on the other: an old water pump. He wondered if it still worked. Beyond it was a small structure butting against the back of the house, with small open windows and a wooden door slightly ajar. Cámara could make out the low sound of someone singing gently from inside.

He walked silently to the door, listening, then rapped his knuckle against the frame.

'¿*Hola*?'

The singing – more a lilting mumble than an actual tune – stopped.

'Who is it?' said a suspicious voice.

'Can I have a word?'

A woman's face appeared from inside, framed with short white curly hair.

'Oh!' she said.

Cámara peered down into eyes yellowed with age and sunlight. Lines ran across her face in a myriad directions like tracks on desert sand. Her mouth was small and tight with anxiety and a tiny crescent of dried saliva curled around the edge of her lip.

'Can I help you?' she said.

'Vicenta?' said Cámara.

She didn't reply.

'I'm from the police,' continued Cámara. 'I'm here about—'

'Oh, oh, oh!' said the woman. 'Terrible business. Such a tragedy. I haven't been able to think of anything else all day.'

'Yes, it is,' said Cámara. 'Can I come in?'

'Please, yes,' she said. 'I'll put some coffee on.'

No questioning, no inspection of his ID. Vicenta belonged to a generation who had never lost their respect – or fear – of a policeman.

Cámara stepped into a small scullery kitchen with a flagstone floor and ceramic sink at one side. Large brass taps were set into the wall, while opposite was a small inglenook fireplace with a blackened, round-bottomed pan suspended from iron chains hanging over the grate. No fire was burning, yet fresh ash on the hearth and the smell of woodsmoke told him this was a very traditional kitchen where the traditional ways were still employed. Vicenta filled a coffee pot with water, spooned in the coffee and placed it over a tiny gas ring next to the sink.

When she turned round, her eyes were glistening.

'We heard last night,' she said. 'Abi called from the hospital. I'd been praying for him ever since the ambulance took him away. My husband thought there was little hope – they got to him so late, you see. But, well, miracles can and do happen sometimes. But not yesterday. Not for José Luis.'

She pulled out a white handkerchief from the pocket of her apron and wiped her nose.

'I'm very sorry,' said Cámara. 'It must be a difficult time.'

'He was such a kind man.' Vicenta sat down at the tiny table, staring into space. Cámara eased himself down into the other chair. On the hob, the coffee pot began to hiss as the water heated. Over the sound came another, almost identical, yet more like a whine. Cámara turned and looked down: there on the floor, curled on top of an old, grubby cushion, was a little white-and-grey Shih Tzu dog, staring up at him with dark, mournful eyes.

'You're going to miss him, aren't you, Blanquita,' said Vicenta. 'I think she knows. Dogs are clever animals. Wouldn't be surprised if the grief kills her. They're not the strongest dogs, these little things.'

Cámara leaned down to pat the animal on the head; it nuzzled the bridge of its nose against his finger, happy to accept his affection, then dropped its head back down on to the cushion.

'She was José Luis's dog?' he asked.

Vicenta nodded.

'Probably not the only one round here wondering what's going to happen now,' she said.

The coffee pot gargled. She got up, poured a small amount of thick dark liquid into a single cup and brought it over to the table.

'Sugar?' she said.

Cámara held up a hand.

'That's perfect.' He had barely eaten any breakfast that morning and his stomach was already starting to growl for something. He sipped at the coffee: it was bitter and scorching hot.

'Have you heard anything?' he asked. 'About the future of the place? Paco said anything?'

'That Paco,' Vicenta mumbled. 'It's certainly not going to survive if he's thinking of taking it over.'

Cámara waited.

'We've been here since the beginning,' she continued. 'My husband and me. Ever since José Luis took it on. That was twenty-seven years ago. I've seen some things going on here, not all of them to my liking, but I never thought it would end like this, with poor old José Luis taken away from us so suddenly.'

She pulled out her handkerchief again, dabbing at her eyes.

'It was his birthday yesterday. Turned sixty. Abi was preparing a surprise party, get all their friends round. Then this. It's such a shame.'

'Were they happy together, José Luis and Abi?' asked Cámara.

She looked up.

'So you know, do you?' she said.

'That . . . they were a couple?'

'It's not right, of course,' she said. 'Not as nature intended. But I wasn't going to judge. Not for me to say what people can and can't do. There are plenty of others who do that if they want.'

'And José Luis . . . ?' he said.

'There were others in the past. I remember some of them. But Abi's been around the longest. Eleven years. They loved each other, I suppose, in the way that two men can. Had their ups and downs, but stayed together. I think José Luis was genuinely fond of him. Wouldn't have let him stay so long otherwise, don't you think?'

Cámara nodded.

'Did you notice any tension between them recently?'

'No more than the usual bickering between couples. My husband and I could easily give them a run for their money on that score.'

'Do you remember what happened yesterday?'

She sighed deeply. Cámara was concerned not to upset her. Such liberal attitudes among her generation were not common, but not unheard of. He thought of his own grandfather, Hilario. Compared to the old anarchist fiend, Vicenta was a hardened conservative, yet she had come to terms in her own way with whatever went on at Sunset, none of which, he was sure, had formed the backdrop to her own youth. Yet for every finger-wagging killjoy in Spain he sensed there was at least one old character like Vicenta, perhaps unable to understand the ways of those younger than herself, yet reluctant to pass judgement either.

'Abi was out at the time,' she said. 'Although I only found out later. His phone was on the ledge by the front door. He's never usually separated from it. Then I heard him come back – he'd been down to the village. Getting some things for the party, I suppose. He asked me where José Luis was. I didn't know. Then Paco said something about that

Enrique, that he'd called, or something. No one did anything for a while – I got on with my chores. We thought José Luis would just come back when he'd finished.'

'What happened?' asked Cámara.

'Abi got worried, said José Luis was taking too long, that he wanted to start the party. He went up to the Chain.'

'The Chain?'

'It's up on the track, where Enrique's land starts. You know, one of those chains across a track to keep people out.'

Cámara nodded.

'Anyway, that's when . . .'

She wiped her nose again.

'That's where he found him?'

She nodded, half-covering her face.

Cámara paused, waiting for a chance to ask more questions. Down on the floor, the dog gave a whimper and flicked its eyes. From outside on the patio came the sound of heavy footsteps, clomping over the paving stones.

'*Me cago en la puta madre*,' said a growly voice. Fucking hell.

Vicenta looked up, a worried expression on her face.

'Fucking stupid . . .' continued the voice, getting closer.

Vicenta stood up, casting an anxious look in Cámara's direction.

The footsteps entered the scullery and the light from the door was suddenly blotted out by the shape of an elderly man.

'Fucking—'

'*Cariño*,' said Vicenta loudly, cutting him off midstream. 'This man is from the police.'

She nodded towards Cámara, who stood up from his chair.

'He's come to ask questions about José Luis.'

FOURTEEN

Carlos admired the ordinary appearance of the *CNI* building. The vast majority of people rushing past along the motorway probably didn't know what it was or the nature of the work carried out there – just another office block on the outskirts of the capital. Unvetted civilians were not allowed to enter, of course, yet had they done so they would have seen little to make them think that they weren't at the headquarters of a large company. The national flag flew from a mast by the main entrance, lawns and gardens – of the type that pay lip service to the natural world but in reality feel far removed from it – curled around its outer perimeter, while a piece of modern, self-aggrandising sculpture had been placed outside reception expressing messages of power. Inside there was a degree of security, but even this was becoming increasingly normal in the commercial world as businesses as well as government institutions became targets for various kinds of attack. Armed guards might be privately hired or part of the actual staff, but they were almost invisible in the modern world through their ubiquity.

Once past the main entrance, the air of normality continued: corridors stretched in various directions leading to a handful of ground-floor offices, a canteen, a comms room, the archive and library. Lifts or stairs offered access to the four upper floors, where various departments had their own fiefdoms with – in inevitable fashion – the larger and higher-up spaces reserved for the more superior officers. The director's office was at the centre of the structure with easy access to all other limbs of the organisation, like a plump heart pulsing at its core. Carlos had been inside it only once, just over a year before, when he had been promoted. The director had congratulated him on his position, shaken his hand and stressed the importance of the task he had been given.

All quite ordinary, all quite unremarkable. What set the place apart from the rest of the world was something intangible, something quite subtle – it was the feeling in the building. The usual emotions of office life were present: petty rivalries, daily grind, a sense of excitement at times, high levels of stress, even financial worries and moments of release at the successful achievement of a goal. Ambition, frustration and status-play were as much a part of the experience within the *CNI* as anywhere else. What set it apart was meaning. Companies might convince themselves that they were changing the world and making it a better place by developing and distributing their products – in fact, entering into the spirit of such a fiction was *sine qua non* for almost all their employees. But in the end a piece of software or a cuddly toy or a new chemical compound had a limited effect on people's lives. It might be useful, enjoyable or even increase their safety to some degree, but it did not radically alter their world, despite the claims of their respective marketing departments. At the *CNI*, however, such language was superfluous. Everyone within the organisation knew at a deep level, that the entire security of the nation rested in their hands. And even if they received scant thanks from the public it mattered little to them because the certainty of their own usefulness and necessity outweighed any desire to be loved or appreciated beyond the narrow confines of their own world.

Carlos had made the usual greetings to his colleagues, making certain to nod and acknowledge each one as he walked it through the open-plan section towards his own office at the side. There he took off his jacket, hung it on the hook behind the door, placed his case on his desk and sat down in his chair. For a moment he did nothing, allowing his eyes to unfocus and drift while he savoured this instant – the brief sensation of having resolved a problem. He had learned to enjoy them as much as possible – they were less common than he would have liked yet were the sweetener in what could at times be a bitter occupation. Drawing on them, like some reservoir of life force, gave him energy to carry on, gave him the meaning that this job, above all others, could offer.

He allowed himself no more than a couple of seconds to register the sensation, breathing it in, before a slight dizziness reminded him that he was in need of more coffee.

Some hours later, still at his desk, his internal phone rang. He picked up the receiver.

'I need you in here immediately.'

The voice was deep, treacly and uncompromising.

Carlos got obediently out of his chair and made for his door, setting off down the corridor for thc larger office at the far end.

Beyond idiots, useful idiots and the enemy, Carlos had a fourth category for people, special and rare. It was: superiors. Superiors were there to be obeyed. Without obedience the entire structure would fall apart. And it was to his immediate superior's office that he now made his way.

Fernando was a large man – fat, if not quite obese in Carlos's opinion. His chin was rarely clean-shaven and despite wearing the regulatory suit and tie, his top button was always undone, revealing the greying hairs from the top of his chest, which sprouted like weeds pushing through cracks in the pavement. A male secretary was tasked with providing a regular supply of caffeine and sugar to his desk in the form of a stream of *cafés solos* and cakes of one form or another, usually *madalenas*, but occasionally doughnuts or even brownies, depending on what Fernando's latest cravings were for. Carlos had nothing but admiration for Fernando – what others might have condemned as a slovenly appearance, a certain candidacy for type 2 diabetes and a chemical addiction to stimulants, Carlos viewed as an act of great selflessness and sacrifice in the name of the fatherland. Fernando, in his mind, placed the security of the nation above all other things, even his own health. He would almost certainly die one day at this very desk, struck by a heart attack or seizure as he worked for the safety of his fellow countrymen and their values. No one could ask for more.

'*¿Señor?*' he said as he walked into the office. Fernando noted his arrival, drained the cup of coffee in his hand and swept the crumbs from the top of his desk.

'I've just had a call,' said Fernando. 'From Palma.'

Carlos's senses became more acute at the mention of the name.

'We've got a situation,' continued Fernando.

'A leak?' asked Carlos.

'Not clear. But a journalist – a woman – has been asking questions.'

'Do we know who she is?'

'I've got her particulars here.' Fernando held out a piece of paper with details scribbled in his small, light handwriting. Carlos took it and gave it a quick glance.

'I'll investigate her immediately,' he said.

'Do that,' said Fernando with some emphasis.

'You think . . . ?' Carlos began.

'She mentioned Clavijo,' said Fernando. Then, as though to confirm the information, he looked Carlos in the eye and nodded.

Carlos returned his gaze, the full importance not lost on him.

'I understand. I'll make it top priority.'

'Find out exactly what she knows,' said Fernando. 'And how she knows. For the time being the Minister doesn't need to know anything about this, not until we're clear on what the situation is.'

'And then?'

'And then we'll assess things and make a decision,' Fernando answered testily.

Carlos nodded and made to leave.

'The *Suiza*,' Fernando called to him in a low voice. Carlos stopped mid-step.

'Sir?'

'You've had some trouble recently, correct?'

'It's been taken care of,' said Carlos.

'Are they fully operational?'

Carlos paused, choosing his words.

'Rest assured, sir, the *Suiza* will be able to undertake any task presented to it.'

Fernando appeared satisfied.

'The green light may come at any moment,' he said.

Carlos nodded.

'We'll be ready.'

FIFTEEN

Vicente stepped across to pour himself a glass of water at the sink, avoiding Cámara's gaze. Cámara guessed him to be in his late seventies, around the same age as his wife. He had the dark, well-used skin of someone who had spent most of his life working outside: there was a black mark near the bridge of his nose that looked like some kind of tumour, while the top of one of his ears had clearly been operated on, sliced straight at the top, perhaps where another growth had been removed. Cámara was aware of thick, giant-like arms with paw-like hands, incongruous against his ordinary-sized frame and curiously small and round head. His hair was thinning, but still covered most of his head, and was a natural brown, with only the slightest wisps of grey scattered at the sides and back. His neck had deep folds in the skin like trenches on a war-scarred terrain, while the lines about his mouth spoke more of a scowling frown than the laughter that his wife's face promised. He would be a straightforward man, Cámara imagined. Crabby and bad-tempered, perhaps, but a man who saw things in simple terms: good or bad, acceptable or unacceptable.

Vicenta shuffled towards him, trying to help him with his glass of water, but he shrugged her off.

'I've been telling the policeman here about what happened yesterday,' she said. 'About José Luis.'

Cámara stood up.

'Chief Inspector Cámara,' he said.

The man took his hand.

'Vicente Felici,' he said. 'You've already met my wife.'

Cámara nodded.

'*Policía Nacional*?' Vicente asked. 'We don't usually see your lot round here. *Guardia Civil* show up sometimes. Must be important if they've sent a chief inspector.'

Cámara forced a smile.

'You suspect foul play, or something?'

'Do you?' asked Cámara.

Vicente paused.

'It looked straightforward enough,' he said at last. 'Assume it was a heart attack. He was a big man, José Luis. Not the healthiest sort.'

He stepped away from the sink and sat in the chair recently vacated by Vicenta. Cámara returned to his seat across the little table.

'But now you're here,' Vicente said. 'You must have your reasons for coming.'

'Someone called us yesterday saying José Luis's death was no accident,' said Cámara. 'That it was deliberate.'

From the sink, Vicenta put a hand to her mouth. Vicente nodded that he understood.

'Do you know of anyone who might have wanted to harm José Luis?' continued Cámara.

Vicente thought.

'Close this place down? Yes, almost anyone round here in the sierra would like that. Don't approve of what goes on.'

He shook his head.

'But kill him? I don't know. Can't see it.'

'What about Enrique?'

Vicente took a deep breath, chest rising, a frown burrowed on his face.

'I've known Enrique almost all my life,' he said. 'We were at school together. He's got set ideas, didn't get on with José Luis . . .'

Cámara waited.

'He's been on his own,' said Vicente. 'Wife died about two years back. They had a son but Enrique doesn't speak to him. He moved to Barcelona years ago. It's just him with his dog. He's got a few almond trees to keep him busy, but . . .' He shrugged.

'What's the business about the Chain?' asked Cámara.

'*Uff!*' Vicente threw his hands in the air. 'Been going on for ages.'

'What's the story?'

Vicente shook his head.

'The problem round here,' he said, 'is that the boundaries between people's land aren't always clear. Or at least they're clear in locals' minds – we've grown up with them, know exactly which rock or tree marks the beginning of one man's land and the end of another. But people from the city have different ideas, want it all marked out. Then there's the differences between the Land Registry and the Tax Office's Registry – they don't always say the same thing. One might give you double the amount of land of the other. And the two registries hate each other and won't talk to each other, so . . .'

He frowned.

'So there's a dispute with Enrique over who owns what?' Cámara prodded.

'They both have a right to use the track,' said Vicente. 'That's where the Chain is. Enrique put it across the track to stop people getting past. Gave a key to José Luis, but didn't want anyone else getting through.'

'Why not?'

'Just didn't want strangers there.'

'It's more than that,' said Vicenta, giving her husband a look. 'It's all about the river. Tell him.'

'I'm not going to bother the man with that,' he snapped.

'Please,' said Cámara. 'Anything might be useful here.'

He turned to Vicenta.

'What's this about?'

Vicenta nodded to her husband, urging him to speak. Cámara noticed their old-fashioned ways: it was the job of the man to speak to State officials. Quite how they fitted into Sunset, with their traditional kitchen and mountain mannerisms, he could not fathom.

'It's nothing,' said Vicente. 'The track leads to the river.'

'River?'

'More of a stream, but people round here call it the river. It's over the hill behind us, in a fold in the mountain. It's the source, where the river begins. People sometimes go there and swim.'

'It's beautiful,' Vicenta chirped up. 'There's a waterfall and a natural pool with a cave. We used to go when we were young, didn't we?'

Vicente grunted.

'We don't tell many people about it,' he said. 'Otherwise the place would be full of city types, dropping their rubbish everywhere and spoiling the place.'

Cámara was surprised. Many elderly country folk he had come across cared little for the beauty or upkeep of their environment, viewing it more as a means to make a living, with any chance to exploit it further embraced with open arms. Anyone else might have welcomed the chance to bring people in, thought of a way of making money out of them, but not this couple, apparently.

'This place . . .' Cámara began.

'We call it the *Molino*,' said Vicenta.

'There used to be a watermill there,' explained Vicente. 'Years back. Nothing left now, just a few stones.'

'Does it belong to Enrique?'

Vicente shook his head.

'The river authority own all the streams and gorges. Enrique just owns some of the land that goes down to it.'

'And José Luis?'

'You can't get there on his land, but he has rights to the track which takes you down there.'

'The track where Enrique placed the chain.'

'That's right,' said Vicente impatiently, as though he had already explained this.

'So,' began Cámara tentatively, 'why did Enrique put the chain there?'

'He didn't want people using his track to get to the *Molino*.'

'Who was going to use it? I thought no one knew about it.'

'José Luis,' said Vicenta. 'He was . . . Well, go on,' she urged her husband. 'Tell him.'

Vicente tilted his chin at her, as though telling her to mind her own business.

'I don't know the details,' he said after a pause. 'It's nothing. José Luis wanted to turn the *Molino* into some kind of attraction. Allow people from the club to go down there. Not quite sure when, because this is a nightclub.'

'In the mornings,' said Vicenta. 'They're here all night, then in the mornings he thought people might want to go down and have a swim. It is such a lovely spot. There's nothing wrong with it.'

'They'd just make a mess of it,' growled Vicente. 'Or drown in it. Enrique was right. Put the chain across, don't let them near it.'

The couple had clearly disagreed about this in the past. Cámara needed to get more information out of them, hopefully without prompting a row.

'I imagine,' he said, 'that José Luis wasn't too happy about the chain going up.'

Vicenta threw her husband a look.

'He was furious,' she said.

'But there was nothing he could do,' added Vicente. 'It's Enrique's track, he's absolutely in his rights to chain it off. José Luis has access, that's true, so he gave him a key to the padlock. But José Luis can't let anyone else go down there. Just him. That's how things are.'

He fell silent, staring at the floor, mouth as tight as a fist.

'My husband tried to explain to José Luis,' Vicenta said. 'But he wouldn't listen.'

'That's enough,' Vicente barked. She stared hard at him. If he hadn't been in the room, Cámara wondered if she might not have reached for a pan and brought it down over her husband's head. She looked as though she'd thought about it a few times.

There was silence for a moment, broken only by a slight breeze beginning to blow outside. The sound seemed to stir something in Vicenta as well, and after a roll of her eyes she stepped away from the sink and crouched down at the inglenook, where she began to place some kindling in the grate.

'We'll be having lunch soon,' said Vicente, watching her. 'You'll join us.'

It felt more like an order than an invitation. Cámara nodded his acceptance.

'About yesterday . . .' he said. Vicente looked him hard in the eye. 'Can you tell me what happened?'

'I was on the far side of the estate,' said Vicente. 'By the old oak. The gorse has got out of control up there, grown like mad after the rains we had this spring.'

From the inglenook, Vicenta tutted at the memory of the weather they'd had, striking a match to light the fire she'd set.

'So you were nowhere near . . . ?' Cámara asked.

'Only heard about it when my wife came to find me and tell me what had happened,' he said. 'By the time we got back here the ambulance had arrived and they were putting him inside.'

He sighed.

'Never got to see him.'

'My husband might not have approved of everything José Luis did,' said Vicenta, 'but you liked him in your own way, didn't you.'

'Things they get up to here,' he said, shaking his head. 'But he was a good employer. Fair. Looked after us.'

'What's going to happen now, do you think?' said Cámara.

'Don't know.'

'Abi will know,' said Vicenta. 'We'll be all right. José Luis will have thought of us, don't you worry.'

'José Luis is dead,' he snapped. Vicenta turned her back on him, muttering. The flames were beginning to grow in the hearth, a thin trail of smoke steaming up the chimney, small flames licking the bottom of the blackened pan.

'Your first thought was that José Luis had had a heart attack,' said Cámara.

Vicente shrugged.

'I suppose that's what passed through my mind. Paco said something about some bee stings. Bees can't kill a man, but perhaps the shock? He wasn't a healthy man, as I say.'

'And the bees?' asked Cámara. 'Are there some hives nearby?'

'I told that Abi,' Vicente muttered darkly. 'He's doing it deliberately, putting them right there.'

'Who?'

'Enrique. Put a dozen hives right at the chain.'

'They're Enrique's bees?' said Cámara.

'I mean the chain itself, fair enough. But the hives? That's unnecessary, provocative. I said, he doesn't want anyone going round there, I said. Trying to frighten people off. And they're a nasty, aggressive strain. Stung me a couple of times, they have. It's his land, of course, he can put them where he likes. But right there?'

He gave an indignant snort.

'How long ago did Enrique put the hives there?' Cámara asked.

'About a couple of weeks ago?' He looked up at Vicenta

for confirmation. His wife kept her back to him, busying herself with lunch.

'About that,' she said, after an appropriate pause.

Vicente gave Cámara an exasperated look. Then he got up, reached for some small glass tumblers from a cupboard and sat down again, an unlabelled bottle in his other hand.

'Here,' he said, pouring light red wine out for both of them. 'You won't mind home-made, will you?'

Cámara lifted the glass and they drank at the same time. It tasted of vinegar.

'I saw a black BMW when I was driving up,' he said, placing the glass back on the table. 'Tinted windows. Couple of men inside. Don't know who they might be, do you?

'Can't say,' mumbled Vicente, looking uncomfortably at the floor. 'Don't have anything to do with them. Having fun is one thing. But ruining young people's lives is something else.'

SIXTEEN

She found Marisol's details in an old contacts book that she kept in a drawer, a record of her pre-digital self when she had written down numbers and addresses on paper. Almost all of them were now on an electronic device of some sort, but a handful had escaped the transition and remained in this old-fashioned format. She thanked herself for not having tossed the book away.

It was a mobile number, from the time when they had last been in touch. And she tried to remember when that had been. Perhaps ten years before. Marisol was the kind of person from whom she was happy having long breaks. Fleeing the nest was as important a step with one's former mentors as with one's parents.

Would she still be at the Ministry? It was a good job, the kind of secure, well-paid, not-too-stressful kind that everyone hoped to land in order to see out the years before full retirement. Perhaps she had already left, been given the push with all the cutbacks and changes over the years. But if anyone could survive, it would be Marisol. Toughness, doggedness – these were the qualities she had always stressed to her protégées. They had to be consistently better, harder, more stubborn and flexible than the men around them. It was the only way they might ever be treated as equals.

Her hand paused over the keypad, waiting to punch in the numbers. Would Marisol be at the other end? Would she be happy to hear her? Alicia felt a pang of self-doubt as she prepared herself – the feeling that speaking or being with Marisol always produced.

It doesn't matter, she whispered to herself. I could never have lived up to such high expectations. None of us could.

She listened as the phone at the other end rang a couple of times, and felt the pulse in her temples.

'Alicia! Darling!'

Marisol's voice rang clear like a siren, as though she were standing in the same room.

'What a wonderful surprise! How are you?'

'Hello, Marisol,' Alicia said. 'It's good to hear you again.'

'And you. And you. My goodness, how long has it been? No wait, don't tell me.'

They chatted for a few moments, going through the motions of reconnecting, recalling their last conversation – during a rare trip Marisol had made to Valencia, when Alicia was still at *Llevant* – and making the expected noises of pleasure at being able to speak on the phone again.

'I think of you so often,' said Marisol. 'Almost every day, in fact. You were my favourite, Alicia. You know that.'

Alicia let the comment pass.

'We shouldn't let such a long time pass without getting in touch,' Marisol continued. 'It really won't do. It is so wonderful that you called. Now, darling, you must tell me everything – what you're doing, where you are, all your projects. I look out for your byline all the time, but can't find you anywhere. And I know you're not wasting all that talent you have, Alicia. You're too good for that. So there must be something big brewing, I can feel it. You're on to something. And you must tell me all about it.'

Alicia smiled to herself.

'Actually,' she said, 'I was calling to find out about you.'

'About me?' Marisol said theatrically.

'Yes,' said Alicia. 'Listen, are you still working at the Ministry of Defence?'

'Oh, they haven't managed to get rid of me yet. Not for want of trying. But I know too much. About everyone here. That's a press officer's real job – not communicating with the outside, but finding out everything about the organisation you're working for. Especially the dirty secrets. So firing me would be dangerous, no matter who is in government.'

Alicia laughed.

'Am I amusing you, darling?'

'It reminds me of what you used to say.'

'What was that?'

'It became a kind of unofficial mantra for us,' said Alicia. 'Your motto. "In the end a journalist is judged not by what they say, but by what they know." '

'And my views haven't changed one bit,' said Marisol. 'If anything I'm even more convinced of the truth of it.'

'So perhaps,' said Alicia, 'you may be able to help me.'

'Of course, darling. I can tell there's something on your mind. Delightful though it is to chat, you're fishing for something. And if I can help, then you know you can count on me.'

Alicia picked up a pen, her hand hovering over the notebook on the table at her side.

'It's just some background, really,' she said. 'I'm trying to find out what's really happening on the island of Cabrera. You know, that uninhabited rock just off the south coast of Mallorca.'

She paused, but Marisol made no sound.

'And something to do with the term "Clavijo". It might be a military code word. Do you know anything about that?'

SEVENTEEN

On Carlos's desk was a framed photograph. It showed the colour image of a woman perhaps in her early or mid-thirties, with brown hair held up with clips on the sides of her head and cascading down the back – very straight, very combed. She wore a blue-and-white striped top buttoned up at the neck with a small rounded collar. Her face was soft and pretty – in an ordinary, not exceptional, kind of way. She smiled at the camera with just the slightest shine on her bottom lip from where the flash reflected on her pale lipstick. Her nose was small, straight and unthreatening, and her eyes, which were faintly outlined with black pencil, were dark brown and shone with a polite yet not overly generous kindness. She looked like the sort of person one might see attending mass (although only once a week, perhaps – not *too* regularly), an impression confirmed by the delicate silver cross that hung from a chain around her neck – more a token of her upbringing than any statement of religious fervour. Anyone seeing the photo would have the impression of a woman of conservative social values and politics, dependable, dutiful, not overly burdened with ambition or a particularly active imagination. She would, in fact, make a very decent wife – Carlos's wife, which was why the photo was on his desk. She was quite young, but judging from her clothes the photo had been taken some years before and she was doubtless much older now. Closer in age to Carlos himself, although how old she actually was no one could say. Asking too many questions about a colleague's private life was frowned upon in the community – that was what vetting officers were for.

Carlos made certain that the photo was always visible, never taking pride of place, but its presence noticeable without being distracting. It was about the size of a postcard, framed in solid dark wood and placed on the other side of his desk from his keyboard and screen, perched near the corner next to a simple, unprepossessing lamp. Sharp-eyed colleagues saw it the first time they entered, others might need two or three visits. But everyone who stepped inside his office was aware of it to some degree: a little reminder of life beyond work, beyond their duty. What it was all for.

Occasionally Carlos wondered about changing it, updating it with a newer, more up-to-date image. But such a task would bring complications. As it was it served its purpose, like an icon: an image that represented, in his companions' subconscious, Carlos's normality, his espousal of the kinds of values that the organisation set itself to defend. His wife.

There were no photographs of children on his desk, a fact that would not have gone unnoticed. Perhaps the couple were childless. Perhaps, for whatever reason, they couldn't have any. Some felt sorry for Carlos, others admired his pragmatism: child-rearing could sit ill with their line of work.

The truth was, however, that Carlos would never have children, nor a family of any sort. The woman in the photo was not his wife, nor any relation. In fact, he had never even met her. He knew her name and something about her life – he at least went to some lengths when he found her image and decided to use it. He knew that she had died some twenty years before – from complications after contracting pneumonia. He was also certain, to the best of his knowledge, that she had no connection with any of his work colleagues. She was not Spanish at all: she was French, from a village near Perpignan. But she easily passed as Spanish. That was all he needed.

And so María – he quickly rechristened her from her original Marie – had been his desk companion these past years, his quiet, dutiful wife, playing her part, not getting in the way, fulfilling to perfection the role he had assigned her. For everyone at the centre was supposed to *have* a life beyond, at least nominally. It was all part of the pretence. Long hours and dedication to the work were expected and demanded – to the extent that maintaining a personal life of any description was all but impossible. Yet openly to admit this, to declare an absence of any personal hinterland – effectively your addiction to the job – was impossible. If there was nothing else, what, in fact, were you sacrificing by staying in so late every night? Fernando showed them all the way, not only forgoing the pleasure of the family life waiting for him at home, but also laying his own health on the line. That was the standard, and they all had to aspire to it.

Carlos had caught himself wondering from time to time

about his boss and his home life. The family photograph in Fernando's office showing a woman with two small children on her knee had not changed for the entire time Carlos had known him. Nor did Carlos's secretary fail to remind him the first week in every May that she needed the afternoon off because it was her little boy's birthday, making sure to bring some cake in the next day to share around the office. Always uncut – not quite the leftovers that she intended it to be. Small mistakes like that kept her where she was, meant she would never rise any higher than her current position. And Carlos would feel warmly reassured by his greater observational skills; there were times when he imagined the entire building was engaged in the same pretence, with trinkets and photos and tiny reminders – silent signifiers of imaginary private worlds.

He thought briefly about María now – the María of his imagination, conjured into existence by the flick of his wand – as he looked down at the file on his desk. Most of the time he was content to do this kind of thing on screen, but for important and urgent cases he preferred to revert to hard copies. The woman in this photograph was a far cry from his 'wife': her hair was on the short side and had highlights of more than one colour; she wore a tight-fitting, low-cut T-shirt which revealed a small but clearly visible amount of cleavage; one of her ears had clearly been pierced more than once with two unmatching earrings hanging from it; and the glint in her eye spoke of wilfulness, an independent mind, rebellion.

Carlos read through the file on her, detailing her place and date of birth, her education, university degree, how she had become a journalist soon after, working eventually for a local newspaper in Valencia, then in Madrid, before falling off the radar in the past few years having been fired from her job during the cutbacks. Yet he had enough to go on: a clear image of her and her name. Alicia Beneyto.

He paused. Something about the woman had been nagging in the back of his mind since picking up the file. The fact that she was a journalist? They could be troublesome at times, but not always. No, it was something else . . .

He turned over the page and glanced at her address. He knew that street: central Valencia, not far from Barón de Cárcel. It was a bit run-down and sleazy: an area where prostitutes and drug dealers congregated. But what was it about the address itself that rang a bell?

His eyes glanced down the page. Someone else lived at the same address, Alicia's partner, no doubt, her lover, as there was no record of her having remarried after her divorce.

And his eyes rested on a name he had not expected to see – certainly not today, perhaps not ever again. The name of a chief inspector in the *Policía Nacional*, a man he had worked with in the past, a former useful idiot who had been successfully placed back into the category of mere idiot – which undoubtedly he was.

Except that now, with Alicia's file on his desk, Carlos was forced to think again. There was only one other group.

He looked up from the file and turned to the photograph of María. And with a smooth and well-practised shift of thought, he slotted two new names into his third classification: Alicia Beneyto. And Max Cámara.

EIGHTEEN

'I'd like to see the Chain,' said Cámara.

'I'll take you up there after lunch,' answered Vicente.

Cámara checked his phone: no signal, still, but the time showed it was almost two. There was no sign of any clock in the kitchen and neither Vicente nor his wife wore a watch, yet they seemed to know by instinct that it was time for the midday meal.

The kitchen was filled now with the smell from the bubbling pan over the fire, meaty and rich and creamy. Vicenta had thrown in some chunks of carrot and leek, as well as several handfuls of rice, but the base of the dish appeared to be something that she had been cooking for some time before, perhaps since earlier that morning.

'You eat boar?' asked Vicente. Cámara nodded.

'Don't hunt myself,' said Vicente. 'But some of the locals pass on a few pieces most years towards the end of the season. Keeps well in the freezer.'

Cámara was amazed that they were in possession of such a modern piece of equipment. There was certainly no sign of one in the tiny kitchen.

'Thing about boar,' Vicente continued, 'is you have to soak it in wine for a long time, then cook it for several hours. Otherwise it's too tough to chew.'

He nodded towards the pan.

'My wife started this last night.'

'And you put rice in it?' said Cámara. 'I've never seen that before.'

'Makes a nice wet rice dish,' said Vicenta, turning with a smile. An *arròs caldos*. 'My mother used to make it like this.'

'Mountain recipe,' said Vicente. 'You won't find many people down in Valencia eating this.'

He took another sip of the acid wine.

'Or so well.'

Cámara raised his glass, smiled, and forced down another mouthful. Almost immediately, Vicente was offering him some more.

'Thought policemen weren't supposed to drink on duty,' he said. 'That's what they're always saying on the television.'

'There are certain perks to being a chief inspector,' said Cámara.

Lunch was placed on the table in front of them, large bowls of steaming boar stew with floating grains of rice. Cámara spotted shredded green stalks and recognised another ingredient that he had smelt earlier: fresh garlic. His mouth watered.

Vicente stood up, went to the back of the room, pulled out a folding chair and placed it at the table. Then he sat in it himself, freeing the chair he had been sitting in before for Vicenta. Once the three bowls were served, and more wine poured, they began, using large pewter spoons to eat with.

Any doubts that Vicenta's food might be as challenging as Vicente's wine were dispelled with the first mouthful. It was rich and flavoursome, with a thick texture like velvet. The rice was cooked through yet still firm, and had absorbed the earthiness of the boar, while the wine that the meat had been marinating in gave a neat kick to the back of the throat.

'Delicious,' he said almost involuntarily. Vicenta smiled. He wished Alicia could be there to share it with him. He almost wanted to thank Rita for putting him on this case: any demotion, he reasoned, was worth this moment.

They ate in silence for a while, but the policeman in Cámara was eventually reawakened and he tried to start a conversation again.

'I suppose people in the village will have heard about José Luis by now,' he said.

Vicente shrugged.

'There won't be many sad faces down there.'

'You'd think Father Ricardo might make an appearance at least,' said Vicenta.

'That *maricón*?'

'He's not a poof,' said his wife.

'He's a fucking priest. What else is he going to be?'

Vicenta pulled a face, shrugging her husband's comments away.

'Father Ricardo is the village priest?' said Cámara.

'You'd think he might show up,' said Vicenta. 'Pass on his condolences.'

'Do you—?' Cámara began.

'My wife believes in all that superstitious shit,' said Vicente with a mouthful of stew.

'I haven't been to church for years,' she hit back.

'Still believe in it, though.'

'What kind of a man is Father Ricardo?' asked Cámara. There were moments when it felt like being with a couple of bickering children.

'Been here for years,' said Vicenta. 'Used to be a chaplain in the armed services, I think, then he came—'

'He's the last person who'd come with condolences,' Vicente butted in. 'Hates this place even more than the rest of them. Probably organising a celebratory mass as we speak. Might pack out the church for once.'

'Vicente!' his wife hissed.

'It's true, woman,' he said. 'Tell me I'm wrong.'

Vicenta was silent.

'He won't be coming. And neither will any of them. They'll be praying this place closes down.'

Cámara lapped up the last of his stew, pushing his spoon hard against the bottom of the bowl.

'Is there anything specific about Sunset that people in the village don't like?' he said.

'Stuff goes on here,' said Vicente. 'But mostly it's kids having fun. They've got a right to enjoy themselves. We're not around for very long, so you might as well get some pleasure out of life while you can, that's what I say.'

'Yes,' said Vicenta. 'But even still.'

'I'm not saying I approve of everything that goes on here. Not my thing, that's for sure. It's their life, though, and they can do what they want. Of course, people start talking rubbish, talking about rituals and dark magic—'

'Satanism,' Vicenta butted in.

'It's all nonsense.' Vicente waved a hand dismissively. 'People talk, want to make it sound worse than it is. It's that Father Ricardo, I'm telling you. Spreading false rumours. Even Enrique started to believe it.'

'Enrique?' asked Cámara.

'The priest is about the only person Enrique has any contact with. But he preys on the feeble-minded, trying to scare them into believing his nonsense. He's the Satanist, that one. If there's anyone round here trying to pervert people's minds, it's him.'

'Paco doesn't mind him,' said Vicenta.

'Paco?'

'I've seen him going to church.'

'Don't talk rubbish, woman!'

Vicenta bit her lip and got up to clear away the plates.

'Only thing Paco cares about is money.'

Vicente reached for a plate of oranges from the side and placed it in the middle, cutting into the skin of one as he peeled it with expert skill.

'Help yourself,' he said, passing Cámara a knife with a cracked plastic handle. 'They're the last of the season, but all right for eating.'

After peeling his own, Cámara munched on the sweet, juicy fruit. It was the perfect way to wash down the stew. And cleanse his mouth of the taste of the wine.

Vicenta was pouring coffee when they heard the sound of a car arriving. The couple exchanged a glance and a nod.

'That'll be Abi,' said Vicenta.

Cámara drank his coffee quickly, trying not to burn his mouth. Vicenta busied herself with clearing the table. Her husband sat motionless.

When Vicenta stepped out of the kitchen, Cámara

followed her. A dark blue Audi was pulling into the back courtyard, wheezing with the sound of the air conditioning. The engine cut out and the door opened. Vicenta rushed over, tears beginning to flow once more down her cheeks. Cámara watched as she bustled around the door. Out stepped a slim man in his mid-forties with short black hair, dressed in a white shirt and tan-coloured trousers. His eyes were red and puffy, and he smiled down affectionately at Vicenta as she stepped forward to kiss him on the cheeks. As she did so, something in him appeared to break, and his shoulders slumped, the simple kiss of welcome turning into a prolonged embrace of sadness and tears. The man's shoulders heaved as he sobbed, Vicenta crying with him and placing a hand with maternal affection on the back of his neck.

After a pause, the man gathered himself, pulling away, his face wet. Vicenta said something to him in a low voice. He turned to look at Cámara, and Vicenta continued, explaining. Cámara saw green eyes glance at him. The man made to approach him, as though wishing to shake his hand, but Vicenta turned him away, leading him towards the entrance of one of the stable buildings on the far side of the courtyard. There, she opened the door and ushered him in. Cámara caught sight of him breaking down into more powerful sobs as the door was closed behind them.

Cámara now realised that Vicente had been standing in the doorway to the scullery, watching everything. He stepped forwards, closed the car door and turned to Cámara.

'I think Abi's going to need a bit of time,' he said.

'Come.' He motioned with his head. 'I'll show you where everything happened.'

NINETEEN

They walked past the stables, along a path that cut through the undergrowth and headed up into the pine forest at the back. It felt cool in the shade. Cámara's feet crunched on pine cones as he followed in Vicente's wake. Tiny brown birds with red tails fluttered silently like arrows from tree to tree in front of them, feeling threatened and seeking safety. At one moment Cámara thought he caught sight of a thrush perched on a branch some metres away, but it flew off before he could get a better look. Behind them, the nightclub quickly faded from view.

They pressed on; the climb got a little steeper. Vicente walked with a sprightliness incongruous with his age, skipping up the path like an athlete. Cámara lagged behind, more used to the dead flatness of the city, sweat beginning to bead on his forehead.

A hissing, whistling sound came from somewhere to their

left. Cámara stopped; Vicente pushed on as though nothing had happened.

'What was that?' Cámara said.

The sound came again: not quite human, but almost. A sharp cutting sound of harsh breath.

Vicente tilted his head.

'Ibex,' he said simply, pointing through the trees.

Cámara stared. It took him a few moments, but eventually, partially obscured by the pines, he made out the form of a large creature with lyre-like horns arching up from its head. It was staring down at them with a mixture of anger and trepidation. Then it lifted its chin and proceeded to make the whistling sound they had heard earlier.

'There's a herd of them living round here,' said Vicente. 'About forty of them.'

'How lovely.'

Vicente tutted.

'Bloody nuisance. Eat everything. Shrubs, leaves, the lot. Haven't been able to plant anything for years what with them roaming about.'

'They must keep the hunters happy,' Cámara hazarded.

'Hah! Bloody protected species,' said Vicente. 'Not allowed to shoot them. Bloody ecologists slapped a protection order on them. Now they walk around like kings of the mountain. And there are more of them every year.'

'They can't be shot?'

'Not unless you pay thousands for the privilege. Got to get a special permit. Only one or two killed every year. They take out some of the older ones, that's all. Useless for eating.'

He turned and pushed on up the hill. Cámara looked back through the trees: the ibex had vanished.

For the final section of the climb, rough steps had been cut into the rock, like a rustic staircase. They were narrow and worn and covered with loose stones, making the walk almost harder, not easier. Cámara wondered about stepping off and going up the side, but prickly bushes barred his way.

'If anything killed José Luis,' said Vicente, 'it was probably just coming up here. Put strain on his heart. As I say—'

'Yes,' interrupted Cámara. 'He wasn't a healthy man.'

He was beginning to wonder if Vicente and Paco were right, that this was simply an accidental, or natural, death. Plenty of people might have had motives for disliking, even hating, José Luis. But enough to murder him?

Yet there was the anonymous phone call to explain. His own need for this to be a murder fed on that one fact like a bat sucking the last dregs of juice from a rotten piece of fruit. Only when he could say categorically that this was not a murder would he let it go.

After the climb, the path flattened out a little, the trees thinning and letting in more light. Ahead, Vicente stopped dead in his tracks. Head down, watching his step, Cámara only saw at the last minute and pulled back. Vicente thrust an arm out to block his way. Cámara waited, confused, then Vicente beckoned him forwards. He pointed at the ground a few metres ahead, where a shaft of sunlight was burning into the ground. And there, at its centre, perfectly coiled like a piece of rope, was a snake.

'Viper,' said Vicente in a soft voice.

Cámara stared down in fascination at the grey-brown form, with the darker, diamond-shaped pattern stretching down its back. It was small, perhaps the size of a side plate, and its eyes were closed.

'Sleeping,' said Vicente. 'But they can lash out.'

Cámara felt a light but uncontrollable trembling in his knees as though some primitive memory in him had been awakened.

'What do we do?' he asked.

Vicente cast an eye about.

'Here,' he said. 'Pass me that stick.'

Cámara gingerly reached down behind him and picked up a crooked pine branch from the ground. It had a fork at one end. Vicente took it from him wordlessly and inched towards the snake. Then, with a swift, sharp motion, he hooked it into the fork and tossed it low and fast towards the undergrowth at the side of the path. The snake uncoiled as it flew, hitting the side of a tree before falling to the ground. Then it quickly slithered away, disappearing from view under the rocks.

'There,' said Vicente, tossing the stick away. He grinned back at Cámara and started walking again. Cámara's legs still wobbled. He looked across to where the snake had vanished and carried on behind Vicente. This landscape felt anything but friendly.

A few metres further on they came to a boulder with a small white cross painted on it.

'This is where Enrique's land begins,' said Vicente.

Beyond the boulder was a dirt track. To one side it wound down the hillside, presumably heading towards the village. To the other, it pushed through more pine trees to what looked like a stone farmhouse not far on the other side.

'That's where Enrique lives.'

'Will he be in?' asked Cámara.

Vicente frowned.

'His dog's not barking. If he was there, we'd hear the dog.'

'So you can drive here as well,' said Cámara, indicating the track.

'It's quicker to walk from José Luis's place,' explained Vicente. 'Long way by car. You have to go round the mountain.'

Cámara nodded, walking up on to the track itself. A few metres further on he could see where it split in two: to the right it veered off to Enrique's farmhouse; to the left it carried on straight. And there, draped across from one steel pole to another, was a chain. Cámara pointed.

'That's right,' said Vicente. 'Enrique put it up.'

'And further along there's the *Molino*?'

Vicente nodded.

Cámara could understand why José Luis might have wanted to exploit this for the clubbers at Sunset. This little spot was delightful enough as it was, with clean, invigorating mountain air and the heady scent of pine. If there was a place to swim just further on in some secret fold in the mountainside it could be quite an attraction. But equally he could understand why anyone would want to protect it, keep the hordes away.

He leaned down and brushed his hand through a low bush at his side, then lifted it to his face and sniffed the deep, warming scent of rosemary carrying memories of every paella he had ever eaten. What looked like lavender plants were also scattered about, with bright little spots of lilac at the ends of their stalks.

'It's a lovely spot,' said Vicente. 'Enrique might not be all right up here –' he tapped the side of his head – 'but he was right to put the chain there, stop people from coming up. They wouldn't appreciate it anyway. What with the amount of drink they take. And other things.'

It took Cámara a moment, but there was a sound in the background, like a faint hum. Then he noticed a number of grey-painted wooden boxes lined up on the far side of the track. The sound appeared to be coming from there. He crossed over to investigate.

'Enrique's beehives,' explained Vicente.

'And they've been here . . . ?'

'A couple of weeks. Not much more.'

Cámara approached cautiously. Apart from the humming sound, there was little activity. A small gap in the wood near the bottom of each box appeared to be the entrance. At each one, two or three bees dozily sat, like guards. Occasionally a solitary bee would appear and fly off, disappearing into the trees, or buzzing around the rosemary and lavender bushes looking for some previously missed droplets of nectar. They didn't seem the kind of bees one might have to be careful with.

'They'll be sleeping now,' said Vicente. 'Having their siesta. Bees like the mornings. That's why the openings are facing east, so the dawn wakes them up. That's when they're busiest.'

Cámara walked back along the track towards him.

'What time was it when José Luis came up?'

Vicente thought for a moment.

'Must have been around midday,' he said. 'Perhaps a bit after. Before lunch, anyway.

'Bees still active at that time?'

'They're beginning to quieten down by then,' he said. 'Usually.'

'But these are an aggressive strain, you said.'

'Well, they must be,' said Vicente, a defensive tone creeping into his voice. 'They stung José Luis, didn't they?'

Cámara nodded.

'Where was José Luis when they found him?' he asked.

Vicente pointed to a patch of ground near where he was standing, at the edge of the track.

'But you didn't see him yourself,' Cámara said.

'My wife brought me, showed me where.'

Cámara narrowed his eyes.

'And you call this place the Chain.'

'That's right,' Vicente said. 'On account of the chain over there. Didn't have a name before. Or not that I remember.'

'Paco told me that José Luis was up here to have a meeting with Enrique.'

Vicente frowned.

'I wouldn't know anything about that,' he mumbled.

'Did they often meet up here?'

Vicente looked uncomfortable.

'First time I've heard of it,' he said. 'They usually met down in the village, at the bar, I thought. That's when they were still talking to each other, at least.'

They headed back down the slope towards the nightclub.

Cámara scoured the ground for the viper, but there was no sign of it.

TWENTY

Marisol had done considerably better than the military spokesman at Palma. Her tone of voice had not wavered, her fluency unhindered by any doubt or concern. As the head of the press office at the Ministry of Defence, shielding inquiries from journalists over sensitive information was a daily occurrence, and the fact that she had survived in the job for so long was testament to her skill. Alicia had been impressed and reflected that she might even, at some future date, listen to her recording of the phone conversation as an example to study. Despite all the time they had spent together in the past, Marisol still had something to teach her.

She spoke almost continuously for ten minutes, producing such a barrage of words that it was impossible for Alicia to butt in or stop her midstream. That in itself was admirable, for in those ten minutes she gave away virtually nothing more than what Alicia already knew – that the island still belonged to the military despite being declared a nature reserve, that military manoeuvres were under way as part of a build-up to bigger war games that were due to be played with other NATO countries, that this was not a permanent measure but that no date could be given for when the island would be returned to its previous state. How, in effect, nothing unusual was actually taking place. The whole thing might not be exactly routine – nothing like this had happened on Cabrera before – but it was as good as. And she stressed in the most emphatic terms that no harm would come to any of the wildlife on the island, that the military respected the local ecosystem, that its being a military possession in fact was beneficial to the natural habitat and that the real threat was from the *masificación* of building projects designed to cater for tourists and holiday homes of the kind that had caused so much damage on the rest of the Balearic islands.

It was perhaps this last point that had set Alicia's alarm bells ringing, although if truth be told she had suspected something almost from the moment she had heard Marisol's voice on the other end of the line. When the conversation ended shortly after – Marisol having to dash off to a meeting, but so lovely to hear from her again and they really must get together as soon as possible – it was this emphasis on Cabrera wildlife that had stuck in Alicia's mind. Since when did the military care so much about a few jellyfish and a handful of plants? That, and something else. Not so much what Marisol had said, but what she hadn't. The obvious line of defence – not just from a Ministry press officer but from Marisol specifically – would have been to wonder why Alicia was sniffing around this in the first place, to question her journalistic judgement for spending any time at all on it. *There was no story*, was the obvious thing to say – the same line Sergi at the newspaper had used. And while the suggestion had been there, with talk about the measures on the island being almost routine, it had not been spelled out or stated clearly. And that, more than anything else, persuaded Alicia that there was, in fact, something to be investigated. That there was, to use a phrase that Max was fond of, *un gato encerrado* – a dead cat locked up somewhere, invisible but letting off quite a stench.

It was time to dig a little deeper. It was already early evening and the street outside was beginning to buzz to the sound of children coming home from school and the honking of horns as traffic built up. She felt the thrill of excitement, a sensation she had not enjoyed for several years – the possibility that she was on to something, something that no one else was even remotely aware of.

She rubbed her hands together and sat down at the computer, her fingers moving rapidly over the keyboard. It was time to do some background checking on Cabrera. Some clue might lie in the open air waiting for her to stumble upon it.

She brought up a handful of web pages on the island. The photos showed a beautiful, unspoilt place with limestone rocks breaking out of crystalline water to low peaks perhaps two hundred metres high. The landscape was covered with typical Mediterranean scrub plants, spattering the paleness of the rock with a light coating of olive green. There were few buildings apart from a lighthouse, the remains of an old castle and a handful of temporary structures in what was known as the 'Port' – the bottom point of a cove cutting into the northern coast of the main island that served as a natural harbour.

The history of Cabrera centred on this natural formation – Phoenicians, Greeks and Romans had all used it at various times as a place to shelter their sea vessels. There was even a legend that the great Hannibal had been born there. During the Middle Ages a monastery of some kind had been set up, but the monks appeared to have gone over to the enemy after the island became a base for Barbary pirates. The castle was built around this time, but the place was virtually deserted for the following centuries.

The next time Cabrera played a role in history was during the Napoleonic Wars in the early 1800s.

And as Alicia read on she discovered something – something that set her teeth on edge.

TWENTY-ONE

Vicenta appeared at the sound of their footsteps, crossing the courtyard to meet them as they descended the path towards the nightclub.

'Abi says he'll speak to you now if you want.'

Cámara nodded. Vicente headed back to the kitchen while Cámara followed the old woman to the door that Abi had passed through earlier.

'He's upset, still quite weepy,' said Vicenta. 'He's taken a sedative.'

'When?' asked Cámara sharply.

Vicenta looked concerned.

'Oh,' she said. 'Have I done something wrong? I just gave him one now. A minute ago, no more.'

'Never mind,' said Cámara. 'It'll need a few minutes to take effect.'

She opened the door and he stepped inside. Vicenta made to come in with him.

'I'd rather speak to him alone,' he said, turning and standing in the doorway.

'Of course,' she said. And she closed the door behind him.

Cámara took a step into the room. It was dark inside and he was partially blinded from the harsh sunlight outdoors.

'Come in,' said a drowsy voice. 'Please, take a seat where you like.'

Cámara felt his way forward, holding out his hands to avoid bumping into anything.

'Can I offer you anything to drink?' said Abi. Cámara still couldn't see where he was. The tone of voice was sorrowful; the offer might be genuine yet the underlying hope was that Cámara would refuse.

'I'm fine,' he said.

'As you wish.'

After he had stumbled a few more steps, the room came into focus. There seemed to be no windows in what was a large, high-ceilinged room. At the side were some metal steps leading up to a mezzanine area where a mattress and an unmade bed were just visible. Down on the ground floor was a living room with a tiny kitchen area tucked into one side. A door at the back presumably led to a bathroom.

The living room had a table in the middle, a very large television screen on one wall, and a dark brown L-shaped sofa opposite. On it, draped with a fuchsia-coloured blanket, was Abi, his head resting on white satin cushions. One arm, uncovered, lay at his side. It was long and thin, like a dancer's. Judging by the length of the man, stretched out horizontally now, he was quite tall – taller than he had looked when he had got out of the car.

A single lamp on a sideboard near his head cast a faint

light. Cámara got a better view of his features: a long, thin, prominent nose; hollow cheeks; pronounced Adam's apple. There was barely a gramme of fat on him.

In his hand, Abi loosely gripped a white cotton handkerchief not unlike the one Cámara had seen Vicenta with. Perhaps she had lent him one of her own.

Cámara sat down in a chair on the other side of the glass-topped table. A couple of gossip magazines were stacked neatly at the corner.

'Forgive me,' said Abi. He slowly lifted himself and sat up on the sofa, pulling the blanket over his shoulders. He looked older and weaker than his age.

'Vicenta just gave me a sedative,' he said. 'Perhaps we should talk before it kicks in. Although my head's spinning already.'

'I have a few questions,' said Cámara.

'About yesterday,' said Abi. 'Vicenta mentioned.'

'Yes.'

Abi shook his head.

'I was out,' he said. 'Went to the village.'

'Why?'

Abi closed his eyes.

'It was José Luis's birthday,' he said at length. 'We'd . . .' He paused. 'We'd had an argument earlier in the morning. I wanted to make it up to him. I drove to the village to find him a present. Something special.'

'What was the argument about?'

'Just, you know, couples' stuff.'

'Like?'

Abi shrugged.

'José . . . I usually called him José, not José Luis. He didn't like it. José said I wasn't doing enough for his birthday. That it was special – he was turning sixty. He could be like that, sometimes, a bit spoilt. I didn't want to tell him about the party I was planning – it was meant to be a surprise. But, well, he got cross. And I left.'

He sniffed and put the handkerchief to his nose.

'Which was clearly the wrong thing to do, in hindsight.'

'That's when you went to the village,' said Cámara.

Abi nodded.

'Is that your own car?'

'Yes. José didn't like driving. Preferred to be driven.'

'Did he have a licence?'

'Oh, yes,' said Abi. 'I saw it once. But he had delusions of grandeur. He was like that. Thought it would make a better impression to have someone else at the wheel, like some kind of pasha.'

'Can't have made life easy, living out here.'

'It's why he always needed someone like me around, to be his chauffeur.'

Abi's mouth flattened into a humourless smile.

'But you were more than just his chauffeur, weren't you?'

A tone of defiance crept into Abi's voice.

'I was his partner,' he said. 'His lover.'

'Did he live here with you?' Cámara's eyes darted around the small, rather cramped living space.

'No, no,' said Abi. 'We shared a bed sometimes. But José has . . .' He checked himself. 'Had his own living quarters across the courtyard. Much grander than this little hole.'

'You didn't . . . ?' said Cámara.

'Separate living areas,' said Abi. 'Each person with his own space.'

He shrugged.

'It's not a bad arrangement. If you can afford it.'

'But you'd been together for a few years.'

'Over a decade.'

He sniffed.

'Perhaps that's why we stayed together for so long. Not getting on top of each other all the time.'

'What about enemies? It sounds as though he – this place – was quite unpopular among the locals.'

'It's certainly not the locals who tend to come to Sunset,' said Abi. 'Although I'm certain that secretly a few of them would like to give it a try.'

He squinted at Cámara.

'But you're not suggesting . . . ?' he said.

'These are routine questions,' said Cámara.

'Surely not . . .' Abi began.

His shoulders began to shake under the blanket.

'We need to look at these things thoroughly,' said Cámara.

Perhaps even too thoroughly, he thought to himself. He had spent most of the day on this case already. Was it really the best use of a chief inspector's time? And yet he got the sense that there was something to be uncovered here, even if it wasn't a murder.

'I don't know everything that was going on here,' said Abi, 'and I don't want to name names, but things had been tense with Enrique recently.'

Cámara waited.

'What was going on?' he asked when Abi said nothing more.

'I don't know. I just know it was getting worse. All this business about the Chain. José was angry – it was beginning to get to him. I heard him cursing. He was getting grumpy about it. It's one of the reasons why I wanted to throw the party for him. Not just for his birthday, but because things had been getting to him. This Chain business.'

He was starting to drawl a little and he was swaying slightly from side to side. The sedative was starting to take effect.

'People round here are different,' Abi went on. 'Mountain people. They're strange, closed folk, hold grudges for years. Families up here still not speaking since the Civil War.'

His eyes were closed; he looked as though he were about to fall back down on to the sofa. Cámara spoke quickly.

'Did José Luis ever take drugs?' he asked.

Abi waved a limp hand in his direction.

'All the time.'

He checked himself.

'Well, not *all* the time. But often enough. Kind of goes with the job.'

'What did he take?'

'The usual.' Abi's eyes were rolling, the whites just visible under his eyelids.

'There's so much cocaine up here sometimes you could scour the floors with it.'

He giggled softly.

'Anything else?' Cámara asked. 'Did he ever use needles?'

'There was some new stuff around,' said Abi. 'Didn't try it. Don't know what it was.'

'Do you know who supplied it?'

Abi's head hit the cushion with a soft thump. His body was close to rolling off the sofa. Cámara walked across and pushed him firmly into place, lifting his legs and doing his best to drape the blanket over him.

He looked around the room, glancing at the door through which he'd entered.

'You won't mind if I have a little snoop around now I'm here,' he said.

Deeply asleep now, Abi made no reply.

'I'll take that as a no,' said Cámara.

TWENTY-TWO

He entered the main building of the nightclub through the front doors. The entrance was large and semicircular and had a high, domed ceiling, with a crystal chandelier on a long chain suspended from the keystone and a black-and-white chequered tiled floor. Large, leafy pot plants stood in classical urns on top of white stone pillars near the windows. It was bright and grand and gave the sensation of entering a palace rather than a discotheque. Cámara wondered how it looked so immaculate and well kept. It smelt of fresh, watery perfume.

At the side was the cloakroom: a counter, with rows of empty coat hangers suspended from steel bars. A wicker basket at the side for ticket stubs had been emptied and a cloth wiped over the marble top: Vicenta must have passed through here not long before.

A passageway to the left-hand side led to the toilets. The door of the first showed a picture of a buxom woman lifting her skirt and placing a hand between her legs; the second a silhouette of a man with an oversized erection. On the third a sketch was drawn in felt-tip pen of someone with both exposed breasts and a penis.

Not much room for confusion there, thought Cámara.

In front, through double swinging doors, was the main body of the disco. He pushed and stepped through.

The contrast to the entrance was remarkable. The fresh smell gave way to something more akin to what he had expected from the start: the sticky staleness of spilled drinks, the toxic combination of sweat and bleach. Here everything was dark: the windows had been painted black on the insides and only tiny rays of sunlight managed to penetrate where the paint had peeled or cracked, shooting across the empty space like splinters of glass. It was just enough, once his eyes had adjusted, to find his way around. He looked, but saw no sign of any light switch.

The floor was wooden and, like the windows, painted black. Steps led up to a main dance area. To the right was a long bar with dozens of bottles of liquor stacked neatly along shelves at the back. The walls had tall mirrors that came down to the floor at regular intervals for people to watch themselves as they danced.

Four pedestals no larger than a dining-room table were placed at various points for young, semi-clad dancers – the go-gos – to stand above the heaving mass of bodies and perform: something to look at and admire, something to aim for, even. They were a common feature of most discos: a focus for lustful imagination. What kind of dancers performed here?

The ceiling was a labyrinth of exposed piping and air-conditioning units, all painted black. Speakers and spotlights were placed at various points, while disco mirror balls hung forlornly like little moons, waiting to come alive with new light to reflect.

Cámara looked around: nowhere could he see anywhere to sit down.

A staircase shot up the left-hand side, doubling back on itself to an open upper floor which led to a booth for the DJ. Mirrors on the ceiling inside gave a clear view of the mixing decks and a laptop computer with a shiny chrome cover. Whoever was on shift up there would be clearly visible to those below, yet majestically lifted above them, like a musical deity.

He took the stairs and came up to a smaller area at the side of the DJ's booth. This had the air of an executive lounge: a second bar stood at one side, while doors at the other indicated more bathrooms. Black-painted metal railings divided it from the larger dance area, but whoever was up here would still have a clear view of below – and the people dancing. Black leather sofas and chairs were also arranged in a U-shape for greater comfort. The sense of hierarchy was evident in everything from the furnishings to the cleaner, less suffocating air. He had the sense of entering the bridge of a large, steaming ocean liner, the point from where the captain stared out and viewed the horizon while reassuring his crew as they powered towards the next sea port.

José Luis must have spent a great deal of time here, he thought, watching over his creation.

A door with a circular window led to a dark corridor. He felt for the lights, but could find none and had to creep forward using his fingertips. As he made out the beginnings of a door frame and edged closer, thinking he might find a source of light on the other side, he heard a click and fluorescent strips on thc ceiling shuddered into life.

'You still here?'

It was Paco, shutting a door further down the corridor behind him and locking it with a key.

'That your office?' asked Cámara.

'If you want to look inside, you're going to need a warrant.'

Paco walked up the corridor and brushed past, heading towards the executive lounge. Cámara watched him go.

Alone again in the corridor, he tried the various doors to see what lay behind. There were a couple of small, cramped changing rooms with crates of bottles stacked at the sides. A third room was the main store area for the bars, with shelves weighed down under hundreds of bottles of booze, with more stacks of plastic crates. The one nearest was full of Coke.

Cámara tried the handle, but Paco's office was securely locked. To his surprise, however, the room opposite was not: it was another office. A walnut desk stood in the middle, with a large executive chair behind, like a throne. A globe – one of the illuminated kind, judging by the flex trailing from the bottom – was perched on a corner. A cabinet in walnut stood against one wall, with bottles of vodka and gin placed on a special mirrored shelf next to a silver cocktail shaker, a bottle of bitters, and various other materials, as well as an engraved crystal jug with a long silver stirring spoon and a silver ice bowl.

The floor was tiled, but a large, brightly coloured Oriental carpet covered the space between the doorway and the desk. On it was the design of a creature that looked like a stylised peacock.

But for one thing the room looked like the office of some small-scale mogul in a bad 1970s spy film – it felt clean and unused, the furniture trying to make a statement but one that had no heart to it, could not take itself seriously. And what underlined this was the gigantic photo on the back wall of Dolly Parton wearing a white Stetson and black-and-red check shirt, tilting her head coquettishly to the side and smiling at the camera through blonde curls. It was housed in a gilt frame to which fairy lights had been attached: when switched on it must have appeared like an altar.

Smiling a polite greeting to the Queen of Country, Cámara passed round the room, trying to gauge what impression it gave him about José Luis – for something told him clearly this was his space – but the messages were confused and unclear. Flamboyant and sensual on the one hand, yet with a streak of conservativism.

He glanced down at the back of the desk. A small safe sat at the bottom to one side. He tried to open it, but, not unexpectedly, it was locked.

He left, wondering who now might have the key.

Cámara found José Luis's apartments in the larger building adjacent to the stables on the far side of the courtyard. The door was open and he passed through into a hall with steps leading to the first floor. At the top, a white security door with golden edgings was ajar. The air from inside the apartment was stuffy and thick, tinged with a hint of sweet perfume. He felt at the side and turned on the lights.

José Luis's home was open-plan and very big. Shuttered windows, each one about two metres across, were in every wall, yet looked as though they were rarely, if ever, opened. With the blinds up, they would have given a panoramic, almost 360-degree view. Cámara walked across to one of them and pulled on the cord. With a dusty rattle, afternoon sunlight began to filter through, eventually revealing vistas down the mountainside, through the pine trees to the Mediterranean in the far distance. He lost himself in it for a moment, wondering why anyone would choose to close themselves off from something so beautiful.

He felt a sudden urge to allow more daylight and fresh air into this dank space. Jerking hard on the cords of the blinds, he lifted them all, then opened a couple of the windows to the full to allow a cross-breeze to enter.

His eye was immediately caught by a large golden Chinese cat standing in the middle of the apartment waving its arm in perpetual motion. He had seen them before – they had been everywhere a few years earlier – yet never so big. There was something sinister and uncomforting about its fixed grin, as though it echoed the presence of the man who had been living here only hours before. It certainly hadn't brought José Luis much luck. Who the hell was it waving to now?

He shook himself, forcing himself to turn his attention away from the cat and take a proper look at his surroundings, wondering in the back of his mind what was making him so uncomfortable there.

Most of the fittings were in white or pale tones. Cream-coloured rugs lay on a floor of shiny, brilliant tiles; a white coffee table was surrounded by a U-shaped combination of soft white sofas, with fluffy white pouffes for people to place their feet on. A gigantic television near the middle of the room on a white stand had a white plastic frame and back rather than the usual black or grey. A couple of free-standing bookcases used to create divisions within the diaphanous space were equally white, with porcelain figures – no books – painted in pale glazes on the shelves: a shepherdess gazing into the distance, a man sitting mournfully with a guitar. Yet there were also more eye-catching ornaments: a couple of indistinct gender held in an erotic embrace; a phallus, proud and unembarrassed. And white.

It was all luxurious, if not to Cámara's taste, and well kept – there was barely a grain of dust in the entire apartment. There was also something self-indulgent about it. Mirrors were everywhere, seemingly on every spare patch of wall. A place of darkness, where no natural light entered, yet which spoke of brightness and reflection, as though desperate for the very thing from which it had cut itself off. Why go to so much trouble? thought Cámara. Why not just open the windows? What had José Luis been afraid of?

Only one piece of furniture provided a different tone: a glass cabinet on one wall with old toys displayed in neat rows, as though in a museum. They were familiar to him from his own childhood: whistles, tin cars, wind-up trains – decades old yet immaculate, as though they had just been purchased. Cámara would never have thought of hanging on to them himself, still less put on show like this. What had they meant to José Luis?

A king-size double bed stood on a raised platform a few centimetres higher than the rest of the room. The floor nearby was littered with scraps of purple tissue paper. The bed itself was unmade and in the middle sat a small pile of presents, all – but for one – unopened. Cámara peered at them: there were no cards or signs of who they were from. The open box was made of golden card, yet there was nothing nearby to suggest what it had contained. Had José Luis only had time to open this one before he had been called out? Cámara left the others as they were: something about opening a dead man's birthday presents made him uneasy.

At the foot of the bed was a smaller television in a set of shelves. Cámara opened the drawers beneath to reveal a collection of DVDs. He smiled: José Luis had just turned sixty. Was he still watching these things? Certainly Cámara did.

He lifted one out. The cover showed a photograph in garish colours of three naked men having sex, with small silver stars covering their genitals and cheap-looking graphics framing the scene. The others in the collection appeared to be in a similar vein, although one or two showed both men and women.

A glass door on the far side of the bed led to a bathroom. A shelf at the side was home to a large array of colognes and perfumes. Cámara leaned over and sniffed tentatively. Most were in expensive-looking glass bottles, with one or two more ordinary-looking, the kinds sold at the supermarket. He lifted one, a black can, and sprayed it just in front of his face. It was sweet and dark, with a clinging, cloying quality about it that almost made his eyes water. Who on earth wore this stuff?

A second cabinet in the bathroom, below the sink, captured his attention. A box contained over a dozen throwaway hypodermic needles. In his mind flashed the sight of José Luis's corpse at the Forensic Medicine Centre earlier that morning and the pinprick marks he had seen on the left arm.

But what kinds of drugs had José Luis been injecting himself with? The bottles next to the syringes were the ordinary kinds one found in any medicine kit: paracetamol, omeprazole, aspirin, antihistamines.

Cámara stood up and went back to the bed. He lifted one corner of the sheet to reveal the frame underneath the mattress: as he suspected, there were drawers, probably intended for storing linen. Yet the rattle that sounded when he pulled on one spoke of quite different contents.

With daylight shining directly down through the open window, he lifted out a handful of small plastic bottles. Most contained liquids; a few had pills; others simple white powders. Cámara counted: there were over a dozen bottles with 'GHB' written on them in different, multicoloured fonts. A handful of the others contained mephedrone, while the majority – over twenty in total – were filled with methamphetamine, or 'T', as the bottles claimed on their labels. At the bottom of the drawer, squeezed in at the side, was a used syringe.

Next to it, lying sleepily like a bird in its nest, was a small handgun, a 6.35mm Astra 2000. Cámara picked it up: it was partly scuffed around the handle, the trigger looked worn, and it had the appearance of something picked up from an antique dealer rather than a potentially lethal weapon. He opened the magazine and counted six bullets before putting it back in its place, making a mental note.

He went to every window, closing the ones he had opened and letting the blinds down again. He had seen enough. After one look back at the golden Chinese cat, he closed the door behind him and went downstairs out into the courtyard.

His feet took him round to the front of the main building, near where he had parked his motorbike. The Mercedes that had been there when he arrived – the car he assumed was Paco's – had gone.

TWENTY-THREE

Everything was silent. The light breeze had stilled and in the later afternoon heat a bright, blinding sense of emptiness had come over the place. No birds sang, no insects chirruped, no animals moved, as if some sleep of death had entered into every living thing.

Cámara listened. There was one, distant noise breaking through the vacuum; he heard it once, then it stopped. Yet it was unmistakable, coming from higher up the mountainside in the direction of the Chain: the harsh, rasping bark of a dog.

It was time to visit Enrique.

He checked his phone again, hoping that through some miracle he might have picked up a signal. Yet the screen stubbornly insisted that there was 'no service'. He thought for a moment about looking for a landline and giving Torres a call. What had he been able to find out?

He had seen a phone back in José Luis's apartments. And

it would be simple enough to find others. He was curious. José Luis had been using powerful narcotic cocktails to boost his sex life. The 'chemsex' phenomenon was well established up here in the sierra, by the looks of things. Mephedrone to keep you awake, methamphetamine to give you power and confidence, and GHB to raise your libido. Sex on a combination of those could last for days on end, no need to eat or sleep.

Would any of this be in the police computer system? Anything be reflected in the files? If so, Torres would find it. He had always been so much better than Cámara at using the intranet to dig up information. And he needed him now as much as ever.

And yet he hesitated – concerned that something in those files would show very clearly that this was anything but murder. What exactly had killed José Luis would become clearer the following day when the autopsy report came through. Yet Cámara wondered whether Torres already had something that would make his investigation pointless.

Vicente and Vicenta emerged from the kitchen as he was about to start on the path back towards the Chain.

'We're going now,' said Vicente.

Cámara turned.

'Abi's all right on his own,' said Vicenta. 'I think the best thing is for him to sleep now.'

'We'll be back in the morning,' added Vicente.

Cámara was confused.

'I thought you lived here,' he said.

'We've got a little house on the other side of the wood,' said Vicenta, 'where we spend the evenings. It's a five-minute walk.'

'Will we be seeing you tomorrow?' asked Vicente.

'Probably not,' said Cámara.

'Enrique should be back.' Vicente nodded up the path. 'Heard his dog a minute ago.'

'Thanks for your help,' Cámara said. 'And for lunch.'

Vicenta nodded. The couple turned and walked off through the trees. Cámara waited until they were out of sight before heading up the path.

It was darker now, the sunlight slanting in at a low angle through the branches, laying diagonal stripes pregnant with tiny motes of dust. He watched carefully when he reached the spot where the viper had been sleeping.

At the Chain, the hives appeared to have more life about them. He went over to take a closer look: dozens of bees were circling the tiny entrances and many were flying off, catching the sunlight on their wings as they darted past.

Almost immediately, however, he noticed that his presence was unwelcome. The buzzing increased in volume and pitch, a clear aggressive intent noticeable purely from the sound. Instinctively, Cámara made to step away, yet already a bee had burrowed its way through his hair into his scalp. The sting, when it came, was excruciating – sharp, piercing and with a cold, acidic bite. His eyes watered, back arching with surprise at the intensity of the pain. It was swiftly followed by a second sting, this time on the back of his shoulder, the bee managing to penetrate the cloth of both his jacket and shirt underneath.

He let out a low scream of agony, drawing away as quickly as he could from the hives. Yet to his astonishment, the bees came after him, over a dozen of them still darting from side to side around him. Cámara threw his hands into the air, swatting in vain as he tried to defend himself. Another piercing needle of flame shot into his right hand, then a fourth sting near the back of his neck.

His legs finally took control and he started running as fast as he could, turning right at the Chain and sprinting up the track leading towards Enrique's house, his muscles pumping as hard as they could. When he had put over a hundred metres between himself and the hives, he threw a glance over his shoulder, expecting the bees to have given up on him. Yet amazingly, two of them were still with him, flying straight for him as he paused mid-step. With a final, panicked burst of energy, he flew off again, running until he was almost at Enrique's house. Only then did he stop, leaning against a nearby tree, panting and out of breath. It took several minutes to convince himself that the danger was finally past.

His whole body throbbed with pain, as though he could sense the poison not only where the bees had stung him, but flowing through his bloodstream. He was dizzy and in a state of shock, legs trembling, a coldness creeping under his skin, harsh, metallic taste in his mouth. He longed to sit down on the ground, yet he knew it would only make standing up again that much harder. The four stings on his body seemed to be linked by some invisible thread, sharp waves of agony passing from one to the next, like a spider spinning its web.

Cámara tried to remember whether he had been stung by a bee before. It was the kind of thing you wouldn't forget. Perhaps, based on his reaction now, this was one childhood rite of passage that had passed him by. It felt like nothing he had experienced before.

Time passed – he was unsure how long. Perhaps as much as an hour; or as little as a minute. He checked the position of the sun, but it was invisible behind the wall of trees. A few yards ahead lay Enrique's farmhouse. He took a deep breath and started walking towards it.

The house was a simple, unprepossessing structure with small windows and thick stone walls smoothed over with decades of whitewashing. The roof was covered with light terracotta tiles and a small chimney with a ceramic flue jutted out at the top. To one side of the building was a field with over a dozen well-tended olive trees, the light red soil beneath them entirely clear of weeds. A rusting abandoned car – an old Renault 4 – sat under the shade of the largest tree, useless now even for spare parts, but too difficult, presumably, to get rid of.

Cámara approached slowly, more through discomfort than any sense of caution. He was hoping that Enrique might be prevailed upon to offer him a glass of water at least: the shock of the bee stings had left his mouth dry.

Something, however, was puzzling him: if Enrique was there, why hadn't the dog barked? Both he and Vicente had heard it from down at Sunset. Had Enrique left in the meantime? Cámara had heard no car. Yet if Enrique were here, the dog would surely have made a noise by now, have signalled the presence of a visitor, of a stranger.

Cámara stepped around the corner of the house. Beyond, on the far side, was a garden area, with vegetables growing in neat rows. A green container next to the building collected rainwater from the roof, with a black plastic irrigation pipe running from it and branching out into smaller ones over the lines of sprouting plants. The soil was newly damp, stained dark against the drier earth nearby. Someone had switched this on in the past few minutes, for there was no sign of any automatic or timed switch to make the water flow.

'Hello?' Cámara called out. 'Anyone here?'

There was no reply.

Around the next corner was a covered patio area with a couple of red plastic bar chairs. Beer advertisements on the backs had faded and been almost entirely blanched by years of sunlight. One door from the area was closed and appeared to lead into the house, while a second, at right angles to the first, was open. Beyond was a single room with a concrete floor and a tiny opening near the top of one wall to let in some light. Cámara stepped inside. It was dark and there was a tangy, disturbing smell, like the tight winds of an approaching storm. As his eyes adjusted he made out a large white chest against one wall, while opposite was a long, wide counter at waist height made out of a single slab of marble. On it were dark, indistinguishable shapes, yet the sound of flies buzzing fiercely about them made him lean in closer to see more clearly. He prodded at one with his finger: it was hard and cold and damp. The flies jumped up as one and formed a cloud around him, then the object fell to one side with a thud. Cámara looked into a single yellow eye bulging out of a fur-lined socket; it was the sectioned head of an ibex.

A quick glance at the other objects revealed their identities as more pieces of some once-living beast – or perhaps beasts. Cámara couldn't tell if they were all ibex, or if other animals had also been cut up and put on display in this amateur abattoir. The counter surface was sticky with old, infected blood.

'You should turn around now.'

He heard a voice from behind, trembling yet certain. It was accompanied by two other sounds: that of a dog growling very softly, as though desperate to lash out; and the unmistakable sound of a firearm being thrust against a man's shoulder and raised to take aim.

Slowly and carefully, with his hands clearly displayed at either side of him, Cámara began to turn around. Standing in the doorway, with an Alsatian glowering obediently from his side, was an elderly man with a tattered black baseball cap on his head, a deep scar running down the left side of his face, and a Remington hunting rifle pointing directly at Cámara's head.

'That's it,' said Enrique. 'I prefer to look a man in the eye before I shoot him.'

TWENTY-FOUR

She thought it would be Max, but instead a woman's voice came on the line.

'Marisol?'

'How soon can you be in Madrid?'

Alicia blinked, then checked her watch: it was past eight o'clock in the evening.

'I think the last AVE leaves at around nine,' she said cautiously. 'What . . . What is it?'

'If you make it . . .' Marisol began, then halted.

'What?' insisted Alicia.

'I'll tell you.'

Alicia breathed in.

'You mean—?'

'No, Alicia!' Marisol butted in. 'Not now . . . You know that much at least.'

'I . . .' Alicia was trying to think: throw a few things in a bag, catch a taxi to the station. She probably just had time to buy her ticket. She could be in the capital by about eleven o'clock. And Lucía would be happy for her to use the flat. She still had the key her friend had given her with the invitation to stay there whenever she needed. The place was empty anyway – it was good to have people in and out.

'It has to be tonight,' Marisol said. 'Otherwise . . .'

'I can do it,' Alicia said. 'But it'll be late.'

'No matter.'

'I'll call you when we're pulling in.'

'No.' Marisol's voice thudded like a heavy rock falling into a stream. 'I'll call you. And you'll do exactly what I say.'

Twenty minutes later Alicia was ready to go, spongebag, laptop, notebooks and clean clothes packed into a small wheeled suitcase. As she was leaving she remembered her phone charger and quickly grabbed it from the counter in the kitchen where she kept it plugged in, stuffing it inside her coat pocket where it jangled next to the keys to Lucía's flat. She would call her on the way, make sure no one else was staying there that night. But in the meantime she dialled Max's number just to fill him in on what was happening.

His phone, however, did not ring, passing straight to voicemail. Wherever he was and whatever he was up to he had either switched the damn thing off or had no coverage. Normally he would have been back by now. Something must have come up. It sometimes did.

No matter. She had her own investigation and had to dash. There would be time to talk – or exchange text messages – later.

She made sure all the lights were switched off, bolted the windows and checked everything was OK. Then she closed the door behind her and turned the key, listening for the double clunk of the bar as it shot across, firm and secure.

TWENTY-FIVE

'Shooting me is not a good idea, Enrique,' said Cámara. 'I'm a police officer.'

Something glinted in Enrique's eye: a look of suspicion and fear.

'*Policía Nacional*,' continued Cámara. 'I'm here investigating the death of José Luis, from the nightclub.'

Enrique's rifle lowered marginally from the side of his face.

'Prove it,' he said.

Cámara's right hand began to move very slowly.

'I'm reaching into my jacket pocket to get my ID,' he said. 'I'm unarmed.'

Enrique's hands gripped the weapon tighter. Cámara pulled out his wallet and fished out his police card, offering it. Enrique appeared more focused on Cámara himself, staring him hard in the eye before finally lowering the rifle to his side and snatching the card.

He spent some time reading it, the struggle to understand its few words visible in his eyes. Cámara waited.

'Don't see many of your kind round here,' said Enrique, handing the card back. Cámara slipped it inside his wallet again and reinserted that into his jacket pocket. As he did so, a renewed throb of pain from the bee stings coursed through his body, making his head spin.

'You all right?' asked Enrique.

'Got stung,' explained Cámara. 'Back at the Chain.'

'Perhaps the bees don't like the smell of policemen.'

Another glint in his eye, of defiance and pride.

'I could do with a glass of water,' said Cámara. 'Could I get one?'

Enrique pursed his lips. There was something impenetrable about the man. His face was set, like concrete. Deep dark lines ran across his forehead and down the sides of his cheeks near his mouth, and his complexion was like toasted bread, hard, pockmarked and burnt in places. The scar that sliced the skin on one side was visible more for the lighter tone of the healed tissue, with clear, almost white, slash-like marks running across it in places. A knife cut, perhaps? Had Enrique been involved in a fight? It seemed possible.

The eyes were the only thing that gave anything away, yet reading their expression was made difficult by their smallness, mere dots partially veiled behind folds of wrinkled, well-used skin, with a final curtain of thick grey bushy eyebrows that trailed downwards, almost covering the apertures of his eye sockets.

He was a small man. Yet he stood erect and proud here in his own home, with powerful limbs and an animal-like sense of purpose about him. Enrique was no thinker; he was a man of action, of deep and perhaps thwarted passions; and he was dangerous.

'What are you doing here?' he said. 'Where are the *Guardia Civil*?'

He was still holding the rifle by his side in his right hand.

'It's a *Policía Nacional* case,' said Cámara. 'José Luis—'

'José Luis got what he deserved,' interrupted Enrique.

'Meaning?'

Cámara could sense the pain building up to pulse through him again, like the pull-back of the sea before sending out another crashing wave. He leaned his weight against the counter behind, trying not to touch the coagulated blood. He braced himself; the crescendo flashed into his brain as he forced his eyes to remain open, show no sign.

'He wasn't mountain people,' said Enrique. 'Not from round here. Didn't fit. Things will be better without him.'

Cámara tensed what felt like every muscle in his body, sweat trickling down the centre of his back. The pain subsided. He let out a breath and looked Enrique in the eye.

'Is that why you killed him?'

Enrique's immobile face performed the impossible and froze even more. The eyes were dead still behind their walls of protection, the expression as motionless and unrelenting as before. Cámara noticed his knuckles turning white where he gripped the rifle.

'You hated José Luis,' Cámara continued. 'You hate the nightclub and everything that goes on there. And you had a long-standing feud with him over the Chain. That's why you put the bees there.'

He barely registered the tiniest flicker in the eyes.

'Not just to frighten people away, to keep the clubbers

from Sunset off your land, or from going down to the *Molino*.'

Enrique tilted his chin. Cámara could sense a momentum building.

'But because you wanted the bees to get rid of José Luis for you. So you put an aggressive strain of them right at the edge of your land, where it borders José Luis's estate. You know he's not a fit man. You demand an urgent meeting, get him up to the Chain supposedly to discuss matters, then let the bees do the rest.'

Yet just as the momentum had appeared to be growing, it was lost. Cámara could feel it draining away even before he had finished. Enrique's dark, impenetrable eyes opened a fraction.

'If I'd wanted José Luis dead,' he said simply, 'I would have shot him years ago.'

From somewhere in his body, Cámara could feel another wave rushing towards him. Had the stings unbalanced him?

'I don't know if you're accusing me of José Luis's murder,' continued Enrique. 'From the sound of it you're saying I got the bees to kill him for me.'

His little mouth almost cracked as it curled into something like a grin.

'Now, I know bees. Had them all my life, as did my father before me. And I know their ways – what they like and what they don't like. And I could make another animal attack someone at my command. This dog, for example.'

The Alsatian had not moved its gaze from Cámara's face the entire time.

'One command and he'll tear into a man without any hesitation.'

Cámara swallowed hard and gripped the counter behind him with both hands.

'But even I can't make bees attack someone when I ask them to. And I don't know anyone who can.'

The tremble returned, sweat building up once more as Cámara's blood pressure rose with the tide of pain. A searing sensation, like a band of hot iron, crossed his brow and seemed to bore into his skull. And he felt certain that Enrique was aware of his condition, was watching him the way a child might observe a dying fly on its back, flailing its legs furiously in the air. There would be no glass of water.

'You're the strangest-looking policeman I've ever seen,' said Enrique. 'You sure you're in the right place? I've half a mind to go and call the *Guardia Civil*. I know Corporal Rodríguez. He'll be able to tell me what this is all about.'

It was desperate, but Cámara had got this far and could only carry on.

'The call,' he said through gritted teeth. 'You called José Luis yesterday and demanded to meet him at the Chain. Why did you do that?'

The eyes narrowed.

'What?' spat Enrique.

'I know about the call,' insisted Cámara. 'You wanted to meet José Luis at the Chain. Said it was urgent. Why else would you do that if you weren't luring him into a trap? I know it was unusual. You'd never done anything like this before.'

'Never done it before, and never done it at all!'

Enrique thrust out his chest. At his side, the dog stood up, readying itself.

'What call are you talking about?' he demanded.

'You called Paco, the manager at Sunset,' said Cámara, looking at Enrique while keeping an eye on the Alsatian. 'You left a message. Said you wanted an urgent meeting at the Chain.'

'Paco?'

For the first time there appeared to be a clear expression on Enrique's face: confusion.

'I've never spoken to Paco in my life,' he said.

'You know who he is.'

'Course I know who he is. But I've never spoken to him. Never want to speak to him. Why would I call him? Don't even have his number.'

The throbbing had eased a little. Cámara tried to clear his head.

'You're saying you didn't call Paco yesterday,' he said.

'Not yesterday. Not never!' cried Enrique. 'I don't talk to people like him.'

'People like him?'

'You know what I mean,' spat Enrique. 'You're supposed to be the policeman. That Rodríguez from the *Guardia Civil*—'

'Will be informed of everything in due course,' interrupted Cámara. He held up a hand.

'Your phone records can be checked,' he continued. 'Both landline and mobile, if you've got one.'

'No signal out here,' said Enrique. 'Only use it when I'm in the village if I have to. But it comes to the same. You'll find nothing. Not about me calling Paco.'

Cámara paused, trying to deepen his breathing.

'You've got José Luis's number, I take it,' he said at length.

'Not much use to me now.'

'Did you ever use it?' asked Cámara. 'Did you ever call José Luis on that number?'

Enrique shrugged.

'Well, did you?'

'Once or twice, maybe in the past,' said Enrique eventually.

'When was the last time?'

'Years ago.'

'When you were still talking to each other.'

'Huh?'

'When you and José Luis were still talking.'

'I suppose.'

'And when was that?' asked Cámara.

Enrique thought.

'Perhaps a couple of years ago,' he said.

'You're saying you hadn't spoken to José Luis for at least two years?'

Enrique nodded.

'About that.'

'Did you arrange a meeting with him yesterday?' Cámara asked.

'No, I've already told you.'

'Did you have any reason to arrange a meeting? Was there anything new to discuss?'

'We went beyond discussing a long time ago.'

'So there is no possibility that you might have wanted to see him yesterday at the Chain.'

Enrique shook his head.

'I've already—'

'Answer the question,' ordered Cámara.

'No,' Enrique said at length, his eyes boring into Cámara's head.

'Tell me where you were yesterday,' said Cámara. 'What were you doing late morning?'

From Enrique's side, the dog began to growl, as though obeying some unspoken command from his master.

'If you're not going to arrest me,' said Enrique, 'then it's time you left. I've answered enough of your questions.'

With a flick of his wrist he motioned with the gun barrel, indicating for Cámara to step outside.

Cámara sniffed and did as he was told. He had got what he wanted.

The dog's head lurched towards him as he stepped past, as though making to take a bite out of his leg. After a pause, Enrique ordered it to stop.

'I'll be telling the *Guardia Civil* about this,' said Enrique as Cámara made to leave. 'They're proper police, they are. Know what they're doing.'

Cámara walked with heavy steps back down the track in the direction of the Chain. And the hives.

TWENTY-SIX

The sun would be setting before long. Cámara reached the Chain, trying to leave as much space between himself and the hives as possible. It was difficult to tell in the fading light and from a distance, but the creatures appeared less active, less aggressive now. He dodged through the trees to a safer space some metres away.

He was exhausted. The stings had drained his energy and he longed to go home. The path back towards Sunset – and his motorbike parked outside – lay in front. In a few minutes he could be putting on his helmet and riding away. Within just over half an hour, he could be pushing through his front door once again, and into the arms of Alicia. And quickly taking a couple of painkillers.

It was tempting and, leaning against a tree, he had resolved to head off, finish his working day, when he heard a rustling sound to his right. He turned to look: a long-tailed lizard was scuttling off, hugging the ground and kicking up tiny nebulae of dust as it disturbed the pine needles in its way. Cámara followed its progress as it sped along, passing under the chain and away down the path that led to the *Molino*.

He checked the position of the sun: it was low, but there was still time. If the place was as beautiful as people claimed, it would be good to see it, especially now as the sun was setting. He might even have a quick swim down there, ease the stings a little with fresh water. Then come back with Alicia one day, when this business was over.

He took a breath, pushed himself off the tree and headed down the track, carefully lifting his feet over the chain, and began his descent.

The earth soon changed from the light grey of lime to a softer, more orange sandstone as the path emerged out of the pine wood and continued along a short flat section. On both sides, he could see the valley stretching away, curling and sweeping in tight arcs as it followed a course millions of years old and slowly wended its way down towards the fertile plain of the city, and the sea beyond. Above, the sky appeared to have been painted by a child's bright crayons, with streaks of red, orange, yellow and purple shooting in many directions from the smiling disc of the setting sun. At last the birds had come to life in the cooling, more forgiving air, tweeting light bursts of song as they flew like shadows in front of him, darting from tree to bush to rock. Cámara kept his eyes open for any snakes basking in the last rays of light, yet he already felt certain that there would be no danger here, that he had entered an altogether more benign and less threatening world. This valley, unlike the forest, had a welcoming feeling about it, as though it beckoned him, promising beauty and shelter, a place to heal and recover.

His thoughts wandered through the dying day as he walked along the path. There was, he decided, no murder to answer for here. He had seen it in Quintero's eyes that morning at the Forensic Science Centre; had heard it in Torres's voice. There had been an anonymous call suggesting something more sinister, yet as Azcárraga had insisted, there was nothing to it, no clues, not even a name to go on. Just some crank, probably one of the regulars at the club, distraught that José Luis had left them so suddenly. Perhaps the caller was stoned. Certainly there were enough narcotics inside José Luis's apartments to keep a small army in a state of altered consciousness for several days. Drugs, he suspected, were in no short supply at Sunset, and if anyone was involved in providing them, then his first suspect would be Paco, the manager.

But Paco being a drug dealer didn't make him a murderer. Neither did Enrique's long-held grudge against José Luis.

He grinned to himself at the thought of the interview back at Enrique's farmhouse. Yes, there were questions still to be cleared up. If Enrique hadn't called Paco, then who had? Perhaps no one. Perhaps Paco made the whole thing up. Perhaps he needed José Luis to be off-site for a time while he conducted some of his business. There could be many reasons. Perhaps some of them involving illegal activity. Yet despite being suspicious, even important, none of them pointed directly to murder.

And what was he thinking? That the bees had somehow been used to kill José Luis? The very thought had been floating somewhere in the back of his mind, yet was clearly absurd. Had he actually accused Enrique of murdering José Luis by getting bees to sting him to death? He shrugged and carried on walking. Perhaps it was getting stung himself, perhaps it was the mountain air, perhaps it was delayed shock from being kicked in the balls by Rita that morning. Whatever it was, he seemed to have temporarily lost his senses.

Still, there was one thing he could carry away from this day, and that was discovering a hidden beauty spot in the mountains.

The path veered to the left, the descent becoming steeper as it passed through a cluster of holm oaks, with dusty-green leaves and gnarled, knotty trunks. Cámara crunched acorns underfoot, skidding slightly on the loose stones and holding himself upright by pulling on the branches of a nearby rosemary bush. A cloud of comforting scent was released as he let go, and clung to him as he carried on.

The path zigzagged down the slope, heading towards the bottom of the valley. The sun was starting to clip a ridge of mountains to the west. At the sound of rushing water from below, he picked up his pace, crouching and lowering his weight so as not to trip over the uneasy rocks along the path.

After crossing what looked like a couple of ancient and unused water channels, he inched his way down a flat slab of rock before finally reaching the river. The water gushed and bubbled joyously near his feet, as though revelling in its own youthful energy and escape from the insides of the mountain into this vibrant stream. The bare rock just below was smooth and rounded, like polished marble, sculpted by the tiny hands of many thousands of years' flow into a myriad curling, twisting shapes.

Along the banks of the river, leaning across the water and forming an arch, were dozens of oleanders, with bright pink and red flowers like torches held aloft. Beyond them, in the middle distance, stood the remains of what had once been the waterwheel, its walls crumbled until they stood barely a metre above the ground. Nothing remained of the wheel that had once turned with the force of the stream.

The place was magical, thought Cámara, in the true sense of the word. The last sunlight reflecting off the rippled surface of the water; dragonflies, bright blue and green, darting from side to side like fairies; the deep, calming sound of the stream, the scent of flowers and herbs. It was, he thought, the kind of place where one could step out of time, where the strain of everyday slipped away and was discarded like an unwanted skin. It was wonderful just to absorb the sensation for a moment, to let it soak into him like ink into paper.

The oleanders and dragonflies, the ruined watermill and the sunlight dancing in the eddies of the stream were almost as nothing, however, to what had caught his eye as soon as he had arrived: the waterfall, where the river shot over a ledge some three metres above a large pool of dark blue water, like an image of paradise from the brightly coloured films he had seen as a child. The pool was deep and clear and inviting; he knew, as soon as he set eyes on it, that he must jump in.

It took almost no time for him to rid himself of his clothes, leaving them in a loose pile on an outcrop of dry limestone at the river's edge. There was no need to check if he were alone: the time of day, the day of the week, even the time of year – late June, before the real summer had begun – all told him that he had this place, this moment, to himself. With not a scrap of clothing on, he worked his way to the top of the waterfall, standing where it cascaded into the pool below. He paused for a second, gauged the angle of his jump, felt the stings throbbing once more, closed his eyes, and launched himself.

The water was cold, much colder than he had imagined. He sank deep under the surface, eyes suddenly open to the full with shock. He saw a light green and turquoise world, its outlines blurred, yet with shapes and patterns scattered like some code or language whose meaning he could not decipher. Light streamed in from above, a single pale finger slicing through the surface and illuminating his chest, as though the sun had cast its final ray and found him, lost in this sacred pool, arms and legs flailing about like the limbs of a newborn child.

He pushed upward, breaking through the surface of the water into the evening air with a yell. A moment longer, he thought, and he would freeze. Yet almost at the same moment, a burning sensation began in his chest and spread over the rest of his body as a reaction kicked in and his skin responded to the sudden change. He allowed himself to float for a few seconds, turning on his back and staring up above the falling water at the sky beyond. It was turning a dark violet now, the sun having passed over the edge of the mountain and working its way towards the inevitable horizon.

He lingered a few moments more before gradually drifting towards the edge and standing up to get out. He was cold and invigorated. Alicia would adore this place; he would bring her as soon as he could.

The path back up to his clothes proved trickier than he expected, and he had to jump up on to the bare rock, pulling at a bush lodged in a crease in the stone to help himself up. He cast a disparaging glance at his ageing body as he stood and dried himself in the light breeze, then arched his back and gazed at the canopy above his head. He himself was no beauty, but nothing mattered when all this surrounded him and offered so much.

It had been worth it, he thought, as he pulled his clothes back on. Today, everything that had happened. All of it worth it for this moment alone, discovering this wonderful corner of the sierra. Any amount of trouble could be wiped clean by such a place.

He put his jacket on and slipped on his shoes. It was getting quite dark now, with just a faint glow of twilight to guide him. Just enough to see him back to the nightclub, and his bike.

He stuck his hands in his pockets and made to step towards the path leading back up the slope.

Which was when the shooting began.

TWENTY-SEVEN

Cámara dropped to the ground. A moment later, a second shot came blistering across from his left, smashing into a rock just metres in front, sending splinters of stone scattering, the bullet ricocheting off into the bushes beyond.

Whoever was firing was aiming to kill.

Without thinking, he lifted himself in the pause after the second shot and sprinted off up the river bed, in the opposite direction to the firing, bending low, keeping his weight as close to the ground as possible. It was impossible not to make a noise as he splashed against the current, pushing his way past oleanders and other plants, prickly and less friendly that suddenly appeared in this previously idyllic spot. Yet he had to move, get out of sight, or out of range, of his attackers. A deep, animal instinct within him understood that if they found him he would be dead.

His right hand had already reached round for the pistol that he normally carried on duty, only to find an empty space where the heavy piece of metal usually nestled against his body. He was unarmed and alone; there was no way he could either defend himself, or, with zero mobile coverage, call for assistance or backup. Any cry for help would only give his position away. He would have to face this – and whoever was trying to kill him – like an ordinary man. No longer a policeman trying to resolve a murder, but suddenly and without warning a lone individual trying desperately to save his own skin.

He pushed on up the river, staring with wild, open eyes in the increasing gloom. If there was one element in his favour, it was that night was falling and he would become a more difficult target. Yet he had to put enough distance between himself and the shooter first. And with every step he was making more noise.

Still he pushed on, throwing an occasional glance behind, yet intent on getting up the valley as quickly and as far as possible – the only direction open to him. The water grew shallower as he climbed, falling below his knees and pushing against his shins, yet still it was an effort to make progress. The banks at the sides were too dense with bushes and trees for him to be able to break out on to dry land.

He heard noises in the distance behind him, the sound of a voice calling. To an accomplice? Was there more than one person trying to kill him?

A sudden break in the undergrowth, and he tumbled out on to a flat patch of rocky ground. To one side the water gathered in a shallow rippling pool before rushing down the valley. This must be the source of the river, he thought, with relief. From here on he could stay on dry land, head up the remainder of the valley bed without having to struggle against the stream.

He darted across, cursing every stone and pebble beneath his feet as it turned and crunched loudly under his weight. At the far side was the thick trunk of what looked like a weeping willow, a steep rock face arching up behind it towards the top of the valley wall. He sprinted over to it and threw himself behind, lungs straining for breath, heart pounding like an engine.

With the tree as protection, he turned back to see if he was still being followed, straining his eyes against the slowly intensifying darkness to catch a glimpse of any movement back down in the river. The sun had long gone over the horizon, leaving a faint glow in the sky. Soon even that would vanish and he would have even more cover of darkness in which to lose himself. Yet first he wanted to see who was trying to kill him.

Thoughts raced through his mind like the blood speeding through his veins. The first suspect was Enrique. Had Cámara disturbed him? Perhaps triggered something with his accusation of killing José Luis? Had Enrique followed him down to the *Molino* to finish him off, here in this lonely, distant setting? There would be no witnesses and, if he did things right – disposing of the evidence efficiently – no body to point to either. Only the shots themselves might have to be explained away. Sound travelled far out here. But that wouldn't be difficult; he could easily put it down to a spot of furtive, out-of-season hunting.

Yet almost immediately he had doubts. More than one attacker didn't fit. Enrique was a loner. Also, where was the dog? The Alsatian would have tracked him down by now, have sunk its sharp white teeth into some soft part of his anatomy. The animal had looked fast and obedient: it would have had no trouble catching Cámara. Yet here he was, cowering behind a tree, with no sign of a dog, not even a growl to indicate one nearby.

He stared out, watching for any signal that he was still being followed. Slowly, his breathing began to settle, yet every muscle was taut and prepared, ready to sprint off again into the undergrowth at the first opportunity.

Something in the sky distracted his attention: he looked up at the radiant glow high above the edges of the valley. For some inexplicable reason it was getting brighter, not duller. And with a sinking heart he realised that what he had assumed was the fading glow of the sun was actually the sharpening light of the rising moon, and from the brightness he could tell it was in its fullest phase.

He swore to himself: the darkness he had been relying on would not provide the thick cover that he needed. He had a choice: stay where he was and hope that he had lost his attackers. Or start moving again, covering as much ground as he could before the moon came over the mountain and illuminated the valley.

The crack of a bullet slamming into the trunk of the willow made the decision for him. Pushed backwards by the force of the shot, he saw that the blast had come from beyond the source of the river, directly in front of him. Far from having lost him, the gunmen were on his tail and closing in.

He reached for a branch of the tree and hauled himself up on to the rocks behind. A fortuitous foothold helped launch him upwards and he grabbed at whatever he could to bear his weight, using arms, legs, fingers and nails in his ascent. Breaking out from the cover of the willow and trying to run up the dry valley bed was too dangerous now. His only possible escape was to climb upwards, head for the top of the valley wall and try to break out into the land beyond.

Another shot rang out, slamming once again into the

tree, which was now a few metres below him. Had his attackers not realised where he was going? Surely they could hear him, yet the direction of the sound might be distorted in the narrow confines of the valley. He heard a voice again, low, querying, then silenced by a second. Two men, that much was clear now. Were they both armed? Unlike many of his police colleagues, Cámara was no firearms obsessive, yet the sharp, high pitch of the shots made him suspect they were using handguns, not rifles or anything more powerful. Which gave him some degree of hope: an accurate shot with a pistol over distance – and in the dark – was difficult. Staying as far away as he could from these men would be key to surviving, and doing so before the rising moon betrayed his position.

A smooth ledge of rock along his climb allowed him a moment to pause. Down in the valley he thought he could make out two shadows crossing towards the willow, perhaps to see if they had hit him. Had they not heard his climb? When they saw that he was not there, their attention would soon turn to finding him again. And logic, and the evidence of their senses, would give his position away once more.

He slipped over the ledge, clinging on to a low branch of a tree, finding his way feet first in the absence of any clear light. He felt a step in the ground, smooth stone cut with a 90-degree angle. He leaned forwards and fingered it, his hands creeping up to feel for another, and then another above. His blood seemed to give a jump. Here, perhaps, was a way out: what appeared to be a path leading up the mountainside, away from the river bed below.

He began crawling on all fours, reaching for each step with the palms of his hands before following behind with his feet. The path rose steeply, pushing past angry gorse bushes and long tentacles of bramble that pierced his skin, scratching at his face as he forced his way up and through. This was his only chance, a stairway out of danger, and he had to make the best use of it that he could.

From below he thought he could hear angry voices: the men had realised that he had escaped and were cursing. A couple of shots rang out, then stopped abruptly. The bullets flew wildly, far to his left. And for a second he thought that he would make good his escape, that they would not be following him.

Panting and scraping his way along the path, ignoring the thorns and needles, he climbed steadily to the top of the valley wall. The path began to flatten out, and he was able to stand upright, staggering forwards, trying not to trip over the rocks and stones that littered the way. He glanced up: the moon had now emerged and was shining down with angry determination. With a shudder, he realised that he would be clearly visible from below, his shadow sharply defined against the earth.

He could barely take another step, yet he could not stay here: he wasn't safe. The gunmen had already shown that they were out to kill. There was every chance that they were following him still, had perhaps found the same path and were coursing their way up to him even now.

He threw a look of defiance at the face of the moon, then turned to carry on. He had reached the top of the valley wall: from here on it would be downhill. Yet whether safety or more danger awaited him in the next valley, he could not say.

The path soon entered a wood of what looked like oak trees, smaller and more crooked than the pines he had grown used to. He stumbled as he sped through them, allowing gravity to pull him down the slope, catching branches and pulling himself back upright where he lost his balance, caught the edge of a stone with his foot and almost fell to the ground. Adrenalin had done much to get him this far, yet he could feel its effects beginning to wane, tiredness creeping into his legs, pain crying out from his ankles and knees, and from the thousand cuts he had suffered from the prickly bushes.

So far, this valley was proving more benign, as though drawing him down into a more friendly embrace. Yet the landscape had tricked him earlier, back at the *Molino*. He must keep going; keep going until he could go no further, until he could be certain that the gunmen had been lost.

He began to flounder: the very thought of stopping brought him close to collapse. He thought he could see something ahead. Were those lights in the distance? Perhaps someone had heard the shots. Hunters? The *Guardia Civil*? Was he safe at last?

He broke out into an orchard of olive trees, their tiny leaves shining with a dull, deathly glow in the moonlight. One was larger than the others, and he fell towards it, finding a hollow in its trunk and pressing hard against it, feeling its rough hands creep around him in a cold embrace.

He could run no further. Lungs, blood, heart, brain – all called out for him to stop. Had he managed to lose his attackers? Had they followed him this far? He could barely think any more, eyes closing as exhaustion took hold of him, pulling him down into the ground with steely fingers.

He listened, blood pumping in his ears: silence.

Then the slow, deadened sound of footsteps coming closer.

TWENTY-EIGHT

The train pulled into Atocha station shortly after eleven o'clock. All the cafés, kiosks and shops were closed. Alicia stepped on to the platform and without looking around her, quietly joined the thin trickle of passengers heading out past the gate, through the atrium with its tall tropical trees and out into the street. To avoid a surcharge – but also following instructions – she bypassed the taxi rank and crossed the wide boulevard opposite the station before hailing the first taxi passing her way. The driver wanted to get out and place her suitcase in the boot, but she opened the door and asked him to drive off straight away. At the roundabout he curled in with the late-night traffic before peeling off and heading north up the Paseo de la Castellana.

'Plaza de España,' Alicia said simply.

The driver eyed her through his mirror.

'Had a long journey?' he asked jovially.

'It's been a long day,' answered Alicia.

He got the message; no more was said until they pulled up a few minutes later and Alicia paid the fare.

'*Gracias*,' he called. Her back was turned and she was already walking away.

She made certain that he had driven off, watching from the corner of her eye before doubling back on herself and walking the other way. A pedestrian crossing took her into the centre of the square. Despite the sounds of the city, still reverberating at this relatively late hour, the wheels of her suitcase made a considerable noise. She stopped by a bench and picked it up: it wasn't too heavy, she would be able to carry it the short distance.

At least, if her instructions did not change before then: Marisol had already given her three sets, each one contradicting the last. Now she was told to loiter in the centre of the Plaza de España until Marisol herself appeared. Then she was to follow her without calling out or making any gesture of recognition.

Alicia had had secret meetings in the past, but never quite like this, never one where she was asked to cross half the country at the drop of a hat and then engage in cloak-and-dagger games in order to speak with a contact. A simple meeting in a bar was usually enough, somewhere quiet and small. Somewhere like the bar that Nacho had insisted on that morning.

She carried on walking, forbidden to stop or draw attention to herself. Meanwhile her eyes darted from side to side in the lamplight looking for any sign of Marisol. From which direction would she appear? How would she be dressed? Would she look quite different from the last time? Years had passed, after all. She might be much slimmer, or have put on weight. Would Alicia recognise her straight away?

And then she noticed a figure walking to her right on a parallel path, a few paces ahead, a long, lightweight coat hanging below her knees – despite the time of year – and carrying a plastic shopping bag in each hand. She looked – well, she looked like someone who might be searching for a place to sleep that night, someone who did not always know where home was. Yet her shoulders were just a little too straight, her gait fractionally too confident. And despite wearing simple rubber-soled shoes, there was a swagger in her hip that spoke of power – and the struggle for power.

Alicia checked the slight shake of her head and, feigning nonchalance, fell into the woman's wake, keeping a distance and placing a hand in her jacket pocket. Everything was normal, this was something she did quite regularly, it said.

She had still not seen Marisol's face and now they walked away from the square, crossing a road and heading up a path where a park area curled round and incorporated ancient Egyptian ruins – the Temple of Debod, gifted to Franco by President Nasser in thanks for Spanish assistance with the Aswan Dam. It was a curious, incongruous place, one of Madrid's less successful attempts at appearing like a monumental European capital. Yet it was here, just behind the squat stone building, that Marisol was clearly taking her, for as they passed it she turned to the left and crossed towards it, finding a spot less illuminated by the lamps and perching on the edge of a low wall.

Alicia continued in the same direction, finally coming close and, still wordless, sitting down beside her.

'Hello,' said Marisol. Alicia looked: her face was lined, her eyes dark, as though veiled by some subtle fabric, and she grinned from ear to ear through small tobacco-stained teeth.

'It's so nice to see you.'

'What's going on?' asked Alicia. 'All this . . .' She glanced around the empty park, then back at Marisol. The grin was wavering, less certain.

'Are you frightened?' said Alicia.

Marisol's eyes dropped to the ground for a moment and she clenched her hands together. In all the years that Alicia had known her she had never seen her like this. Always so strong and confident, always radiating an energy that spoke of possibility, of nothing ever getting in her way. It became a common remark among those who knew Marisol that she had more balls than most of the men around her. She was the reason why Alicia had become a journalist in the first place, showing her and her contemporaries that young women could not only break into that world, but also excel in it and even, perhaps one day, take a lead. Yet now here she was, at the tail end of her career, and she looked almost broken. She was as slim as she always had been, with thin, lizard-like skin. Her hair was darker than Alicia remembered – a new shade of dye, perhaps. Each finger still decorated with a gold ring, nails painted what looked – in the pink-orange glow of the lanterns – like a dark purple. She was still the Marisol that Alicia had known and admired, yet the change was striking: something about her posture, her head sitting less comfortably on her shoulders.

'We need to be quick,' said Marisol.

'What . . . ?

'You asked me on the phone about Cabrera,' she continued. 'About Clavijo.'

'And you gave me the official response,' said Alicia.

Marisol twisted her mouth and stared Alicia in the eye.

'I'm now going to tell you what I know,' she said. 'What I really know.'

Not taking her eyes off her, Alicia thrust a hand into her bag to reach for her phone.

'No.' Marisol shook her head. 'No recordings. This is off the record. And no notes, either. I just want you to listen.'

Alicia let her hands drop passively into her lap. For a moment she felt uncomfortable, so she changed her position, crossing her legs and propping herself up against the edge of the stone wall where they sat.

'OK.'

Marisol cast a quick glance around them, eyes darting from side to side, before turning back to Alicia.

'Something's happening on Cabrera,' she said. 'Something big.'

'What?'

Marisol paused.

'I don't have the whole picture,' she said. 'But I know it's more than just military manoeuvres. That's the story we've been ordered to put out, but there's more to it.'

She reached into her pocket and pulled out a packet of Fortuna cigarettes, half pulling one out and offering it to Alicia. After a pause, Alicia reluctantly, dutifully, took it out and placed it between her lips. Marisol put her own between her teeth, lit it, then passed the lighter to Alicia, who twisted it between her fingers waiting for Marisol to speak.

'The order came a week ago,' said Marisol. 'A direct command from higher up on the story we were to tell. Not a story we should actively disseminate, you understand. Just what we were meant to say should anyone – like you – come asking questions.'

She shrugged.

'That kind of thing is fairly normal. A lot of the time I'm party to decisions and discussions within the Ministry and I get on with my job, telling the press what it needs to know. I've been around for long enough and I'm trusted not to make mistakes. But every now and again a story is passed down in this way without my prior knowledge or my being involved in its creation.'

Her cigarette glowed in the night air as she pulled on it.

'It happens when something sensitive is taking place. Which is fair enough for somewhere like the Ministry of Defence – I've learned simply to go along with them. What was different about this was the addendum to the order. We were asked to take note of who – if anyone – was making inquiries about Cabrera. That in itself, again, is not unusual. But then we were meant to send this information on through the usual channels to the *Centro Nacional de Inteligencia*.'

Marisol crossed her legs and leaned away from Alicia slightly, tapping her cigarette repeatedly to flick the ash to the ground.

'Now, as you probably know, the *CNI* is not part of the Ministry of Defence any more. Although there are links, naturally, it now reports to the Prime Minister's office. So we were being asked effectively to work for the country's spying agency. And that was what made me . . .' She tailed off.

Alicia nodded. She took the unlit cigarette out of her mouth and pocketed it.

'So you started snooping around.'

'Of course I did, darling. I am first and foremost a journalist, after all. My job may be to act as mere mouthpiece, but our training runs deep, does it not? It's why we're both sitting here on this wall in the dark at this very moment.'

She snorted mirthlessly.

'So,' said Alicia, 'what did you find?'

'I already told you,' snapped Marisol. 'I don't know everything.'

There was a pause.

'But . . . ?'

'But for one thing,' she continued, 'we were supposed to make particular note of any enquiries in which knowledge of certain key words was demonstrated.'

'Clavijo,' said Alicia.

'Exactly. And there were others.'

'Which were?'

'I looked through my files, stretching back several months,' Marisol said. 'Certain things, in the light of the command about Cabrera, began to leap out. Various orders for materials to be sent to the Captaincy General in Mallorca. Items which you would imagine them either to have over there already, or which now seemed odd for the Balearics.'

'What are you talking about?'

'Perhaps individually they didn't stand out, but put together . . .'

She took a final drag of her cigarette and stubbed it out with her heel.

'For example a large shipment of razor wire,' she continued. 'Taser guns, infrared imaging equipment – the very latest and very expensive. Then there were things like food rations – lots of them, enough almost for a whole division. And blindfolds.'

'Blindfolds?'

Marisol shook her head, as though trying to work it out herself.

'That was just the beginning,' she said. 'But there was more, a second wave of material, only in the past few days. Building materials – breeze blocks, cement, rebars.'

She looked Alicia in the eye with a studied expression of confusion.

'Surely there is a vast amount of all that on Mallorca itself. Why send more out there? Unless it wasn't destined for Mallorca at all, but somewhere else.'

'Cabrera,' said Alicia.

Marisol pursed her lips.

'I don't know. There was nothing to say where it was destined.'

'What about the money?' asked Alicia. 'The country's supposed to be broke. How can they afford to pay for all this?'

Marisol nodded and smiled.

'Good,' she said. 'I'm so glad, my dear Alicia, that it's you sitting here by my side tonight. The very same thought occurred to me, naturally. In fact, it was one of the other proscribed words that put me on to it. Although I insist I don't know what's happening over there. Not entirely.'

'What word?' Alicia said. 'What do you mean?'

'Abravanel,' said Marisol.

'Abra . . . What?'

'It was the one element that linked all these curious orders. Somewhere, buried in the paperwork of all of them was that word. I don't know what it is or what it means. I don't know if it's a person, an operation, or what. But it was there. And it was also one of the words we were meant to look out for if anyone came asking questions about

Cabrera. No explanations – just pass the information on directly to the *CNI*.'

She stopped and stared into space for a moment.

'I think it's that which annoys me most about this. I work for the Ministry of Defence as head of the media office. I'm not an employee of the *CNI* and nor should I bloody well spy for them. If they want me to work for them, let them come and recruit me, pay me. How dare they treat me like some minion at their beck and call.'

Her voice rose slightly as she spoke, losing her self-awareness for a second. But then immediately she composed herself again. And now, conscious that she had lost control, the fear returned to her eyes.

'You did everything I said, didn't you?' she asked Alicia suddenly.

'Of course.'

'You weren't followed?'

Alicia looked at her with a compassion tinged with sorrow. What had happened to the indefatigable Marisol she had always known?

'No,' she said. 'Not as far as I know.'

Marisol got up hurriedly to leave.

'I've told you everything I can,' she said, stepping away.

'But . . .' Alicia said.

'Don't call me,' Marisol insisted, already backing away. 'Whatever you do, don't call me.'

And she disappeared into the shadows between the trees.

Alicia got up slowly from the wall. It was the second time that day she had heard that.

TWENTY-NINE

The moon shone steadily on to the olive trees. Cámara opened his eyes wide at the sound of footsteps behind. With dread, he shifted his weight and turned to look up, readying himself to make a last, desperate run.

Pale, milky light glimmered from the skin of a woman walking slowly across the field. Her hair was tied in a plait that curled from the back of her head and lay over one shoulder, streaks of grey visible against the black of her tresses. Across the other shoulder, digging into the flesh, was the strap of a rope bag swinging gently against her hip. Apart from the bag, she was naked, her skin exposed to the warm caress of the night air. Cámara guessed her to be in her late fifties; she had a proud air about her, with an athletic, graceful pose, almost like a panther. And her limbs were long and powerful, yet with a lithe energy about them, like one who lived ever conscious of her body, its strength and its energy. Either side of the bag strap, her breasts hung low on her chest, nipples splayed to the sides. Below, her belly was taut and firm, yet the skin sagged in small crescents beneath the navel, where the first hairs of her pubis crept up, heralds of the dark silhouetted triangle of her sex.

Cámara watched in awe. But for her age, and the signs of motherhood, she appeared like an embodiment of Artemis, the Moon goddess herself out hunting during the hours of night. What had happened to those unfortunate enough to catch a glimpse of her? He tried to remember from childhood stories. Whatever it was, it wasn't good.

As he watched, the woman crouched low to the ground and picked up a handful of stones, dropping them in her bag before standing again and continuing, scouring the ground for more.

When she was just a few metres away, to the side of the hollow trunk where Cámara was hiding, she stopped. With a start, Cámara realised that she had seen his own tracks scratched in the soil moments before as he had scrambled for the safety of the olive tree.

She turned and peered down at him, trying to make out who was there.

'Enrique?' she said with a powerful voice. 'Are you spying on us again?'

Cámara edged his way out and showed his face in a ray of moonlight.

'My name's Max,' he said. 'I'm lost.'

The woman took a couple of steps closer, bending down fearlessly to take a look at him. She read his expression, the look of exhaustion in his eyes.

'Come with me,' she said.

*

Moments later, leading him by the hand, she walked down smooth steps to a patio and the door of a house nestling in a fold in the hillside. She pushed the door open and beckoned him inside.

The first thing that Cámara saw was a naked male backside pointing up in the air as its owner knelt down and pushed his face hard to the tiled floor.

'Bloody plectrum,' said the man as he shuffled about, trying to peer underneath a chest of drawers at the side of the room. 'I know I dropped it here somewhere.'

Cámara glanced around: he was in a large, dusty room with ancient-looking sofas and armchairs scattered about. Sitting proudly on one of them was an electric guitar, the lead plugged into a small amplifier on the floor at the side. Brightly coloured sheets of cloth were draped over much of the furniture, and there was a sweet, dense, choking smell of incense hanging in the air. In one corner of the room was a large, scruffy dog with light brown curly hair, lying cosily on a sky-blue rug thrown in a heap next to what looked like a fridge. The animal raised an eyebrow and lifted its ears slightly on Cámara's entrance, but kept its chin resting firmly on its front paws, mildly interested but essentially unconcerned by this new arrival.

'Bloody thing,' said the man on the floor, still searching. 'Bet the dog's eaten it.'

The dog seemed to understand it was being blamed and turned its head, closing its eyes nonchalantly and going back to sleep.

The woman closed the door behind her. Cámara noticed small lamps standing in niches in the walls; they gave off a warm, comforting glow. He had the sense that the entire place had been built by the people living in it.

The woman reached for a cloth from one of the armchairs and wrapped it around her nakedness.

'Jimmy,' she said, taking a second cloth and throwing it loosely over his backside. 'We've got a visitor.'

At the sound of her voice, the man slowly lifted his head and, with his haunches still high in the air, turned his head to look.

'Oh,' he said with a surprised grin. 'I thought you were having me on for a minute.'

He turned, sat on the ground, wrapped the cloth around his waist and stood up. His hair was grey and hung long over his shoulders. His face was fleshy and sunburnt, with a long thick nose jutting down from bright, friendly eyes. A pointed grey beard cascaded from his chin, almost touching his chest. Halfway down it was tied by a bright yellow rubber band.

'I was going to do some recording,' said the man almost apologetically. 'It's always a good time, when there's a full moon. The energy's different, makes for a clearer sound.'

'Jimmy, this is Max,' said the woman. 'He's lost.'

'Oh, right,' said Jimmy. 'Introductions.'

He thrust out a paw-like, rough-skinned hand.

'Welcome,' he said. 'Anyone who's lost is welcome here. We specialise in them.'

Cámara shook his hand gratefully, yet fear still coursed through him.

'I'm Max,' he said. 'And . . .'

'You've already met Estrella,' Jimmy said, smiling to the woman. 'It's a good job she found you.'

'Listen,' said Cámara. 'I'm a policeman . . .'

From the depth of his belly, Jimmy suddenly let out a long, loud and deep laugh. And with a cackling chorus, Estrella quickly joined in.

'Policeman?' Jimmy bellowed, his face reddening with mirth. 'That's a good one.'

'But . . .' Cámara began.

'There's no way you're a policeman. No policeman looks like that.'

Cámara glanced down at himself: his clothes were torn, trousers almost shredded at the knees, and he was streaked with dried blood.

'If you're a policeman,' Jimmy continued, 'where's your gun?'

'I don't have . . .' Cámara went to reach into his pocket to get his ID, then let his hand drop. Was it worth it? Besides, some instinct told him he might be more welcome here if he went along with this.

'Listen,' he said. Jimmy's laughter was beginning to die down. Estrella was still giggling, but had walked to a kitchen area through a side door, pushing a bead curtain aside which was still rattling in her wake.

'Listen,' said Cámara again. 'I don't want to scare you, but I've been chased by armed men.'

'Armed men?' Jimmy's face was more serious of a sudden, yet there was still a hint of doubt in his eyes.

'Have you got a phone?' Cámara said.

The laughter began to creep back into Jimmy's face.

'Did you hear that?' he called to Estrella. 'He wants a phone.'

'Ooh!' called Estrella in a high voice. 'Well, he's not going to have any luck here.'

'I'm sorry, Mr Policeman,' said Jimmy.

'Please, Max,' insisted Cámara.

'Well, Max, we're off the grid here. That's the way it is and that's the way we like it. No mains electricity, no water, no phone cables, not even a mobile signal. We try our best to live as nature intended.'

He pulled at the cloth wrapped around his waist and grinned.

'But we make some allowance for the occasional visitor, like yourself. Don't want to upset anyone.'

'These men,' Cámara said, exasperation creeping into his voice. 'They've been trying to shoot me.'

Jimmy sat down on one of the sofas, his legs stretched open. Then he realised he was revealing himself and quickly covered his groin with a loose corner of cloth.

'Right,' he said. 'I was going to say you looked more like a man on the run than a pol—'

His voice was interrupted by a bullet crashing through the window and slamming into the wall on the far side. Had Jimmy still been standing, his head would have been caught in its trajectory. Cámara fell to the floor.

'Get down!' he screamed. 'For God's sake get down!'

To his amazement, however, Jimmy calmly got up out of the sofa, cast a look of disgust at the shattered rendering on the wall where the bullet had impacted, and leaned down to open a drawer in a nearby chest. Then, with no sense of rush or urgency, he lifted out an Uzi sub-machine gun and flicked off the safety catch at the side.

From the floor, Cámara stared up in astonishment and disbelief. Jimmy smiled down at him.

'I know what you're thinking,' he said with a steady voice. 'But don't worry – the magazine's full. I checked only this morning. Had a feeling I was going to need it today.'

He stepped over Cámara's prostrate body, and reached for the door.

'Wait!' cried Cámara, but Jimmy had already turned the

handle and was stepping outside. Then, taking a couple more paces and checking that he wasn't too close to the house, he got his bearings, gauged the spot from where the bullet had been fired, and pointed the Uzi with both hands, letting off a short angry burst of fire that illuminated his face with peppery light in the darkness. Cartridges pelted the stones by his naked feet as they fell, scattering in all directions, faint wisps of smoke drifting from them as they cooled on the ground. One fell close to Cámara's nose as he stared open-eyed at Jimmy.

The magazine was emptied, the firing stopped, and Jimmy's face was engulfed in darkness again. He stepped back to the house, closed the door behind him and returned to the drawer to deposit the machine gun.

'Right,' he said, rubbing his hands together. 'I reckon that should see them off.'

Gingerly, Cámara lifted himself from the floor.

'Do you . . .' he stammered. 'Do you know who they are?'

'Of course,' grinned Jimmy. 'That's Dorin and Bogdan. Don't worry about them. They're a couple of cowards. Won't be troubling us any more tonight.'

THIRTY

Cámara got to his feet and fell into one of the armchairs. Jimmy grinned at him.

'Don't worry,' he said. 'Only they would shoot through the window like that. And they know there are guns everywhere in this place. If they did try again they'd be shot to pieces. You ever used a gun?'

'Once or twice,' Cámara nodded.

'Right, well, in the pocket of your chair, under the arm next to the remote control, there's a Glock.'

Cámara leaned down and felt the smooth steel of the pistol between his fingers.

'If they give us any more trouble,' continued Jimmy, 'use that. But I tell you, there's no chance of that. They'll be off home now.'

Cámara wanted to ask questions, but exhaustion and shock got the better of him and he sank deep into the chair. Jimmy took a small wooden box from a ledge and sat down with it on his knee. Then he opened it, pulled out a cigarette paper and began the process of making a joint, mixing the tobacco and marihuana in the palm of his hand, then placing the paper over it and turning both hands over before squeezing it all together, rolling and licking it closed. An initialled Zippo lighter let off a tall shot of flame, which he used to light it, drawing hard and quickly filling the room with sweet, clammy smoke.

'Ah,' he sighed with a deep voice of satisfaction. Then he passed the joint over to Cámara.

Cámara hadn't smoked marihuana for months. In the not-too-distant past it had been a regular habit of his, gratefully consuming the home-grown that his grandfather, Hilario, grew for him in pot plants on the back patio, trying to ensure that his wayward, law-enforcing grandson kept one foot at least in what he saw as the 'real' world – the world of ordinary law-breaking lives far removed from the artificial conformity of the police. The Cámaras were anarchists, Hilario insisted, and if one of them had betrayed this tradition by actually becoming an agent of the State, then the least he, Hilario, could do was throw out a rope on to which his errant grandson could cling. That rope came in the form of the home-grown, dutifully nurtured and watered, much as a priest might take care over the sacred wine. And Cámara had smoked it willingly, as much to dull the strains of being a murder detective as to forget painful memories – not least the killing of his own sister when he was still a child – that lingered in his heart.

Hilario had died years before and the supply of home-grown had quickly dried up, or been thrown away eventually – Cámara felt less and less need for it. Yet now, here was a man suddenly appearing and saving his life, someone who, in his own way, reminded him a little of

Hilario – fearless, eccentric, master of his own domain – and he was offering him the same dose of green weed which had been such a part of his previous life. He had vowed never to touch the stuff again, but right now, after a long and frankly complicated day, he wanted nothing more.

He leaned over in his chair, thrust his hand out, took the joint from Jimmy and brought it to his lips. The smoke ran hot and sharp down his throat. He felt the kick in his lungs, the rush to his head, then the slow treacly sensation begin to flow through his limbs.

'See,' said Jimmy, his smile broadening. 'Told you you weren't a policeman.'

Cámara threw him a glance.

'Although there's something I'm not sure about you,' Jimmy continued. 'I reckon you're a spy.'

It was Cámara's turn to laugh.

'Or a master criminal on the run,' said Jimmy. 'You really do look a bit of a mess. Whatever you did, you certainly pissed off Dorin and Bogdan.'

Cámara nodded, and the nodding seemed to continue for a long time, like the swinging pendulum of a clock.

'I'll have to find out more about those two.' He paused. 'Eventually.'

'Time for that later,' said Jimmy. 'Tomorrow, perhaps.'

Cámara looked around at the room, which he felt he was sinking in deeper and deeper.

'There's a spare bed,' said Jimmy. 'And you're welcome. Especially if you know how to use a gun.'

He got up to walk to the kitchen. Cámara took another draw on the joint.

'I love guns,' said Jimmy.

*

Cámara wasn't sure if he had fallen asleep, but moments later he was sitting at a small table in the kitchen with plates of food being served: salad, a simple tortilla and some bread. In the middle was an unlabelled bottle of thick green olive oil.

'We're almost self-sufficient,' said Jimmy.

'These eggs are fresh from this morning,' said Estrella, who had clearly been busy all this time preparing the meal. 'Jimmy collected them just after breakfast.'

A glass of wine was placed in front of him. It looked very much like the home-made stuff Vicente had offered at lunchtime, and a shudder went through Cámara at the thought, yet as he brought it to his lips he was relieved to find it was much more drinkable, if not quite the kind of thing you would pay money for.

'I've been meaning to ask,' he said as the wine warmed through him and brought him back to life. '*Jimmy*?'

Estrella giggled.

'Jaime,' explained Jimmy. 'But I was in a rock band when I was young and everyone called me Jimmy. The name stuck.'

Cámara took a mouthful of tortilla. It was deep yellow and richly flavoured; for a moment he was cast back to his family kitchen, his mother preparing food while he sat at the table and watched in fascination. For the past years he had been eating supermarket eggs that tasted nothing like this; he had even forgotten what the real taste of eggs was. Now here he was in the middle of some lost valley in the sierra, with people he didn't know, having been shot at and almost killed, half-stoned from the joint, eating simple, delicious, home-produced and home-made food. It was as if this place, these people, evoked some childlike pleasure, a sense of fun and play that he felt he had lost in recent years. Hilario had done his best to keep him in touch with that side of himself. But Hilario had died, and Cámara had been drifting ever since, as though unable to locate the sane, healthy silliness within him that acted as a bulwark against all the rest, all the shit. There was almost a feeling of coming home.

'Is there just the two of you?' he asked.

'Now,' said Estrella. 'There have been more of us in the past.'

'Children?'

'A couple. They've left home.'

'There used to be quite a community of us, years back,' said Jimmy. Estrella smiled at him.

'I went down to Seville one day to learn flamenco guitar,' he continued. 'And when I came back a couple of months later, four women had moved into the house.'

He grinned, a mischievous sparkle in his eye.

'So, well, I just had to get on with it,' he said. 'Four wives. It was fun.'

He poured more wine into their glasses.

'Two of them were lesbians,' he continued. Then he stared Cámara in the eye.

'But even lesbians need a night off every now and again.'

He guffawed and Cámara laughed with him, casting a look in Estrella's direction. But she was smiling as well.

'The great thing about having so many wives,' Jimmy said, 'is that it's brilliant for the kids. Every time they fell over and banged their knee, there was a mother close at hand to pick them up and kiss them better. Worked really well.'

'So what happened to them, the other women?' said Cámara.

'Oh,' said Estrella, 'they left eventually.'

'The lesbians set up together in their own place,' said Jimmy. 'The other one went travelling. We still hear from them.'

Cámara carried on eating: the food really was delicious.

'Is that all right for you?' asked Estrella.

'Wonderful,' he said.

'We fertilise everything ourselves,' said Jimmy. 'There's a thunder box out in the garden. Makes excellent manure.'

Cámara stared questioningly at the piece of lettuce on the end of his fork.

'Should have mentioned that at the start,' said Jimmy. 'Hope you don't mind.'

Dinner ended and they passed through to a smaller living room on the other side of the house. Jimmy lit a fire: the air grew colder up in the mountains at night. After a few minutes, Estrella reappeared wearing a Moroccan djellaba with the hood pulled up over her head. In her hands was a pile of men's clothes.

'Jimmy never wears these,' she said. 'You might want something else to put on in the morning.'

'Help yourself,' insisted Jimmy. 'I don't need them.'

'You got far to go?' asked Estrella.

Cámara shrugged. Thoughts about the next day were far from his mind.

'I can give you a lift to the village after breakfast if you like,' said Jimmy.

Cámara must have nodded, for the matter appeared settled.

They sat around the fire for what felt like a long time, watching the flames begin to rise and consume the firewood, reach a blazing peak and then gradually die down again to a steady, tranquil glow. Jimmy rolled another joint and they smoked in hazy silence, their eyes droopy and unfocused, never wandering from the hearth.

There was something essentially happy and balanced about this place, he felt. Yes, the house appeared to have a small arsenal of its own – for reasons he had yet to ascertain – yet it felt good, welcoming, gentle and at peace with itself. He could not help but contrast it with the sensation over in the other valley, at Sunset and Enrique's house. Much of the countryside there was beautiful, with views down to the coast, yet the feeling had been one of tension, conflict and unhappiness. This side of the valley – and he had yet to see it in daylight – was like another world, somewhere he was much more at ease, and could imagine himself spending considerable time. At some point, when he got a chance, he would look on a map to see exactly where he was: running away over the mountains in the darkness meant that he had quite lost his bearings.

He heard a riffling of playing cards nearby and glanced over to see.

'Oh,' said Jimmy, his teeth glinting in the glow of the fire. 'You're privileged.'

Estrella had a deck of tarot cards in her hands.

'She doesn't do this for everyone,' said Jimmy.

Estrella handed the deck to Cámara and asked him to cut.

'Think of a question,' she said.

He split the deck in two and passed the cards back to Estrella. As the fire lit one side of her face, he thought back to his first impression of her among the olive trees, when she had appeared like a goddess of the Moon. At the time he'd felt he was almost hallucinating with fatigue, yet now he had a similar sensation.

Estrella spread the cards out on the floor, illuminated by the flames. Cámara glanced down with incomprehension at the various figures and pictures staring back at him. All he could see was that Death wasn't present and he gave a sigh of relief.

'The High Priestess,' said Estrella, pointing to a card showing a seated woman in flowing robes. 'Does that mean anything to you?'

Cámara shook his head.

'Then there's the Tower and the Wheel of Fortune,' she continued. 'And the Moon.'

She paused, staring long and hard at the images.

'It's confused,' she said at last. 'There are several women here, at least two, perhaps three, and they're all having a very powerful effect on your life.'

She looked up at him, her eyes deep dark pools of ink.

'Change is coming,' she said. 'Sacrifice and real change.'

THIRTY-ONE

Carlos opened the iron gate of his block of flats and stepped into the marble-cool of the entrance hall. It was late and the concierge had already left. Ignoring the lift, Carlos walked the three flights of stairs to his front door, his coat over his arm and briefcase dangling from his hand. He was tired, but this routine of taking the stairs – avoiding lifts where he could – was all part of a regime to fight against the ill-health brought on by a desk job. Opportunities for exercise were far fewer since he had been assigned to the Centre, but small measures such as this might go some way to maintaining a certain level of fitness. Or at least stop him from descending too quickly into stiff, overweight immobility.

Puffing slightly and with the blood pumping in his cheeks, he reached his floor and pulled out the key to open the door. As he did so his phone vibrated against his hip where he kept it in a holder on his belt. He waited until he was inside and with the door closed behind him before answering. It could only be work at this late hour and so far his day had not gone well. He just hoped this brought better news.

He placed the briefcase on the floor, draped his coat on the hook, flipped open the stud of his belt-holder and lifted out his phone.

'We've found her,' said a flat voice.

'Where is she?' said Carlos. He walked into the kitchen, where the previous night's bottle of whisky stood on the table. He quickly rinsed out the tumbler in the sink and poured himself a healthy shot.

'In Madrid,' said the voice.

'She left Valencia?' Carlos asked.

'Caught the AVE. Must have been just before we put the tail on her. But we found her name on the passenger list.'

'Where is she now?'

Carlos checked the time on his watch. It was almost one o'clock in the morning.

'At an address on Calle Santo Domingo, near Opera. We've checked – it belongs to a journalist by the name of Lucía Valderrama. Not her main residence, however. She lives out of town.'

'Some kind of meeting place,' said Carlos. 'A safe house. Do we have anything nearby?'

'Nothing.'

'How long has she been in Madrid?'

'The last AVE got in at 2310.'

'And how long have you known about her whereabouts?'

'For the past forty minutes. She tried to make another phone call to her partner. That's how we—'

'Did she speak to him?'

'No. There was no answer.'

Carlos took a swig of whisky, feeling it burn his throat and send a rush up his spine.

'So you're telling me there's a gap of well over an hour between her arriving and you locating her.'

The voice at the other end didn't answer.

'Well?'

'Yes, sir.'

'*Joder*! I shit on . . .' Carlos checked himself.

'It's the Valencia team's fault, sir. They didn't . . .'

'Too late for that,' said Carlos. 'Concentrate. We need to know what she was doing during that time. This is crucial, do you understand? Where did she go? Did she meet anyone?'

He closed his eyes, trying to keep calm. Passion – anger – was in danger of getting the better of him.

'My God,' he said in a low voice.

'What was that sir?'

'Just find out what she did during that missing hour. That is your top priority, do you hear?'

'Yes, sir. And you still want her monitored here, correct?'

'Of course I bloody do.'

'Yes, sir. It's just that our staffing levels—'

'Sort it out!' Carlos bellowed.

He switched off the phone and tossed it on to the kitchen table. Then he breathed in and out again, letting his shoulders drop.

The whisky bottle stared up at him like a temptress. But he shook his head and walked away, a grim, self-congratulating smile on his lips at his powers of self-control.

THIRTY-TWO

They ate breakfast on the patio underneath a grapevine, with views over a garden that sloped down in terraces to the bottom of a gorge. On the far side, an oak-covered mountain rose to a jagged, diagonal edge, slicing the cool morning air like a rusty knife. A plate of peeled and sliced fruit stood next to a large coffee pot, with bread and a jar of honey. Cámara cut himself a piece and spread some of the sweet, thick paste over it. It had an aromatic taste, an echo of the many thousands of flowers from which it had been made.

He had slept deeply on a thick rug by the fire. Jimmy had brought blankets and cushions from a cupboard and placed them out for him. Cámara could remember little else that had happened after that. When he woke, he found a shower room across the passageway and had washed himself clean in the healing water, pulling thorns out where they had lodged the night before. His own shirt and jacket were still all right to wear, but he had cast away his trousers and pulled on a pair of Jimmy's instead. They were a little short in the leg, but good enough.

Estrella was sitting silently beside him, drinking coffee, a breeze blowing through her hair, which had been loosened from the plait and hung about her shoulders.

'Is that the way to the *Molino*?' Cámara asked, making out what looked like a path heading up beyond the gorge.

'You found the *Molino*, did you?' said Estrella. 'You did come a long way.'

Jimmy came in as Cámara finished his piece of bread and stretched out for another, smothering it with the delicious honey.

'Do you like it?' asked Jimmy.

'It's wonderful,' said Cámara. 'Have you got your own hives?'

'They're round the back. Don't want them too close to the house. But you've got to be careful with that honey.'

Cámara gave him a quizzical look.

'I laced some of it with opium,' explained Jimmy. 'But I didn't label which ones. Stupid of me.'

Cámara stuck his tongue into his cheek.

'Funny thing, opium,' said Jimmy. 'It's like death. Makes you lose sense of time.'

He bared his front teeth and showed them to Cámara: they looked brighter, shinier than the others.

'See these?' he said. 'I ate some of the laced honey once and after a while I started to feel really sleepy. So I thought, I'll just lie down here where I am, really slowly, and have a bit of a rest. When I woke up later, I'd smashed my front teeth out. You see, I'd thought I was lying down slowly to go to sleep, when actually I'd crashed to the floor face-first. Taught me a lesson, it did.'

Cámara grinned at him, then took another bite of the bread. *De muertos al río,* he thought to himself. In for a penny, in for a pound.

'I met Enrique over in the next valley yesterday,' he said. 'He's got bees.'

'Our honey's much sweeter,' said Jimmy simply. 'Ours is made with love. Enrique doesn't know what love is.'

'You know him well?'

'Bees are beautiful animals,' continued Jimmy, 'if you treat them right. You give them what they need and they pay you back over a thousand times. They have tremendous healing power, yet people think they're only good for honey and nothing else. And they're busy killing them with their pesticides and poisons they're putting on the land.'

'They cured me,' said Estrella.

'That's right,' said Jimmy.

'I had a melanoma on my back a few months ago,' she said. 'The doctors cut it out, but it was already quite thick – they thought it had spread to the lymphatic system.'

'But we got the bees to sting her right there,' said Jimmy. 'Kept them in the fridge then placed them where the cancer was and got them to sting her.'

'When the results came back the doctors were amazed,' said Estrella. 'The cancer hadn't spread at all. The bees cured me.'

The talk of bee stings stirred a painful memory in Cámara's body of the stings he had endured the previous day. Had they cured him of something as well? He had heard of bee stings being useful for arthritis, but never for curing cancer.

'That's a great story,' he said. 'More people should know about it.'

'That's what I said,' Jimmy cried, turning to Estrella. 'We should write a book.'

Estrella raised her eyebrows and pursed her lips.

'Maybe,' she said.

After drinking several cups of coffee, Jimmy took Cámara for a stroll around the garden while Estrella went indoors. A neat, stone-covered path led them down from one terrace to the next, olive trees growing at the sides, their roots curling into the bare rock in places where the soil thinned.

'It must be hard work keeping this going with just the two of you now,' Cámara said.

'We get some help,' Jimmy said, and he pointed to a small wooden structure where a donkey poked its head out of a barn door, flies buzzing around its face.

'Boris there does a lot of the heavy stuff.'

They walked down to the stable. Cámara patted the animal affectionately on the nose. Jimmy unbolted the bottom half of the door and let the donkey step out into the paddock. He opened a large box at the side, where a pile of discarded vegetables was kept. Strapped to the inside, glinting in the sunlight, was another pistol.

'Breakfast for Boris,' said Jimmy, pulling out a few scoops of the vegetables with a shovel.

'These weapons you've got scattered about the place,' Cámara said. 'What's that about?'

He cast a glance over the mountains, wondering if last night's assailants might still be there, or have returned to finish the job.

'The way we live,' Jimmy said. 'It makes people nervous. They instinctively want to shut us down, or make us conform. Brings out the worst in many of them.'

He shrugged.

'I don't understand it either, but I've learned the hard way that it's better to defend yourself properly. That way people tend to leave you alone. Most of the time.'

'What about the *Guardia Civil*?' asked Cámara. 'Don't they give you trouble?'

'I've got the right paperwork. They leave us alone, mostly. We don't bother anyone else, so they don't bother us.'

He closed the lid of the box. The donkey was munching merrily at the pile of slightly rotten carrots and potatoes.

'But you never know what's going to happen from day to day. Like you showing up last night.'

'Listen,' said Cámara, reaching into his jacket pocket. 'There's something you should probably know.'

Jimmy's eyes bulged at the police ID card held in front of him. Then he bent backwards and roared with laughter.

'A policeman!' he cried. 'You really *are* a policeman. I don't believe it.'

Tears began to stream down his cheeks and into his beard.

'A policeman sleeping in my house!'

He put his hands on his hips.

'Well, I think I've seen it all now.'

Cámara shrugged.

'I did try to tell you,' he said.

'So, Mr Policeman,' beamed Jimmy. 'You here to arrest me?'

Estrella appeared less surprised when Jimmy told her about Cámara's real identity, as though she had guessed, or actually believed him when he'd mentioned it.

'The question is,' she said, 'are you a policeman in your heart?'

'Course not,' said Jimmy. 'He's like one of us. Almost.'

'It's certainly a beautiful set-up you have here,' said Cámara. 'I wouldn't mind having a place like this for me and my . . .' he paused. 'For me and Alicia.'

'Is that her name?' said Estrella. 'I saw her last night in the cards. You should bring her round some time.'

'She's a city woman,' said Cámara. 'But I think she might like this.'

'So, Mr Policeman.' Jimmy was curious. 'What brings you out here into the sierra?'

They sat down again on the patio in the shade of the grapevine. The sun had risen higher and the air was growing warmer. Cámara told them about José Luis, about Sunset, and about the things he had learned the previous day. The two of them listened with concentrated fascination.

When he finished, he watched their expressions.

'You must have known José Luis,' he said. 'What did you make of him?'

'Are we suspects now, Mr Policeman?' grinned Jimmy.

Cámara shrugged.

'José Luis was all right,' said Jimmy. 'But not mountain people.'

'That's funny,' said Cámara. 'Enrique said the same thing.'

'The mountain has its own power,' said Jimmy. 'It tends to accept those it wants to stay, and find ways to get rid of those who don't really belong.'

'I see,' said Cámara.

'But if I were a policeman – which clearly I'm not.' He laughed. 'If I were you, I'd be taking a close look at Dorin and Bogdan. If they're trying to kill you, it must be for a reason.'

'They sound like Romanian names,' said Cámara.

'Moved to the village seven or eight years ago,' Jimmy said. 'Bogdan's the big stupid one; Dorin is bigger and stupider. They've got a grocery shop, which their wives run. Dorin and Bogdan themselves are plumbers.'

Estrella snorted.

'Well, they're drug dealers. But they've got a business as plumbers. But it's never open. Everyone knows what they're really up to.'

'Why doesn't the *Guardia Civil* shut them down?'

Jimmy shrugged.

'Not my concern,' he said.

Cámara's mind was churning. Why would a couple of Romanian drug dealers be going to such lengths to get rid of him?

'You don't happen to know what kind of car they drive, do you?' he asked.

'Changes pretty often,' said Jimmy.

'No,' said Estrella. 'We saw them last week, don't you remember? They've got a big black car. Dark glass in the windows.'

'Oh, that's right,' said Jimmy. 'Looked like one of those expensive German cars. Mercedes, maybe. Or a BMW.'

'With tinted glass?'

'Yes,' insisted Estrella.

Cámara nodded: the same car that had tried to run him off the road.

'And you know about these two because . . . ?' he asked.

'Well,' said Jimmy, 'I'm assuming you're not going to put us in jail, after everything we've done for you.'

'Not unless you murdered José Luis.'

Jimmy hesitated for a second.

'Dorin and Bogdan wanted to get me involved in their business,' he said at length. 'Few years back. They know about my home-grown. Thought I could plant some more out here, provide them with marihuana to sell. But I wasn't interested. This is all for our personal use; I don't want to turn it into a business. Besides, it's natural, what we do. Whereas they're into these modern chemical drugs, made in a lab or something. Reckon the government's behind it all, anyway, making money while keeping young people stupid: bread and circuses, just like the Romans. I don't want anything to do with that. I just stick to what Mother Nature gives us.'

'So you said no,' Cámara said. He ignored the comment about a government conspiracy.

'I said no. They didn't like it, tried to set fire to the house once, drove round and took some shots at us. But then they saw us firing back . . .' He glanced at Estrella, who nodded. Clearly she could handle a gun herself.

'And with much bigger guns,' she said.

'Yeah,' said Jimmy. 'Much more powerful than their little handguns. Well, they didn't bother us after that. Not until last night, anyway.'

'But you think they may have something to do with José Luis's death,' Cámara said.

'You think there's something suspicious going on?'

'I can't prove anything at the moment.'

'Dorin and Bogdan are the drug suppliers for Sunset,' said Jimmy. 'It's common knowledge. I say follow the money. They were trying to put a bullet into you last night, so I reckon something serious is going on.'

Cámara raised a quizzical eyebrow.

'You still think José Luis's death was just an accident?' said Jimmy.

THIRTY-THREE

Torres sat at his new desk staring at the computer screen. He spent a lot of time staring at computer screens these days. More and more. And less and less time out on the street. Which was where he wanted to be. Yes, a great deal of crime-fighting could be achieved using the Internet and diving into the darker corners of the digital world, yet the pay-off for the policeman was never as high. The adrenalin rush of tracking and chasing a criminal and then the release of actually catching him and taking him down could never be matched by tapping away at a keyboard. Success sometimes came, but it lacked something real, something tangible.

He had been through enough shit to lose any romantic notions about policing. In fact, it took him less than two hours on his first day of proper employment to realise that police work was laborious and largely tedious. But he had stuck it out because of the occasional moments that made everything worth it. That, and the luck of spending a lot of his career with Chief Inspector Cámara. Their partnership had come under strain at times, and faced attempts to break it up, but they had somehow managed to stick together, becoming the object of a certain amount of envy among colleagues who recognised the bond between the two men. Yet now, as he stared at the glowing pixels, Torres wondered whether this was finally it, whether his time with Cámara had really come to an end. A simple order from the top and their working relationship had been snuffed out like a cockroach crushed by an angry shoe.

It was his second day in Narcotics, but the frostiness of his new colleagues was still in evidence. Torres had arrived early that morning – a demonstration from his side at least that he was prepared to make a go of it. And so he sat at his computer bringing himself up to speed on past cases, investigations that were on-going, trying to get a sense of how the unit operated. All he could see so far was a fucking shambles. No clear sense of direction, total chaos. And he thought Cámara was disorganised.

His mobile rang and for a second he was distracted from the screen.

'Hello?'

'Torres,' said a voice. 'It's Alicia.'

'*Hombre*, Alicia.' Torres smiled, half-guessing the reason for her call. 'What's up?'

He had spoken on the phone with Alicia before – occasionally the three of them socialised. But there was only going to be one reason why she would be ringing this early in the morning.

'Don't tell me,' he said. 'He's gone missing.'

'I can't reach him,' said Alicia. Torres thought he detected something in her voice. Not quite fear, but nervousness, perhaps.

'Don't worry,' he said. 'He'll be fine.'

'I haven't spoken to him since yesterday morning,' said Alicia. 'Has something happened?'

'Oh,' said Torres. He sucked his teeth. 'So you haven't heard?'

'Heard what?'

'We've been shut down. No more Special Crimes Unit.'

Alicia drew a breath.

'Wow.'

'Yeah,' said Torres. 'That was kind of our reaction as well. Totally out of the blue.'

'What the hell happened?'

'It's this new commissioner, Rita Hernández.'

'Max mentioned her.'

'Well, no surprise there. She's had it in for him since she arrived. She's, er, how shall I put it? Not like us.'

Alicia sniggered drily.

'I get it. But what was the reason?'

'I don't know what she told him. She got us in separately. But it's something to do with centralising all investigations into Islamic extremists.'

'What?'

'They're shutting down all the *Policía Nacional* and *Guardia Civil* investigations. Now there's a dedicated unit in Madrid. Bloody stupid if you ask me. All the legwork we've put in, and all our local knowledge and contacts – Bang! All up in smoke.'

'Sounds mad,' said Alicia.

'Oh I'm sure it's even madder than that. Things usually are. We'll be hearing about Operation Covadonga at some point in the future – probably when the whole thing blows up in their faces and we get parachuted back in to clear up the mess.'

'Operation what?'

'Covadonga,' said Torres. 'The papers were on Hernández's desk. I spotted them while she ranted on about . . . well, about Cámara, really. About why she was closing us down. Christ, you'd think he ran over her dog or something.'

'So where are the two of you now?'

Torres sighed.

'There's no *us* any more,' he said. 'She made certain of that. We've been split up, made to sit at opposite ends of the class.'

'Oh for God's sake.'

'I'm in Narcotics and your other half is back in *Homicidios*.'

'*Homicidios?*'

'And not in charge of it either. Laura Martín is still very much in control. So he's just had to slot back in, become a foot soldier. For someone of his rank and experience it's ridiculous. But that's Rita for you. She's putting the thumbscrews on him, trying to force him to resign. That's what she really wants – to get him out of the Jefatura.'

Like many taciturn people, once he finally got started Torres could talk at considerable length.

'So do you know where he is,' Alicia butted in. 'Max?'

'He's almost certainly up in the sierra,' said Torres. 'Some routine case. You know the guy who owns Sunset?'

'The disco?'

'Found dead. Cámara's on it. I suspect he's still up there. The phone signal won't be great. But don't worry, I'm sure he'll be in touch soon. If I hear from him first I'll tell him to ring.'

'OK,' said Alicia. 'Thanks. Tell him I'm in Madrid. Something's come up.'

'Sure, will do. Anything interesting?'

'I don't know,' said Alicia, 'Possibly. Although quite what and how big . . .'

She paused.

'Listen,' she said. 'You know that tiny island off the coast of Mallorca?'

'Cabrera?'

'Just wondering if that's flashed up anywhere, appeared on your radar.'

Torres thought for a second, then shook his head.

'No. Why?'

'And a couple of code words,' continued Alicia. 'Abravanel mean anything to you?'

'Sounds Arabic,' said Torres. 'Or Jewish. But no, means nothing.'

'Clavijo?'

Torres chuckled.

'Only from school. That sends me back.'

'From school?' asked Alicia.

'Battle of Clavijo,' said Torres. 'Didn't you do it? Some battle in the Middle Ages when Santiago miraculously appeared and slayed all the Moors. Or something like that.'

'It's ringing a faint bell.'

'All that *Reconquista* stuff. When Spain was cleared of the Infidel and turned into a pure Catholic nation, the sword and shield of the one true faith. Come to think of it, Covadonga was some other battle against the Moors during that time.'

'Must have been asleep during that lesson.'

'Ah! See what you were missing?'

'Clearly. But, Paco . . .' Alicia lowered her voice. 'If you do hear anything, can you let me know? Perhaps ask around?'

'I'll see what I can do,' Torres said. 'I'm being mostly ignored at the moment, but there are a couple sniffing me out, trying to work out what I'm about. If the opportunity arises . . .'

'Brilliant, thanks.'

'You watch yourself,' said Torres.

'Oh, I'm fine,' said Alicia. 'Absolutely fine.'

THIRTY-FOUR

Jimmy's battered old Seat managed to make it over to the village without – miraculously, Cámara thought – breaking down. The front wheels had a definite wobble, and every time they went over one of the dozens of potholes along the mountain road he thought the axle might snap. That was not to mention the lack of functioning seat belts, the passenger door that had to be fastened with a piece of elastic, and the cloud of blue smoke billowing out from the exhaust pipe.

'Here,' Jimmy said when they reached the main square of the village. He reached across to the glove compartment and pulled out a small Browning handgun. 'It's yours if you want it.'

Cámara hesitated. He was used to being armed; guns could be useful. Yet despite his admiration for and gratitude to Jimmy, he couldn't take a weapon from him.

'Thanks,' he said. 'I'll be all right.'

'Watch yourself, Mr Policeman,' said Jimmy. 'This may look like a sleepy mountain village, but there's more going on here than meets the eye.'

Cámara nodded and got out. Jimmy tied the door closed again with the elastic and set off, leaving Cámara coughing in his wake.

He was in a small square with a public fountain in one corner and an arcade of what looked like Gothic arches along the opposite side. Various shops and municipal offices took up the ground floors of most of the buildings, some of which dated from the late nineteenth century, others built more recently in shiny brown brick.

Cámara walked to the side of the square, found a quiet spot in the shade and took his phone out. After a couple of seconds it registered a signal; he sighed with a mixture of relief and trepidation.

The first message to reach him – a text – came from Dario Quintero at the Forensic Medicine Centre. It had been sent late the night before.

– *Call me.*

Cámara pressed the buttons and soon heard the phone ringing at the other end with a steady, hissing beep. No answer came and he thought it was going to go through to voicemail when there was a click and he heard a voice.

'*¿Si?*'

'It's Cámara.'

'At last,' said Quintero. 'I texted you last night.'

'I'm out of the city. Didn't have a signal,' said Cámara.

'Listen,' said Quintero. 'I'm just about to start another autopsy. Can I call you back?'

'You mean you've already worked on José Luis?'

'Of course, last night. That's why I texted you.'

'I thought—'

'A slot came up,' Quintero explained. 'And I thought, as a favour—'

'What did you find?' Cámara interrupted. 'And thanks.'

'Well, look, quickly,' Quintero said. 'Because I really have to go.'

'Yes, yes,' Cámara said.

'Well,' Quintero began. 'José Luis died of a heart attack.'

'I see.'

'I mean, that's what killed him eventually.'

'Eventually?'

'The man was anaphylactic.'

'Anaphy-what?'

'He was allergic to Hymenoptera.'

'Which is?'

'The venom in bee stings.'

Cámara drew a breath.

'So the bees did kill him,' he said.

'In a manner of speaking,' answered Quintero. 'Firstly I established that those were indeed bees' stings that we saw on his skin. There were seven of them, which ordinarily wouldn't kill anyone, certainly not a grown man of his age. But once we took a proper look at him the telltale signs were there.'

Quintero appeared to forget momentarily that he had another autopsy to perform, detailing the manner of José Luis's death with a professional enthusiasm.

'The throat and tongue tend to swell up in such cases, leading to shortness of breath, the bronchial muscles go into spasm and, as was the case with our friend, a cardiac arrest is eventually caused by a spasm in the coronary artery.'

Ever respectful to the bodies under his knife, Quintero

had clearly enjoyed this one. Cámara doubted if he had seen many cases like it before.

'So it was all there once we got inside: an empty heart – virtually no blood inside it – caused by the reduced venous return from vasodilation . . .'

Cámara's mind began to wander as Quintero trailed out a string of words that held no meaning for him: laryngeal oedema, eosinophilia, myocardial hypoperfusion . . .

'Which is how,' Quintero concluded, 'we can say that the bee stings were the prime cause of death.'

'One thing,' said Cámara. 'You're certain it was the bees. Couldn't have been some other venom. Say from a viper.'

'A viper?' Quintero was surprised. 'No, we found traces of Hymenoptera in the blood. Very definitely the bees.'

'Thank you,' said Cámara. 'I'm simply wondering . . .' he continued.

'You're wondering if this rules it out being a murder,' Quintero finished his sentence for him.

'Yes, I suppose I am.'

'I thought you would. Which is why I ran some other tests.'

'Other tests?' said Cámara.

'The bees clearly killed José Luis,' explained Quintero. 'But is there any way that the bees might have been drawn to him and induced to attack?'

The idea sounded insane. Cámara had had the same thought the day before, when he had accused Enrique, yet had dismissed it almost immediately.

'Well,' he said. 'Is there?'

'Bees are sensitive creatures,' said Quintero. 'Particularly to smell. I've known them to become quite aggressive if they don't like the way someone smells.'

'Are you serious?'

'Very much so. Certain scents on a mammal, for example, can trigger an attack response in them. Makes them feel threatened so they respond aggressively. I remember taking a walk in the country once with my wife when she was heavily pregnant with our first son. When we passed a beehive, they flew out at her and attacked. Didn't bother with me at all.'

Cámara shook his head, trying to understand.

'Quintero,' he said. 'Please don't tell me José Luis was also pregnant.'

He was breaking a taboo. Quintero always worked with a total and iron-held respect for the dead. Jokes about them were strictly off-limits. There was a pause; Cámara waited, then a rhythmic wheezing started from the other end of the line. With a sense of relief, he realised that Quintero was laughing.

'Pregnant,' he coughed at last. 'Well he was certainly big enough. Ha, ha.

'No seriously,' he added. 'And I really do have to go now. I ran some tests, trying to see if there was anything about José Luis which might have attracted the bees.'

'And?'

'I found pheromones on his skin – a greater quantity than you might expect. And I'm not sure because I'd have to do some more work on the samples. But there's a faint chance that they're artificial ones, not ones produced by his own physiology.'

'And pheromones might have caused the bees to react in the way they did?' Cámara asked.

'They could be a trigger.'

'How could the pheromones have got on to his skin?'

'I'm afraid I can't answer,' Quintero said. 'Now I really must go.'

The line went dead. Cámara checked the time: it had just gone ten o'clock. For a moment, when Jimmy dropped him off, he had wondered about heading back to Valencia. Now he knew he had to stay.

His phone had beeped in his ear a few times during the conversation with Quintero as it registered other missed calls and messages.

Don't worry, began the first one on his voicemail, sent late the previous evening: it was Torres. *I've had a word with the police union. They can start proceedings now if they want. Well, I think we can take that as read. She* is *going to start proceedings, but there's an automatic period of grace – and I bet she hasn't bothered to read this. But there's six months before she can actually kick you out, and during that time you have all kinds of opportunities to defend yourself, prove that the allegations are groundless. So I reckon you're covered. Of course, the simplest thing would be to do as she asks, but I'm just letting you know. Thought it might be useful.*

Cámara stared at the phone with incomprehension. Then he saw that there were two previous calls from Torres. He listened to the one sent immediately before.

Well I can only assume there's no signal wherever you are, he said. *That's the obvious explanation. But you-know-who doesn't see it that way. And this is all about you undermining her authority and not showing due respect, blah, blah, blah. So, just to let you know, in case you manage to hear this, the shit has hit the fan quite definitively. So, if you do hear this, you might want to have a think about calling in. If you get a chance. Just a simple report, tell Laura where you are, what you're up to. That kind of thing. I know it's not your style but, well, it might help smooth things over a bit. If it's not already too late.*

Cámara sighed. Office politics. It felt like a very long time had passed since he was last in the Jefatura, yet it was only the previous morning. How easy it had been to forget it all for a while, become immersed in the simple act of detection.

He pressed the screen and listened to Torres's first message of the previous day, sent some time before lunch.

Right, he began. *I've had a quick look at what's available on José Luis.*

Cámara let out an involuntary sigh of relief.

Sixty years old, that's confirmed. Nice way to spend your birthday. Born in Sueca. Father was in the Air Force, but died when José Luis was young. Brought up by his mother. Did all right at school and it looks like for a while he wanted to follow in Daddy's footsteps – signed up for the Air Force when he was 18. Did two years' training in Seville, wanted to become a pilot. But then he left suddenly. Didn't complete and dropped out. The papers don't explain why, but I've done a bit of digging around, found a contact in the Air Force Ministry. Anyway, turns out that poor old José Luis had an allergy to bee stings. Got some complicated Latin name. But that's why the Air Force wouldn't take him. Ran some standard tests and when they discovered that, bang, he was out. Anyway, he drifts around for a bit after that, was in Madrid for a few years, then came back to Valencia and got into the nightclub scene. Then he bought Sunset *and the rest you probably know. That's it for now. I'll call again if I get anything else.*

Cámara pondered for a moment. There was one more message to listen to. He didn't have to check who it was from.

Chief Inspector Cámara, Commissioner Hernández began. *You are a disgrace to the* Policía Nacional. *Even by your own standards, not reporting in . . .*

Cámara rolled his eyes and pressed the delete button, not waiting to hear the rest.

He had police work to do.

THIRTY-FIVE

'The situation has become more serious, sir.'

Carlos stood in Fernando's office and watched while his superior picked up a fresh cup of burning hot coffee and drank it down in two gulps. Quite what the man's gullet was made of, Carlos couldn't say, but whatever it was it had the fire-retarding properties of asbestos. Any other mortal would have screamed in agony.

Fernando reached for a *madalena* cake, pulled off the case, threw it into the overflowing bin at the side of his desk and took a large bite, chewing slowly and deliberately before swallowing. His secretary was still in the room, standing at his side. Fernando pointed silently at his empty coffee cup and it was immediately whisked away for a refill, the secretary striding past Carlos to step out of the office in the direction of the hot drinks machine.

When the door closed, Fernando looked up, wiping crumbs from his mouth with the back of his hand. Carlos watched as they tumbled down his chin and came to rest on the upper curve of his belly, nestling in a fold of his shirt.

'Fill me in,' ordered Fernando.

'The Beneyto woman,' said Carlos, 'the journalist from Valencia – she's in Madrid.'

Fernando sniffed. Carlos recognised that look. Others misinterpreted it as one of unconcern, even a lack of interest. But Carlos knew it disguised a deep and very focused concentration wrapped in a layer of studied calm. And he viewed it with unalloyed admiration.

'When did she arrive?' Fernando said.

'Late last night. She caught the last AVE from Valencia.'

'Which gets into Atocha at 2310,' said Fernando. He nodded to himself. 'I'm assuming this is abnormal behaviour.'

'We've checked,' said Carlos. 'She travelled on the AVE before, but never the late one.'

'Where is she now?' Fernando asked.

'At a flat on Calle Santo Domingo.'

'Is she alone?'

Carlos nodded.

'Has she gone anywhere this morning?'

Carlos shook his head.

'It's already ten past ten,' said Fernando without looking at his watch. 'Which means that if she caught that last train it was in order to do something or meet someone late last night.'

Carlos didn't react.

'And now you're going to tell me exactly what she did when her train got in,' said Fernando.

Carlos took a breath.

'There's a gap,' he said.

'Go on.'

'About an hour. Between her arrival and our picking up the trail.'

Fernando lowered his eyes and nodded. His secretary came in through the door behind Carlos carrying another cup of steaming coffee. He placed it down on the desk and stepped away.

'Leave us,' said Fernando to him.

Walking towards the door, the secretary pursed his lips and gave an involuntary raising of the eyebrows. There was trouble afoot.

The door clicked shut. Fernando picked up the coffee and sniffed at it, then he placed it back without drinking. Carlos could feel a tremor in his right knee.

'There's . . .' The words stuck in his throat. He brought a fist up to his mouth and coughed. 'There's more.'

Fernando tapped his fingers together, staring at him to carry on.

'The Beneyto woman made a phone call this morning. She's . . . she's found out more.'

Fernando's eyes didn't blink.

'Who did she call?'

'Someone in the Valencia Jefatura. An inspector by the name of Francisco Torres.'

'Who is he?'

'A colleague of her partner, of Chief Inspector Max Cámara.'

Fernando breathed in heavily.

'You've mentioned that name to me before,' he said.

'I believe he's out of the picture,' said Carlos. 'Neutralised in the course of Operation Covadonga.'

'But?'

Carlos felt the quivering now in both knees.

'But Inspector Torres has clearly seen more than he should have,' he said. 'He knows about Covadonga for a start.'

'How?' demanded Fernando.

'An oversight at the Valencia Jefatura,' said Carlos. 'It'll be taken care of.'

'Does this Beneyto woman know they're connected? Covadonga and Clavijo.'

'Not as far as I'm aware, sir,' said Carlos. 'They're completely separate as far as she's concerned. But . . .'

'But what?'

'Well, the names, sir. She might work out a connection herself.'

Fernando nodded slowly and silently.

'Bloody soldiers,' he said. 'This is what happens when a bunch of elderly generals get given too much to do. Make basic mistakes.'

Carlos shuffled his feet; the tension in his legs was becoming quite uncomfortable.

'I'm afraid the Beneyto woman knows something else as well, sir.'

Fernando gave him a dark, unwavering look.

'She's found out about Abravanel,' said Carlos.

There was a lengthy pause where the only thing in the office that moved was Fernando's chest as it slowly rose and fell with his breathing.

'Who was her source?' he said at last.

'We don't know,' said Carlos. 'We have to assume it was someone she met during the hour that we lost her in Madrid last night.'

'You need to find out who that was,' said Fernando calmly. 'If we have a leak we need it blocked immediately.'

'Yes, sir.'

'This is your responsibility, Carlos,' said Fernando. 'Security for the whole of Operation Navas is on your shoulders. I vouched for you, said you were the man for the job. I don't need to tell you what is at stake here.'

'No, sir. Should I . . .'

'Put the *Guardia Suiza* on high alert,' said Fernando.

Carlos nodded.

'When the time comes,' said Fernando, 'it's on you. You're the one who'll be pulling the trigger.'

THIRTY-SIX

Cámara walked down stone steps to the arcade. He passed a bank, a hairdresser's and a hardware shop before reaching the door of Los Arcos bar. A couple of empty tables stood on the pavement. Cámara pushed through the beads hanging in the doorway and went inside.

There was a long dark passageway before the actual bar area. Next to a public phone he saw colourful posters pinned to the wall: the village would soon be celebrating the first of its summer fiestas. In the gloom he saw an image of a bull running full-speed at the camera, a flaming torch blazing from the end of each horn.

Two men were sitting at stools at the bar, hunched over small glasses of coffee. One of them had a shot glass of brandy at the side and was mixing the two drinks to make a *carajillo*. No one seemed to notice Cámara entering, but within a few moments of his sitting down at a side table, the two men had finished and were leaving money on the counter, hitching their trousers up and marching out.

Cámara was alone: there was no sign of anyone behind the bar. He got up and walked over.

'Hello?'

'In a minute,' came a voice from the kitchen.

Presently, a short man in his forties with greasy black hair and close-set eyes appeared, wiping his hands dry on his hips, a look of mild annoyance on his face

Cámara already had his police ID out.

'Oh,' said the man, checking himself, an expression of some confusion in his eyes. Cámara dived straight in.

'I'm investigating the death of José Luis, the owner of Sunset,' he said. For a moment he had almost said 'murder'.

'Did José Luis ever come in here?' he said.

The man hesitated.

'Your name is?' Cámara demanded.

'Ramón,' he said.

'So, Ramón. Did you ever see José Luis in this bar?'

'He wasn't a regular,' Ramón answered. He had a nervous, high-pitched voice, like a twittering sparrow.

'But he did come in sometimes.'

'Once or twice. Perhaps a bit more often. Had a meal here in the evenings occasionally. But not for a while. Hadn't seen him for some months, in fact.'

'You know he's dead,' said Cámara.

'Yes, I heard something.'

Cámara paused.

'Did he ever meet people here?'

Ramón looked circumspect.

'His neighbour, perhaps? Enrique, who has the farm up near Sunset?'

'That's right.' Ramón grinned with relief. He was naturally suspicious, perhaps had a sense of loyalty to his customers, didn't want to pass on anything that he shouldn't – almost like a priest with his sacramental seal – but Cámara had already answered for him.

'Yes, with Enrique,' Ramón said. His teeth were pitted with black streaks. Did he ever – had he ever cleaned them, Cámara wondered.

'When was the last time you saw them here together?'

Ramón paused, a knot of concentrated yet hesitant thought on his brow.

'Recently?' Cámara asked.

Ramón shook his head.

'No. Not for a long time,' he said. 'Maybe a year or more.'

'You know what they came here to discuss?'

Cámara had crossed a line.

'Oh, I never listen in on customers' conversations.'

'You know about the argument between Enrique and José Luis over the Chain.'

Ramón frowned.

'Don't know anything about that,' he said with emphasis.

Cámara tried a different tack.

'Can you tell me,' he asked, 'was José Luis liked in the village?'

Ramón shrugged. And thought.

'He wasn't popular with everyone,' Ramón said at last. 'I don't know what goes on up at Sunset. Not my business.'

In Cámara's experience, it was the business of every bar owner to know exactly what was going on in his or her local area, yet Ramón continued with his pretence.

'There were rumours. Don't know if any of it was true, but a lot of people round here didn't approve. Old people can't understand that kind of thing. Belong to a different generation.'

Cámara wondered about Vicente and Vicenta for a moment: people of the previous generation who appeared to have accepted Sunset and what went on up there in their own way.

'Did you ever hear Enrique speaking about José Luis when he was in here?'

'What, during their meetings?'

'When he came here alone.'

'No,' Ramón said categorically. Then he looked Cámara in the eye. 'This is a small village,' he said. 'Small community. People tend to watch what they say.'

'I get it,' said Cámara. He decided it was time to leave.

'Some of the hunters used to grumble occasionally,' Ramón said. Cámara pricked up his ears.

'What about?'

'Don't know the details,' said Ramón. 'You should talk to the mayor.'

'Whose name is?'

'Javier Santos. He's one of them, keen hunter. Something about a protection order José Luis had slapped on his land. Stopped the hunters from roaming on his property.'

Cámara nodded.

'Can I find the mayor at the Town Hall?' he asked.

Ramón looked at his watch.

'You might just catch him. Should be halfway through his round.'

'His round?'

'He does the local mail delivery as well.'

Cámara stepped back out into the square. At the far end of the arcade he noticed a grocery shop with fruit and vegetables displayed on two wooden tables at either side of the entrance. A woman wearing a work overdress was arranging the bananas and swatting away flies. She had dark hair and olive skin, but there was something about her features and body language which Cámara could not quite put his finger on that made him suspect she wasn't of Spanish origin, was possibly an immigrant.

He turned and headed across the square towards a large, ornate building on the far side with *Casa Consistorial* written in pale blue letters above a large, open double doorway. Inside was a spacious, empty hall with a brightly coloured tiled floor, geometric patterns in green, red and white spreading out from beneath his feet with dizzying complexity. A woman wearing glasses and holding a sheet of paper walked past.

'I'm looking for the mayor,' said Cámara. Like Ramón, she looked at her watch before answering.

'He's . . .' she began. Then she looked behind Cámara out into the square.

'He's just coming now. There.'

She pointed. Cámara saw a small yellow van pulling into a parking space outside the door.

'Thank you.'

He waited for the mayor to get out of his van and greet a couple of locals who were passing, before approaching.

'*Policía Nacional*?' said the mayor when Cámara introduced himself. 'We don't tend to see your lot . . .'

'Is there somewhere we could talk?' Cámara said.

'My office.'

The mayor was a small man, barely reaching Cámara's shoulders, but he was used to being in charge. Cámara judged him to be in his mid-sixties, perhaps close to retirement. His hair was cropped short and his chin was freshly shaven that morning, with a hint of cheap, traditional old-man's cologne about him. He removed his grey postman's cap and slipped it under his arm, as though to signify that he was moving from one municipal duty to the other. With it, his bearing stiffened and his clothes – white shirt, dark trousers and dark, but not matching, cotton jacket – almost took on the air of a suit.

Cámara followed as they walked up a large marble staircase to the first floor. The building was probably a hundred years old or more: there must have been more money about back then. Certainly today, judging by the shops and the general appearance of its inhabitants, the village did not have a look of wealth about it.

At the top of the stairs, the mayor pulled out a large bunch of keys hanging from a chain on his hip, unlocked three bolts on his office door and beckoned Cámara in. They passed into a large, well-lit chamber with views through a balcony window on to the square below. It felt almost like a throne room. Cámara was immediately struck, however, by the large number of stuffed animal heads on the walls: wild boar, mostly, but there were others, including an ibex with its distinctive horns like the one he had seen the day before, and animals that were not native to the Iberian peninsula.

'You a hunting man, Chief Inspector?' the mayor asked, mistaking Cámara's curiosity for approval.

'No,' Cámara said bluntly. 'I just shoot people.'

The mayor froze, eyes staring, uncertain how to react.

'But only bad guys,' Cámara added with a smile.

'I see,' said the mayor. He went to sit behind his desk, easing himself down into a tall oak chair with a red velvet covering.

'So what can I do for you?' he said. 'It must be quite important if someone of your high rank has been sent.'

'These animals,' Cámara said, pointing at a zebra and what he felt certain was a gazelle. 'Where do you hunt them?'

'I travel all over the world,' said the mayor proudly. 'I've hunted on almost all the world's continents.'

'And you bring your spoils back home with you?'

'I don't travel with them myself,' he said with a condescending smile. 'They're couriered to Spain. Then a specialist works with them and they eventually reach me here. I have more at home. These are just a sample.'

'Must be an expensive hobby,' said Cámara. 'All the kit, all the travelling.'

The mayor's face was impassive.

'So, Chief Inspector. Are you here to talk about hunting? I'm afraid I have the second half of my postal run to complete. And then there's a plenary council meeting to attend. And other duties.'

Cámara walked to the window, hands on hips, and looked down into the square. People were moving about, none of them at any great speed. He wondered if a village like this ever experienced the sense of rush that almost always prevailed in the city.

'José Luis,' he said. 'Sunset.'

'Very sad business,' said the mayor, shuffling in his chair. 'I heard yesterday.'

'Did you know him?' Cámara asked.

'Of course. Not intimately, you understand. But as mayor I have dealings with most people at some point.'

'My understanding,' said Cámara, 'is that there was tension between José Luis and the local hunters.'

He raised his eyebrows and looked pointedly at the rows of dead animals on display.

'You'd know all about that.'

The mayor placed his elbows on the table, his fingertips together, and spoke in a flat voice, as though addressing an official meeting.

'Any private land measuring less than forty hectares,' he said, 'is part of the local hunting area, as I'm sure you're already aware.'

Cámara nodded.

'Meaning members of the local hunting club have every right to roam and hunt on any such land.'

'How many hectares did José Luis have?' Cámara asked.

'Eighteen.'

'So less than the minimum needed to seal it off from the hunters.'

'That's right.'

'And did local hunters – did you – hunt on his land?'

'When you're chasing down a wounded boar . . .' the mayor began.

'All right,' said Cámara. 'And I assume José Luis wasn't too happy about it.'

The mayor paused before answering.

'There's a loophole in the law,' he said. 'And he used it.'

'The nature reserve?' Cámara asked.

'You've already heard,' smiled the mayor. 'He found a sympathetic biologist to identify some species of moss on his land. Quite rare, apparently. Anyway, it was enough to declare his land a mini nature reserve. Meaning—'

'Meaning that the hunters no longer had a right to go on his land.'

'Correct.'

Cámara walked across and stood over the desk, looking down at the mayor.

'Must have caused quite an annoyance.'

The mayor shrugged it off.

'The hunting areas around here are ample enough,' he said. 'And there were never many boar near Sunset in the first place.'

'Still,' Cámara insisted. 'Not many among you will be mourning his death.'

'On the contrary,' the mayor spat. 'It's a blow to this village.'

Cámara was dubious.

'Brought in much-needed income from outside,' the mayor went on. 'Villages like this are dying on their feet. Young people moving out, almost nothing keeping the local economy going. You can't sustain a community like this on some small-scale almond and olive farming. Sunset is vital for us.'

'So you wouldn't want to see it closed.'

'Closed?' The mayor looked genuinely shocked. 'Heaven forbid. It could mean the death of this village.'

He stood up, leaning on his fists over the table.

'Have you heard anything?' he asked, a perturbed look on his brow. 'Is it possible it might not reopen?'

THIRTY-SEVEN

The taxi pulled in at the top of the Plaza de la Reina and came to a stop. Commissioner Rita Hernández handed the driver a twenty-euro note, waited for the change, then opened the door and stepped out into the unforgiving midday sun. She quickly put on large, angular sunglasses to shield her eyes and began weaving her way through a small huddle of tourists towards the baroque south entrance of the cathedral. A man was standing by the gold-leaf-covered doors wearing thin grey trousers and a stained shirt. Hernández did her best to ignore him as she stepped past. Then, hesitating, she fished out a fifty-cent coin from her purse, thrust it into his grubby, thick-fingered hands and continued into the cool, musty shade of the church.

It had not been a good morning at the Jefatura. The day before had shown so much promise, had seen the final implementation of a plan she had been dreaming of almost since she had arrived in Valencia. And she had fallen into the trap of imagining that the smoothness with which it was carried out was an indication of things to come. Yet now she was wondering whether it had been nothing but a false dawn, a far cry from the happy control that she had believed she was imposing on her domain.

It began as soon as she arrived at the Jefatura: the guard at the gate did not return her wave for some inexplicable reason, and her space – the space meant for *her* Range Rover – was taken by another car, a Porsche Cayenne. Upon making a complaint, it was explained to her that a visiting commissioner from Madrid – and a personal friend of the *Jefe Superior*, her own boss – would be needing it for the duration of his visit, which was expected to last three days.

She eventually found another place to park – down a side street five blocks away – but it took her almost twenty minutes and by the time she walked back to the Jefatura she was late – for the first time ever in her career. That in itself might have been enough to disturb her tranquillity, but her bad mood was intensified when, shortly after reaching her office, she learned that Chief Inspector Max Cámara was again causing problems. Not only had he failed to resign the day before, he had taken on the routine case she had insisted on for him and was now apparently missing – uncontactable and with no sign of any progress report on his investigation. She could at least add this to the long list of his misdemeanours which would provide ammunition for an eventual misconduct hearing, but her plan was to be rid of the man without having to resort to something so complicated and uncertain. It was as if there were a mercurial quality about him, slipping through her fingers the moment she thought she had finally caught him.

Yet even this had not been the sum of her morning

difficulties. If there was anything worse than the festering wound that was the Cámara problem, it was that she herself should fail in her duties as a loyal servant of the State. Which was exactly what she had done.

The phone call came halfway through the morning as she returned to her office from the joint commissioners' daily meeting. It was Madrid, from the Centre, and the man she only knew as Carlos. A mistake had been made, someone had been careless and as a result confidential information had fallen into the wrong hands.

His voice was steady and businesslike. There was something calm and unruffled about him that she immediately admired. But there was no mistaking his seriousness, and the fact that she, Rita Hernández, had been the cause of this security breach.

He did not name her personally, naturally. These people were too good for something so crude. Yet the implication was clear enough. She remembered the meetings in her office the morning before, first with Cámara then with Torres. And her mind's eye fell directly on the papers from Madrid that had still been lying on her desk at the time. What a fool she had been! How could she have made such an elementary blunder? These men were police, they were trained to see, to observe. So of course they had caught sight of something they were meant to remain ignorant of. But which of the two had it been?

'Was it Chief Inspector Cámara?' she asked Carlos, trying to stifle the tremor of loathing in her voice.

And he had paused before answering.

'I am not at liberty to say.'

And her remorse only deepened for having the temerity to ask in the first place.

Carlos had not been unaware of her distress, she now realised. She needed forgiveness, a redemption of sorts, and so he had given her a name and suggested she go to the Cathedral. Her own priest, her normal confessor, would not do in these circumstances. And she had thanked him profusely for his understanding, repeated her apologies several times over and insisted that she was still, should he ever need her, at his service. Would always be.

His final words had given her hope: 'Keep me informed about Cámara.'

Still, she needed this. Perhaps more than ever before.

Dipping her fingers in the font, she crossed herself and genuflected in the direction of the altar. A nearby priest walking towards the Chapel of the Holy Grail pointed her to a confession box on the left side of the nave.

She crossed under the wide Gothic arch and approached the wooden box. Black leather shoes jutted out from behind a velvet curtain. She knelt down on the cushion at the side and heard the priest turn towards her.

'I . . .' she began. 'I was told to ask for Father Bartolomeo,'

'You are speaking to him,' came the warm, immediate reply.

'I was sent by Carlos,' she continued. 'From the Centre. He said . . .'

The priest's robes ruffled as he shifted in his seat.

'He said you were a member of the Brothers of Cáceres,' she said.

This time the priest paused before answering.

'What is your name?'

'Rita,' she said. 'Rita Hernández. I'm a commissioner with the *Policía Nacional*.'

She waited, longing for him to say something.

'Welcome, Rita,' said the priest. 'I am listening. What would you like to tell me.'

Hernández breathed out, the embryo of a tear pricking at the corner of her eye.

'*Padre*,' she said, '*me arrepiento . . .*'

I have sinned.

THIRTY-EIGHT

The grocer's shop was small. Cámara caught the typical smell as soon as he walked in: a mixture of bananas, bleach and spices. Two elderly women were huddled at the far end of the counter with well-used shopping trolleys parked by their ankles, ready to be filled. On the right, next to the soaps and perfumes, stood three teenage boys chatting loudly and giggling over a present they wanted to buy for a friend.

Cámara took a step inside and let the door close behind him, the bell ringing for a second time as it did so. No one looked up. He stuck his toe into a hole in the dirty grey linoleum floor, wondering how many customers had tripped over it. The place felt cramped and unloved: a layer of dust had settled on the shelves of canned food along the left-hand wall, while paint was peeling off the ceiling in long patches and hanging down like limp stalactites.

Behind the counter he saw the dark-haired woman he had caught sight of earlier. Next to her was a small, more intense woman with bleached hair, lips painted bright pink with an acute cupid's bow, and eyebrows entirely plucked in favour of pencilled alternatives which arched high up her brow. Both women were dutifully attending the elderly ladies at the counter, pausing to listen to their stories and gossip.

Being immigrants, these women would have to work extra hard to capture and maintain their customers. There was no doubt in his mind that they were the wives of Dorin and Bogdan, the two Romanians. Not too long before it would have been difficult, even impossible, for an enterprise like this to succeed. Yet the influx of foreigners over the previous decade or so had changed the country, not least parts of the countryside where locals – particularly the young – were often moving out and the only people replacing them were immigrant workers. After some hesitation most had learned to accept them, remembering that not so long before in the past they, too, had been migrant workers, flocking to Germany and Switzerland in the fifties and sixties, and that even today hundreds of thousands of their own children had had to leave the country, seeking work in Berlin, London, or wherever they could.

The first of the elderly women had finished and was inching past Cámara to leave. On the other side of the shop, the teenagers appeared to have given up on their quest and were heading out as well. There was only one elderly lady remaining at the counter, who was being attended to by the dark-haired Romanian. The other opened a door behind the counter leading through to what looked like a living room, where a television was flickering in a corner. Cámara tried to see if there was anyone there, perhaps the two husbands. But the door closed before he could see.

He waited. There were some bread rolls on a shelf behind the counter. He might buy one along with some ham and cheese and make himself a quick lunch.

The elderly lady wanted to chat; she was talking about her grandson, who was finishing his end-of-school exams; was worried about having to do retakes. The woman behind the counter listened patiently.

The conversation stuttered towards an end. The woman placed her items in the shopping trolley. Cámara went to open the door for her. She passed through without giving him a second glance. Cámara turned back to the shop, facing the counter. But the door through to the living room closed before he even took a step, the remaining Romanian disappearing from view. For a moment he could hear muffled voices, then silence. He waited: would they be returning?

After a pause, the door opened a fraction. He saw a single eye peep through, catch sight of him still standing there, then vanish.

He pulled the door hard as he left, signalling his departure with the loud clanging of the bell.

Across the square, near the fountain, he spotted a baker's. He ambled over and joined a small but chaotic mob.

'*¿El último?*' he asked.

A man wearing a flat cap signalled that he was indeed the last in the queue, such as it was. Cámara hovered until it was his turn, then ordered a couple of tomato-and-tuna pasties and a slice of onion and vegetable quiche. With a bottle of water tucked under his arm, he took them outside to the fountain, where he sat on the edge, unwrapping his lunch and eating hungrily.

This was probably the busiest moment in the village day, he thought as he watched the comings and goings in the square. Just as in the city, the rush to get things done before lunchtime brought a surge in activity, yet here it was marked simply by the presence of an extra car or two driving past. A delivery lorry laden with bottles of soft drinks had just arrived, parking badly in front of Los Arcos bar. A man who now found his own car blocked in was arguing with the driver. The bar owner himself had got involved. The car owner was getting irate, his face reddening as he shouted abuse. The bar owner had to hold him back, preventing him from physically attacking the lorry driver, who eventually, after much fist-waving and shouting, moved the lorry and let the man drive away.

It was odd, just a minor dispute, and yet to Cámara it captured something about the place: there was an underlying tension, a feeling that passions – and perhaps grudges – ran deep here. Everyone knew one another and had probably done so since childhood. Many of them would be related in some way. And while they did their best to get on and not ruffle any feathers too much, he could not help but feel that there was anger bubbling under the surface and that very little would be required for it quickly to boil over.

He looked up at the mayor's balcony on the first floor of the Town Hall. The curtains were drawn, yet he felt certain someone had been watching him from up there.

He finished his pasties and drank the last of his water. It had already turned two o'clock and most of the shops had closed their shutters, people heading home for lunch. After the brief spike in activity, the square became quiet, deserted but for the odd person or two rushing off to get their midday meal. Cámara scrunched the wrappings into a tight ball and tossed them into a nearby litter bin, rinsed his mouth with water, and set off to have a wander. Nothing would be happening for the next hour or so, but he wanted to make certain of the first stage of his plan.

He took a street that meandered away from the far end of the square, heading up a slope that became steeper and narrower as he went along. He passed the simple sandstone facade of the church. It had large doors decorated with goldleaf. To the side, written in faded paint, were the names of local Francoist soldiers who had died during the Civil War of the 1930s. Elsewhere in the country such one-sided commemorations of the Civil War dead were being erased, or replaced with something more inclusive. Yet nothing like this had taken place in this village.

Cámara continued. The street was a cul-de-sac, with small, mostly whitewashed houses on either side. It could have been a pretty place, he thought, and perhaps indeed had been at some time in the past, yet every so often a newer, much uglier building had replaced a more traditional structure, leaving unsightly scars.

A narrow stone stairway led up the hill at the end of the street. He climbed to a tiny walled square next to a large building that might once have been a castle. From here he looked out over two valleys that converged where the village sat on an outcrop of rock. For a moment he allowed himself to be lost in the sweeping carpets of pine and holm oaks, the orange and grey streaks of rock on sheer cliff faces, the gushing waters of the river far below, where strips of land had been carved out of the valley floor for olive and almond groves. The air was clear and unhurried, the vistas spectacular. To his left, almost hidden by a curve in the valley, he could just make out Sunset. Further up the valley he imagined must be where the *Molino* was, with Jimmy and Estrella's farm over the other side, in the next valley.

A road took him down the hill on the other side of the square, curving round until it swept back in towards the village. On a parallel street to the first he found a mirador with mulberry trees providing ample shade over a bench. Interestingly the bench did not face the valley, but the street, and in particular the shuttered facade of a building that Cámara eyed with curiosity. He sat down on the bench and stared across at it. In blue letters that were almost invisible under the heavy coating of dust, was the word '*Fontaneros*'. What the remainder said was irrelevant. Cámara knew instantly that he had found what he was looking for.

Now all he had to do was sit and observe.

THIRTY-NINE

'Of course, if you can prove any of this, show documentary evidence, then we'll publish – no question. But as things stand it's just a theory. And a pretty crazy one at that.'

Alicia stared into her glass of wine, watching it swirl up the sides as she turned it slowly between her fingers. Then she lifted it to her lips and took another sip, enjoying the heavy, oaky taste lingering in her mouth as she looked her former colleague in the eye.

'I know,' she said. 'You're right.'

She shook her head.

'But it's not just a crazy theory. They've used Cabrera for this kind of thing in the past. There'll be a paper trail somewhere. And I think I know where I can find it.'

She watched as Quico Romero chewed on his last piece of chicken, swallowed and reached for his own glass. His beard had greyed in the three years since she last saw him, the few white hairs that had been sprouting at the sides now covering most of his chin, save for a small, dark V-shape beneath his lower lip. The tip of his nose had darkened in colour as well, moving from a simple scarlet to something more violet, with indentations on its bulbous surface, like a lunar landscape viewed through a purple haze of late sunset. She wondered about the glass of wine now in his hand, the urgency with which he had ordered a second bottle, and the amount he had already drunk that morning before they had met. His breath had given him away in the instant they had kissed each other on the cheeks.

Now he grinned at her in the professional, cynical, flashing way that he had. *El Diablo*, some at the office had called him, in an only partially endearing kind of way. An editor at a national newspaper had to be hard with his employees, had to push them to their limits. It was tough working in print media these days. Others had fallen by the wayside. Only a miracle and a dedication to bloody good reporting was keeping his publication going. Or so he claimed. Yet he stepped over the mark frequently; the drinking didn't help. The story about Marga was almost legendary, about the woman who had been fired for not showing up for work years back on some busy news day. When, later, she told Quico her absence had been due to her father's sudden death, he had brushed aside her excuse as lame and unacceptable. In his eyes loyalty to the paper outweighed even personal family grief.

Sitting across the lunch table now, Alicia wondered how much longer he could keep going. The booze, the stress, the anger, the long hours: he was looking so much older so very quickly.

He finished his wine with a gulp and reached for the

bottle to pour them both some more. Alicia pulled her glass away. He shrugged and helped himself.

'You get me the story, Alicia,' he said. 'Get it properly – paperwork, sworn affidavits, the works. And I promise you now we'll put you on the front page. And not just a one-off – probably for several days. This story – if it's true, and I'm not doubting your word, but until you can prove it I have to treat it as only a theory – this story will run and run. It will be picked up by everyone. And it will be my honour – and your honour – to break it.'

He raised his glass, leaned over the table and clinked it against Alicia's.

'That's worth a toast, I should say.'

Alicia nodded, lifting her glass from the table and gesturing towards him. 'Deal,' she said. 'I'm going to hold you to that.'

Quico grinned. 'You recording this?' he said.

'Something tells me I should be.'

'Don't worry. I'll be true to my word.'

They both drank, Alicia watching Quico closely; Quico cast his eyes up at the restaurant ceiling as he tipped his head back.

'Besides,' he said, putting his glass back down. 'I'm going to have to justify the expense of this lunch. And the bean-counters won't buy it if I put it down as simply catching up with a former employee. Someone who, I seem to remember, I actually fired.'

'I think the term is laid off,' said Alicia.

'Same difference. Still, I'd have you back in the blink of an eye if I could.'

She raised an inquisitive eyebrow. Quico shrugged.

'I don't know,' he said. 'The finances are still in a complete mess. But get me this story and . . .'

He raised his hands in a noncommittal gesture. Alicia nodded.

'OK,' she said. 'I get it.'

The waiter came and took away their empty plates. Neither of them wanted anything else to eat, so they ordered coffees. Quico wiped his mouth with the linen napkin and put on a more serious expression.

'You know,' he said, 'if this is true, what you've told me, all this Cabrera thing, the military, the history of the island, these bizarre connections with the *Reconquista* and the Moors, you should be watching your back. I hope you've been taking precautions.'

A chill passed down Alicia's spine. She thought of Marisol: had Alicia's name already been passed on? With a sense of dread she realised she had been betrayed by her own sense of invulnerability. Far from making her sensibly cautious, past experiences had left her foolish and open. Quico seemed to read the expression in her eyes.

'You *have* been careful, haven't you?'

She pulled a face. Quico understood and nodded.

'You've been out of the game for a while,' he said. 'It's understandable. It may not be too late, but you need to start now. This kind of thing is basic these days. One of the first things they teach kids when they study journalism.'

Her eyes widened.

'Oh yes,' he said. 'You and I are from a different generation, but it's no excuse. And remember' – he pointed down at the mobile phone on the table beside her – 'that thing can be your worst enemy.'

She picked up the phone and placed it guiltily in her bag.

'Whatever you do,' he said in a lowered voice, 'don't use

it for anything associated with this. In fact the best thing might be to ditch it.'

He fell silent as the waiter brought their coffees and placed them on the table. Quico picked his up.

'From now on,' he said, watching the waiter walk off again, 'you need to take it as read that they're on to you.'

He drank the coffee in one gulp and placed the cup back down with a clatter in its saucer.

'And be very, very careful.'

FORTY

Carlos's phone had barely begun to buzz when he pressed the button and brought it to his ear.

'Yes?'

'Ready to report, sir,' came a voice.

'Proceed,' said Carlos.

'The subject has finished lunch and is heading out on foot from the restaurant.'

Carlos quickly switched the phone to his other ear and pulled out a pen and piece of paper from the top drawer of his desk.

'Who did she have lunch with?' he said.

'We've just identified him, sir,' said the voice. 'It's Quico Romero, the editor of—'

'Yes, I know who Quico Romero is!' Carlos blurted out. 'Where is Romero now?'

His breath caught in his throat, chest hard like concrete. With something of a start he realised that he was losing his cool and slowly and deliberately forced his breathing further down into his abdomen, trying to loosen the tension. The pen pressed deep into the paper, leaving a dent in the wooden desktop beneath.

'Romero just left,' said the voice. 'Took a taxi.'

'Where to?'

'Presumably back to the newspaper offices, sir.'

'*Presumably?*' coughed Carlos. 'You mean you don't know?'

'Our orders were to shadow the Beneyto woman, sir. We don't have enough manpower to follow—'

'All right!' barked Carlos. 'Never mind. Beneyto is the key subject. She must on no account be lost. Is that understood?'

'Yes, sir.'

'What is she doing now?'

'She's . . .' The voice hesitated.

'Well?'

'She's just gone into a phone box.'

'What?'

'She's dialling a number, sir. Reading it off her mobile phone and punching the digits in on the public phone.'

Carlos closed his eyes, temporarily unable, once again, to breathe. He pressed two fingers against his temple.

'What do you want us to do, sir?' said the voice.

'Carry on as before,' said Carlos after a pause. 'But from now on with extra vigilance.'

'Sir?'

Carlos silently swore the most irreverent oath that he knew, cursing the imbecilic operative at the other end.

'She's on to us,' explained Carlos. 'She knows she's being tracked.'

FORTY-ONE

The phone box smelt stale and dusty. Alicia held the phone to her ear and heard it ring at the other end. There was a prickling feeling at the back of her head where she had an urgent desire for a second pair of eyes. After four rings, she heard a click.

'Hello?'

'Hello. Is that Marine Biology?'

'Just put you through.'

The line pipped for a few seconds as her call was transferred. Eventually a female voice answered.

'Marine Biology Department.'

'Hello,' said Alicia. 'I'm trying to get in touch with a friend who works there.'

'Sure. What's the name?'

'Ignacio Alberola.'

'You mean Nacho?' said the woman.

'That's right. Can I speak with him?'

The woman at the other end paused.

'Is there a problem?' asked Alicia.

'Nacho isn't here,' the woman said.

'Do you know when he'll be back?'

'Well . . . I don't know.'

'Could I leave a message?'

'Maybe,' said the woman. 'It's just that . . . We haven't seen him for a while. He's been in the Balearics. I can't say when I'd be able to give it to him.'

'Didn't he show up yesterday?' asked Alicia.

'Well he was meant to. But no one here saw him come in. And several of us were here till late.'

'Are you sure?'

'Yes, positive.'

Alicia shook her head.

'I saw him yesterday,' she said. 'In Valencia. He told me he was going straight there, to the department.'

'Well, he didn't show up.'

Alicia paused.

'And today?' she said. 'Any sign of him today?'

'We haven't seen him,' said the woman. 'I think someone tried his mobile, but there was no reply. Which is strange in Nacho – usually he's easily contactable. Perhaps you should try, yourself. You might have more luck.'

'Perhaps I'll do that,' said Alicia.

'What did you say your name was?' asked the woman. 'I can tell him you rang when he turns up.'

Alicia placed the phone firmly back in its place, pulling down heavily to make sure that the line was cut. She closed her eyes, blotting out thoughts of Nacho, where he was and what might have happened to him.

For a moment she stood motionless, willing an alertness

to come to her, a steady, sharp state of mind which, she now coldly realised, she was going to need. She was on a trajectory, and would need all her wits about her if it was going to have a different ending to the one intended for her.

There was no one she could turn to; she was alone.

She opened her eyes and stood up straight. On the wall of the phone box was a small map of the city centre with indications of the various public transport options. She allowed herself ten seconds to study it, refreshing her knowledge as quickly and thoroughly as she could. Then, without casting a second glance around her, she stepped out of the phone box.

At the second street on her left, she turned and walked purposefully, unhurriedly, towards the centre.

FORTY-TWO

The *Guardia Civil* office was on the outskirts of the village opposite a petrol station. Cámara sauntered over, watching for signs of life. The place appeared to be closed, but as he approached, he saw a squad car pull up outside, park in its designated spot, and an officer step out, jangling a bunch of keys. Cámara stepped through the door seconds after he'd opened it and entered.

A portrait of the King hung on the wall above a desk. Grey filing cabinets stood obediently in single file beneath a tall, barred window. Above his head, next to a bare light bulb, was a rotating fan covered in thick layers of dust.

'*Buenas tardes*,' the officer said stiffly on seeing Cámara. He looked to be in his fifties, with cropped grey hair and a grey moustache. The three red bars on his shoulder indicated his rank.

'Corporal Rodríguez?' Cámara asked.

The man looked at him with suspicion. Cámara took out

his ID and passed it across. 'The José Luis Mendoza case,' Cámara said. 'I've been looking into it.'

Rodríguez cocked his head and handed the ID back with a salute and a knowing look. There was no need to say anything, but he said it anyway.

'So they've sent a chief inspector.' His upper lip barely moved as he spoke, as though the weight of the moustache kept it immobile. 'Must be important.'

Cámara had had good relations with individual *Guardia Civil* officers in the past. Indeed, he had only been able to solve a number of investigations thanks to their help. Yet the professional rivalry between the two police forces was always an issue, something to be overcome on the occasions when their cases overlapped.

Rodríguez had no choice but to cooperate with the high-ranking police detective who had suddenly appeared in his office. Yet cooperation could take different forms. Cámara was alone in the sierra, operating in *Guardia Civil* territory. His investigation could only progress if he managed to get Rodríguez on his side.

'We all have to perform our duty, Corporal,' he said. 'Even when we don't want to. But that's what makes us who we are.'

Rodríguez stared.

'*Unos sacan las castañas del fuego*,' Cámara continued with a resigned grin, '*y otros se las comen*.' Some do all the hard work while others reap the reward.

Rodríguez nodded, and signalled to a chair on the other side of the desk. Yes, he would welcome this police officer for the time being. They all knew what it meant to be shat on by their superiors: he just hadn't expected something like this happening to men of Cámara's rank.

He sat down himself.

'So José Luis died at La Fé,' he said.

'Two days ago,' Cámara answered. 'I came up yesterday morning.'

Rodríguez gave him a look.

'Last night,' Cámara continued, 'someone tried to kill me.'

Rodríguez sat up straighter in his chair.

'I was shot at several times,' Cámara said. 'Near the *Molino*.'

He deliberately left out any mention of Jimmy.

'My suspicion,' he went on, as Rodríguez listened in silence, 'is that it was Bogdan and Dorin, the Romanian, er . . .' He paused. 'Plumbers.'

Rodríguez placed his hands together, as though in prayer, his moustache seeming to bristle under his nose.

'I know,' Cámara said, 'that they're both involved in the drug trade, and that they've been supplying Sunset for some time.'

Rodríguez shot him a glance.

'I have a theory,' said Cámara, 'but I'm still not certain why they would want me dead.'

'Can I ask you a question?' Rodríguez said.

Cámara nodded.

'Did you happen to come up here yesterday on a motorbike? I mean, an unmarked, private motorbike?'

'That's correct.'

Rodríguez sighed, nodding to himself.

'Well,' he said after a pause. 'Your information corroborates our own. Dorin and Bogdan are known drug dealers here, and the main source of their custom is – or certainly has been over the past few years – Sunset.'

'What kind of stuff are they dealing in?'

'Pretty much what you'd expect: cocaine, MDMA, ketamine.'

'Anything new?'

'The drug culture has been changing recently,' said Rodríguez, 'as I'm sure you know. The new stuff has been around for a while, but it's coming in greater quantities.'

'You're talking about methamphetamine,' said Cámara.

'And the others: GHB, mephedrone. I'm sure you don't need me to explain what they're being used for.'

Cámara shrugged.

'It's not for me to judge, and it's not my job to judge,' said Rodríguez. 'But these . . .' He paused. 'These sex orgies they have up there. Last for days on end. All fuelled by drugs. Ruining young men's lives.'

'Just men?'

'It's mostly a gay scene at Sunset,' Rodríguez said. 'But not exclusively. Women there as well. I mean, straight women. Prolonged bouts of casual sex with multiple partners, lowering their inhibitions, keeping themselves going with these new drug cocktails. And the risk of infection is growing. Not just from the sex, but they're injecting themselves with this stuff. It's like the eighties and nineties again. HIV rates haven't been this high for years.'

'Have you ever heard of pheromones used as part of these cocktails?'

Cámara detected a nervousness in Rodríguez's voice. He felt certain he was hiding something. The wedding band on the corporal's finger glimmered as he spun it around with his thumb.

'Haven't heard anything,' said Rodríguez. 'It's meant to make you sexually attractive, right? Perhaps they're using that as well.'

'Can you tell me more about the Romanians?' asked Cámara.

'The plumbing business is just a front,' Rodríguez said. 'Place is never open.'

'How are they laundering their money?'

'Through the grocery shop.'

'The one next to Los Arcos bar.'

'That's the one.'

'I was in there earlier,' said Cámara.

'There used to be three in the village,' said Rodríguez. 'But the others couldn't compete. It's run by the wives, but they used the drug money to buy supplies then sell the goods at reduced prices. The other two shops quickly closed down. Now they're the only grocer's left and they've recently started putting the prices up – created themselves a monopoly.'

Rodríguez shook his head.

'Was José Luis involved in the drug business himself?' Cámara asked.

'José Luis was very clever,' said Rodríguez. 'He kept himself completely apart from that side of things.'

Cámara remembered the collection of drugs that he'd found inside José Luis's apartments: not so separate, he thought, that he did not partake himself on occasion.

'The drugs are one of the attractions of the place, one of the main reasons why people go. They're not so readily available elsewhere. Although some of the other clubs are starting to follow the trend, and it's probably just a matter of time before they're as ubiquitous as cocaine and everything else.'

As the local *Guardia Civil* officer, it was clearly Rodríguez's job to know as much as he could about what went on in the village and the surrounding area, but Cámara was still surprised at how much detail the corporal appeared to have on what went on at Sunset.

'José Luis needed the drugs there in order to attract the clientele. And he needed to keep them concentrated at *Sunset* – not spreading to the other clubs – for as long as he could. That way he could make more money. But he didn't want any of this to be traceable directly to himself.'

'So he used cut-outs?'

'Exactly,' said Rodríguez.

'And one of them, I'm assuming, is Paco Jaén, the manager.'

'Paco is the hub,' said Rodríguez. 'The central man. Without him, it all falls apart.'

'And he deals directly with Dorin and Bogdan?'

'Probably,' said Rodríguez. 'Although I'm still not clear on that.'

Cámara thought about Paco, about how he had lied directly to his face about not knowing Bogdan and Dorin, the men in the BMW.

'I met Paco yesterday,' said Cámara. 'But there was no one else at Sunset apart from Abi and the old couple. I expected there to be more.'

'They'll have fled. As soon as they heard about José Luis. I'm surprised you even found Paco there, to be honest. Everyone will be keeping their heads down till they know what happens next.'

'Do you have any ideas in that respect? I met the mayor earlier today. He seemed quite concerned that Sunset might close down.'

Rodríguez shook his head.

'I heard talk once about José Luis having a nephew in

Madrid. But I've no idea what's happening to Sunset now. It was all about José Luis. He was one of those larger-than-life characters, made the place in his own image. Hard to imagine how it could carry on without him.'

'Just to get back to the Romanians,' said Cámara. 'Do they drive a BMW with tinted-glass windows?'

'That's their latest car,' said Rodríguez. 'They change fairly regularly, think it will put us off their scent.'

He grinned like a sly cat.

'But it never takes us very long to work out what they're driving. It's not as if they go for inconspicuous vehicles.'

'You see,' said Cámara, 'I think they may have tried to kill me more than once. You asked a minute ago about my motorbike.'

Rodríguez's moustache twitched.

'Relations haven't been good recently with Paco,' he said.

Again, Cámara was impressed by how much the corporal knew. He could only assume that he hadn't put Dorin and Bogdan away for lack of evidence to convict them.

'The Romanians are essentially middlemen,' Rodríguez continued. 'They're supplying stuff sold to them by a gang operating down on the coast. It's a common modus operandi.'

'So what happened?'

'The guys on the coast find someone locally to supply their drugs. They watch how things go for a while, perhaps a few months or even a few years. They're clever. Then, if they see a market begin to take off, they move in themselves, undercutting their own middleman and eventually running him out of business.'

'And this was starting to happen here?'

Rodríguez nodded.

'About a week ago. Made Dorin and Bogdan very twitchy. That BMW they've got is the second new car in ten days. It was clear something was up. And then there were rumours of new people appearing in the village, strangers . . .'

He looked Cámara in the eye.

'One of them was reported to have come up on a motorbike, a man about fifty years old, the kind who could look after himself.'

He shrugged.

'Never saw him myself, but . . .'

Cámara smiled.

'I've been mistaken for several things in my life,' he said. 'But never a drug dealer before.'

FORTY-THREE

'Listen,' said Cámara. 'Dorin and Bogdan still don't know who I am. I want you to arrange a meeting with them.'

Corporal Rodríguez leaned back in his chair, scratching his chin with a sudden urgency.

'With all due respect,' he said at length. 'I think that would be a bad idea.'

'I'd like you to do it nonetheless,' insisted Cámara. 'Is it possible?'

Rodríguez pushed out his chest. 'Well of course it's possible,' he said.

'Good,' said Cámara. 'Then I'd like you to get a message to them. I don't care how. Tell them to meet me at their plumber's office tonight. Tell them . . .' he paused. 'Tell them the suppliers are prepared to talk.'

Rodríguez tapped his finger nervously on the desk.

'If you wouldn't mind,' added Cámara.

'It's not that,' said the corporal. 'It's just . . . I'm wondering about the protocol here. Is this still a *Policía Nacional* case? Or is the *Guardia Civil* now officially collaborating in the investigation, taking its share of the responsibility?'

Cámara understood: there would be forms to fill in, reports to be done, costings and justifications for each step that the corporal made. Such matters were time-consuming enough when operating alone or simply within the confines of the *Guardia Civil*. Coming in like this on a *Policía Nacional* case meant the amount of paperwork would be tripled at least. Which only made sense if, in the event of a happy conclusion, Rodríguez could put it down as a *Guardia Civil* success. The pay-off had to justify the expense of energy and resources. Cámara had made a connection with Rodríguez on the basis that they were both foot soldiers of a kind – in spite of his rank. He could not break that common bond now.

'I'm happy to go along with whatever makes this feasible from your point of view,' he said.

Rodríguez nodded: it was the answer he'd been hoping for.

'Just one thing,' he said. 'I'm assuming no one saw you coming here? Otherwise your cover story might already be blown.'

Cámara frowned.

'I was careful,' he said. 'No one followed me, as far as I know. Except maybe the man at the petrol station.'

'We don't have to worry about him,' said Rodríguez. 'He works for me.'

'One thing,' said Cámara. 'How come you've never put any of these people away – Bogdan, Dorin . . . ?'

Rodríguez gave a mirthless laugh.

'We know almost everything,' he said, 'but still need hard

evidence to convict. We don't know where or how they drop the drugs, despite putting them under surveillance. Must be somewhere in or around the village, but Paco and the Romanians never meet.'

He shrugged.

'A mystery.'

Rodríguez got up to leave. It was almost six o'clock. Behind him, Cámara noticed a steel cabinet with a heavy lock on it.

'Armoury?' he asked.

Rodríguez glanced back.

'The usual. Nothing special. Why?'

'I'll explain later,' said Cámara.

Rodríguez slipped his cap on and headed towards the door.

'I'll lock this behind me,' he said. 'As far as the outside world is concerned, there's no one inside and I'm off on my evening patrol.'

Cámara nodded: there was an interesting change in the man now that he knew this was a *Guardia Civil* case: not quite so deferential to the high-ranking *Policía Nacional* officer, more of an equal.

'I shan't move,' Cámara said.

Rodríguez clicked off the light and closed the door behind him, turning the key in the lock twice to secure the bolt.

A few minutes passed in silence, the light inside the office gradually dimming. Cámara felt a buzzing in his pocket and pulled out his mobile phone.

The number on the screen was unrecognised. He pressed the green button and pulled the phone to his ear.

'Chief Inspector,' said a voice that Cámara failed to recognise at first. 'It's Azcárraga.'

'*Hombre*,' said Cámara, surprised.

'Can you talk?' said Azcárraga.

'Yes, now's good.'

'OK, it's just that there are some rumours going around. Wasn't sure if you were still on this case.'

'Until you hear otherwise directly from me,' said Cámara, 'assume that I'm still in charge of the investigation.'

'Right, right.'

'So what have you got?'

'I went to the judge you mentioned,' said Azcárraga. 'Judge Jurado. He totally cooperated, as you said.'

'Good. So you got the warrant?'

'Yes.'

'And have you been able to run a trace on the call?'

'Yes.'

'So,' said Cámara. 'What did you find?'

'I've got a name,' said Azcárraga. 'But that's it. I'm really sorry. I haven't been able to do anything else yet. Things are pretty hectic here today.'

'Don't worry,' said Cámara. 'That's great. Who was it, then?'

'The line is in the name of someone called José Montesinos.'

'He made the call?'

'Well, it was made from a line in his name. That's it, all I've got.'

'It's a start,' said Cámara.

'Does it mean anything?' asked Azcárraga.

'Not at the moment.'

'I've . . . I've really got to go,' said Azcárraga. 'I'm on a cigarette break. And they're actually timing them these days. Can you believe that?'

'Yes,' said Cámara. 'Unfortunately I can.'

Azcárraga rang off. Cámara put the phone down on the desk in front of him. Almost as soon as he did so, the bolt on the door clicked and Corporal Rodríguez came back in. He closed the door behind him before walking over to the desk and speaking to Cámara in a low voice.

'The message has been relayed,' he said. 'I can't guarantee they'll show, however.'

'What do you think?' asked Cámara.

'I don't . . .' began Rodríguez.

'What does your instinct tell you?'

Rodríguez looked surprised. Cámara guessed that no superior had ever talked to him like this before.

'I think they'll show up,' he said. 'And I think you're putting yourself in danger.'

'I shall go alone,' said Cámara. 'I have yet to report back to the Jefatura. As far as the *Policía Nacional* know, none of this is happening. Should anything go wrong – and it won't – but should things go badly, then there's nothing to stop you saying you had no part in it and that some maverick *Policía Nacional* officer got his fingers burnt up here while working on his own. That he got what he deserved. You get me?'

Rodríguez nodded reluctantly. This was not the *Guardia Civil* way of doing things, but the man had seen enough service, Cámara guessed, to know that sometimes breaking standard procedure was the only way to get things done.

'I said midnight,' Rodríguez said. 'Things will be quiet by then. The village mostly closes down by about eleven o'clock.'

'Good,' said Cámara. 'I'll wait here.'

'There's a camp bed,' said Rodríguez. 'And some bottles of water. I'll be back later.'

'I'll be fine,' said Cámara.

He seemed to know that the call was coming in seconds before his phone buzzed again. He picked it up quickly and answered.

'Hello, chief,' said Torres at the other end. 'Did you get my messages?'

'Not until this morning.'

'What?'

'I'll explain later.'

'Dodgy signal in the sierra?'

'Something like that. Are you near a computer?'

'Funny you should mention that.'

'Good. Can you look some things up for me?'

'I'll do it right now,' said Torres. 'There's no one around. They've all gone off to a drinks party. Arranged some time ago. I wasn't invited.'

'Nice.'

'Better this way. So what is it you want me to look up?'

Cámara gave him the names of the Romanians, mentioning their connection with the drug gang operating on the coast.

'Well, I can tell you quite a bit about the coastal gang without checking the computer,' said Torres. 'One of the biggest groups in the region.'

'OK,' Cámara. 'What's their makeup?'

'Colombians at the top, dealing with the suppliers on the other side of the Atlantic. Most of the others are locals, but they're sometimes known as the Colombians because of where the stuff's coming from.'

'Are they still shipping everything over from Colombia?'

'Well, the cocaine, obviously via Venezuala. But they're expanding, producing their own stuff here, on site. These new chemical drugs. Got various labs dotted about.'

'I'm aware of them.'

'It's a big operation,' said Torres. 'Got lots of different offshoots, like an octopus, as you can imagine. And they're a bit cleverer than the usual types. Dress well, but not too flash. They work a lot on image, know how to appear invisible. Respectable, middle class. No cars worth more than a certain amount – absolutely no Mercedes or SUVs. You're more likely to see them in a Skoda or a Renault.'

'Or on a motorbike?'

'That's the kind of thing. Not a biker in leathers, but a guy wearing a jacket, perhaps the kind who commutes to work on a bike. You know the kind of thing. A bit like you.'

'Thanks.'

There was a pause: Torres seemed to have guessed what this might be about.

'A couple of things might be useful,' he said. 'These guys always refer to their drugs as *material* – that's their jargon.'

'OK,' said Cámara. 'And specific names for each narcotic?'

Torres listed off the code words for each drug they sold.

'OK, that's probably enough,' said Cámara.

'So these Romanians you mentioned,' said Torres.

He tapped on the keyboard while Cámara waited. Then he clicked his tongue.

'Not the kind of guys you'd want to meet in a dark alley,' he said. 'Suspected of drug dealing – nothing proved yet, but they've been under surveillance in the past, according to this. *Guardia Civil* keep a file on them.'

'Anything else?'

'Moved to Spain eight years ago with their wives. No children as far as I can see.'

'What did they do back in Romania?'

'There's something here about a boxing gym . . .' he paused. 'Wait, there's something more here, in the *Guardia Civil* notes. Looks like Dorin and Bogdan pump themselves up with drugs before carrying out acts of violence. There was a case of assault two years back against a man called Enrique Fuster Polo.'

'Not Enrique?' said Cámara. 'Got a place up here?'

'You know him?'

'We met. What happened?'

'No charges. But they made quite a mess of him. Left a scar down one side of his face. Old guy.'

'That's it. Anything else? A motive?'

'Nothing. Sorry. Just that the two were suspected of carrying out the assault when they were high on some drug or other.'

Cámara let out a sigh.

'You sure you know what you're doing, chief?' said Torres.

FORTY-FOUR

She's on Carretas, heading towards Sol.

This is Carlos speaking. Do you hear me?

Yes, sir.

Who am I speaking to?

Number 1, sir.

Are you the team commander?

Yes, sir. But there are only two of us, sir.

You will both be taking direct orders from me. The subject is extremely valuable. She must on no account be lost. Do you understand?

Affirmative.

I'll be listening the entire time. I want regular updates. This is top priority.

I understand.

Who else is with you?

Number 2.

Does he have an earpiece?

Yes, sir.

Number 2, do you copy?

Hearing you clearly, sir.

A female, I hear.

Yes, sir.

Good. You are both fully briefed and aware of the situation. Now carry on.

Yes, sir.

Yes, sir.

Where is she now?

Just entering Sol.

Fewer shops in the centre of Madrid closed at lunchtime now, staying open through the hotter hours of the day, but shoppers themselves – at least of the local kind – still obeyed the old rhythms and as Alicia came out into the open space of the Plaza Puerta del Sol she noticed with a certain relief that the afternoon rush was in full flow. The area was more pedestrianised these days – in the past the streaming cars had been even more of a threat than the pickpockets and hustlers who made it their theatre of operations – and she was able to cross over towards the statue of Carlos III with relative ease, skipping behind a passing taxi and throwing her handbag over her shoulder. It felt warm and the top of her brow prickled with beading sweat. The air conditioning of the restaurant was already a distant memory, the safety of lunch with Quico like a quickly disappearing island dropping behind the horizon astern. She was in far choppier waters now, with an unknown and unseen foe almost certainly in pursuit. Surviving, and reaching her final destination, would require her to employ full awareness and clean instinct.

The shop window of a chain store on the far side of the square caught her eye. Barely changing her course, she made for it, wending her way through the thickening crowds.

Has crossed the square. Handbag thrown over her shoulder.

I have eyes on her.

Heading towards north side.

How is she walking?

Come again, sir?

Describe her way of walking. Is it fast? Slow? Give me more information.

I'd say it's . . .

Meandering, sir. Normal. Neither fast nor slow. Typical shopper.

OK. Where is she heading?

Towards the Cortefiel store.

Is she going inside?

She's . . . She's standing outside, looking in the window.

Alicia stared patiently at the window. The mannequins on the other side were only partially visible with the sunlight reflecting on the glass, but she didn't mind. She wasn't really interested. At least not today. Behind her, in the mirror image, she could clearly see the tobacconist's kiosk that she had just walked past. And she wondered about popping back to buy a pack of cigarettes: an urge to smoke was growing in her. In fact, a younger woman was purchasing some now. A woman with short light brown hair and a black leather jacket with a double front – like a motorcyclist's. It was surprising that tobacconists could survive these days, with the number of people giving up.

How much longer, she wondered, before they all closed for good?

She glanced up and a sign caught her eye. Not thinking twice, she stepped in through the shop door and headed for the first floor.

She's in.

I'm on it.

Wait!

What?

She's heading upstairs. You can't go there.

Oh, shit.

What is it? What's going on?

Number 2's right, sir.

What?

It's the lingerie section. I'll stick out, she'll notice me.

Number 2! Get in there!

Yes, sir. Going in now.

I'll be outside.

Alicia was greeted at the top of the escalator by a faceless, tall and unnaturally thin mannequin dressed in purple knickers and bra with white lace edging, one knee bent inward slightly to emphasise the curve of her hip. Alicia stepped past a pair of teenage girls standing at the edge of the bikini rail and headed down the aisle to the far end, where packets of tights in numerous shades and sizes hung from metal pegs attached to the wall. Less eye-catching merchandise, perhaps, but possibly one of the bestsellers. It was odd that they should place that particular section in a far corner, but it suited her. An elderly woman – a widow, judging by her black dress – walked away dragging a shopping trolley as Alicia approached, padding carefully to the counter near the top of the escalator to pay. Alicia watched as the escalator brought up two new shoppers: a dark-skinned woman wearing a necklace with large, brightly coloured beads and a man in a beige jacket holding her hand and with a look of tension around his jaw.

Alicia turned her attention back to the tights. There was nothing there that she needed, or even wanted. A window looking back out on to the square was just to her right, the sunlight partially blocked by a dark plastic coating on the glass. Would she be visible from outside? She glanced out at the tobacconist's kiosk. The woman in the black leather jacket had gone.

She's on the move.

Got it. I'm on her. Heading east across the square.

I'm leaving the shop now.

Stay behind me. Don't get too close. Did she see you?

No. Definitely not.

Stay with her and keep the chat between you to a minimum. You'll give yourselves away.

Yes, sir.

What's her current position?

Turning left up Montera.

How's it looking?

Very busy.

Alicia threaded her way through the crowds, hauling her handbag back on to her shoulder to make herself larger, something for the scores of people coming towards her to avoid. The press of bodies squeezed in. She felt caught in a tightening storm. An instinct told her to bring her bag round to her front again, hold it against her chest like a shield. But as she pulled on the handle, it caught momentarily, would not budge.

She turned swiftly on her heel. The pickpocket was lightning quick, immediately pulling her empty hand out of the gap where she had opened the zip. But she was not fast enough to dissimulate entirely: Alicia had caught her off guard and she stared with bulging eyes. Alicia shoved her away. The woman stumbled backwards with an expression of manufactured outrage.

'HEY! HEY!'

Alicia didn't stop to listen. She glanced quickly around then spun on her heel once more, bag squeezed tight around her belly.

Shit!

What happened?

A pickpocket. Some woman just tried to put her hand in her bag.

Did she steal anything?

I don't know. Don't think so. Couldn't see.

What's happening now?

She pushed the woman off and is carrying on. But . . .

What?

I think she saw me.

Saw you?

When she turned round to push the pickpocket away. I think she caught sight of me before turning back again.

Are you sure?

Not positive.

Where's Number 2?

Coming up behind, sir.

Number 1, you fall back. Number 2, take the front position.

Yes, sir.

For Christ's sake! Do your job. I shouldn't even have to be telling you this!

Two sets of eyes had been staring at her. She hadn't just caught the pickpocket by surprise – someone else had been looking intently when she spun round. And not at the suddenness of her action. The pickpocket had betrayed a look of surprise, but that second pair of eyes had had a different expression: one of steely keenness.

It had all happened quickly, and she hadn't managed to take in the face that went with them, but the eyes had been registered.

It was enough to confirm what her instinct already knew. And the certainty brought both a chill and greater clarity. Keep going, she told herself. Stick to this route, the plan that had formed inside the phone box. The urgency of what she needed to do was greater than ever.

Number 2, do you have eyes on the subject?

Yes, sir. Just coming up now.

What's happening?

She's stopped. In the middle of the street. She's got her hand in her bag, looks like she's rummaging around for something.

Her phone? Perhaps someone's calling her.

Thank you Number 1. We're monitoring her phone live here. No incoming calls at present.

Right, sir.

She's on the move again.

OK. Did she take anything out of her bag?

Negative. Just rummaged inside and is now continuing up towards Gran Vía. Can't see anything in her hands apart from her bag.

Right. Keep on her. And keep out of sight.

She's reached Gran Vía. She's turning left.

Stay with her. Number 1, you get up there as well, but keep well back. We can't have her seeing you again.

Yes, sir.

Edging along the pavement, trying not to get knocked into the bus lane by the crowds, she allowed herself a half-smile. She hated shopping: it was one of the things that Max said he loved most about her. Now she had to pretend to be as interested as everyone else in the stuff on sale, an endless array of things – clothes, mostly; she felt sure there used to be a greater variety of shops not so long ago.

On the other side of the street she caught sight of a familiar sign. At the crossing she waited for the light to turn green, aware of the bodies closing in around her. The light changed. She walked. The shop grew larger before her, wide open doors, windows on either side.

Thank God for reflections, she thought as she cast a quick glance towards the shop front before passing inside, through the cool shower of icy air conditioning.

She's gone into Zara.

Copy. Get in there.

I'll be outside.

Good.

Can you hear me?

Loud and clear.

I'm inside. She's crossing the shop, heading towards a rack of T-shirts.

What are you wearing?

Sir?

I said, What—

A pair of jeans, blue trainers, cream top, jacket . . .

Take your jacket off.

Sir?

Have you changed your appearance since you started tailing her?

No.

Then take off your jacket. She may have spotted you earlier.

Yes, sir.

For God's sake.

Jacket removed.

Congratulations. Now, what is the subject doing?

She's at the counter.

Buying something?

Yes, I think so.

What is she buying?

Can't see. She's got her back to me. She must have picked something up while I was taking my jacket—

Get in there now and find out what it is!

Can't, sir.

What?

Too late. She's paid and is heading for the—

Number 2? . . . Number 2?

Number 1 here, sir. I see her. Leaving the shop now.

Where's Number 2?

Don't know, sir. Do you want me to check in on her?

For Christ's sake, no, man. Stay with the subject!

Yes, sir.

Number 2?

Here, sir.

What happened?

Had to break communications. Subject brushed past me.

She what?

Shop's a bit crowded. She bumped into me to get through to the exit.

She pushed you over?

Not exactly. I stayed on my feet. But I dropped my jacket.

What?

She picked it up and handed it to me.

Do you think . . . ?

Barely even looked at me, sir. Just gave me back my jacket and sped out the door.

Oh, for Christ's sake.

I'm sure she hadn't seen me before.

Maybe not. But she'll recognise you if she sees you again.

She's getting in a taxi, sir!

Number 1?

In a taxi heading east.

Get after her now!

But what if she sees us?

It doesn't matter. Just follow her. I need to know where she's going!

So there were two of them. The woman had taken the jacket off, but Alicia knew at once it was the same one she had seen before – twice before and both times in reflection:

at the tobacconist's and then behind her as she crossed to go into Zara. And despite having taken it off, perhaps to disguise her appearance, it was definitely her, definitely the same jacket. Alicia had contrived to bang into her a little too hard, made the woman stumble. When the jacket fell to the floor it took just an instant to pick it up and hand it back. And although it was turned inside out, she felt the smooth leather against her fingers, knew at once who the woman was, what she was doing.

And the taxi seemed to float effortlessly towards her as she stepped back out into the street. As though he had been waiting for her. So she had got in. Given an address for him to drive to.

And he was looking at her through the mirror. Was he working for them as well?

I'm in a taxi. We're tailing. She's three taxis ahead.

Number 2, where are you?

I'm getting in a taxi myself.

Good. Number 1, have you got the licence number of the taxi she got into?

Negative. Didn't have time.

Where are you now?

Crawling down Gran Vía. Traffic's terrible, very slow.

Well that can work to our advantage. Just make sure you don't lose her.

It was slow. Way too slow. If she'd managed to give them the slip they were almost certainly back on to her now. Assuming that the man behind the wheel wasn't one of them as well. She avoided his gaze, trying to disguise her annoyance. What had got into her head, getting into a taxi like that? With traffic at a virtual standstill? Just following instinct. But her instinct appeared to have let her down. Should she tell the driver to stop and make a dash for it now? Perhaps there was still time. But where could she go?

She closed her eyes and thought back to the map of the city centre on the wall of the phone box, and the plan that had formed in her mind then. Tracing steps and lines across the city in a giant spider's web. It could still work.

She opened her eyes. The taxi had fed on to Alcalá and was picking up speed as it headed past the Banco de España building.

'Atocha!' she called out as they reached the junction. 'I've changed my mind. Take me to Atocha.'

The driver swung the wheel to the right and they slipped through the traffic lights just as they turned red. The driver glared at her through the mirror. She ignored him.

They've turned down Paseo del Prado, heading south.

Are you with them?

Negative. They shot through the lights.

Did you get the licence plate?

GPE9284. Mercedes. Didn't catch the model.

Have we got backup?

No, sir. Just myself and Number 2.

Get after her. Just fucking get after her!

'Plaza or station?'

'What?'

'Do you want Plaza Atocha? Or the train station?'

Alicia thought for a second.

'The square,' she said. 'Drop me by the Bar El Brillante.'

The traffic was more fluid here, if not quite as fast as she would have wanted. She noticed with some relief that they had passed through the traffic lights just as they were changing. Her tail might be thrown off.

But for long enough?

She resisted the temptation to look back through the window, but could almost sense the wall of cars coming in behind them. Would one of them contain her pursuer?

She took the money out of her purse and had it ready to hand over. She opened the door before they came to a full stop.

'Hey! Watch out.'

She thrust the money in his hand without waiting for the change, then darted out into the street in front of the taxi as the last pedestrians on the crossing were hurrying over. She felt the bow-wave of air from a beer truck as it swung centimetres from her shoulder, pressing herself into the sea of commuters as they huddled on the far side, waiting to get through and down towards the station building.

Lots of people, lots of bodies, all in a hurry. This was good. She could lose herself. Lose them.

Number 1, report in. What is your position?

Atocha Square, sir. Making chase.

Have you located the subject?

No eyes on her yet, sir, but I know where she's headed.

Explain.

Found the taxi, sir. The one she was in. She'd already left. Driver was counting his money, about to leave. Said I was her husband. He told me which way she went.

Which is?

Atocha station, sir. That's where I am now, just heading inside. Assume she's catching a train to Valencia.

Possibly. But make no assumptions. Do you have eyes on her?

Negative.

Number 2, report.

Pulling into Atocha Square now.

Proceed to the station and wait for instructions.

Understood.

She walked through the atrium towards the platforms. The place was so much busier than the previous night. She fed into a stream of commuters stepping through the glass doors at the far end and turned to the left, past coffee stalls and newsagents. Should she stop, perhaps browse for a magazine? Watch for anyone holding back to stay with her? Perhaps see those eyes again, the ones that had been staring back on Montera. She doubted the woman with the black leather jacket would make a return. But there would almost certainly be others. Not just two. Unless money was *really* tight.

Something told her to continue, allow herself to be carried along by the crowd. At the end the passageway opened into a large hall. The trains were over on her right. In front, just a little further on, was the metro station.

She fed into the crowd pushing forwards. At the turnstile she pushed in quickly behind someone else. No time to buy a ticket. But the small eyes of security cameras peering out from a high corner told her to remain on her guard.

She carried on, taking the escalator down, joining the flow of those in a greater hurry, walking instead of allowing themselves to be carried by the great turning machine. At the bottom she got on the platform for trains heading south towards Congosto. And waited.

Number 1, listen. She's not on the passenger list for any trains heading for Valencia. Or anywhere else. She is not, repeat not, getting on any train.

Understood. I've got eyes on her now, sir.

Where is she?

In the metro station, heading down to the platform.

Follow her, man.

But sir, we'll lose the radio connection. It's too far below ground.

Just do what I say! Keep eyes on her at all times.

Yes, sir. Heading down now, sir.

Number 2, come in.

Yes, sir.

Where are you?

By the taxi rank outside the station.

Get inside the building now and head towards the metro station. Report when you get there.

The train came. The commuters crushed their way in. Alicia was one of the last, pressing herself into the tiniest gap just within the door space, her back to the mass of people, facing out. She had a clear line of sight up and down the platform. Others were already mingling, deciding to catch the next train, hoping for more space. She glanced at them, examining their faces: two Moroccans; a huddle of young men in shiny, overpriced suits; a woman wearing brightly coloured, tight-fitting Lycra. She was in conversation with a balding man in his forties; he was . . . what? Trying to chat her up? Here on the platform in the middle of rush hour? Alicia sniffed with a kind of admiration. The woman in Lycra was not interested, ignoring him, but already there was little room on the platform for her to walk away. Alicia glanced further up the platform, then back again. What was holding the train up? The Lycra woman was still there, but now the balding man had gone. Alicia scanned the other commuters, trying to see him. A movement to her left caught her attention, down at the other doors into her carriage: someone squeezing in to the annoyance of the other passengers. She stood up on tiptoe to see just as the doors hissed and began to close. Over the tops of the commuters she could just make out the bald head. And the eyes. The eyes from Calle Montera. The eyes that had been staring at her from behind the pickpocket.

Her foot shot out as the doors closed, catching them where they met. She thrust out both hands and heaved with all her strength, pushing through the tiny gap, smearing her face against the black rubber edges.

'Hey!'

'Careful.'

'What are you doing?'

She was on the platform, but her bag was still stuck in the door. She could hear beeping, an alarm of some kind. She felt a pair of hands reach out. With a final heave she pulled on the bag. And the train shunted into motion.

She looked up. The woman in Lycra had a concerned expression on her face.

'You all right?' she said. 'Too many people? Know how you feel.'

'Thanks,' said Alicia. 'Thanks for helping.'

She glanced up and down the platform quickly. There was no sign of the balding man.

'Thanks,' she repeated. 'I must get going. Just remembered something.'

And she hurried away.

Number 2, report in.

Just reaching the metro entrance now.

We've got a live feed at this end of the security camera footage. Scanning it now for when the subject entered. Do you remember what she was wearing?

Black jeans, red-and-white striped top and a light, off-white coloured cotton jacket.

The bag?

Large, some kind of woven material. Striped – light and dark brown. Leather handle.

Shoes?

Didn't catch sight of them.

Never mind. That's enough. We're scanning the footage for her now, checking the other cameras along the Line 1 stations. Number 1 will be reporting back as soon as his radio signal returns.

Yes, sir. No sign of her here.

Alicia walked off the platform taking quick glances to either side. No one seemed to notice her as she pressed against the flow of fresh commuters and made her way back to the bottom of the escalators. At the side was a round structural column with a tiny gap behind. She fought her way across and squeezed in. Looking up over the heads of the crowds of people streaming past, she could make out no security cameras. Satisfied that she was not being watched, she took off her jacket and fished into her bag from Zara for the top she had bought. Then, as quickly as she could, she pulled off her striped top, stuffed it into the Zara bag, and put on the new top: it was simple, a chocolate brown, made of light, matt cotton. Nothing too eye catching. Yet it also had a loose piece of cloth around the shoulders, like a shawl, something which she could, if she chose, drape over her hair, like a veil.

She looked into her bag. From her purse she could fit her money and cards into her trouser pockets. Other things – tissues, a long-forgotten packet of chewing gum, a small torch for emergencies – could all be left behind. She squeezed a number of keys into another trouser pocket. Then there was her phone and the charger. No better time, she thought, to get rid of it. After pressing a few buttons she made certain that all her contacts and information were stored on the SIM card, then she switched it off, took the SIM out and pushed it back into her pocket. For a second she thought about smashing the phone as though it, rather than her own carelessness, had betrayed her. But she held back, simply letting it drop. After one last glance inside, she let the bag slump on to the floor. A shame: she had liked it.

She stood in her little space, watching the people coming and going. And waited.

Number 1 reporting.

We hear you. What is your position?

I lost her.

What?

In Atocha. She got off the train just as the doors were closing. It was too late. I couldn't get out.

Which train?

It left just a few minutes ago. Line 1 heading south.

We'll find the footage.

I got off at Menéndez Pelayo, came straight up to re-establish radio connection.

Get back down and catch the next train back to Atocha.

Understood.

Number 2.

Sir?

Have you seen the subject come up from the platform?

Negative.

Then get downstairs immediately. We need eyes on her.

On my way.

We've got live feed of all the Atocha security cameras here. Between us we'll find her.

It was the same woman, this time with her leather jacket back on. She was turning this way and that, standing on tiptoe to peer above the heads of the commuters. Alicia slid further into her corner and watched as her tail crossed the central reserve between the two platforms, carefully looking at almost every person there, an expression of frustration on her face. She took several seconds to scan the area, but although Alicia could see her, she was shielded from view by a new wave of travellers pouring in from a recently arrived train. When the woman peeled off to inspect the platform, Alicia took her chance and slipped out into the flow of people, stepping on to the escalator and rising up towards the top.

With a simple movement of her hand, she pulled the shawl from around her shoulders and brought it over her hair, keeping her gaze fixed firmly on the floor.

Number 2, report . . . Number 2, can you hear me? Report in. I can't believe this. Where the hell has that woman got to? Number 2! Number—

Number 2 here, sir.

What's going on?

Lost her, sir.

What?

No sign of her.

That can't be!

I've checked everywhere, sir. Even the toilets, the tunnel entrances. She's not here.

That's impossible. She must be there. We've checked the footage at this end. She hasn't left the station. Go back and find her. Liaise with Number 1. We must find her at all costs!

And if, I mean, when we do find her, sir?

. . .

Sir?

End it.

Out through the glass doors again and into the open air. It was properly dark, now, easier to walk the streets without being seen. The street lighting was less intense in Madrid than in Valencia. All that lobbying about light pollution. It had its advantages.

She headed up across the square towards the Retiro park, where the streets were shaded by mature trees, and even darker. There she would find a spot to sit, to rest, and to make certain she was on her own.

And then, only when she was sure, she would move on to her destination. She had about another hour. The timing was just right.

FORTY-FIVE

The shutters at the Romanians' plumbing shop had been partly raised – enough to see the glass door behind them. No lights were switched on but it was a sign that they were there and expecting him. Cámara stood in the little mirador opposite, underneath the mulberry tree, listening for any sounds, his eyes adjusting to the darkness. He had taken up Corporal Rodríguez's offer of the camp bed, but had been unable to doze off, instead lying silently with his eyes closed, trying – and largely failing – not to think. Rodríguez had returned and offered him something to eat, but Cámara refused, only drinking water from the bottles and getting up once or twice to use the toilet next to the single cell at the back of the building. When the time came, Rodríguez helped him prepare, then led him out a side door so as not to be seen. He wanted to come with Cámara, act as backup, but Cámara refused. The more people involved, the greater the risk to his plan. And although he trusted Rodríguez to a degree, he could not vouch for him: the wrong move at the wrong time could prove disastrous.

At the last minute, just as they were leaving, Rodríguez pulled a listening device out of a drawer: a tiny wire with a microphone and a battery pack.

'Just a suggestion,' he said.

Cámara thought for a second, then nodded. He slipped off his shirt and they stuck it to his chest with a piece of tape. Once he was dressed, they tested it, his voice and movements clearly audible on the office receiver.

'I'll be recording everything,' said Rodríguez.

Now, as Cámara stared at the open shutter, choosing his moment to go in, he could feel the wire nestling in his chest hairs, rubbing against his skin. It felt like a parasite living off his flesh, one that could endanger the life of its host.

It had gone midnight, and the village was silent and asleep. Unlike the city, this was a community of early risers, people whose rhythms were dictated by the land and their animals. The only sign of life was a single street lamp fifty metres away, staring at the ground like a Cyclops, with the bright flickering of insects darting about the light beaming from its singular eye.

Cámara took one last, long breath and stepped forwards.

The shutters were stiff, wouldn't rise any higher. He bent almost double to get under them, then pushed against the door. It yielded instantly, swinging open silently into darkness.

Cámara hesitated. He sensed, rather than saw, other people inside: a warmth from their bodies; a crackling, almost electrical spark in the air, and a smell that he recognised but could not identify.

'Step inside,' said a man. 'And close the door behind you.'

The sound of the voice gave Cámara a rough location and distance for at least one of them: somewhere on the opposite side of the room, several metres away, certainly beyond striking distance. The voice was deep and steady; he tried to detect any signal that its owner might be drugged – a sharpness, perhaps, or acceleration in speech – but could sense none. So much for the first one, but the second would also be present somewhere, perhaps much closer, ready to land a blow, and he had to proceed cautiously.

He took a quick step inside, closed the door audibly behind him, then slipped as silently as he could to his left, crouching low, pressing his knuckles against the gritty cement floor and scrambling several metres to the side.

There was a crash, the sound of cracking glass, followed instantly by a stifled, urgent grunt of pain. Cámara heard mumbled, angry words, oaths sworn in a language he did not understand. He dashed several more metres away from the door, using the backs of his hands to feel his way in the dark, trying to avoid a second attempt to knock him out.

He heard heavy footsteps, the sound of someone being pushed to the ground, and the door being opened. Then the shutters were pulled down, the door closed again and the lights inside were switched on. In an instant, Cámara raised both his hands.

The Romanians were by the door. One, the larger of the two, was on the floor, lying on his side and nursing his hand, which had blood pouring down the back from a wound. The other, slightly smaller than the first but no less menacing in appearance and stature, was on his feet, one hand on the light switch on the wall next to a crucifix, the other nestling a revolver which he was waving about, trying to locate Cámara in the room. As soon as he spotted him he raised the gun and held it with outstretched arm, fingers tensing as though about to pull the trigger. And then he saw, his eyes widening at first, mouth opening with fear and surprise. Eventually his hand dropped.

'What?' he said. 'What are you doing?'

The larger of the two glanced up from the floor, saw what was happening, and quickly forgot his injured knuckles, hauling himself quickly to his feet.

Cámara's hands were raised to shoulder height, and the grenade that he gripped in each one was clearly visible, as was the cord tied to each clip which passed up into his sleeve.

'Just in case you haven't worked it out,' he said clearly, 'yes, these are real grenades from which the pins have been removed. And yes, if I drop them for whatever reason – let's say because you try to hit me again, or perhaps shoot me – then we shall all, in this small, confined space, very certainly die.'

The Romanians stared aghast.

'Do you understand?' asked Cámara with deliberation.

The larger one – Dorin, Cámara surmised from the description Jimmy had given him – nodded. Bogdan simply stared in anger.

'Now,' continued Cámara, 'that's three times you've tried to kill me. And three times you've failed. Don't you think it's time to change tack? And isn't it a little short-sighted? Getting rid of me won't change anything. It would only make my people more determined in their plans, and bring greater problems for you. Believe me.'

Dorin's eyes were darting from side to side. If either of them was on something, Cámara reasoned it was the larger of the two. Bogdan, meanwhile, stared at him with a bovine stillness, his eyes boring into Cámara like drills.

'What we need to do,' said Cámara, 'is begin a conversation. Here and now. Nothing else is going to settle this. You've tried violence, and I know that is your preferred method. But I think you will have to agree that so far it has failed. And,' he glanced at the grenades in his hands, 'I don't think it's going to work now either.'

He nodded at them.

'What do you say?'

He could see the wheels turning in Bogdan's mind as he tried to work out how to play this. It was time to pull out another card, to keep him in a state of confusion.

'I know that you might be hesitant about speaking openly,' said Cámara. 'And I agree. It's always better to be cautious in such circumstances. I myself took precautions before coming here.'

He nodded at the grenades.

'And I don't just mean these.'

Bogdan gave a questioning look.

'Now I'm going to hang on to these,' said Cámara. 'But as a gesture of goodwill, what I'm going to do . . .'

Still clutching the bombs, he brought his hands in front of his chest and using only his forefingers and thumbs, undid the top two buttons and exposed the wire stuck to his skin. With a jerk, he pulled it off, ripping it out of the battery pack stuck to his waist, and tossed it on to the floor at the Romanians' feet.

'Is get rid of this,' he said.

Dorin crouched down and picked up the wire. Bogdan stared Cámara darkly in the eye.

'My people,' said Cámara, 'like to have some kind of insurance. Which I'm certain you'll understand.'

For an instant, he thought of Rodríguez back in the *Guardia Civil* office, cursing him.

'But we need to get off on the right foot,' Cámara went on. 'If we're ever going to continue working together.'

Dorin held the wire in his thick paw. The blood was drying now, leaving a bright red streak across his skin. Dark splashes on the floor by his feet showed where drops had fallen. The glass in the door was reinforced with mesh, yet he had managed to leave a deep, fist-sized dent in it, with shattered lines radiating in all directions.

But Bogdan was still holding a revolver, and he was clearly the decision-maker, a dull intelligence flashing in his eyes that was absent from his companion. After a pause, he lowered the gun to his side. As he did so, Cámara buttoned up his shirt again and let his hands drop, palms facing forwards with the grenades in full view.

Bogdan nodded. Dorin seemed to read his command and knelt down, placing the wire on the floor in front of him. Then he located a loose brick lying at the side of the room, lifted it above his head and brought it crashing down, smashing the listening device with blow after blow, and using – Cámara noticed with interest – his left hand to do so.

The act of destruction seemed to go on for too long, Dorin letting out pent up anger and pain as he brought the brick down again and again, sending splinters and brick dust flying about. At the sound of Bogdan's grunt, he stopped, kicking the remains of the shattered wire away, panting for breath, his eyes on the floor, as though in shame at having lost control.

Bogdan patted him on the shoulder. Then he turned to Cámara and spoke.

'All right,' he said. 'Now we can talk.'

FORTY-SIX

'I should say that we are starting from first principles,' said Cámara. 'Nothing that has happened in the past has any bearing on what happens now. No grudges, no prejudices. And I have the authority to strike a new deal right here. That's why they sent me.'

Bogdan nodded; Dorin was silent.

'José Luis's killing changes everything,' continued Cámara.

He watched for any sign – a reaction – in their eyes. But there was none.

'Clever that,' he said. 'Using the bees.'

'José Luis was the problem,' said Bogdan, his voice deep and bitter.

Cámara nodded slowly.

'On that we are agreed,' he said when Bogdan failed to expand.

'Everything was fine,' said Bogdan. 'The whole set-up,

running smoothly. Everyone happy. He was the one trying to cut us out, deal with you directly, not through us.'

'We were impressed by your organisational skills,' Cámara improvised. 'The system has been working without a glitch. The *material* has been delivered as and where it was supposed to be.'

'We're not idiots!' Dorin suddenly appeared to be granted the gift of speech, spitting the words out in a rapid tumble. 'We have friends.'

He was certainly high, Cámara thought. Or so nervous that it made little difference.

Bogdan threw a reprimanding glance to his side and Dorin fell silent.

'The locals, it's true,' he said. 'They've been welcoming to us.'

'What happened with Enrique?' said Cámara.

Bogdan's expression darkened.

'Old man. Got a place beyond Sunset,' Cámara went on.

'That was years ago,' said Bogdan.

'Two years,' Cámara butted in.

Bogdan paused.

'OK. Two years. This was never brought up before. Why are you asking now?'

Cámara frowned.

'We need to clear the air. Of everything.'

Bogdan gritted his teeth.

'Enrique was spreading rumours around the village.'

'To everyone,' screeched Dorin. 'Even to the priest!'

Bogdan shot a hand out to his side to silence him.

'I hear Enrique is good friends with Father Ricardo,' said Cámara.

'As is everyone,' said Bogdan. 'As are we. We go to mass,

just like most people here. But we are foreigners; it is not always easy for us. People are too ready to believe bad things about us. We need to protect our reputation.'

'And Enrique was spreading rumours about . . . ?' Cámara asked.

'No,' said Bogdan. 'Not about that.'

'About the shop,' said Dorin. 'Blamed us for his wife's death.'

'Her shop went out of business,' explained Bogdan with a shrug. 'Shortly after, she died. She was old. She was going to die anyway. But Enrique blamed us.'

'Said we were pushing prices down deliberately.'

Cámara nodded.

'So you went to have a chat with him,' he said.

'We made him stop,' said Bogdan. 'No more talk.'

'Left a nasty scar on his face.'

'He brought it upon himself.'

'Has he said anything since?'

'Not a word!' spat Dorin.

'And I suppose he keeps his distance from you now.'

'He wouldn't dare take a step in our direction.'

Bogdan eyed Cámara.

'How come you know so much about this?' he asked. 'What's going on here?'

'I paid Enrique a visit,' said Cámara. Bogdan looked suspicious.

'My job,' explained Cámara, lowering his voice, 'is to clear up any mess. You understand? Which means I have to know what people around here know and don't know.'

He cleared his throat.

'And I'm happy to see that when it comes to Enrique it looks like you did a thorough job. I don't imagine he'll be causing trouble any time soon.'

'We saw you at his place,' said Dorin. 'Followed you through the woods.'

'Then you trailed me down to the *Molino*,' said Cámara.

'We lost you for a bit,' said Dorin. 'Thought you'd head back to Sunset. But we found you in the end.'

With his simplified, drug-damaged brain, he seemed to desire approval, as though Cámara should praise him for his tracking skills. Cámara nodded to him.

'I'm so glad you didn't manage to kill me,' he said. 'Otherwise we wouldn't be having this conversation now.'

Dorin's mouth broke into a curled, sneering grin.

'Enough of this shit,' said Bogdan.

'Yes,' said Cámara. 'Now, as we said, with José Luis gone, everything is changed.'

'We don't even know if Sunset will close,' said Bogdan. 'Everything could fall apart. No Sunset, no market, no business.'

'Paco's still there,' said Cámara.

Mention of Paco's name brought silence to the dank little room. At length, Bogdan nodded.

'Your distribution network is still in place,' continued Cámara. 'Sunset is popular, makes a lot of money. You think whoever takes it over is going to close it down?'

'Abi isn't the same man as José Luis.'

'But Abi needs a home, and Sunset is his life,' said Cámara. 'Of course he'll carry it on. And he'll need Paco even more than José Luis did.'

He gave them a knowing look.

'By my reckoning,' he said, 'you'll be in an even stronger position than before. Certainly that's how things are looking from our end. Which is why we want to continue with the old system. Dealing with you.'

Bogdan stared hard.

'Only dealing with us?'

'Your system works,' said Cámara. 'And as you said, José Luis was the one who started the problems. Now he's gone we can go back to how things were before.'

Bogdan's face barely betrayed any expression, but Cámara thought he could catch a glimmer of raw greed flashing somewhere within his eyes.

'By the way,' Cámara said. 'Your methods are commendable. The *Guardia Civil* have been keeping an eye on you, as you might suspect. But so far they can't work out how you get the *material* to Paco.'

'How . . . ?' began Dorin.

'We have informants,' said Cámara. 'On the inside.'

Both men looked impressed. Dorin smiled broadly; Bogdan tittered softly.

'I knew,' he said, pointing a finger at Cámara. 'These guys, I said. These guys must have good contacts. How else can they survive for so long. Get so big.'

Cámara smiled with them.

'Now,' he said. 'You'll agree that I've been very frank with you. And I hope that we can mark this moment as a new beginning. All obstacles removed. Clean slate.'

'Clean slate,' said Bogdan.

'What we need to do now,' said Cámara, 'is establish a new working arrangement. Collection and distribution should continue as they have done. No point fixing something that isn't broken. But the quantities involved will be changing.'

'We've been supplying Paco with steady amounts,' said Bogdan. 'A kilo of *grava*, half a kilo of *mercancía* and the same of *melocotón*.'

'What's the cocaine situation like?'

Bogdan looked uncomfortable, as though he'd swallowed something he shouldn't.

'It's fine,' said Cámara. 'No one's listening: no need for code words. And besides, they'll be changing soon.'

'Demand for cocaine drops sometimes,' said Bogdan at length. 'Kids want the newer drugs. But it's steady in the long run. People come back to it.'

'Like an old friend,' grinned Dorin.

'Paco still takes a kilo off us each delivery.'

'That's a lot of cocaine.'

'There's a lot of kids at Sunset.'

'OK,' said Cámara. 'But we want these numbers to grow. From now on I want you to double all of that.'

Bogdan's eyes widened.

'You reckon you can handle that much?'

'Sure,' said Bogdan. 'What about Paco?'

'Don't worry about Paco. He'll take it. I've been speaking to him as well.'

Bogdan nodded. Something in him seemed to be relaxing, the guard beginning to slip. Cámara had just one more question to ask.

BANG!

The door blew open with an explosive force, bright lights flashing, the sound of hurried, shouting, urgent voices echoing in the room. Instinctively, Cámara gripped the grenades tight in his hands and drew his arms into his chest. He felt an impact to his side, a hard, armoured weight hurtling into him and throwing him to the floor. His breath was pushed out of him as he smashed into the cement, staring up at a gun barrel as it was thrust into his face.

'*GUARDIA CIVIL! GUARDIA CIVIL!*'

He couldn't make out how many were there: he saw a

forest of legs clad in black, high leather boots over their ankles, knee pads, and holsters strapped to their thighs. On the far side of the room, Dorin and Bogdan had both been pushed head-first to the floor, men kneeling over them and pinning them still, pulling twisted wrists up tight behind their backs. Neither said a word, no grunt of pain or complaint.

Meanwhile the men in uniform continued to bellow orders, as though needing to shout, as well as wrestle, them into submission. Gloved hands began to move over their bodies. Cámara saw Bogdan's revolver being placed into an evidence bag before he, too, became the subject of a thorough frisking.

The gun barrel was removed from the end of his nose and eyes that he recognised stared into his face. Corporal Rodríguez gave him a hard, unforgiving look, then unhooked Cámara's fingers from the grenades.

'I'll take these,' he said, being careful to unhook the cords from the clips and prise them away safely.

Cámara closed his eyes.

'Oh, God,' he said softly. Everything around him, the room, the men inside it, his world, the investigation, everything that he had been working for, seemed as glass and now proceeded to shatter in front of his eyes.

All those promises, all those words, all gone. Rodríguez had got what he needed, had got the glory that he so desperately craved, the medal that would crown a long and – until then – undistinguished career. And Cámara was left with nothing. Not even any crumbs. Just a pawn in some other, greater game.

He let his body go limp as the *Guardia Civil* officers continued with their farce, offering no resistance when they cuffed his wrists behind his back, reacting with customary resignation when he was officially informed that he – and the others – was under arrest. Marching dutifully with head bowed out into the street. And sitting in gloomy silence between two guards in the back of a *Guardia Civil* van for the short ride to the station.

He wondered how long this would last, how long they would have to keep it up. He was led back into Rodríguez's office and forced to sit down. Keeping his gaze fixed on the floor he didn't look into their faces when Bogdan and Dorin were marched in behind him. When the Romanians were bundled out again, led back to a van to drive them to a larger *Guardia Civil* office in Bétera, Cámara thought that he might finally be released, that the charade might come to an end.

He looked in vain for Rodríguez, the only one there who could vouch for him. But Rodríguez had left with others for Bétera. Cámara was alone with two officers he had never seen before.

They cast him into the single cell, closed the door and turned the key.

Cámara rubbed life back into his wrists, put his head down on the floor, and went straight to sleep.

FORTY-SEVEN

The bar on Calle General Yagüe stayed open till late. The irony of the street name – dedicated to one of Franco's most successful and bloodthirsty commanders from the Civil War – was not lost on her. Here, of all places. There had been talk about changing it.

She sat by the window with a clear view out across to the drab, grey office building on the other side, and the inconspicuous doorway at its middle.

Over two hours had passed now, but still there was no sign. Had she arrived too late? She pushed the thought away as she sipped her coffee: such behaviour would be so untypical as to be impossible. Yet it was now approaching eleven o'clock.

The bar was empty save for the barman and a blind lottery-ticket salesman catching a last cognac before heading, presumably, for home. There was no sign of the balding man with the staring eyes, nor of the woman – with or without her leather jacket. She had caught no sign of either of them – or anyone else tailing her – since she had left Atocha station. Which did not mean that she was no longer being tailed. But she felt as confident as she could be that no one knew where she was right now. No one was watching her.

To be doubly sure she had gone up to the blind man and bought a ticket from him. Everything about him – his mannerisms, the tilt of his head, the smell about him that spoke of an entire day out on the street sweating and drinking and smoking – had an authenticity about it. From what she had seen of the others who had been tailing her, they were not so good as to be able to fake this. The guy was real, she felt certain.

Now she was doubly glad for the shawl attached to her new top. The temperature had dropped a little, and, jacketless, she could wrap it around her shoulders, help keep herself warm. The coffee helped too, milky and sweet to smooth her nerves. She'd been rattled earlier, but now she was here. She had made it.

She drank the last of the coffee and swirled the dregs around in the bottom of the cup. It was already paid for: if she needed to, she could leave without delay.

And the thought seemed to herald something, for no sooner did she look up than she caught sight of what she had been waiting for: a lone figure emerging from the doorway on the other side of the street and heading down the pavement, head slightly dipped, hurried steps.

In an instant Alicia was out on the pavement herself. No cars were coming and she crossed over, falling in behind her quarry, keeping a distance, treading as lightly as she could so as not to be heard.

They walked three blocks in a straight line. The area was largely made up of office and apartment buildings: it was relatively quiet at this time. An occasional car passed.

At the fourth crossroads, her quarry turned right on to a narrower street. A few paces further on the hazard lights of a car flashed as it was unlocked. The quarry climbed into the driver's seat and closed the door.

Less than a second later, Alicia opened the door on the passenger side and climbed in hurriedly, slamming it closed behind her.

'Whatever you do, don't ever come to me looking for a job as a secret agent,' said a voice from the driver's side. 'That's the worst tail I've ever had.'

The engine burst into life, they pulled out and the car slipped into the grid of the surrounding streets.

'But at least you didn't call me. That's one thing to be thankful for.'

'I've thrown my phone away,' said Alicia.

'Under the circumstances I'd say that's probably wise.'

'Did you know? Know that I was being tailed?'

Light from a nearby street lamp flashed through the window as they rolled past: Marisol's face had a tired looseness about it, like a cliff face about to collapse into the sea.

'It was to be expected,' she said. 'You've stumbled on something, and there are very worried people trying to . . .' She hesitated.

'To what?' asked Alicia. 'To just keep tabs on me? Or should I be more concerned for my safety?'

Marisol kept her eyes on the road ahead, fingers gripped tight against the wheel.

'Perhaps it was wrong of me,' she said at last, almost whispering the words. 'To get you involved.'

'If you're worried about yourself, you needn't be. I shook them off several hours ago. No one knows I'm here with you now.'

Marisol's shoulders lifted as she breathed in, her lips tight like a knot.

'That's your mistake,' she said. 'They'll know, all right. It's what you have to assume at all times. The moment you think you've given the slip is when you make mistakes.'

The traffic lights ahead were red. Marisol ignored them, slowing to make sure no one was coming before pulling out and turning left.

'Were you waiting for me in the bar across the road?' she asked.

Alicia nodded. Marisol shrugged.

'Then they know.'

'The barman?'

'The barman is one of those stubborn types,' said Marisol. 'Refuses to be bought. It's his clientele you need to watch out for.'

'The only other person there was a lottery-ticket salesman,' said Alicia. 'A blind man.'

Marisol shook her head, glancing at the street behind them through her mirror.

'Then just about now they'll be hearing all about you.'

'What?'

'Oh, he's genuinely blind,' said Marisol. 'And a genuine lottery-ticket salesman. But for an extra bit of cash he'll pass on a bit of gossip.'

'But he couldn't see me! He's blind!'

'Well, only partially. But the sketchiness of his vision will be filled in by a host of other details: the sounds you made, your smell, that kind of thing. And he'll know that you walked out in a hurry. And at what time. If they're not on to us already, then they soon will be.'

Alicia slumped into her seat.

'That's why I'm sorry I got you involved,' said Marisol. 'I blame myself.'

'I thought, once I'd given the others the slip . . .'

'Waiting for me right outside the Ministry of Defence building? Did you think that was a good idea?'

'I had no choice. Besides, I was convinced I'd lost them. How would anyone know I was there?' She sighed. 'Too late now,' she said. 'How long have we got?'

'They know my car registration,' said Marisol. 'Once they work out what's happened, which may already be the case, they'll put out an alert for my car, get the traffic police involved. I suspect we'll be pulled over soon on some minor count, then held until bigger fish come to collect us and take us away.'

Something stirred inside Alicia, deep fears burnt into her consciousness by previous experience, years before, of incarceration, of abuse and torture. She could feel the physical scars flickering, like antennae picking up signals of danger. Of the need to flee.

She could open the car door, jump out at the next junction, or when Marisol slowed down. But would there be any point? What were the chances that she would be found sooner or later? And she had come here for something. What use was it getting caught without at least obtaining what she needed?

The car swerved as Marisol pulled the wheel to the left, taking the smaller streets, avoiding the wider boulevards where there was greater danger.

'You'll have guessed why I came,' said Alicia.

Marisol said nothing.

'You know more than you let on last night,' Alicia continued. 'All the stuff about not having the whole picture, it's nonsense. You know everything. It was just some kind of test, you wanted to see if I could work it out.'

The car swerved again. Ahead was a rubbish truck blocking the street, men hauling a large container round the back to be lifted and emptied. It was too late to reverse out; another car had come in from behind and trapped them. Marisol watched it through the mirror; Alicia caught her nervousness and cast a glance at the headlights over her shoulder.

'Them?'

Marisol paused.

'Don't know,' she said. 'Maybe.'

Alicia leaned over and grabbed her arm.

'Listen, Marisol, there may not be much time. I don't need you to tell me the whole story; I've pretty much worked it out for myself. All those code words from the Middle Ages: Clavijo, Abravanel, Covadonga. And then there's the history of Cabrera itself. It's pretty bloody clear what they're doing there, what's going to happen. But I need documentary proof, I need paperwork, something to demonstrate that this is all true. That the government is going to—'

'It's all right,' interrupted Marisol. Her eyes were fixed on the mirror, staring at the car behind. In front, the rubbish men were finishing with the container, wheeling it back to its position.

'You don't have to argue your case.'

'You want me to know the truth,' said Alicia. 'You want people to know. That's why you called me to Madrid. Now one person is already missing as a result of this. Nacho, my marine biologist friend. My life is possibly in danger, and perhaps yours as well. You just need—'

'I get it. That's enough.'

The rubbish men trotted back to the truck, grabbed the handles at the side and the wheels started rolling. Marisol put her own car into gear and followed closely, eyes flicking constantly back to her mirror. After a pause, the car behind stirred into life.

At the junction, the rubbish truck swung left. Marisol went to follow it, slowing down to a near standstill. When she saw that the car behind was coming in the same direction, she suddenly jerked the wheel to the right and pressed the accelerator, hitting the kerb as she spun round and went the other way.

'Are they following us?' she asked.

Alicia looked back through the window.

'They've stopped where they are,' she said.

'Have they pulled in behind the rubbish truck?'

'No. It looks like they don't know exactly where they're going themselves.'

'Then it's them,' said Marisol. 'They don't want to give themselves away but they don't want to lose us either.'

The car gave a surge and Alicia was pushed back into her seat.

'Hang on. We're going to have to put some distance between us.'

For the next few minutes Marisol swerved this way and that as she sped along the largely empty streets. They were lucky: most of the traffic lights were in their favour, and where they weren't, Marisol ignored them. Neither of them spoke, both concentrating on the road, both looking out for any tails, or any sign of the police.

Minutes later, having weaved a criss-cross route across the north of the city, they pulled out on to a wider street. Alicia thought it looked familiar. Trees appeared, and in the distance, in the middle of a park area, some ancient stone structure.

'Here?'

'Some anomaly,' said Marisol. 'I don't know why, but there are hardly any security cameras around this area. I know, because I know where the others are.'

She found a space away from the street lamps and brought the car to a stop, turning off the engine and letting her hands fall from the wheel.

Alicia looked out through the windows.

'Can't see anyone,' she said. 'Perhaps we've—'

'Never assume they don't know where you are,' repeated Marisol. 'It's a basic and dangerous mistake. Do you have any cash on you?'

Alicia nodded. Marisol reached for her bag and pulled out her purse.

'You'll need some more,' she said, handing over all the notes she had. 'Don't use your cards for anything, particularly not public transport.'

She paused and looked Alicia in the eye. Neither could see the other well in the gloom of the car, but a silent communication passed between them.

'I thought you would be coming,' said Marisol. 'And I know exactly what you want, what you need.'

Her hand was hovering over the bag now sitting on her lap. It was large, not unlike the one Alicia had left behind at the Atocha metro station. And a file of papers was poking out of the top.

'At some point in our lives we have to do something we

can be proud of,' said Marisol. 'For me, to date, there's precious little. Except perhaps teaching a few things to a handful of young women, like yourself.'

She put her hand on the file, clutching it between her fingers.

'But . . .' She hesitated. Alicia watched her like a hawk.

'They're going to get me anyway,' said Marisol at length. And she pulled the papers out and handed them to Alicia.

'So it might as well be for something worthwhile.'

Alicia took the file from her, flicking her thumb through it: it was at least two or three hundred pages long.

'Take it, use it,' said Marisol. 'And tell the world what it needs to know.'

'Thank you,' said Alicia.

'Don't,' said Marisol. 'You still don't understand how much danger I've put you in.'

She gripped Alicia's arm.

'Now, darling, it's time to run.'

FORTY-EIGHT

Cámara was woken by Corporal Rodríguez prodding him repeatedly in the shoulder.

'Your phone,' said Rodríguez when Cámara finally opened his eyes. 'It keeps ringing.'

He left it on the floor by Cámara's head and walked out of the cell, leaving the door open behind him. Cámara hauled himself up: the phone was silent now. He rubbed his eyes and took a look around: he was still alone in the cell, but two other *Guardia Civil* officers were in the main part of the office with Rodríguez, looks of studied professionalism on their faces as they did their best to ignore the *Policía Nacional* chief inspector lying on the floor not far from their feet.

There was a smell of coffee in the air, smooth and invigorating like a cat brushing its fur against his fingers. Cámara sauntered over, trying to overcome a spinning at the back of his head. A coffee pot stood in the middle of the desk where all three men were writing reports on the arrests made the previous night. Rodríguez's cup was almost empty. Cámara took it without a word, shook the dregs on to the floor and poured himself a full cup, which he downed in three mouthfuls, the coffee already lukewarm. Then he filled it again, draining the last of the coffee pot, and took another gulp.

'The bathroom's that way, isn't it,' he said flatly, pointing towards a door at the back.

The three *Guardia Civil* men looked at him with unconcealed scorn as he stepped across, still holding the coffee cup, and let himself in.

When he emerged several minutes later, Rodríguez pushed mugshots of Bogdan and Dorin across the desk in his direction.

'Have they said anything?' Cámara asked, tucking his shirt into his trousers.

'Don't have to,' said Rodríguez. 'We recorded everything that was said last night.'

Cámara looked at him darkly.

'The wire,' he said. 'There's no way it could have survived. Dorin destroyed it. I saw him.'

Rodríguez shared a knowing glance with the other two men. Then he reached into a drawer in the desk and pulled out one of the grenades that Cámara had carried the night before. Holding it up carefully in one hand, with the other he gently twiddled with the cord that was still tied to the pin.

'I know this looks like a standard grenade,' he said. 'But it's actually a recording device.'

Cámara stared in disbelief.

'There's a microphone in the fuse section. We could listen

to every word, even though you threw away our other wire. But as you yourself said, it's important to have some security, a backup. So that's why I gave you this.'

'You mean,' said Cámara, 'I was totally unarmed in there. I was carrying two duds.'

'Oh no,' said Rodríguez. 'The other grenade was real, all right. You would all have been blown up if you'd dropped that one.'

Cámara could see the other two officers smiling – at their glee at having outwitted not only the Romanians, but also a member of the *Policía Nacional.*

'Congratulations, Rodríguez,' Cámara said. 'Fine piece of work. You must be pleased.'

Yet instead of the look of pride that he expected, Cámara only saw resignation in Rodríguez's face.

'I have to go,' said Rodríguez.

He collected his papers, put them in a file and placed them in a drawer which he locked with a key. Cámara was silently impressed that they were still doing things with pen and paper up here. The digitalisation of everything appeared to have bypassed this particular corner of the policing world.

Rodríguez picked up his green cap, put on a jacket and walked to the door. One of the other men obeyed a silent command and went with him.

'If there's anything you need . . .' said Rodríguez as he was stepping through the door. He left the sentence unfinished. A formal, un-heartfelt offering. The door closed behind him before Cámara could respond.

'You'd think he'd be a little bit more pleased,' Cámara mumbled to himself.

The remaining officer pushed his chair back from the

desk, turned to make sure the door was closed and that Rodríguez had gone, then spoke.

'It's a personal thing for the corporal,' he said.

Cámara looked into unforgiving brown eyes. The man was in his late thirties, a *Guardia Civil de primera*, just under Rodríguez in the chain of command.

'What happened?' asked Cámara.

'A couple of years back,' said the officer. 'A young lad died at Sunset of an overdose.'

Cámara nodded.

'I remember.'

The man's facc twisted.

'It was the corporal's son,' he said.

Cámara sighed and nodded.

'I understand,' he said.

'No you don't,' said the officer. 'None of us can understand something like that.'

Cámara rubbed his face and prepared to leave.

'Yes. I'm sure you're right.'

He stepped out of the station and into the street. Two cars were waiting at the petrol station. The pump attendant came out, watched Cámara coming down the steps, and looked away, pretending he hadn't seen him. Cámara turned left and headed up the hill back towards the village square. As he did so he remembered his phone. The screen showed that Torres had been trying to call him. He dialled the number to ring him back, but a robotic voice told him that the number he was trying to contact had no signal, and to try again later. Cámara pocketed the phone and walked on.

He was tired and his body ached from having slept on the cold cell floor. He needed a shower badly, a slimy, unpleasant layer of sweat clinging to his skin with the smell of stress and dirt hanging around him like a cloud of flies. He needed to get home, lie down in a proper bed and forget everything – this case, the people involved, all that he had learned since arriving in the sierra. There was nowhere further for him to go: his plan had backfired spectacularly; he had no suspects. Should he hand in his resignation now? Go straight to the Jefatura and have done with it? He needed some means of transport. Perhaps he could find a taxi in the square, someone prepared to give him a lift back to Sunset, where he could pick up his bike and ride back to the city.

His feet took him up the street and into the sunlight at the top where the cramped buildings parted near the fountain. Pulling on iron railings, he lifted himself up the three steps to where spring water was trickling gently into the marble basin, creating a bubbling, soothing sound. Without thinking he leaned over and pushed his face into the clear liquid, feeling its cool fingers reach up and caress his cheeks, his eyes, his brow. Then with both hands he scooped more of it up and over the back of his head, drenching his hair and rubbing it with his fingertips into his scalp. It was cleansing and calming, as though some spirit of the water penetrated his body through this sudden contact and washed something deeper within him. He breathed out hard through his nose, watching the bubbles underwater as they floated up to the surface like laughing children scampering up a hill.

He pulled his head out, feeling the water cascade down his neck and shoulders and soak into his shirt and jacket.

'You look like a man freshly baptised,' said a voice nearby.

Cámara turned to look.

'It's a perfect day for it.'

Estrella was smiling at him, her skin tanned and creased with laughter, eyes bright like suns.

He leaned over to kiss her on the cheeks. She accepted the wetness of his skin without complaint.

'You all right?' she said.

'Fine,' he answered. 'Just needed a bit of a wash. Jimmy with you?'

She shook her head.

'He doesn't like this place much. Tries to avoid it. I'm just here to pick up a few odds and ends.' She glanced around at the handful of shops in the square.

'We're self-sufficient in most things,' she added. 'But not everything, unfortunately. We need to come in and buy the odd thing or two every so often.'

It was a curious experience seeing her here in the village. She wore a simple cotton dress, patterned with circular star-like designs in red and white. Cámara thought there was something Japanese about it. The first time he had seen her she had been naked. Later, inside the house, she had wrapped herself in a cloth of some sort, yet it had merely been for the sake of the visitor, as though her nakedness and animal grace were only partly veiled from view. Now here she was, dressed to appear in ordinary society, with sandals on her feet and her skin almost completely covered, yet still it was as if he could sense the litheness in her limbs, a majesty and suppleness that mere clothes could never disguise. He felt certain that were it not for fear of arrest or causing unnecessary scandal, she would happily walk the streets of the village as unclad as she did at home.

'As far as I see it,' said Estrella, 'this place is just a distribution point. We come in and we take what we need from it and go. Nothing more. Doesn't mean we have to be a part of this world. We are in our own. Mere presence doesn't signify belonging. But Jimmy doesn't see it like that. He's more sensitive.'

'A distribution point,' Cámara echoed her words.

'That's it,' she said. 'Nothing more.'

Cámara suddenly leaned towards her and gripped her by the shoulders.

'What was it you said a moment ago?'

'When?' she smiled.

'Just now, when you first saw me. Something about . . .'

'Baptism,' she answered. 'I said you looked like you were baptising yourself in the fountain.'

Cámara looked up to the sky, his mind turning.

'But I'm not the one to talk to about these things,' she grinned. 'If it's baptism you're after, you should speak with Father Ricardo.'

'Father Ricardo?'

'The village priest,' she said. 'Look, there he is now.'

She pointed across the square.

'Just going to the church. He's the man for divine intervention. If you run you can catch him.'

He lifted his hands to the sides of her face and planted a quick, passionless kiss on her mouth.

'Thank you,' he said, turning to go. 'I think you've just saved me for the second time.'

FORTY-NINE

Cámara caught up with Father Ricardo just as the priest was letting himself into the church through a side door and closing it behind him.

'I need a quick word,' he said, holding the door. 'Police business.'

He raised his ID clearly in front of him through the gap. The pressure from inside relented and the door opened.

'You'd better come in,' said Father Ricardo. 'But I don't have much time.'

'I shan't keep you.'

'We can talk in the vestry,' said the priest. 'Follow me.'

Father Ricardo was in his late sixties, clean shaven and with short, balding grey hair. He wore large heavy glasses over a thick, sensual nose, a black cassock over black trousers, with black, rubber-soled shoes. Walking behind him as they ascended a staircase into the main body of the church,

Cámara could see where the heels had worn on the insides of his feet: Father Richard was pigeon-toed.

The church was made up of a single, broad nave with simple Gothic arches. The altar was baroque, a riot of gold with statues of saints painted in pastoral colours standing in various niches, holding the symbols of their martyrdom or faith. At the centre, beneath a crucifix with an agonised Christ hanging from nailed hands and feet, was an image of St Christopher wading through stylised water, staff in hand, an infant Jesus sitting peacefully on his shoulders. It looked almost like a simple, domestic scene.

Cámara glanced at the rows of pews filling up most of the nave. They were made of undecorated wood, with a low shelf for the faithful to kneel in prayer. Cámara quickly scuffled over and checked: there was space underneath, ample room.

He hurried over and rejoined Father Ricardo before the priest had a chance to notice, stepping in behind him to the vestry: a small, cold, octagonal room with a high ceiling and a single narrow window above head height that only allowed a gloomy light to enter from outside.

'So, Chief Inspector,' said Father Ricardo, easing his stiff, heavily clad body down into a comfortable chair behind a table. More robes were hanging from hooks in the walls, ceremonial garb for his various church functions. 'What's this about?'

There was the slightest hint of impatience behind the stiffly welcoming smile.

'Two of your flock were arrested late last night,' said Cámara.

Father Ricardo affected a look of concern.

'By you?' he asked pointedly.

'Two Romanians,' Cámara continued. 'Bogdan and Dorin. They said they knew you.'

The priest nodded slowly.

'Yes, yes,' he said. 'I believe I've come across them. What sorry news. What . . . ?'

'They told me they were regulars,' said Cámara. 'Came to mass on Sundays.'

Father Ricardo placed his fingertips together.

'This is a quite devout community, Chief Inspector,' he said.

'So you must know them well,' said Cámara. 'I mean, if you see them here every week.'

'I know them both,' answered the priest. 'As well as their wives. They run the grocer's shop. But do tell me, what can I do for you? It is very unfortunate to hear that these two men appear to have fallen into sin, but I must hurry. Was it some kind of character reference you were looking for? I can vouch for their faith, that is all. What they did outside these walls is, I'm afraid, unknown to me.'

He gave a resigned smile and glanced at the large, heavy watch on his wrist.

'A question has been bugging me,' said Cámara. 'One of those things that, you know, are in the back of your mind and then POP, all of a sudden they spring into consciousness.'

'I see,' said the priest.

'The thing is,' said Cámara, 'Bogdan and Dorin are both Romanian.'

'So I understand.'

'And yet, here they were coming regularly to this church. A church which, I assume, is Catholic.'

'Of course,' said Father Ricardo with some confusion.

'Most Romanians follow the Eastern Orthodox rite, as far as I know,' Cámara continued. 'Which is quite strange. I mean, why would two Orthodox men – and their wives, as you say – regularly attend mass at a Catholic church? You're a man of the cloth, clearly. Perhaps you can resolve this for me.'

'The Church of Rome welcomes all God's children into her bosom,' said Father Ricardo. 'It is perfectly acceptable for those born to a different tradition to be embraced by the true faith.'

'Yes,' said Cámara. 'I thought you might say that. But there are differences between the Catholic and Orthodox systems. Important ones. I mean, important enough to have kept the two churches apart for centuries. Your rituals, for example. Or your symbols.'

Father Ricardo shuffled in his seat.

'Is this going to be a conversation about theology, Chief Inspector? If so, I will have to leave it for another time, for I really must be—'

'The Orthodox Church uses a different crucifix, doesn't it?' interrupted Cámara. 'Please, just another minute or two of your time. How is it different? Could you enlighten me?'

Father Ricardo looked annoyed.

'The Orthodox crucifix,' he said in a hurried voice, 'is more complex than our own. It has a smaller cross-beam above Christ's head for the nameplate, and then another at the feet, which slants down at an angle.'

'That's it,' said Cámara. 'I thought so. Because I saw one very recently. Only last night, in fact. In Bogdan and Dorin's plumbing office. You know, the one they never used for any actual plumbing. It was hanging on the wall and I spotted it just as the two of them were incriminating themselves as major drug dealers. Turns out they were supplying large amounts of narcotics to Sunset, the nightclub. I'm sure you've heard about it. And what happened the other day to José Luis, its owner.'

Father Ricardo stared at him silently.

'Where is this conversation going?' he said at last.

Cámara leaned across the table, his weight on his knuckles, towering over the priest.

'Those men aren't Catholic,' he said with sudden force. 'Any more than I am. And there's only one reason I can see why they would come here to this church on a weekly basis. And that's to drop off their merchandise.'

'What?' Father Ricardo spluttered.

'I suspect you know the *Guardia Civil* have been trying to take those men down for some time,' said Cámara. 'Yet they never had enough on them to put them away. Well, now they have.'

He glared at the priest.

'But there was one mystery that was not cleared up last night,' he continued. 'One element of the story that was not resolved. And that was how the Romanians delivered the drugs to the distributor at Sunset. No amount of surveillance gave them any clues. Yet it always managed to get through.'

Father Ricardo's face began to turn crimson.

'But of course,' said Cámara, 'the *Guardia Civil* never thought to watch these men as they came and went from attending mass on Sunday mornings, did they? And it's obvious to me now that it was right here that they made the drop. Right in your church. Why else would a couple of Orthodox drug dealers come here? And, if I'm guessing right, they did everything with your blessing. Those gaps underneath the knee rests make a perfect spot for little packages. No one would suspect anything in the gloom of this building. Probably wouldn't even notice anything in the first place, what with the low lighting, the drama of the mass taking place.'

'This is utterly preposterous!' spat the priest, struggling to get to his feet. 'How dare you?'

Cámara simply pulled his phone out of his pocket and held it up for him to see.

'One call,' he said simply. 'I can make one call and have a specialised team here in minutes to start running tests on this place. It's amazing how sensitive the equipment is these days. If there's even the tiniest trace of narcotics in this building, the *científicos* will find it. Believe me.'

He stared Father Ricardo in the eye, and slowly, like the shifting of some tectonic plate, the expression on the priest's face changed from rage to fear. The blood faded from his cheeks. With a slump, he fell back into his seat.

'I'm sure you'll agree,' said Cámara, 'that with all the scandals in the Church at the moment, a new one about drug dealing would not go down particularly well, nor be forgotten very soon.'

Father Ricardo stared into space, wordless.

'You've been using this place as a distribution hub for some time, haven't you?' said Cámara.

There was a long pause. Outside, the bell of the clock tower struck a single, clanging note as it marked the passing of the quarter hour. Father Ricardo looked petrified, muscle and skin turned to hard, haunting stone. Then, very slowly, his head moved up and down, almost imperceptibly, his eyes still unfocused.

'You allowed the Romanians to leave the drugs here, then you passed them on to Paco, the Sunset manager, didn't you? I know he comes here as well.'

Again, the silent nod.

'And – what? – you took your own cut? I mean, you weren't going to do something like that out of Christian charity, were you?'

'I thought I could bring it down from within,' said Father Ricardo, his voice thin.

'Bring what down?' asked Cámara.

'Sunset,' the priest said at last. 'Let it fester, be consumed in its own vice and sin.'

Cámara laughed.

'Is that how you justified it? Doing God's work? Combating sin by allowing it to grow?'

Father Ricardo glowered at him.

'The place is an abomination!' he cried. Tiny hair-like veins in his cheeks were turning blue. 'Sodom and Gomorrah! Right here on our doorstep. Something had to be done.'

Cámara looked at him with despair.

'Father Ricardo,' he said at length. 'I am a policeman. But your drug dealing – no matter how you justify it to yourself – does not interest me.'

The priest looked up at him confused, eyes bloodshot and yellow.

'I am in fact,' said Cámara, 'a homicide detective.'

The eyes were blank, searching.

'And I'm trying to find who murdered José Luis.'

The priest sat back in his chair, mouth gaping open.

'José Luis,' Cámara continued, 'was killed by bee stings.'

Father Ricardo shook his head.

'I know,' said Cámara. 'It sounds implausible. But he had an allergy to them. It's rare, but it only took half a dozen stings to send him to the next world.'

'Bees?' said the priest.

'Someone managed to attract the bees to José Luis by applying pheromones to his skin. Someone who had a reason for wanting José Luis dead. The smell makes the bees aggressive, makes them want to sting you, you see.'

Cámara paused before carrying on.

'I thought that person, or those people, were Bogdan and Dorin. José Luis was trying to cut them out, as you probably already know. Wanted to deal exclusively with the gang who supplied the drugs to the Romanians in the first place. So Bogdan and Dorin, I assumed, were angry about this, wanted to put a stop to it. Which is why, according to my earlier theory, they killed José Luis.'

He held up his hands.

'But I was wrong. You see, another person must be involved, for this to work. And that's the owner of the bees. Enrique. The plan could only work with Enrique's cooperation.'

Father Ricardo appeared to be sinking deeper into his chair.

'But the Romanians and Enrique weren't on speaking terms. I'm sure you know why – they gave him a bit of a beating some years ago, left that scar on his face. So they couldn't have been working together to murder José Luis.'

Cámara sighed and crossed his arms.

'But there is one other person in the village who had an urgent motive for killing José Luis, for scuppering his plans to deal exclusively with the drug gang.'

He let his arms fall to his sides.

'That person, Father Ricardo, is you.'

'I . . .' spluttered the priest. 'I . . .'

'Not only would you be losing out under José Luis's new arrangement,' said Cámara, 'but I know that you are a friend of Enrique's. I reckon you must be one of the few people round here Enrique even talks to. Bit of a loner.'

Father Ricardo fell silent.

'You wanted José Luis dead,' said Cámara. 'And you had the means to do it. Because,' he went on, 'you're ex-military, used to be a chaplain with the armed forces. You knew about José Luis's allergy because he himself learned about it when he was an air force cadet. Those tests they run, you know. Once they found that out, poor old José Luis's dream of following in his father's heroic footsteps vanished. His life could have been so different but for one small biological anomaly.'

Father Ricardo sat with a look of terror in his eyes, shaking his head violently.

'Not me,' he mumbled. 'Not me. Not me.'

Cámara's phone began to vibrate in his hand.

'Of course it was you,' he said, pressing the button to answer. 'Who else could it have been?'

FIFTY

'Chief, where are you?' Torres said from the other end of the line.

'I'm in the village,' answered Cámara, confused.

'I'm pulling into the village right now. I've got Azcárraga with me.'

'What?'

'And José Montesinos,' said Torres.

Something focused in Cámara's mind, like a lens sharpening in on its objective.

'Come to the church,' he said. 'Let yourselves in through the side door.'

'Don't tell me you've suddenly found religion.'

'Something like that.'

Torres rang off.

Cámara looked down at the pathetic vision of Father Ricardo squirming like a wounded insect in his chair. It made something in him want to lift his foot and crush him.

Moments later he heard footsteps coming in through the nave.

'In here,' he said. 'In the vestry.'

Three men walked in. Torres and Azcárraga he recognised. The third was a man in his sixties of slight build, with narrow shoulders and a thick head of hair that looked too full and too well coloured for his age. He had a clipped pencil moustache and wore a pale-lemon suit with shiny brown brogue shoes and a light blue shirt.

'We've got him!' said Azcárraga, grinning excitedly at Cámara. 'This is José Montesinos. The man who made the anonymous call.'

He looked pleased with himself, like a cat offering its latest catch to its owner.

'Good,' said Cámara. 'Very good.'

Torres could tell that they had caught Cámara in the middle of something, and he looked quizzically at the image of the priest slithering uncomfortably behind the table.

'I'll fill you in in a minute,' Cámara said in a low voice to him.

He turned to Azcárraga.

'I need you to do something for me,' he said.

'Sure.'

'I want you to take Father Ricardo here to the *Guardia Civil* office in front of the petrol station and lock him up. He's to be detained. Understood?'

Azcárraga nodded. 'What . . . ?'

'You don't have to explain anything. Say you're with me.'

He threw Torres a glance.

'Those bastards owe me anyway.'

He turned back to Azcárraga.

'Oh, and do me a favour – send a very quick preliminary report on events up here to *Homicidios*.'

'Do you want me to stay there with the priest?' asked Azcárraga.

Cámara shook his head.

'Once you're finished, come back here and find me. And if there's a Corporal Rodríguez there, bring him with you. Tell him I insist.'

Azcárraga took a step over to the priest and slipped a hand under his shoulder to lift him up.

'What do I do if he starts talking?' he said. Father Ricardo allowed himself to be eased out of his chair. He looked unsteady on his feet, as though he might topple over like a cut-down tree. Azcárraga held him up and began leading him away.

'Ignore him,' said Cámara. 'Or shut him up. I don't care how.'

The priest began to sob.

'I shall be seen,' he wept. 'Everyone will see me.'

Torres dug a hand into his pocket and pulled out a bunch of keys.

'Use the car,' he said to Azcárraga, tossing them to him. 'And copy Narcotics into your report.' Cámara said nothing.

They waited until the two men had left the building, then Cámara pointed at Montesinos.

'You,' he said. 'Wait there. Don't move.'

He stepped out of the vestry and into the nave of the church. Torres followed. They stood underneath the altar, by the steps leading up to the altar table.

'What's going on, chief?' Torres said. 'The priest?'

'Why are you here?' Cámara asked. 'OK, so you've got Montesinos. But . . . ?'

'I'm in Narcotics now, remember?' Torres grinned.

'So?'

'What happened here last night, the arrest of the Romanians – it came through on WebPol. The *Guardia Civil* weren't going to keep that quiet, wanted to let the whole world know about their success. So naturally, I got to learn about it.'

'So you're here . . . ?'

'I'm here as a representative of the *Policía Nacional* Narcotics unit doing some routine follow-up in case there's any overlap with investigations of our own.'

'Nice,' said Cámara.

'Which I'm sure there is, at some point down the line. But in the meantime I can come up here and see if my old chief, recently of the Special Crimes Unit, but now back in *Homicidios*, needs a hand with his own case: the death of José Luis, formerly of Sunset discotheque.'

He paused, looking Cámara in the eye.

'Or is it actually murder we're talking about?'

Cámara jerked his head in the direction of the vestry.

'Montesinos. Said anything?'

'So far very little. Azcárraga got in touch as soon as he found him. I had my excuse to come up here anyway. So I figured we'd bring him straight to you. Far better than doing anything back at the Jefatura. The moment you got through the door Rita would probably have you lynched.'

'That good, is it?' said Cámara. He shrugged. 'There'll be time for that later.'

He paused, staring at the vestry door, then up at the gilded decoration of the baroque altarpiece. He walked up the steps and stood in front of the altar table, staring out over the empty pews. It was a powerful position; he could sense the energy and confidence building in him: a position of dominance, of lordship.

Torres knew him well: no words were needed. He went back to the vestry to fetch Montesinos. Moments later, he brought him to Cámara, placing him squarely in front of him, two steps down and overshadowed by his colleague like a member of the faithful about to receive the sacrament. Then Torres himself took a couple of steps to the side.

'José Montesinos,' bellowed Cámara, staring down at the man with open hostility.

Montesinos nodded uncomfortably.

'You are charged with withholding evidence and wasting police time.'

Cámara threw his arms out, splaying his fingers in a dramatic, almost operatic gesture. Montesinos cowered before him.

'Do you know how serious a matter this is?'

Montesinos shook his head nervously.

'No,' he said. 'I mean, yes. It's serious. I'm certain it's serious. I didn't mean—'

'Anonymous calls! Accusations of murder!'

From the side, Torres could see that Cámara was enjoying this.

'I didn't—'

'But we have you now, Montesinos.' Cámara's voice echoed around the nave, resonating and growing in power and strength.

'And you're going to tell me exactly what you know.'

'Y-yes,' said Montesinos.

'Everything!'

'Yes, everything, everything. I wanted to tell you in the first place. That's why I called. I just—'

'You lost your nerve,' said Cámara, dropping his arms and placing his hands on his hips.

'Yes,' said Montesinos. 'I did.'

Cámara paused, then spoke again, this time lowering his voice slightly to a gentler, more forgiving tone.

'I can understand that.'

He took a breath and moved his hands behind his back, leaning forwards, still looking down at Montesinos with a priestly air.

'But you want to do the right thing, don't you?' he said. 'It's what you've really wanted to do from the beginning.'

Montesinos nodded. Something stirred inside Cámara: the fact that he was here at all, that he had taken José Luis's death as anything more than an accident, was due to this man and to the call he had made. It was time to find out once and for all what it was all about.

'Tell me,' he said as calmly and invitingly as he could. 'Tell me everything. Why did you make that call?'

Montesinos looked down at his feet.

'I saw José Luis a couple of weeks ago,' he said. 'Came down for dinner.'

'You and José Luis were friends?' said Cámara.

Montesinos nodded.

'Close friends?' Cámara asked. '*Intimate* friends?'

Montesinos paused before answering.

'We were . . .' he began. 'We'd been lovers. In the past. A long time ago.'

His eyes became glassy.

'But we were just friends now.'

'What happened?' asked Cámara.

Montesinos swallowed hard, quashing the emotion welling inside him in order to continue.

'I'd known José Luis a long time,' he said. 'Almost forty years. I probably knew him better than anyone. He was . . .'

He sucked on his teeth. 'What happened to him in the Air Force marked him.'

'He was rejected,' said Cámara. 'The allergy. I know that.'

'It was his dream,' said Montesinos. 'Following his father. Getting turned down like that had a lasting effect.'

'How?'

Montesinos looked at him with a sorrowful expression.

'It made him insecure, vulnerable; he never really got over it.'

Cámara nodded for him to continue.

'I met him shortly after,' said Montesinos. 'Which is when we – our thing started.'

'Did he . . . ?' said Cámara.

Montesinos shook his head.

'No. I was his first.'

'It must have been easier for him, not being in the Air Force,' said Cámara. 'Things weren't so relaxed back then.'

'Perhaps. But I could tell he was wounded. And it seemed to establish some kind of pattern in his behaviour.'

'What pattern?'

Montesinos paused before answering.

'He was desperate to be accepted,' he said. 'He sought acceptance all the time. From new people, friends, lovers, groups in society, whoever it was. It was as if he constantly needed someone patting him on the back, saying he was a good man, that he had a place in the world. But then . . .'

His eyes began to well with tears once more. Cámara urged him to continue.

'But then he would bring it all toppling down,' said Montesinos. 'Do things deliberately that would bring the opprobrium of those he wanted to impress. I saw it happen time and again, like some automatic behaviour that he could not stop or prevent. A self-destruct button. It was . . .'

He pulled out a handkerchief and dabbed his eyes.

'And you saw that this was happening again,' said Cámara. 'When you had dinner.'

'All the signs were there,' said Montesinos. 'A nervousness in him. Even his voice used to change: he would speak in a higher tone, almost as though he was possessed or something. And the drugs didn't help. He never normally took much. But at these times he would take more, pushing himself to the edge.'

Cámara nodded, thinking about the small arsenal of narcotics that he had found back at José Luis's apartments.

'Did he engage in risky sexual activity?' he asked.

Montesinos nodded.

'He told me about the new trends, these drug-fuelled orgies that can go on for days. It's not my scene: it's more a young man's thing. But I could tell he was getting into it. Another sign, more self-destruction kicking in, like a machine.'

'This dinner,' said Cámara. 'What did you talk about?'

'He did most of the talking,' said Montesinos. 'Barely stopped. I thought he might be high, but Abi insisted he hadn't taken anything that night. So we just had to listen.'

'What did he say?'

Montesinos paused.

'It's why I made the call,' he said at last. 'He was talking about how everyone here was against him, how the whole village, the whole valley hated him, wanted him dead.'

'Who?' said Cámara.

'At the time I didn't take it seriously,' said Montesinos. 'I just thought, Oh no, here we go again. The same pattern being played out. That feeling of being under siege, that everyone had it in for him. He started talking about what happened in the Air Force again, about why they chucked him out, like some old, festering wound. But then when I heard he'd died . . .'

'Who did he mention?' said Cámara. 'Who wanted him dead?'

Montesinos shook his head.

'It was like, everyone,' he said. 'Some business about the local hunters and I don't know what. Then there was this crazy old neighbour, a recluse – something about a land dispute. But then there were others, unspecified. I couldn't make it out. People at Sunset, people in the village. Even the priest was mentioned at one point.'

Montesinos stopped.

'That was him, wasn't it? The man who was taken away.'

Cámara nodded slowly.

'Try to remember,' he said. 'What exactly did he say?'

'It's a bit of a blur,' he said, shaking his head. 'I was just so upset for him. I could tell, the same pattern, all over again. He talked about so many things. He wanted to put his affairs in order, about getting in touch with some nephew or other, his only blood relative. That's when the warning bells really began to ring. I said to Paco—'

'Paco was there as well?'

'Yes, three of them. José Luis must have gone to the toilet or something. I said: You've got to watch out for him. I've seen him like this before. Always the same routine, the paranoia, taking himself to the edge.'

Cámara released his hands from behind his back and brought them together in front of his face in a gesture of prayer.

'This dinner,' he said. 'Was it celebrating anything?'

'It was my birthday,' said Montesinos. 'We always remarked that our birthdays were quite close, except I'm Gemini and he's Cancer. He brought me a bottle of cologne. Always did. Bit of an obsession of his. Always smelt good, did José Luis. Always presentable, well dressed, ready to perform. Even when he was on the point of doing something stupid.'

Cámara's hands dropped to his sides, his eyes staring out, unfocused, over Montesinos's head.

Torres took a step forward out of the shadows.

'Chief?' he said. 'Chief, what is it?'

FIFTY-ONE

Cámara sprinted towards the door.

'Stay here,' Torres told Montesinos hurriedly. 'Don't move. Just stay here.'

He chased after Cámara. Out in the street he just caught sight of Cámara turning right past the church facade and heading into the village square. Torres puffed up the hill behind.

'Chief!' he called.

At the corner, a confused-looking Azcárraga and a *Guardia Civil* officer stopped him.

'This is Corporal Rodríguez,' said Azcárraga. 'What's going on?'

The three of them watched as Cámara darted between two parked cars and dived into the shadows of the arcade at the side of the square.

'What the hell's he doing?' said Rodríguez.

Torres didn't wait, making chase once more. The two

others quickly joined him. Torres reached the door of Los Arcos bar just as it was closing behind Cámara. Within an instant there were four law-enforcement officers in the tiny, grubby space. Three customers – two elderly men drinking mid-morning coffee and a younger man in overalls – stared in astonishment at the sudden invasion. Behind the bar, Ramón, the greasy-haired owner, tried to remain calm, smiling nervously through stained teeth.

'*Buenos días,*' he said.

Cámara walked up to the bar and leaned over, pressing his face close to Ramón's.

'That phone in the entrance,' he said loudly. 'It's the only public phone in the village, right?'

His aggression and tone shook Ramón.

'Yes,' he said, his high-pitched voice rising an octave. 'But I've got all the paperwork for it. It's legal.'

'Hey,' said Rodríguez, looking concerned. 'What's going on here?'

'Who uses it?' said Cámara, ignoring the *Guardia Civil* man and boring his eyes into Ramón.

'I don't know,' said Ramón with a shrug of the shoulders. 'Anyone. Most people have mobile phones these days. So it's not used as—'

'Three days ago,' said Cámara urgently. 'I need to know if anyone used that phone three days ago. In the morning, around twelve o'clock.'

Ramón looked at him desperately.

'Steady on, Chief Inspector,' said Rodríguez. Cámara turned and shot him a look of seniority of rank, and the *Guardia Civil* man immediately backed down.

'I can't remember,' said Ramón. 'I can't really see the phone from behind the bar. And people are coming and going all the time. I mean, I remember some things, but not everything. It's impossible.'

Cámara leaned across the bar, grabbed him by the scruff of the neck and pulled him close.

'I'm beginning to tire of your memory problems,' he said. 'I want you to think very carefully and tell me if anyone used that phone.'

Ramón went pale. From the side, Rodríguez took a hesitant step forwards, but Torres pushed out an arm and held him back.

'I really . . .' said Ramón. 'I really can't remember. Honestly. I swear.'

'I can remember.'

A small, deep voice spoke from the other end of the bar. Everyone turned to look. Cámara dropped Ramón back down behind the bar.

The man wearing worker's overalls stood up from his seat and took a step towards them.

'I was here that day,' he said. 'Usually come in around this time.'

'That's right, that's right,' said Ramón excitedly. 'Jorge was here. That's true. I remember.'

Cámara shot him a glance; the bar owner fell silent.

'Did you see someone using the phone?' Cámara asked Jorge.

The man nodded.

'Who was it?'

They waited as Jorge's mind churned.

'I didn't get a good look at him,' he said.

'Doesn't matter,' said Cámara impatiently.

'Just saw his silhouette in the doorway, but I thought I recognised him.'

'Who was it?' asked Cámara.

'Came in, made a quick call, then left. I don't know his name,' said Jorge. 'That man from Sunset.'

'Which one?' said Cámara.

Jorge paused.

'Well, people get so sensitive these days.'

'Which one?' insisted Cámara.

'Well, you know, the one who's . . .'

'Who's what?'

'*Mariquita*,' said Jorge.

Cámara took a step closer, almost bearing down on the man.

'You saw him come in, make a call and then leave. Is that it?'

Jorge nodded.

'Around twelve o'clock.'

'Just a bit before. 'Cause I'm usually out just before twelve myself.'

Cámara stepped back, his mind racing. Then he turned to the rest of the room.

'Azcárraga,' he said.

'Yes sir.' The young policeman stepped forwards.

'Call Judge Jurado again,' said Cámara. 'We need the call records for that phone.'

He pointed to the public phone on the wall near the entrance.

'Everything for the past week,' he said. 'But specifically—'

'I've got it,' said Azcárraga. 'Three days ago just before twelve.'

Cámara nodded.

'I'm on it,' said Azcárraga, taking his phone out of his pocket and heading towards the door.

'Go to the *Guardia Civil* station,' called out Rodríguez. 'My colleague's there. He can help.'

Azcárraga nodded and disappeared.

Cámara turned to Torres and Rodríguez.

'You two,' he said. 'Come with me.'

The doors of the grocer's shop were closed.

'After what happened last night,' said Rodríguez, 'I'm not surprised.'

'Did you speak to the wives?' asked Cámara. 'Have any contact with them?'

'Not yet,' said Rodríguez. 'But we will be doing. They're almost certainly accessories, if not fully implicated in the drug dealing themselves.'

'They live here, right?' said Cámara. 'Behind the shop.'

'Both couples,' said Rodríguez. 'Although they also have a place outside the village. Built it themselves: pool, garden.'

'The wives,' said Cámara. 'What are their names?'

'The blonde one's Ileana,' said Rodríguez. 'The dark-haired one's Cosmina.'

'Do you know where they are now?'

Rodríguez drew in a breath, then glanced at the cars parked nearby at the edge of the square on the other side of the arches.

'That's their car,' he said, nodding at the BMW with tinted-glass windows. 'Chances are they're holed up inside the shop.'

'I need to speak with them,' said Cámara. 'Urgently.'

Rodríguez shrugged, taking a step towards the door.

'I suppose at some point you're going to tell me what this is all about,' he mumbled. 'There's still lots of processing to do with Dorin and Bogdan. And then there's Father Ricardo of all people sitting in my cell.'

'I'm asking you personally,' said Cámara. 'As a favour.'

Rodríguez sighed and gave a reluctant nod.

He pulled on the door. It wouldn't open.

'Locked,' he said unnecessarily.

Torres took a step forward and hammered on the door.

'Open up!' he shouted.

Rodríguez put out a hand for him to stop. Then he knocked on the door himself, not quite so loudly.

'*Guardia Civil*,' he said, putting his mouth close to the door. 'We need to talk to you.'

He waited: there was no sound from inside.

'It's about Bogdan and Dorin,' Rodríguez continued. He glanced up at Cámara and shrugged.

Still no sound.

'Open the door!'

Cámara was losing his patience. Behind Rodríguez's back he tapped Torres on the shoulder and put his hand out, palm upwards. Torres hesitated, then understood, pulling his pistol out and handing it over. Cámara took a step towards the door and pushed Rodríguez out of the way, pointing the barrel of the gun at the lock in the door.

'Wait!' shouted Rodríguez.

They heard a sound from inside: footsteps shuffling across the floor. A key clunked in the lock. Cámara stuffed the pistol into the back of his trousers just as the door opened and a head framed with bottle-blonde hair appeared.

'We need to come in,' said Rodríguez.

The door opened and the three of them stepped through into the shop.

Ileana had not put on her make-up that morning; her

face was pale, dark bags under her eyes, her lips thin and dry. Cámara thought he could see murder in her black, open pupils. Behind the counter, standing in the doorway through to the living quarters, stood Cosmina, hair loose and ruffled, cheeks stained with red marks from tears.

'Have you come to arrest us?' she said.

Ileana backed away from the three men as they entered, pressing herself against the counter and trying to slip away to the side, thoughts of escape clearly flashing through her mind.

Cámara held the gun out and pointed it at her.

'Don't,' he said. 'Or I'll shoot.'

Ileana froze. Cámara gestured with the gun at Cosmina.

'You,' he said. 'Close that door and come out here in front of the counter.'

Cosmina did as she was told: the door clicked shut and she shuffled out into the shop. Both women, Cámara noticed, were barefoot. Cámara turned to Torres and nodded towards the door through which she had just passed. Wordlessly, Torres walked up the length of the shop and stood next to it, blocking the women's path.

'I need some information from you,' said Cámara.

Neither woman moved; they simply stared at him without blinking.

'Corporal Rodríguez here will be talking to you in due course about your husbands, about what happened last night.'

Cosmina's left eye twitched.

'But right now I need you to forget about that, to think about something else.'

He dropped his arm and tucked the pistol back into his belt. Then, moving slowly and deliberately, he went to the side of the aisle where he was standing and reached out to grab something from the shelf: a black canister with a plastic lid. He brought it down, pulled the lid off, and pressed the button at the top: a spray of cologne shot across the room in front of his face. Instantly he recognised that unmistakable smell, sweet and earthy.

'That's the third time I've smelt that since coming here,' he said.

He turned to Ileana and Cosmina.

'Your husbands wear it, don't they?' he said.

No reply.

'I smelt it last night, in their office. Just as they were telling me everything about their real business. The one that pays for all this.'

He gestured around the shop.

'So why do they wear it?' asked Cámara. 'I mean, if it smells so foul.'

Neither woman responded.

'You see, I'd forgotten,' said Cámara. 'But then a while ago I remembered when this stuff came out. Years ago. People were talking about it, saying it was special, saying it could attract people, like magic. Basically, if you sprayed this on yourself you were guaranteed a partner that night.'

His expression lightened.

'That was it, wasn't it? And do you know what's in it that gives it this magical effect?'

He shook his head as the women remained totally still, scared stiff by this armed policeman suddenly talking in their shop like some demented schoolteacher.

'No?' Cámara said. 'Well, I'll tell you. It's a chemical they contain called pheromones.'

Something in Cosmina seemed to break: she nodded her head gently.

'That's it,' said Cámara. 'And that's why your husbands wear it. To make themselves more sexually desirable.'

Cosmina's head bobbed up and down, as though hypnotised.

'But they're not the only people who wear it, are they?' continued Cámara. 'Teenage boys tend to buy it, don't they? I saw some of them in here picking a can up just yesterday. You remember me coming in yesterday, don't you?'

'Yes,' said Cosmina softly.

'Those boys left without buying any,' said Cámara. 'I watched them closely. But someone else did buy a can of this in the past few days, didn't they? In the last week.'

Ileana had almost disappeared from Cámara's mind. Cosmina was buckling, and he could sense the information he needed on the tip of her tongue.

'And you're going to tell me who that was.'

Cosmina nodded silently.

'Not some teenager,' said Cámara.

She shook her head.

'But someone else.'

Cosmina nodded.

'A man.'

She nodded.

'A man from the nightclub.'

More nodding.

'Yes,' she said almost inaudibly. Cámara took a step closer.

'Who?'

Her voice dropped to a whisper. Cámara leaned in to hear.

There was a loud scream of a car engine outside in the square, the hurried honking of a horn.

'RODRÍGUEZ!' shouted a man's voice. 'RODRÍGUEZ!'

Cámara turned and headed towards the door, with the

Guardia Civil corporal following quickly behind. Outside Enrique was scampering around the square.

'What is it?' Rodríguez said, catching Enrique by the arm. 'What's going on?'

'I thought you should know,' said Enrique, a look of apology in his voice. 'I didn't think anything of it at first, but then I thought I should tell you.'

'What?' said Cámara.

'Earlier on, about an hour ago' said Enrique, 'I was out walking near the hives.'

He looked Cámara awkwardly in the eye.

'I heard strange noises coming from the direction of Sunset.'

His eyes shifted from side to side.

'It was gunfire.'

FIFTY-TWO

Carlos read through the typed letter once more, his pen poised over the bottom to finish it with his small, angular signature. It was not the finest piece of prose that he'd written, there were a couple of turns of phrase that felt slightly awkward, but such things did not really matter at moments like this.

He did not go into the details of why he was resigning. The letter was no place for such things. There would be files and documentation in the system to explain why he had decided to go. Fernando would know everything anyway, and would understand. Carlos had failed in his duty; the disaster of the previous evening's operation, its sheer amateurism, made him wince with embarrassment. And even though they had discovered the leak from the Ministry of Defence and dealt with her, the Beneyto woman had vanished. And she was precisely the person he had been tasked with finding and stopping. After so many years' good service, of working selflessly for the benefit of the State, he had cocked up spectacularly. And there was only one honourable course of action for him to take.

He could sense an emotional response to the situation growing within him, yet he held it back, applying a force like a clenched fist on his more primitive self. Self-control, calm at all times, not giving in to lesser passions – these were his rules, and he would stick to them now more than ever before.

He read through the letter once more, checked the spelling and punctuation, and then lowered his pen to write.

There was an urgent knock at his office door. Carlos paused, lifted his pen from the sheet of paper, and barked an answer.

'What?'

His secretary entered.

'Something I think you should see, sir,' she said, nodding in the direction of the computer on his desk.

'Just come in from Valencia.'

Carlos nodded for her to leave. He placed his pen down and pressed a button on his keyboard to bring the screen back to life. After a couple of clicks of his mouse, he started reading a report sent in from the Valencia Police Jefatura.

The breath caught in his throat as he read the name mentioned in the first line.

'Cámara,' he said in a whisper. 'What *have* you been up to?'

He checked the date and time at the top. It was from that very morning, sent only ten minutes before. It had been drafted by Commissioner Rita Hernández herself and sent straight through to his special account. Good girl, he thought to himself with a smile. Trying to make it up to teacher. You might yet become a *very* useful idiot.

As he read on, thoughts about resigning dissolved like salt in boiling water.

There had been a murder, somewhere in the sierra not far from Valencia. A nightclub owner. A routine case: Chief Inspector Cámara had been sent up on his own to investigate.

But as part of his investigations, Cámara had uncovered something else: a drug operation in the area of the nightclub involving a couple of Romanian immigrants, men who were working in conjunction with the local priest, one Father Ricardo Benavent.

Carlos knew that name and he read on with increasing discomfort. The two Romanians – Dorin and Bogdan – were now in *Guardia Civil* custody along with the priest. Their case was due to be passed on imminently to the judicial authorities.

Rita Hernández ended the report with a final comment: she explained her haste in getting the news to Carlos. For this was, she said, not only a case involving a respected member of the Church, but she had learned through Father Bartolomeo at the Cathedral that Father Ricardo was no ordinary priest. He was, in fact, a member of the same special organisation that he himself belonged to, the Brothers of Cáceres. And it was imperative that he be delivered from his *Calvario* with immediate effect.

Carlos read the last line twice. Useful, yes, very useful. Yet still an idiot. Rita Hernández knew that the Brothers of Cáceres existed, knew now that they were a group of churchmen linked to the more secretive corners of government, perhaps even guessed that they played a key role in the smooth functioning of the State. Yet she did not know *what* they did, beyond giving confession to believers with sensitive information in their hands. Did not know that they were a key element in the whole success of *Operación Navas*, and more specifically in the very sensitive and highly illegal financial side of it, *Operación Abravanel*.

Yet through her ignorance she had stumbled on something of great importance. Losing Alicia Beneyto was one security problem. That her partner, Max Cámara, should unwittingly have broken up a large segment of *Operación Abravanel* – threatening exposure of the Brotherhood in so doing – was very different, adding multiple layers of greater complexity and threat.

Carlos's eyes darted between the report flickering on his screen and the dull matt ink of the letter lying on his desktop. Just as he appeared set on one course, something new had appeared before him.

What to do?

His phone buzzed. Automatically, his hand went down to pick it up.

'We've located her.'

It took Carlos a second to register what he'd been told.

'You've located . . . ?'

'The Beneyto woman,' said the voice.

Carlos cleared his throat.

'Where is she?'

'Back in Valencia.'

'What?'

'At the flat. No order had come through to stop watching it. We've just heard from our operative on the ground.'

'How long has she been there?'

'Can't say. Perhaps she came back late last night.'

'She must have caught a bus,' said Carlos. 'Or got a lift on one of those bloody car-sharing websites. Her name would have flashed up if she'd caught a train.'

'How do you want us to proceed, sir?'

Carlos thought for a moment. There was still a chance.

'Wait for me there,' he said. 'I'm coming to Valencia, taking charge of this personally.'

'And if she leaves?'

Carlos pursed his lips.

'Green light,' he said.

The line went dead.

Carlos picked up the letter, carefully tore it into four pieces and dropped it in the litter bin. Then he stared back at the screen and Rita Hernández's report. There was a detail mentioned there, one which he could use to his advantage. Useful idiots came in all kinds of shapes and sizes.

It was time to bring a new one into the fold.

FIFTY-THREE

Torres came out of the shop, leaving Ileana and Cosmina behind.

'Shots heard up at Sunset,' explained Cámara.

'My vehicle's back at the station,' said Rodríguez. 'I'll get it right away.'

Cámara hesitated.

'Torres and I will make our own way,' he said. 'Meet us there.'

Rodríguez jogged off with an uncomprehending shake of the head.

'Can you take us?' Cámara asked Enrique.

Behind the thick eyebrows Cámara thought he could detect a glimmer of excitement; the scar down the side of Enrique's face twitched.

'All right.'

Enrique had an old Citroen C15 van. Cámara sat in the passenger seat, with Torres in the back. After a sudden jerk forwards as the clutch was released, they set off, heading up the hill and out of the village with a cloud of diesel smoke billowing behind.

'You got any weapons in here, Enrique?' Cámara asked.

The old man drove in silence.

'Any handguns?'

'Never use handguns,' Enrique mumbled. 'Got the Remington in the back.'

'I'll be needing it.'

Cámara took the pistol out from his belt and passed it to his colleague.

The road wound up the mountainside until they came to the sign pointing right and the tarmac gave way to a dirt track.

'Take it slowly.'

Enrique raised his foot slightly off the accelerator.

'At the first sign of any trouble, turn around and get out of here as fast as you can.'

They turned the last corner and the main white-and-yellow building of Sunset came into view. Cámara's motorbike was still parked where he had left it, but there was no sign of any other vehicle.

'Stop here,' Cámara said.

Enrique pulled up in the shade of the pine forest at the edge of the large parking area.

'I want you to turn the van around and leave the engine on,' said Cámara. 'I'll get the rifle out of the boot myself. Stay here and be ready to drive away if need be.'

Enrique shrugged.

'Not quite sure what the point of bringing me all the way up here was,' he grumbled like an upset child. But Cámara had already picked up the Remington, and he and Torres were approaching the main building.

The front door was ajar. After quickly looking around, Cámara motioned to Torres that they should go inside. They tiptoed forward; Torres covered while Cámara pushed the door fully open and darted inside.

He swept the rifle around, pointing in the gloom towards the cloakroom, the entrance to the toilets, the stairway. Nothing. Some other sense told him that no one was there. Still, when Torres entered they continued in the same fashion, each one covering the other as they worked their way into the heart of the building. The main discotheque area was deserted. Torres checked behind the bar and signalled it was clear. Cámara watched closely in the mirrors on the walls for any sign of movement, but none came.

He caught Torres's attention and glanced up the stairs. The two men made their way silently to the bottom then started to creep up. It was impossible, however, to do so without making a noise and the stairs creaked with their weight. Torres rolled his eyes. Cámara took a deep breath, sucked in his lips and started to run: if anyone was up there they would already have heard them. Better to charge up like a bull than make a slow announcement of their arrival. The thing was, he was getting old for this kind of thing, and his strength wasn't quite what it had been.

Torres caught him up at the top of the stairs. Cámara was panting, staring down the corridor at the row of changing rooms and offices. They exchanged a glance: they would have to check each one.

The changing rooms were empty: nothing had changed about them since Cámara had come up here two days before. The room for the bar staff was the same except for a few missing bottles from a crate of Coke at the top of the stack nearest the door. A footprint in the dusty floor signalled that someone had been in there within the last few hours but gave no further clue.

The two offices were at the end. Cámara held his breath as he prodded open the door to Paco's with his fingertips. Torres sped inside.

The place smelt of stale cigarette smoke. It was virtually bare, with a desk, a chair and a sofa at one side. A white-board on one wall was covered in notes written in different coloured inks.

'Engagements for the disco,' murmured Torres under his breath, peering at it. 'Shifts, delivery times . . . routine stuff.'

Cámara tried the drawers of the desk: they were locked.

Cámara gestured for them to leave and try José Luis's office across the passageway. They burst in, Torres leading the way.

'Oh,' he said.

Cámara came up behind.

Papers were lying all over the floor – files, documents, receipts – tossed and scattered.

'Burglars?' said Torres.

'Maybe. News will have spread that the place is in semi shut-down.'

But as he spoke, Cámara's instinct disagreed; there was something about the tilt of the Dolly Parton photo on the wall. He stepped across the carpet of printed sheets and looked behind the desk: the door to the little safe was hanging open, more papers dangling out on the verge of falling to the floor. He put a hand inside and pulled out what was left.

'What is it?' asked Torres.

Cámara shrugged.

'If there was anything of value in here,' he said, 'it's gone.'

'Why else have a safe? Cash?'

'Probably. There would have been enough of the stuff swimming around this place.'

Cámara put the papers back.

'Come with me,' he said.

Back outside the main door, Cámara could see Enrique still sitting in the van. He turned to go the other way, beckoning Torres to follow.

They passed around the side of the building and out to the corner of the back patio. To their right stood the door leading up to José Luis's apartments. Cámara pulled the handle down and stepped through. The air felt colder inside the stairwell. He skipped up the steps two at a time, Torres following in his wake.

José Luis's apartments had not only been ransacked, like the office, they had been deliberately and methodically destroyed. The shelves lay at odd angles where they had been hauled to the floor, piling on top of one another and splintered at the point of impact. The white television lay in pieces, a tangle of plastic, wiring and electronic circuits looking as though someone had beaten it to death. The sofas had been attacked, their covers split and torn with a knife, a plethora of foam and cotton fibres heaped in piles where their innards had been removed and tossed away. Around them, every ornament, every object, every piece of furnishing had been smashed or assaulted. The simple toys that had been on proud display in the cabinet were scattered in all directions, most of them crushed or damaged. The bed had been targeted with specific aggression: the sheets pulled off and ripped into shreds, mattress stabbed and disembowelled with startling viciousness, each pillow split open and its feathers showered around the room. Cámara thought he detected a sharp, sickening smell: a damp patch at the centre of what was left of the mattress looked very like evidence that someone had pissed there.

'What the fuck,' said Torres.

Cámara stepped across and kicked the mattress back on to the bed to reveal the drawers underneath. They were both partially open. José Luis's gun had vanished, while his store of drugs had also been raided.

Torres looked inside the bathroom, then came out, shaking his head.

'Place is deserted,' he said. 'No one here.'

'It's not so much what's here as what's missing,' said Cámara.

'What did you . . .' But Torres's voice stopped as they both heard the sound of a car pulling up outside. Torres made to move. After casting a last look at the scene of destruction, Cámara followed.

Rodríguez had arrived in a 4x4 with a fellow *Guardia Civil* officer, the man who had spoken to Cámara that morning in the station.

'Méndez,' Rodríguez introduced him. They had parked their car right outside the front door. In the back, just getting out, was Azcárraga.

'I'm not happy about having civilians here,' said Rodríguez, indicating Enrique's van still sitting at the edge of the pine trees. The engine had been turned off. Cámara looked: there was no sign of Enrique.

'I've got something,' said Azcárraga enthusiastically before Cámara could say anything.

'What is it?'

He stepped forward

'The phone records from the public phone at Los Arcos. Judge Jurado came up trumps again, then Méndez and I used the *Guardia Civil* system to access the Telefónica files.'

His eyes widened.

'Tell you what, their system's much faster than ours,' he said in a low, impressed voice.

'What did you find?'

'Call made exactly when you thought it had been – just before twelve three days ago. Pretty easy match as there are hardly any calls made on it.'

'Who was it to?'

Azcárraga handed him a piece of paper.

'This number,' he said.

It was a simple row of digits: a landline, but it could have belonged to anyone in the Valencia area.

'Got the ID for the number as well,' said Azcárraga proudly.

'Well?'

'It belongs here,' he said. 'To Sunset. Whoever called from the bar that day was trying to get through here.'

'How long was the call?' Cámara asked.

'Very short. About ten or fifteen—'

His words were drowned by the shrill sound of a scream. They all turned as one.

'It's coming from round the back,' said Cámara.

He pointed to Rodríguez and Méndez.

'You two go that way. We'll go round the other side.'

He nodded quickly to Azcárraga.

'And you stay here.'

The *Guardia Civil* men had already drawn their weapons and were scuttling round the corner of the main building. Cámara and Torres took off the other way. As they came round into the patio, the scream came again, descending into horrified sobs.

'The kitchen,' said Cámara, indicating the small scullery building.

They ran over as the *Guardia Civil* officers appeared from the other way. Cámara and Torres were in first.

Enrique was standing in the centre of the room holding his hands up near his head. He seemed to be petrified, body stiff and rigid but for the pumping of his chest as he breathed in deeply and let out a deafening wail of grief.

On the floor, less than a step away from him, lay two dead bodies.

Vicente had been shot twice in the face, one bullet hole below his left eye, the other below his brow, neat perforations in his skin. He was slumped at the side of the inglenook, one arm crossing his chest, the other lying out across the hearth. The wall behind him was streaked with blood and brain matter from the impact. The second bullet had been fired when he was already down, a definitive *coup de grace* to make sure he was dead. A pool of thick dark blood had formed around his body, pouring out of the shattered mess that was the back of his skull.

Beside him, on the other side of the hearth, lay his wife. Vicenta's face was turned away, her body slumped on its side, lying in an uncomfortable heap on top of two saucepans that had fallen with her. Her head was propped up at an odd angle by the wall, and there, just behind her ear, was the very clear sight of a bullet hole with black scattered burn marks circling it. The shot that had killed her had been fired from behind at close range, perhaps without her even realising.

'He must have shot her first,' Cámara said in an almost inaudible whisper.

Part of his mind was already wondering: the dog – where was it? Then he spotted a motionless heap of white-and-grey fur nestling under Vicenta's shoulder. Even Blanquita hadn't been spared.

He held the rifle in one hand and reached out to Enrique with the other. Turning him as gently as he could, he led him away and back into the sharp sunlight of the patio, sitting him down on a step underneath a window. Enrique looked out vacantly in a state of complete shock.

This man, thought Cámara, has never killed anyone. Could never kill anyone. Animals, perhaps, but humans very definitely not.

Torres came out, followed by the *Guardia Civil* men.

'I need you to put a call out,' Cámara said to Rodríguez. 'Full description of both the man and his car, a blue Audi.'

Rodríguez nodded.

'Wanted for murder,' said Cámara. 'Abdelatif Cortbi. Also known as Abi. He's armed and almost certainly under the influence of narcotics.'

FIFTY-FOUR

Rodríguez spoke briefly to Enrique before the old man drove away.

'I'll be in touch,' he said sympathetically through the window. Enrique nodded sorrowfully.

The van meandered down the dirt track. Rodríguez went to his own vehicle to pick up the radio. Cámara was about to speak to him when he caught sight of another car coming their way. Enrique slowed down to let it pass, glancing without recognition at the driver, then carried on. Cámara stood and stared at the approaching vehicle, a small, silver Ford. It looked clean and almost new. He had the feeling it was hired.

He allowed it to draw close. The driver had noticed the *Guardia Civil* vehicle present, the staring, questioning eyes, and had slowed to a crawl. Cámara put his hand out and he stopped, lowering the window.

'Is everything all right?' came a nervous voice.

Torres stood next to Cámara.

'Could you step out of the car, please?'

The door opened and a man in his late twenties got out. He was dressed in jeans and a black shirt, with sideburns running the length of his cheeks. He wore a confused expression, uncertain about where he was or what he had walked into.

'What . . . ?' he said. 'What's going on?'

Cámara thought he could detect a Madrid accent. Rodríguez was still speaking into his car radio, but Méndez walked over.

'Who are you?' Cámara said.

'Andrés Benítez,' said the man. He looked frightened, glancing back and forth at the policemen surrounding him. 'I can . . . Do you want to see my ID?'

He fished his wallet out from his pocket and handed it to them. Torres took it.

'What are you doing here?' asked Cámara.

'I've just flown in from Barajas,' said Andrés. 'Came straight here.'

'Why?'

'The place is closed,' said Méndez sharply.

'No,' said Andrés. 'I'm not here for the disco. I'm a relative of José Luis.'

Cámara examined him closely, looking for any family resemblance.

'The nephew?' he said.

Andrés shrugged.

'Well, kind of. Not exactly nephew. And I hardly knew José Luis. But his mother was my grandmother's sister, so we're, I don't know, second cousins or something.'

He spoke with a lightness of voice that contrasted wholly

and completely with the mood of the moment. Méndez's eyes narrowed.

'What are you doing here?' he snarled.

'Have you come for the funeral?' Torres asked.

Andrés looked at them with unease.

'I got an email,' he said. 'From José Luis's solicitor.'

Cámara nodded.

'Go on.'

'He told me about José Luis. And said that as executor of his will he was informing me that I was to inherit . . .' He hesitated. 'Well, this. The nightclub.'

The three men stared at him silently.

'I've got a printout with me in the car,' he said. 'He called me as well, said it was all totally true.'

His eyes widened.

'I know, I couldn't believe it either.'

'Show us the printout,' said Torres.

Andrés took a step towards the boot of the car. Méndez tailed him, his hand hovering over his pistol. Andrés took out a laptop case and rifled through a side pocket for a piece of paper, which he handed to Torres.

'When did you hear?' asked Cámara.

'Yesterday morning.'

At the side, Torres was clutching the printout and taking out his phone.

'No signal,' said Cámara. 'Try one inside the building.'

Torres walked towards the main doors as Andrés continued.

'Came completely out of the blue. We haven't had any contact with José Luis for years. Apparently I met him once when I was little, but I can barely remember. I knew about this place, heard about it sometimes, but we never talked on the phone or anything. Not even at Christmas. When the solicitor got in touch I thought he was just letting me know that José Luis had died, passing on the information. But then he told me about José Luis's will and how everything was being left to me. I thought he was joking at first. But I checked the solicitor's website and everything – it's real. Not a fake. But, well, when I realised it was all true I thought I should come round. See what it was all about.'

'You caught a plane,' said Cámara.

'Yeah. Hired a car at Manises and drove straight up here. It's easy to find once you see the sign.'

His face fell.

'But something's happened, hasn't it?' he said. 'I mean, you lot . . .'

Torres was coming back from the main building. Cámara turned.

'It's true,' said Torres. 'Confirmation from the solicitor himself; just had him on the phone.'

From the *Guardia Civil* car came the sound of the radio crackling. Rodríguez went to answer.

'José Luis changed his will one week ago,' continued Torres. 'Everything's going to his relative.'

He glanced at Andrés.

'Our sudden visitor here.'

'Who was it going to before?' asked Méndez. 'Before he changed the will?'

'The solicitor wouldn't say,' said Torres. 'Confidential. But we can find out.'

'We don't need to,' said Cámara.

Rodríguez put the radio back into its slot in the car and stepped towards them.

'Two pieces of news,' he said. 'My colleagues in Valencia

have picked up Paco: he's been arrested and charged with drug dealing.'

'Well done,' said Cámara. 'You must be relieved.'

Rodríguez nodded at him with bloodshot eyes. Paco was clearly the one, in his mind, to blame for his son's death, the personal link, perhaps even the man who had sold him the drugs that killed him in the first place.

'What's the other piece of news?' asked Torres.

'We've found Abi's car,' said Rodríguez. 'It's parked at a petrol station on the A7 motorway.'

He shook his head.

'But no sign of Abi.'

Méndez stayed on guard at Sunset, waiting for the *Guardia Civil* crime scene officers to arrive. Rodríguez offered to drive Torres down to the *Guardia Civil* station while Cámara took his motorbike. Andrés was ordered to leave and head to Los Arcos bar, where he was to wait for further instructions.

'Abi could be anywhere by now,' Rodríguez said, opening his car door. 'If I were him I'd have hooked up with someone on one of these car-sharing websites and caught a lift somewhere. No way of tracing him, totally invisible.'

'Unless we can find the website in question,' said Torres, getting into the passenger seat.

'He'll be miles away before we can do that.'

Cámara stood silently by his bike, slipping on his helmet as he watched Rodríguez and Torres drive away.

'There's got to be a way,' he said to himself.

The bike fired into life; he slipped it into gear, let the clutch out and powered on down the dirt track.

Cámara's mind raced over everything that he had learned

over the past three days. He had joked about Abi back in Rita's office: *Cherchez la femme*. It hadn't gone down well, not politically correct. Yet it had never been Enrique, nor Paco, nor the mayor and the hunters, the Romanians or even Father Ricardo, momentarily forgotten yet still languishing in the *Guardia Civil* cell. It had been Abi all along.

He began picking up pieces from the mass of information, turning them in his hand like shattered shards of a mirror before placing them down, shuffling them carefully as he located each one in its given position, slotting them into place to give him a cracked, disjointed, yet complete reflection.

He had barely made note of the argument that Abi mentioned between himself and José Luis, put it down as some lovers' tiff. It was clever of him to have mentioned it. To put Cámara off his guard? What had they been arguing about? The will? Was that when Abi had learned the truth? Something about the nephew had been mentioned before, during the dinner down in Valencia with José Montesinos, José Luis's old boyfriend. Was that when Abi first began to suspect? He had been with José Luis for eleven years. There was no marriage certificate, but any judge would have regarded their arrangement as a civil partnership in all but name. Abi would likely have inherited in the event of José Luis's death. Yet Montesinos had seen the warning signs that night, the sense that José Luis was about to fall into another pattern of destructive behaviour, of pushing away the very people whose acceptance and love he had sought. Did that include Abi? Was Abi the person really set to suffer from José Luis's impending breakdown? An immigrant here in Spain – his only anchor was José Luis. His entire life devoted to Sunset. And he was about to lose it all.

So what had he done? Had he known that José Luis had already changed his will? Perhaps he thought he still had time to act. And so everything came to a head on his birthday.

There was always something that nagged Cámara about his story of going into the village to buy José Luis a present. What kind of a present could you buy there? A baker's, a grocer's, a hardware shop, a bar and little else. Exactly what gift was he intending to buy for José Luis? The point was that he had already bought him something there – days before in the Romanians' shop: the cheap, black cologne stuffed with pheromones. How had he presented it to José Luis? As a joke, perhaps? It must have been the present in the golden box. What kind of cologne could you buy a man who already had such a wide selection? Had he sprayed it on José Luis himself? Had José Luis tried it, more out of idle curiosity than anything else?

It mattered little how it got there. The point was that once José Luis's skin was peppered with the stuff all it took was to get him to the right place and let things take their natural course. Enrique was wrong: bees *could* be made to sting a person. Why else had they stung Cámara himself when he walked past them the second time? Because he had been covered in José Luis's new, cheap cologne, full of pheromones that made the bees aggressive. 'Perhaps they don't like the smell of policemen,' Enrique had said. There had been an unwitting clue right there in front of him.

Cámara's mind spun like the speeding wheels of his bike, casting back over every scene from the past few days. But he kept returning back to the birthday dinner with Montesinos; the poor man clearly loved José Luis, yet he had unwittingly caused his undoing. Abi hadn't known the full truth about José Luis's rejection by the Air Force until that night. The allergy was a key piece of information. Add to that Enrique's stubborn placing of the hives up at the Chain and everything was in position.

'I told that Abi,' Vicente had said. Yes, Vicente had mentioned the hives to José Luis's lover. Abi had known. All he had to do was get José Luis up to the Chain on his own.

And so the farce of going down to the village to buy a birthday present. He hadn't bought anything at all. Had he lingered before going into Los Arcos? The only public phone in the village. He slips in, lifts the receiver, puts in his money and dials. Not José Luis's number, naturally – there was too much of a risk of being found out. Instead he calls Paco. And he – what? – puts on an accent? Tries a different voice? Whatever he did – and it was a very short call – he managed to persuade Paco that it was Enrique on the line, that he wanted an urgent meeting with José Luis. At the Chain. Paco had then dutifully passed the message on.

It had been quick, and the phone was not in clear view. But someone had seen him, had seen the 'poof' from Sunset making the call.

'The *mariquita*,' the man in the bar had said. Which could only be Abi.

Cámara wondered what Abi had done after the call. He couldn't head back to Sunset too quickly – he needed to give his plan sufficient time to work. José Luis would have to walk up to the Chain in the first place. And he probably wouldn't rush, despite the supposed urgency. Then the bees would have to play their part, and José Luis would have to be left some considerable time on his own as the allergic reaction kicked in. Reach him too soon, get him medical attention, and the chances of killing him would be reduced.

And so Abi spent his time in the village – it would give him more alibis. Nowhere near the scene of the murder when it was taking place. Perhaps wondering – fearing, even – if his complex plan would even work.

Then he had driven back to Sunset relatively quickly. That much was clear because an ambulance did get to José Luis just before he died. It was on his way down to hospital in Valencia that he had breathed his last. Confirmation of death came on arrival.

So what had drawn Abi back? Remorse? Had he had second thoughts, tried to undo what he had set in motion?

Cámara pulled up outside the *Guardia Civil* station and parked the bike.

'I think I know,' said Cámara, walking inside and finding Torres and Rodríguez already there. 'I think there's a way we can find him.'

FIFTY-FIVE

The car was cramped, and he wondered whether it would make it all the way, but he was safely out of the mountains and heading south, unspotted and untraceable. In a few hours they would reach a port. There were ways of getting across the sea undetected. He had enough money in cash: it wouldn't be too difficult to find someone to help him make the crossing.

He was squashed against the door next to a teenage boy, squeezing into a space that wasn't really there. But the father had listened when he'd shown him the hundred-euro note and had made up his mind when there was promise of another at the other end.

His car had broken down, he said. But he had to get to Tangier in a hurry: a member of the family had died. Calling out a tow truck would take too long. Was there room in the man's Peugeot?

The family was driving down from Toulouse as they

usually did at this time of year. The schools had finished and they embarked on their annual journey back to Morocco to visit the relatives, reconnect with their own land. France meant work and money and education. Morocco was about life, about identity.

The roof rack was piled high with cheap chequered bags filled with presents and goods for everyone in Tétouan: blankets, clothes, cooking pots, a few electronic items that were more expensive south of the Strait. They were tied on precariously with lengths of coloured rope that were fraying at the ends after six hours' driving. They had stopped at the service station to wash and rest, have a bite to eat by the grass verge and visit the toilets before getting back into the car and setting off once again.

He congratulated himself on leaving his own car on the other side of the motorway and crossing here, skipping past the speeding cars and jumping over the central reservation. Should the vehicle be located, they would assume he was heading north, had picked up a lift on the road heading to Catalonia and France. It would put them off the scent for a while. To be doubly safe he had switched off his phone: he had seen enough TV cop shows to know they could locate someone by the signal. He wasn't going to make that mistake. He hated disconnecting, but it had to be done. Just as he'd done three days before. He had been certain that Vicenta would see it there on the window ledge; she'd been the one to mention it when he'd returned from the village.

'Have you seen José?'

His voice hadn't faltered, steady, unwavering, calm, with just a hint of concern.

'Paco said something about him having a meeting with Enrique. Up at the Chain.'

'Oh.' And he left it, just long enough. Perhaps twenty minutes, a bit less.

'He's been gone a while. I'll go and see if he's OK.'

Was that when he first caught a glimmer of suspicion in her eye? She nodded silently to him, as if she already knew. Damn her!

And then came the walk. He took his time, resisting every urge to break into a run, pacing slowly and deliberately through the pine trees, his eyes wide open, watching for any movement, any sign.

And then he saw him, his lover, lying in the sunshine, basking in a ray of light that penetrated the canopy and shone down from the sky, accusing, unforgiving, final. José Luis was staring upward, a hand clutched to his throat.

He had watched from a distance for a while. His lover was not quite dead, still in the process of leaving this world. Yet it would not be long. The bees had done their work. As he had hoped they would. Was that the sound of their buzzing he could hear? Were they still flying around him, swooping down to sting even as he struggled to draw his last, pathetic breath?

A chasm opened in him at that moment, dark, vast, like a great tear in the fabric of the universe, a consuming emptiness that stuck to him like glue. Regret? Sorrow? No words came close to describing the experience. He felt love and hatred, tenderness and anger in equal measure, and yet he was removed at the same time: feeling and unfeeling; lover and stranger; murderer and disinterested observer.

Returning to the nightclub he had run as fast as his legs could carry him.

'It's José. Something's happened. Call an ambulance!'

Genuine, confused tears of concern had flowed down from his cheeks. Vicenta had comforted him while they waited.

'It's all right,' she said. 'It's not your fault.'

And again the doubt creeping through his mind like shadows from a setting sun. What did she know? *How* did she know?

He had insisted on driving down behind the ambulance as much to get away from her as to keep up pretences. By the time they made it to La Fé he almost wished José Luis would survive. When they told him, minutes later in a side room by Accident and Emergency, he couldn't take it in, as though they were telling him a sick joke, or a lie. He who had planned everything not able to comprehend that his design had been successful. He had loved José, thought his love was returned. The parties, the orgies, the drugs – they meant nothing. He himself had taken part at times. Yet José, in his heart, loved only him.

Or so he had thought.

José had mentioned Andrés a couple of times over the previous month. Which was unusual. His name had come up before in the past, but very infrequently. Now it was clear that Andrés was, for whatever reason, on José's mind. And he had begun to wonder.

Then Montesinos invited them to dinner, an old lover, José Luis's first. He saw disquiet in Montesinos's eyes that night, watching as José Luis talked endlessly, demanding and receiving every drop of attention that he could get, like a hippo wallowing in fresh cool mud. And there was more talk of Andrés. Watch out, Montesinos had said when José Luis left them for a moment. Watch him: I've seen him like this before. It bodes ill.

Which was when he had told him about the Air Force. And the allergy.

After that, the wheels in his mind had started to turn with a will and momentum of their own. An overheard phone call to the solicitor had given him all the confirmation that he needed. He, José Luis's lover of the past eleven years, was about to be stripped bare and left to rot, like some discarded piece of meat.

'It's a pattern,' Montesinos had said. 'He can't help himself.'

Perhaps not, perhaps he could not prevent it. But he could protect himself. He could . . . The plan formed itself, as though Fate were forcing his hand. Enrique, that ridiculous old man! Who would have thought that the means would have come through him? Yet placing the hives there, as close as he could to the nightclub, had been the trigger, the moment when he had known what was going to happen, and more importantly, how. Supplying the necessary chemical had been easy: cheap and disgusting, the cologne that the Romanian women sold was exactly what he needed. He had heard from somewhere – perhaps a TV documentary? It didn't matter – about the effect pheromones could have on bees. Then he had placed the bottle in the golden box with a smile, a joke present before the bigger, proper one to come later that day.

A joke? What was he thinking? The joke had killed José.

As it had been meant to.

During the argument he had thrown out Andrés's name. Yes, José Luis said. My relative, my blood. My nightclub.

You wouldn't leave me with nothing!

That's just for you to find out.

For him to find out . . . Well, he had found out. The

papers in the safe confirmed everything, that he was too late. It had all gone to the nephew.

But José Luis was already dead by then. Too late to change anything.

There was cash, at least. Plenty of it. He knew where the key to the safe was, hidden behind the hideous Dolly Parton photo. José Luis had told him. A long time ago now. When there was still trust between them.

There's never been anyone like you, he used to say back then.

So hc had money. And it was time to run.

Vicenta knew. Old women were like that. They could sense things. He saw it in her eyes, saw it in the way that she shielded him from the police detective when he drove back to Sunset. She was protecting him. Because she had guessed everything. Perhaps not the details, but the bare bones of what had happened.

Killing her had been the hardest part. Yet he liked to think that he had been considerate, given her no stress, no pain. A shot straight to the back of the head and she had fallen like a stone. The husband had been easier. Shot as he stood up at the sight of his dead wife. And another once he hit the floor, just to be sure. They would pass to the next world together. He had not been cruel. He could find redemption yet.

Only far from here, from the mountains, from Sunset, from everything.

Cramped against the car door, a plastic bag bumping against his head from the mass of luggage squeezed into the boot, he watched the oleander bushes at the side of the motorway whip past in a blur of white and red. Each metre they drove, each bridge they passed, every junction they left behind put more and more distance between himself and danger, brought him closer to safety, to home.

He hadn't been back to Morocco for seven, perhaps eight years. An uncle in Tangier would be able to put him up for a while, then he would press further south, head towards Rabat or Casablanca. It would be easier in a big city: more resources, more places to hide. Then, after a while, perhaps a few months or a year, he would slowly re-emerge. He had enough cash on him to last him a while, perhaps even build something new for himself. Eventually. When all this was past.

Yet there was still so far to go.

A sign to Alicante flashed by. The landscape was already changing: the pine trees he was used to back at Sunset were almost gone, the ground become drier, sandier, like a desert, with a hint of Africa, of home. Even the air, pouring in through the father's open window, smelt different: warmer, dustier, with a promise of vast open skies. He could sense his future reaching out towards him with silvery fingers, drawing him back to long-forgotten horizons.

Just a few more hours. The discomfort, the heat, the noise of the family chatting busily away, a baby crying in its mother's arms as she pulled out a breast to feed him once more, was all worth it. For soon he would be free.

His eyes began to droop as the nerves and drugs lost their grip on him.

By the time the car got caught in the traffic jam, he was asleep.

FIFTY-SIX

The *Guardia Civil* helicopter touched down in a rocky abandoned field by the side of the motorway. As Cámara got out, squinting against the clouds of dust kicked up by the spinning blades, he admired the work done so far: the tailback was stretching back several kilometres into the distance, but there, up ahead, he could make out the *Guardia Civil* patrol cars that had caused this traffic jam in the first place, and the green-and-white motorcycles passing up and down between the stationary cars as more officers looked for their prey. Once the satellites had locked on to the GPS signal emitted from his phone, it became quite easy to locate Abi's whereabouts. The poor man had probably thought himself safe by switching it off, thought Cámara. He should have thrown it away, cut himself off, yet there was no way he could do that. Vicenta had known – 'He can never be separated from it,' she said. She knew Abi so well. Too well, perhaps: was it that knowledge which had brought about her own death?

The sun was beginning its afternoon descent, its rays beaming down with bright heat. Each car flashed a harsh yellow, windows like mirrors, dark, distorting, only partially obscuring those sitting behind. Torres ran up as he approached the crash barriers at the side of the road.

'He's definitely here. We've got a very clear signal.'

Cámara said nothing.

'What do we do? Search every car?'

He pointed towards the *Guardia Civil* officers. The motorcyclists had already got off their machines and were pacing past the stuck vehicles, peering in through the windows, checking the faces inside against the ID shot they had been issued of the man being sought. They would find him eventually.

'Do you think he'll run?'

'He's been running already,' said Cámara. 'Only without knowing we were on his tail.'

The helicopter blades continued to spin behind them, filling the air with sand and noise.

'The *Guardia Civil* will want to claim him,' said Torres.

'The *Guardia Civil* have got their own,' said Cámara. 'This one's mine.'

He climbed over the crash barriers and started moving about the cars himself: ordinary vehicles, some going home from work, perhaps; others, judging by the foreign number plates, on holiday.

He took a few steps closer to the Peugeot: it was French, an entire family and more somehow crammed inside. The driver wound down his window when he saw Cámara approach. Cámara looked him in the eye: there was a pleading in his expression: please, don't drag us into anything.

And the man gestured behind him with his head. Cámara leaned down to look.

Cámara stood in the way of the sun, cancelling its reflection. The mirror-like dazzle of the car windows disappeared. The view inside was clearer now. Cámara saw a sleeping head, pressed against the glass, skin white with the pressure, mouth open, a droplet of saliva perched on the edge of his lower lip.

Abi looked so peaceful, so calm, so deeply relaxed.

Almost, thought Cámara, as though he were asleep at home in his own bed.

FIFTY-SEVEN

Torres sat back down at his desk in Narcotics and stared at his computer screen. The atmosphere in the department had been notably cool since his return that evening. Admittedly he had been on the fringes of an operation which had seen the *Guardia Civil* take all the credit for destroying a drug-dealing operation in the sierra, and he could understand if there was some annoyance that he, as a member of the *Policía Nacional*, had been involved in their rivals' success. Yet he had experienced similar situations in the past and this went beyond that; there was more than mere frostiness towards him from colleagues: he felt certain some were talking about him behind his back, and the expressions on their faces betrayed the uncharitable nature of their opinions.

It was not so much the feeling that he wasn't particularly loved. That kind of thing came and went and was nothing to worry about. No, there was something more to it: an active dislike, hostility, even. And if he felt disturbed by it, it was out of curiosity: he wanted to know why.

Now that he was at his desk and facing his computer, the uneasy feeling he had had since walking in was dramatically, even comically, increased. For on a Post-It note, someone had written a simple message for him and placed it on the screen: *JUDAS*.

Really?

He peeled the note off, screwed it into a ball and threw it nonchalantly into the bin. And for the next half an hour he trawled through the police intranet, looking for some clue or other as to what had happened, why attitudes in the department were so hostile.

He found nothing, however, nothing to shed light of any kind on the matter. If anything, there was more reason to be confused: according to a report he found from the *Guardia Civil*, Father Ricardo had been released without charge. Something about there being no evidence to link him with the drug trade. Dorin and Bogdan, and Paco from Sunset, however, were still being detained and their case passed on to the judicial authorities.

Getting up from his desk, Torres decided to step out into the corridor and get some coffee from the machine. As he did so, one of his colleagues – one of only two who had at least greeted him the previous day – caught his eye then looked away. Torres shrugged and headed out the door.

The man appeared at his side just as Torres was pulling his cup out from the machine.

'Hello,' said Torres, as amiably as he could – a feat that was never particularly easy for him, still less so today.

'I'm amazed you even showed up,' said the man.

'Bit of an overreaction, don't you think?' Torres said. 'Am

I really a traitor just because the *Guardia Civil* took the prize?'

The other officer smiled and shook his head.

'What?' said Torres. 'This happens. To all of us every now and again. But I don't remember ever getting quite so cut up about it.'

The man looked at him, a question in his eyes.

'You don't get it, do you?' he said. 'Don't know.'

Torres leaned in. With his bulky weight and large black beard, he could do imposing when he wanted to. Friendly, not so much. But imposing, yes.

'Don't get what?' he said.

'That outfit you just helped to break up,' said the officer. 'There was much more to it, much more than the surface appearance. And now you and your pals have gone in like a bunch of kids and wrecked everything.'

Torres raised an eyebrow.

'Wrecked everything?'

'You just don't know anything,' said the man, breathing hard and clearly uncomfortable with Torres leaning over him, but refusing to back off, nonetheless.

'I know what I know,' said Torres. 'And I know a crook when I see one. And I'm beginning to get the sense that not all of them are out there.'

He pointed a thick finger towards the window and the street beyond.

'This department has a reputation. There's just too much temptation for some. Perhaps you're happy to be thought of as bent, but that's one thing no one's ever going to be able to throw at me and make stick.'

The officer snorted, his face reddening.

'You're not going to last a fucking week. Trust me, anyone

who interrupts the bigger picture gets given short shrift. And you've caused big ructions, believe me. In fact, if I were you I'd be watching my back. You're up to it well beyond your eyeballs, Torres. When it comes to Abravanel, there's no mercy. And don't think your track record or your friends elsewhere are going to be able to help you with this one. You're dead meat. I'd get out of here now, while you've still got legs to walk on.'

He thrust out an arm and pushed Torres in the centre of the chest. Torres didn't resist, stumbling for a moment as he got his balance. When he looked up again the other man had gone, the doors back into the department swinging behind him.

Torres stood in silence as connections and links furiously criss-crossed his brain.

Abravanel. He suddenly remembered where he had heard that name before.

And a sense of clear, mortal danger appeared before him.

He turned and ran as fast as he could down the corridor. There was someone he had to find very quickly and very urgently.

FIFTY-EIGHT

The papers covered almost the entire floor of the living room. And they included only the most important ones: a whole pile on her desk detailed finer points of the web-like structure which had spun itself as each page brought more details, deeper complexity to this great, secret government enterprise.

Yet a secret for not much longer, for she had already written the first draft of her article and was about to read it for a second time, to edit and polish it, before sending it off to Quico Romero. It would be the first of many articles, probably stretching out over several days and weeks, even longer if its exposure brought more revelations, as she expected it might. There was so much here that it was impossible to detail in only one piece, yet she had the outline, the basic story, and even now, as she read her own words, she felt a shiver run through her blood at the sinister magnitude of it.

It had been risky, getting back to Valencia. And she still did not know if she had done the right thing. She felt like a bull of the meek and docile kind in the bullring, pulling back, in the face of so many wounds, to its *querencia*, its perceived place of sanctuary, somewhere it might feel safe. Yet was she really safe here? Almost certainly not. But she had information, and that information might just save her. As long as she got it out as quickly as possible. Once others were party to it, there would be no point in the security services shutting her down.

Which was why she had to work as quickly as possible. She had tried to read some of the material the previous night on the late bus from Madrid, but the adrenalin from chasing around the city, meeting up with Marisol, had left her drained, and she had fallen asleep. Waking up with a start as they pulled into Valencia, she had seen with relief that the file was still where she had left it, as a pillow for her head against the window.

A quick walk – no more taxis – to the flat, a shower, breakfast, litres of coffee, and she had started work. It had taken her time just to organise the material, put it into some kind of shape, make sense of the many layers and the terminology, decipher the euphemisms that state officials – and particularly the military – tended to use.

The process had taken several hours and she had had to read and re-read the material, making certain that she had correctly understood, that the story was, indeed, what she was about to tell the country it was.

'It's big,' she wrote in a simple email to Quico. 'Have everything. Expect something from me later this afternoon.'

'OK,' came the simple reply. She would have preferred

something stronger, something to indicate greater commitment, give a sense that she was not alone with this.

At least Max would be back soon, communications between them having finally been restored. He had sent her an email – was on his way now. There was so much to tell him. He could be her second pair of eyes before she sent it through to Madrid. She wondered how he was going to react when she told him.

She glanced at the screen, scrolled up to the top of the article, and began to read once more.

> The government is building a secret Guantánamo-style facility on the Balearic island of Cabrera to detain thousands of suspected Islamic militants in the event of a new terrorist attack and collapse of public confidence. The scheme, funded by money from illicit drug dealing, is jointly run by the Ministry of Defence and the *Centro Nacional de Inteligencia* (*CNI*) and has been given the code name *Operación Navas de Tolosa*. Ministry of Defence documents obtained by this newspaper show that *Operación Navas*, and a complex web of sub-operations, has now commenced following a two-year preparation period. The first steps to build the detention centre on Cabrera – a process code-named *Operación Clavijo* – began within the last week under the guise of military manoeuvres in the waters south of Mallorca.
>
> Officially, no public money has been spent on any part of *Operación Navas*. All financing has come through *Operación Abravanel*, a covert government-sponsored drug cartel designed to raise funds for the project. This newspaper understands that among the

drugs sold as part of the scheme are mephedrone, methamphetamine and GHB, narcotics used in the cocktails common to the 'chemsex' trend that has taken hold in certain communities and which has been linked to a recent increase in HIV infections. The drugs have been produced in various laboratories and factories around the country and distributed by European immigrant drug gangs. They in turn have been aided – at least in part – by an organisation known as the Brothers of Cáceres, a classified group of Church priests and officials working directly for the *CNI* and a key element in the working of *Abravanel*.

The security operation for Navas – code-named *Operación Santiago* – is headed by the *CNI*. A key element of *Santiago* has been *Operación Covadonga* – the closing down of units at the *Policía Nacional* and *Guardia Civil* investigating Islamic militants and the concentration of these investigations at the *CNI*. *Policía Nacional* sources have confirmed that such a step has been taken in the past three days.

Other elements of Navas – a large and highly complex project – involve *Operación Lerma*, a plan to forcibly expel Muslims to Morocco. Plans envisaged under this scheme involve the revoking of Spanish nationality from people holding joint citizenship with an Islamic country. Current estimates suggest that as many as a million people could be affected by such a move.

Controversially, all the project's operational code names are linked to key events or personalities involved in the *Reconquista*, the mediaeval campaign to expel Muslims from the Peninsula. 'Covadonga' is the name of the first battle of the *Reconquista*, in the mountains of Asturias in 722. 'Clavijo' was the name of the first – and fictitious – battle against the Moors in 844 at which the Apostle Santiago is supposed to have miraculously appeared and set the enemy to flight. 'Navas de Tolosa' refers to the most famous battle in Spanish history, the great victory over the Moors in 1212. 'Abravanel' was the name of a Jewish moneylender who gave their Catholic Majesties the money for the War of Granada, culminating in the conquest of the last Moorish-held city in 1492. The Duke of Lerma was the man behind the final expulsion of the Moriscos in 1609. The 'Brothers of Cáceres' was the original name of the Knights of Santiago, the military order based on the Templars whose purpose was to rid Spain of the Moors.

The irony that such allusions should be made in the twenty-first century to an operation designed to incarcerate and expel large numbers of Muslims and people of North African origin will not be lost on public opinion – both at home and abroad.

When completed, the detention facility on Cabrera will resemble the US camp for suspected Islamic militants at Guantánamo. It will not be the first time that Cabrera has been used in this way. During the Napoleonic Wars it was turned into a concentration camp – arguably the world's first – for captured French troops. From 1809 to 1814, some 9,000 enemy soldiers were held prisoner there, of whom only 3,600 survived.

> The documents obtained go into great detail about the planning and various stages of the project, as well as the various government departments and even some of the personalities involved in its operation. These include . . .

Alicia looked away from the screen. The window on to the street was open and she thought she heard something, a footstep that was familiar.

With a sigh of relief and joy she realised it was Max, finally coming home. She got up from her desk and went over to see.

FIFTY-NINE

He felt happy, happier than he had for a long time. Even Commissioner Hernández hadn't quite managed to put a dent in his mood.

'For a moment there,' he had told her back in her office, 'I thought you were trying to get rid of me.'

She hadn't responded well to his grinning face, couldn't see the lighter side of it. Not only was there a murder where there shouldn't have been one – in her eyes – but he had successfully solved it. Abdelatif Cortbi had buckled quickly once in custody. He seemed to long to confess. One of those ones seeking forgiveness, redemption, by recounting all their sins.

Except that there would be no forgiveness for him. The sentence would be long and lasting. A triple murder in cold blood. He would be old, probably dead, before his release date.

And unloved. There would be few visitors for Abi in jail.

The others – Bogdan, Dorin, Paco and Father Ricardo – were all, as far as he knew, safely in *Guardia Civil* custody, facing long prison terms for drug offences.

So now there was the question of Cámara himself.

'You know, Rita, you should have said if you were trying to push me out. It might have worked. I'm a reasonable man, after all.'

She looked at him as though she had swallowed the contents of an ashtray.

'I will not be spoken to like that. I am your commanding officer.'

Cámara shrugged. And took a look around her loveless office. He pitied the colleagues brought in here and made to stand to attention while she read them the riot act.

'Listen,' he said.

Her hair stood on end.

'I'm a policeman; I solve crimes.'

He drew his sentences out.

'So, after much consideration . . .'

He nodded to himself, as though confirming the results of a long internal discussion.

'I've decided to stay.'

She stood, watching him with silent loathing, teeth grinding, blood vanishing from her cheeks like morning dew evaporating in bright morning sun.

'There will always be plenty more crimes to solve.'

She couldn't speak, her jaw frozen, muscles tense with rage.

Cámara tilted his head and gave her a quizzical look.

'I sometimes get the feeling you don't like me very much,' he said.

It had been simple in the end. A question that had dogged

him time and again over the years now dealt with, the decision made, no more doubts or self-examination. He was just himself.

It felt like a lifting of some great weight, a rock he had been carrying like Atlas with the Heavens, condemned to bear for eternity. And yet all he had to do was put it down and leave. He felt light, free and unburdened, as though layers of his past, his own self, were slipping away.

I can finally live up to the promise of my name, he joked to himself. Clean, unsullied, with open, non-judging eyes. I am Max. I am a Cámara.

Torres had mumbled something earlier on their way back to the Jefatura about a celebration party for solving the Sunset case. He wondered how many would come.

Just a few drinks in a bar, he had insisted. No need to make a show of it. He would give him a call soon, once he'd seen Alicia.

It was late evening. He had done the minimum necessary – dealing with the paperwork and clearing up at the end of a case. Even now that he was trying to move it on it seemed it could barely bring itself to let him go.

For a moment, it was true, he had thought about leaving the police, of finding a place with Alicia in the mountains, starting something new away from the city and the coast. The severance money would have made it worthwhile, would have been a start, enough to get them going.

'There's some people I met up there,' Cámara would tell her when he got back. 'Jimmy and Estrella. I think you might like them.'

But he could already see the expression in her eyes and knew that it would never happen.

'*De viejo morirás y aprendiz quedarás*,' she would say,

nodding her head in his imaginary conversation with her like a patient schoolteacher. You'll die of old age while still being an apprentice.

'Hold on, since when do you speak in proverbs?'

'I've got a few of my own tucked away, to be used at the right moment.'

He laughed: she was right – as if the conversation had already taken place.

Now Alicia was waiting for him at home. He wasn't sure what he would do: perhaps have a shower, lie down for a while. Then they would be off later in the evening with Torres, and whoever else showed up. Azcárraga would be there. Perhaps some of the others. Even Laura. He would introduce Azcárraga to her, set in motion the process of getting him inside *Homicidios*. Certainly they could do with more like him.

And what would they have to drink? He looked forward to something cold, something fun, something to inspire a relaxed, frivolous mood for everyone. They needed it; they deserved it. Yes, he thought, as his mouth began to water at the idea: a nice big jug of Sangría, with plenty of ice and fruit. That would do it.

Just for starters.

SIXTY

There was a cracking sound from somewhere out on the street, like a single firecracker being let off. Just an ordinary sound in a city like Valencia.

BANG BANG BANG.

A sudden hammering came from the door.

'ALICIA!'

She was expecting Max. It was him, but it wasn't him. For a moment she didn't understand; she knew that voice. Yet the context, the urgency of it, confused her for a second.

'Alicia! You need to run! Now!'

She took a step towards the door.

'Is that—?'

The door swung open. Outside, Torres stood with a younger uniformed policeman she didn't know. Both were armed, their pistols drawn.

With his free hand, Torres grabbed Alicia by the wrist

and jerked her out of the flat, pushing her towards the other policeman.

'This is Azcárraga, a friend,' Torres said, bustling her down the stairs. 'No time to explain. We have to go.'

Alicia looked at Torres with incomprehension.

'They're coming to kill you,' he said.

SIXTY-ONE

He parked the motorbike, locked his helmet in the topbox, then turned the corner of the street and headed down towards his flat. The prostitutes were out, looking sleepy and bored as they stood in the shade of doorways or smoked in groups of two or three by the edge of the pavement. Cámara glanced up at the balcony window of his flat a few metres further on. The shutters were almost pulled down, but he thought he could see Alicia there, waiting for him. He had emailed before leaving the Jefatura, said he was on his way.

The sun flashed, reflecting off a shop window. He was blinded for a second and stopped, rubbing his knuckles into his eyes. When he opened them, he blinked, trying to see. Someone was standing in front of him: a woman. Was she trying to get past?

He stood to the side, but she moved with him. Then he took a step the other way. Who was she? There was something familiar about her, yet still his vision was blurred by the startling sunlight.

He raised a hand, blocking out the light. He saw blonde hair, a heavily painted face: clearly defined cupid's bow and pencilled eyebrows arching like black rainbows high into her brow.

Cámara stopped, his heart suddenly frozen.

How many times had he imagined this moment, only to dismiss it. The only policeman to live in the centre of the city. They all shook their heads at him: no other was prepared to take the risk of being easily found, of reprisals being taken against themselves or their families. The outlying towns and satellite villages were much safer. Only a lunatic like Cámara would be so stupid as to have a flat not only in the centre, but in one of the roughest areas. Yet Cámara hadn't minded. This was life, he thought. Anything else was unreal.

But he had never, in his heart, imagined this moment ever really coming to pass. There was, in his imagination, not fully recognised, a sense that he was protected in some way, that no serious harm would come to him. He had been wounded in the course of his policing years, it was true, but death had never formed a part of his musings on his position, his risk, his openness.

And yet, now, here She was: Death staring down at him through the coal-black eyes of Ileana.

'For Bogdan,' she said. 'For everything.'

He watched in silent resignation as she lifted the gun, pulled the trigger, and felt the kick of the explosion within the barrel.

And the bullet, spinning towards him.

And very slowly he put his hand out and lowered himself

to the ground, just as Jimmy had described. In a world beyond time.

The sun itself reached out golden hands to catch him.

'Hello.'

He heard a voice. It sounded like Hilario, his grandfather.

'Wasn't expecting you so soon.'

SIXTY-TWO

Carlos stood over Cámara's immobile body, watching the blood seep out of him and stain the paving stones around. The street was deserted: the drug dealers and prostitutes had fled at the first sight of trouble, abandoning the stage. Ileana panted heavily at his side, chest heaving violently as she breathed in and out through flared nostrils, lips wrapped tight like a tourniquet. She raised her hand to fire once more, gripping the butt of the pistol that Carlos had handed her with white intensity.

'No!' A single order, barked with clear authority. And she obeyed, slowly lowering her hand again.

'Go,' he said, gesturing up the street.

'Five doors up. The woman is there.' She looked at him with eyes like tar-black pits. White spittle drying at the edge of her mouth.

He nodded to her.

'Finish the job.'

She hurried away, running in near silence and disappearing through the doorway to head upstairs. It was messy, but necessary. Soon the Beneyto woman would be dead, the files recovered, her computer drives erased. All traces – of *Navas*, *Clavijo*, and most importantly of *Abravanel* – gone. The public would learn about the internment camp on Cabrera eventually – such a thing could not be kept secret for ever. But how it was being funded – *Operación Abravanel* and the connection with the drug trade – must at all costs remain classified. No one must ever know about it, or about the role that members of the Brothers of Cáceres – including the unfortunate Father Ricardo – played in its operation. The Brothers' loyalty was first and foremost to the State, not the Church. But in return the State had to look after them. Father Ricardo had been unlucky, but was now a free man – at least for the time being. Everything must be done to remove any suspicion surrounding him, and if necessary he, too, could be liquidated.

Soon – very soon – there would be no one left who could tell. Ignacio, the marine biologist, dead. Marisol, the traitor from the Ministry of Defence, dead. Beneyto, the journalist who discovered too much, as good as dead. And Cámara, the man who never knew quite what he had uncovered, slowly bleeding to death in front of him. It was right that Cámara should die in ignorance: a man who in the past had uncovered some of the biggest scandals, now breathing his last with no knowledge of the vast government project that his little murder investigation in the mountains had come so close to unravelling. Should Carlos bend down now and whisper everything in his ear? Tell of how, through sheer coincidence, his beloved Alicia had stumbled on the same story? And was now going to die for the same reason?

Carlos checked himself. No, that would be cruel. And he smiled to himself: he had come close to losing control.

Besides, there would be much to do now, and quickly. Afterwards it would be easy to make everything stick on the Romanian woman. Ileana, another useful idiot, happily playing the role of embittered, vengeful spouse. Something about her willingness to take up Carlos's offer had scared even him. She could be seen to, once she was taken into police custody. A suicide driven by remorse. There was something of a loose cannon about her. Someone to be taken care of before entering the category of 'enemy'.

Carlos took a last look at Cámara. He was lying on his back, face draining of colour as the bullet wound pulsed life out of him. And for a second his eyes opened, staring up at Carlos in the fading evening sun.

His lips were moving. Was he trying to say something? Utter his last words?

Carlos checked his watch: he had to go. Soon the Beneyto woman would be dead too and the clear-up operation would have to sweep into action. There was no time for this. No time for sentimentality.

He took a step back, lifted his own pistol, and pointed it at Cámara's head.

ACKNOWLEDGEMENTS

Thanks first to Rob, without whom this book would never have been written.

Also to Peter Robinson for his warm-hearted support throughout.

Finally to my Mother and Father, and to Salud, Arturo and Gabi for so much that cannot be expressed here.